LOVE AND MARRIAGE

Celebrate the month of June with three best-selling Zebra authors as they each share a passionate and beautifully moving story about getting married . . .

WHAT BETTER MONTH FOR A WEDDING?

Watch the tender newness of spring become the full blaze of summer as romance blossoms for three lovely women about to embark upon the most thrilling adventures of their lives. Experience the excitement of seduction on the high seas, the delights of home and family on a Montana ranch, and the danger of wild, forbidden love on the Arizona mesa . . .

Join master storytellers Phoebe Conn, Kathleen Drymon, and Susan Sackett in these wonderful tales sure to stir all the sweetness of love in your heart!

HEART STOPPING ROMANCE BY ZEBRA BOOKS

MIDNIGHT BRIDE   (3265, $4.50)
by Kathleen Drymon

With her youth, beauty, and sizable dowry, Kellie McBride had her share of ardent suitors, but the headstrong miss was bewitched by the mysterious man called The Falcon, a dashing highwayman who risked life and limb for the American Colonies. Twice the Falcon had saved her from the hands of the British, then set her blood afire with a moonlit kiss.

No one knew the dangerous life The Falcon led—or of his secret identity as a British lord with a vengeful score to settle with the Crown. There was no way Kellie would discover his deception, so he would woo her by day as the foppish Lord Blakely Savage . . . and ravish her by night as The Falcon! But each kiss made him want more, until he vowed to make her his *Midnight Bride*.

SOUTHERN SEDUCTION   (3266, $4.50)
by Thea Devine

Cassandra knew her husband's will required her to hire a man to run her Georgia plantation, but the beautiful redhead was determined to handle her own affairs. To satisfy her lawyers, she invented Trane Taggart, her imaginary step-son. But her plans go awry when a handsome adventurer shows up and claims to *be* Trane Taggart!

After twenty years of roaming free, Trane was ready to come home and face the father who always treated him with such contempt. Instead he found a black wreath and a bewitching, sharp-tongued temptress trying to cheat him out of his inheritance. But he had no qualms about kissing that silken body into languid submission to get what he wanted. But he never dreamed that *he* would be the one to succumb to *her* charms.

SWEET OBSESSION   (3233, $4.50)
by Kathy Jones

From the moment rancher Jack Corbett kept her from capturing the wild white stallion, Kayley Ryan detested the man. That animal had almost killed her father, and since the accident Kayley had been in charge of the ranch. But with the tall, lean Corbett, it seemed she was *never* the boss. He made her blood run cold with rage one minute, and hot with desire the next.

Jack Corbett had only one thing on his mind: revenge against the man who had stolen his freedom, his ranch, and almost his very life. And what better way to get revenge than to ruin his mortal enemy's fiery red-haired daughter. He never expected to be captured by her charms, to long for her silken caresses and to thirst for her never-ending kisses.

Available wherever paperbacks are sold, or order direct from the Publisher. Send cover price plus 50¢ per copy for mailing and handling to Zebra Books, Dept. 3780, 475 Park Avenue South, New York, N.Y. 10016. Residents of New York and Tennessee must include sales tax. DO NOT SEND CASH. For a free Zebra/ Pinnacle catalog please write to the above address.

A Bride's Temptation

Phoebe Conn
Kathleen Drymon
Susan Sackett

ZEBRA BOOKS
KENSINGTON PUBLISHING CORP.

ZEBRA BOOKS

are published by

Kensington Publishing Corp.
475 Park Avenue South
New York, NY 10016

First printing: June, 1992

Printed in the United States of America

CONTENTS

Apache Caress

by

Phoebe Conn

Chapter One

Arizona Territory
September 1886

Dawn was still several minutes away, but after a dozen years of climbing the rugged path to the top of the butte, Belle found her way with the playful nonchalance of a young woman gracefully seducing a longtime lover. It was a pilgrimage of sorts, not merely an excursion to a spectacular vantage point above her father's sprawling cattle ranch but a journey inward to the land of memory and dreams. When Belle reached the crest, she stood for a moment in a silent salute and then sat down cross-legged, her palms resting lightly on her knees, to await the arrival of the new day.

Iron oxide painted the butte, the nearby cliffs, and the soil, covering the broad terrain with a rich reddish hue. As dawn broke above the horizon, the brilliant rays of the rising sun split the heavens with a blinding exuberance and licked the red earth with tongues of flame. As always, Belle saw the breathtaking natural phenomenon as a sign sent by the mother she had never known. It was only in those few precious minutes when the sun was reborn that she felt loved.

Not nearly so appreciative of the spectacular beauty of the sunrise, weary and sore, Coyote sat up slowly. He squinted slightly to avoid the glare, then, shocked to find the butte where he had taken refuge had been invaded by a man who sat silhouetted against the dawn, he rose to his feet with an agile stealth. His knife was at his belt, but he would not use it on a stranger. His situation was dire, but he was no murderer, at least, not yet. He could not risk being seen, however, and jeopardize his freedom. The rawhide soles of his moccasins made no sound as he began to slowly close the distance between them.

Far more at home atop the butte than in her father's house, Belle felt rather than heard someone approaching. A cold chill unrelated to the temperature of the desert air slid down her back; she knew she was being stalked. Every bit as quick as she was bright, she drew her Colt .45 as she rolled to the side and came up with the barrel pointed directly at the Indian who was standing no more than five feet away. The Army had cleared the area of the last of his kind in the 1870's and her fright was overlaid with surprise.

"You're a long way from the reservation," she announced with near-theatrical bravado, "and I know Indians never get lost. This is my father's land. Just what do you think you're doing here?"

The suddenness of her reaction had knocked Belle's hat askew and freed her thick red curls to cascade over her shoulders and tumble down her back. Looking into the sun, Coyote couldn't see her face clearly, but her flowing hair made it easy to recognize her as a woman. He raised his hands.

"Don't be afraid. I'm not armed."

Belle had the advantage of being able to see him clearly, but the fact he wasn't carrying a gun didn't assuage her fears. She judged him to be close to six feet in height, and he had a lean, muscular build. He was dressed in typical Apache fashion with his shirttail worn outside a pair of close-fitting pants and moccasins with leggings that extended up over his calves like boots. His thick black hair, while tamed by a bandana headband, was long rather than cropped at shoulder length.

He was undeniably handsome, but there was a delicacy to his features that made him appear to be as much Spanish as Indian; and she assumed he had Mexican blood, like so many of the Apaches. His English was softly accented and his voice seductively deep. He was standing in a relaxed pose, but he still looked fierce to her.

"Answer my question," she ordered. "What are you doing here?"

Apparently in no hurry to reply, Coyote glanced toward the south. "Have you heard of Geronimo?"

"Yes. He's a murdering renegade, but I've seen photographs of him in the *Phoenix Herald* and he doesn't look anything like you."

Amused, Coyote flashed a wide grin. "I didn't say I was Geronimo. I asked if you knew of him."

Belle was astonished by the Apache's composure. She had a pistol aimed at his heart and he was teasing her! Ignoring his smile, she grew stern. "I'll ask the questions; you provide the answers. If you're trying to blame your presence here on Geronimo, it won't work. I know he's on a train bound for Florida."

"Yes he is, and I'm one of the scouts who put him there. I was with Lieutenant Gatewood when he brought him in."

Belle knew the Army had Apache scouts, a great many of them if she remembered correctly. "I suppose you know General Crook, too?"

"Yes, ma'am, I worked with him. If he were here, he'd vouch for me."

"Unfortunately, he *isn't* here. Now, while a list of your acquaintances is undoubtedly fascinating, you still haven't answered my original question. What are you doing here?"

"Do you know what happened to the scouts who helped to bring Geronimo in?"

"Lordy, why can't you give me a straight answer?"

Tired, Coyote flexed his shoulders. "May I put my hands down?"

"No! Just talk."

Coyote took a deep breath and let it out slowly, but he could no longer rein in his temper. "The scouts who risked their lives to capture Geronimo were repaid for their loyalty with betrayal. We were all to be transported to Florida with him."

"Obviously you missed the train."

Enraged by her lack of sympathy, Coyote nevertheless refused to react to her taunt. "Chato, and most of the others, were guarded too closely to escape, but I got away."

11

"Wasn't Chato on the warpath himself a couple of years ago before General Crook captured him down in Mexico?"

Coyote was sorry to learn she knew more about his past than he had anticipated. Why had he had the misfortune to meet a woman who apparently memorized every edition of the *Phoenix Herald* rather than one who was content merely to cook and sew? "You're a smart girl," he complimented with bitter sarcasm. "Had we been well treated on the reservation, we would have stayed."

"That may be true, but the fact is, you didn't."

Again the Indian glanced toward the south. There were cattle grazing in the distance, but no plumes of red dust to show riders coming their way. He looked back at his feisty captor and wondered if she really had the courage to shoot him. She was holding the Colt with a steady hand, and he swiftly decided that she did.

"No, ma'am, I didn't, not until the summer of '83, but when Crook forced us to settle near Camp Apache I tried to raise cattle and crops with the others. I left when the Army offered work as a scout but I won't go to Florida. White men are free to live where they choose. Why can't I?"

"There are a lot of dead settlers who would answer that question if they could speak from their graves. The Apaches will have to turn away from their murdering ways before whites can view them as men rather than savages."

Without thinking, Coyote took a step toward her. "Aren't you listening to me? It was because I wanted peace that I chose to scout for the Army. I was repaid with a train ride to Florida. Shoot me if you must, but I won't go back."

In the few minutes Belle had spoken with him, she could not help but be impressed by the young brave's sincerity, but she knew white men were not the only ones capable of speaking with forked tongues. "What's your name?" she inquired in a softer tone.

"Coyote."

He stressed the last syllable as a Spaniard would, and Belle used the same inflection when she replied. "Well, Coyote, if what you say is true, then you have every right to be angry, but how do I know you weren't one of Geronimo's band rather than Chato's?"

Such a possibility had not occurred to Coyote and he shook his head slowly. Then he had an idea. "Had I been one of Geronimo's braves, I would have thrown my knife at your back and you'd be dead. The fact you are alive proves I love peace."

Belle knew there had indeed been time for him to throw his knife at her between the instant she had felt his presence and the moment she had turned to confront him. He seemed so elated by that bit of proof that she was inclined to believe him, but she still remained cautious. "I intend to stay alive," she warned.

"So do I," Coyote vowed with equal sincerity.

"You can't stay here. Isn't the Army out searching for you? You may have missed Geronimo's train, but there will be others."

The brave responded with a derisive snort. "I told you, the Army put all the loyal scouts on the train. There is no one left in the Arizona Territory to track me."

When he broke into a wide grin and began to laugh, Belle was suddenly as amused as he. She had never fired a shot at an Apache, and this seemed like a particularly poor time to start. She slid her Colt into its holster; when Coyote did not immediately dive for her, she gestured for him to lower his hands. "Do you have a horse?" she asked.

"Yes. I hid him in the cypress trees down below, but he is worn out, and so am I. We can't go any farther today."

Belle was about to tell him she was the only one who ever climbed the butte, then realized how foolhardy such an admission would be. "You'll not be safe here for more than a day, so don't tarry. Do you have food?"

Coyote nodded. "Some; enough."

"I don't want to know where you're going. I just want you to be gone by the next time I come back up here. My father would have shot you on sight, and the hands wouldn't have given you time to relate your tale, either. You might have been safer on the train."

When she moved toward the trail leading down to the floor of the valley, Coyote was finally able to see her face clearly. She had brown eyes framed with a thick sweep of long, dark

13

lashes, a nose dusted with freckles, and a mouth made for smiles . . . or kisses. "Wait," he called. "You didn't tell me your name."

Not certain that would be wise, Belle hesitated a moment too long. She saw his disappointment, and decided a man who could make such an eloquent plea for justice could be trusted with that much. "It's Belle."

"Bell? ¿Cómo una campana?"

"No." She spelled the word for him. "It's French. It means beautiful."

"It is a good name for you."

"I think Coyote is a good name for you, too. You're certainly clever and you look fast as well. Leave as quickly as you can."

She disappeared over the rim of the butte before Coyote could think of a reply, but he walked to the edge and watched her descend the steep path with the agility of the big horn sheep who roamed the red cliffs. As he watched her ride away, back toward the ranch that lay in the shadow of the butte, he decided, despite her warning, he was in no hurry to leave.

Belle started for home, then veered wide to the south and swung around to follow the meandering northeasterly course of the Oak Creek upstream. The meeting with Coyote had left her more shaken than she had realized and she dared not return home until she had her emotions under full control. She drew her pinto mare to a halt, then left her to graze in the sparse grass that grew along the creek's rocky shore while she splashed water on her cheeks. She could feel the heat of an incriminating blush and did not sit back until she was certain she had erased it.

That she frequently watched the sunrise from the butte was no secret to anyone on the ranch, but until that morning, she had never shared the experience with a single soul. Not that Coyote had gone there to enjoy the view, but it was disconcerting to find someone else trespassing on property she had always considered uniquely her own. She had never spoken with an Apache before. Her father employed a few Mexican

14

vaqueros who were no more civilized than Indians, but the few words she exchanged with them didn't count.

She rose, brushed away the red dust clinging to her clothes, and turned to look back up at the butte. She was much too far away to see Coyote, or for him to see her, but that didn't dispel the disquieting sensation that her privacy had been invaded. She wished him luck, wherever he was bound, and, remounting her mare, returned home.

"You're late for breakfast again," Aurelia Calderon scolded in a cross whisper. Constantly sweeping away the gritty red dust that seeped into the house each time a door or window was opened, she threatened to give her charge a well-deserved swat with her broom but stopped just short of doing so. An overly conscientious woman, the housekeeper considered Belle's behavior, or *mis*behavior as was usually the case, a very poor reflection on her gallant efforts to raise the motherless girl.

"Hurry on into the dining room before the major gets even more angry than he already is," she urged.

A much decorated Confederate Army officer, Donovan Cassidy had not stopped using his military title just because his country had ceased to exist after Lee's surrender at Appomattox. Because he was a genuine hero with the medals to prove it, no one had ever considered the habit an affectation.

The year Belle had turned ten, she had suddenly come to realize that she was living in a Confederate museum rather than a home. Where other families had colorful paintings to adorn their walls, Major Cassidy preferred to display photographs taken during the War Between the States. Some were casual poses showing him and his fellow officers lounging in front of their tents, others were formal portraits of proud young officers dressed in gray. There was even a photograph of Donovan with General Robert E. Lee taken during the early months of the war when hopes for the Confederate cause had been at their brightest.

The grim progress of the war was etched so plainly in the expressions of the haggard young men in the later photo-

15

graphs that Belle could have laid them out in correct order without ever turning them over to verify the dates. In four years, the young men in her father's battalion had aged ten, and those were the lucky ones. They had survived.

Steeling herself for what would undoubtedly be another of the endless hostile exchanges with her father, Belle handed Aurelia her hat and entered the dining room with a brisk, confident stride. She circled the long table, paused to place the briefest of kisses on her father's cheek, waited for him to flinch as he invariably did, and then took her place at his right. She had once asked him if he despised her because she was not a boy, but he had insisted, in what she thought was one of the rare instances of truth to pass between them, that her sex had never been the issue.

Just what the issue was he had failed to confide, but Major Cassidy did nothing without reason so she knew there had to be one for his failure to love her. She had never felt any love for him, either. Her mother had committed suicide when Belle was only two, and Belle had always known Donovan had driven her to it.

Concha, one of the maids, brought in her breakfast, and having already had sufficient thrills for the week in one morning, Belle quickly picked up her fork and took a heaping bite of the cheese omelet. She followed it with a strip of bacon and an orange slice before glancing over at her father. "Beautiful morning, isn't it?" she commented with a forced smile.

Donovan eyed her coldly. "If you'd arrived any later, I'd have missed seeing you. We have something important to discuss."

"Really? And what might that be?"

Donovan shoved his empty plate aside and rested his elbows on the table. "Your cousin Edwin should be arriving this afternoon, if the fool managed to get on the stage after his train reached Tucson. He can't have much sense if he'd drop out of medical school, but I promised his mother he'd be welcome here and I insist that you make some effort in that direction.

"Coming from Virginia, he'll quite naturally expect to find you wearing feminine attire, which will be a rare treat for the

16

rest of us. I've completely forgotten what you look like when you're not dressed like one of the hands. When he arrives, I want you wearing that gown I bought you so you'd look presentable at your friend Janet's wedding. God knows what Aurelia can find for you to wear tomorrow, but you two can worry about that then."

Belle started to argue, then decided that her father's request she don a dress wasn't unreasonable. But then, it hadn't been a request. Like all of the major's pronouncements, it had been an order. She ate another strip of bacon before responding. She had never been to Virginia, and had always had difficulty keeping her father's relatives straight.

"Is Edwin Moira's son?" she asked.

"Good Lord, no." Donovan shook his head as though he were dealing with someone too dense to understand the obvious. "Moira is my older sister. She's in her sixties. Edwin is her grandson. Moira's daughter Kate is his mother."

After that rebuff, Belle preferred eating her omelet to any further tracing of the family tree. She swallowed a savory bite before asking another question. "How long is Edwin planning to stay?"

Concha came in to refill Donovan's coffee cup and he waited until she had left to continue. "The boy's a quitter. He won't stay long."

"Boy? Isn't he in his twenties?"

"He's twenty-three, but you mark my words, he's still more boy than man."

Belle had heard the story so often, she knew exactly how her father had spent his own youth. "You were only twenty when the war began, but I doubt you considered yourself a boy."

"No, by God, I didn't and neither did any of the others with whom I served. Edwin, however, hasn't had the privilege of fighting for his country and I doubt he'd have survived if he had. I'll do what I can to make a man of him while he's here, but I can't believe he'll stay long."

Belle could only imagine how her father intended to make a man out of Edwin. She didn't envy her poor cousin. "Perhaps a week or two here will be all he'll need to inspire him to return to medical school. Is that what Kate really wants?"

Donovan choked out one of his infrequent laughs. "That could very well be. Perhaps the boy will surprise me and be more competent than I expect. If that's the case, you would be wise to do your best to impress him. With Janet married, you've no more unattached friends. At nineteen, people might already be calling you an old maid; spinsterhood will not become you.

"Unlike your friends, who all know the value of dressing like a woman, you've never had a serious suitor. If Edwin is at all appealing, then do what you can to wrench a proposal from his lips before he leaves. He's likely the best you'll ever do."

Although used to her father's poor opinion of her, to hear him call her an old maid hurt. She didn't think it was her choice of attire that kept the young men away, but rather the major's reputation for being cold and demanding. She could readily understand why a young man wouldn't want Donovan Cassidy for a father-in-law. She had never wanted him for a father.

"I'd prefer to wait for love," she confided softly.

Donovan shoved back his chair and rose to his feet. "You've the same soft, sentimental streak as your mother. The fact is, a woman needs a husband and you're unlikely to get another chance to wed, so don't waste this one. Do the best you can to look and act like a lady tonight. As for meals, you've got to do a better job of arriving for them on time. I should have told Concha to feed your breakfast to the dogs. The next time you're late, I will do just that."

Ending their conversation on that strident note, Donovan turned away. Although his hair was white, he was still slim and erect at fifty-five. He left the dining room with the same proud bearing he'd shown while reviewing his troops.

The trouble was, Belle had never enlisted in his Army.

Chapter Two

Excited by the prospect of Edwin's visit, Aurelia's hands darted through Belle's flowing curls with the whimsical abandon of hiccupping butterflies. A touch of the comb here, a slight nudge with her fingertips there and the housekeeper gradually transformed the unruly mass into a splendid crown. "Just a few more seconds, *querida*," she begged, for she knew full well how little patience Belle possessed when it came to such odious tasks as pinning up her hair.

"There, I'm finished. What do you think?"

It took a long moment for Belle to recognize herself as the elegant young woman reflected in the mirror above her dressing table. On the rare occasions Aurelia had succeeded in winning her consent to style her hair, her uncanny resemblance to her late mother had always unnerved her. There was only one photograph of Isabel, which Donovan kept in his bedroom, but Belle had memorized the contours of her mother's face and the sweetness of her smile as soon as she had been old enough to grasp the astonishing fact that the beautiful young woman in the treasured portrait was her mother.

To again find her mother's sweet serenity reflected in her mirror brought a burst of pain to Belle's heart she couldn't hide. She quickly turned away. "Do you suppose my mother would be pleased that I look so much like her?" she asked.

"She adored you," Aurelia exclaimed, "and she would be very proud of you." She stepped back as Belle rose and straightened the folds in the elaborately draped skirt of her yellow satin gown. "You look even more beautiful than you did at Janet's wedding."

Belle shot Aurelia a disapproving glance. The housekeeper had predicted at least a dozen suitors would begin to call after she had attended the June wedding, but her father's forbidding manner hadn't encouraged attention from the bachelors present at the function and her solitary life had not been interrupted by amorous young men eager to court her. "Please," Belle scolded. "I don't want to hear about how pretty I look when it'll make no difference in the way I live."

Tears filled Aurelia's eyes and she hurried to brush them away before they were noticed. "You will have a long and happy life, *querida*. I just know that you will."

What Belle saw as she again glanced toward the mirror was not the face of a young woman whose future was filled with promise, but instead a ghostly reminder of another young woman who had chosen not to live at all. Aurelia had only effusive praise for Isabel and painted a glorious picture of maternal love, but Belle had never been able to reconcile the housekeeper's flattering description of Isabel with the shocking circumstance of her death. She knew that if her mother had really loved her, even in the smallest amount, she would never have leaped to her death.

Sweeping her sorrow aside, she tried to look forward to having a guest join them for supper. "Thank you for helping me with my hair. I just hope that after all this trouble, Edwin didn't miss the stage."

Aghast at the idea of such a calamity, Aurelia raised her hands to her cheeks. "Don't even think such a horrid thing. Go on downstairs to the parlor so it will look as though you have nothing to do but sit and read when he arrives."

Belle laughed as she went out the door. She spent many an afternoon reading, but it was always down by the creek rather than in her father's parlor. Unaccustomed to wearing a gown, she held the rail firmly as she descended the stairs. Fearful of tripping, she was moving so slowly she was only halfway down when her father and Edwin came through the front door. Certain she looked more awkward than graceful, she paused and waited to meet her cousin.

Having expected a squat adobe house like the ones he'd seen traveling across the Southwest, or perhaps a rustic log dwelling, Edwin had been completely unprepared for his first glimpse of the Cassidy mansion. Built of local pine and sandstone in the Greek Revival style popular for southern plantation homes before the Civil War, the façade of the oddly elegant two-story house was adorned with fluted columns topped with an ambitious Mexican artisan's interpretation of Corinthian capitals.

While whitewashed every spring, the red dust that settled over everything in the area had lent it a decidedly pinkish hue. Completely out of place in a land of red cliffs and spectacular vistas, the home evoked a melancholy reminder of the past glories of Virginia and filled Edwin with a searing homesickness he hadn't felt since boarding the train to come out west. It was with a very tight lump in his throat that he looked up and saw Belle for the first time.

His leather satchel fell from his hand and landed with a dull thud at his side. Embarrassed to appear so clumsy, he whipped off his hat and bowed low. "Edwin Pierce, at your service," he announced proudly. As he straightened up, he regarded Belle with exuberant admiration. "Please call me Win."

Despite the fact that Donovan had encouraged his daughter to inspire Edwin's interest, he had not expected the young man to be so taken with her that no such encouragement would be necessary. Relative or not, he'd not allow anyone to ogle Belle with such unabashed joy. He introduced his only child, and then leaving her on the stairs, ushered Edwin on into the parlor.

Belle had had no real mental image of her cousin, but that he was a handsome young man with wavy blond hair and bright blue eyes was certainly no disappointment. That he had actually looked thrilled to meet her was an additional, and very pleasant, surprise. Grateful for the chance to reach the bottom of the stairs unobserved, she completed her descent, paused to collect her thoughts, and with a blithe step followed the men to the parlor.

The rows of framed photographs were not the only Civil War memorabilia in the room, and as Edwin waited impatiently for Belle to join them, he took it all in. Donovan had hung his sword above the mantel; over it, his battalion's tattered flag was

21

on display. At the base of the wrought-iron fireplace tools sat an artfully arranged heap of small cannonballs, while a drum, which had undoubtedly outlived its drummerboy, was placed nearby.

The rest of the furnishings were not nearly so elegant as Edwin had anticipated, given the home's impressive exterior. The chairs and end tables had been heavily carved and stained the rich shade of mahogany to hide their simple pine origin. A cowhide was thrown over the back of a leather sofa, and a single bearskin rug decorated the oft-swept plank floor. Uncomfortably aware of the intensity of Donovan's gaze, Edwin turned toward him and smiled.

"Thank you for inviting me here for a visit. After leaving Harvard, I had no reason to remain in Boston, and Alexandria has lost its appeal."

Donovan had taken an instant dislike to the handsomely dressed youth and was positive his initial impression of him had been correct. Edwin was not only a quitter, but a spoiled dandy to boot. He had absolutely no reason to coddle him, either.

"I didn't invite you here, son," he corrected him sharply. "Your mother begged me to take you in. I said I'd welcome you to the ranch, and I will, but I'll expect you to work for your keep."

Amazed the dictatorial tone had already crept into her father's voice, Belle would have remained at the door, but Edwin glanced her way in a silent plea for help she couldn't ignore. Again taking care not to trip over her hem, she moved to Edwin's side. "I imagine, Edwin — Win — must be exhausted after his trip. Don't you think we ought to allow him a week or so to recuperate?"

"Your mother and I rode out here in a wagon, not in the comfort of the train, and I don't recall either of us needing any time to rest before we got to work building this place. I'll give you a day just to prove I have a generous nature, Win, but don't press me for any more leisure time."

Disappointed to find his great-uncle was so unfriendly, Edwin was cheered by the fact that Belle had spoken up for him. She would definitely make his visit worthwhile even if Donovan didn't. "I enjoy working, sir. Unfortunately I know nothing about cattle, but I'm certain I can learn."

"I hope you brought more practical clothes."

Edwin looked down at the new suit he had saved to wear for his arrival. He had hoped to impress everyone, not arrive looking like he wanted a job. "Yes, I brought other clothes," he assured him, "but I wanted to look my best when I met you."

"Yes, I knew you would. Come on, let's see if supper is ready. We have a Mexican cook, so you may find some of our food too highly spiced for your tastes. You'll soon get used to it."

When Donovan started for the dining room, Edwin offered Belle his arm and escorted her to her seat. He then slipped into the one opposite hers. He bowed his head while Donovan intoned a lengthy blessing, but responded with a ready grin as soon as he pronounced the amen. "I had no idea you'd be so lovely or I might have dropped out of school long before this."

Having never heard the type of charming flattery Edwin dispensed with practiced ease, Belle glanced toward her father. He was frowning so angrily, she could not help but be amused. It was very easy to be fond of anyone he disliked, and she was positive she and Win would soon become the best of friends.

"Thank you, but I really don't believe you should make light of your decision to leave medical school," she chided. "I'm sure you must have given it a great deal of serious thought."

Concha carried in a platter of barbequed beef, bowls filled with fresh vegetables, and a stack of steaming hot corn tortillas. It wasn't until after their plates had been served and they had begun to eat that Edwin had the chance to respond. "As a matter of fact, deciding to leave Harvard was the smartest decision I've ever made and also one of the quickest. I simply didn't belong there. Medicine didn't come easily to me and I knew I'd make the worst of physicians. The whole profession should be relieved I chose not to complete my training."

"A man should always finish what he begins," Donovan argued.

Believing her to be on his side, Edwin winked at Belle. "Yes, sir, that's an admirable trait, but not when it's carried to extremes and forces a man to follow through with a mistake."

It was now generally agreed that the South had lacked the men and matériel to win the war and that their cause had been doomed from the first whispers of succession, but he had been warned by his mother not to make any remarks derogatory to the Confederacy within Major Cassidy's hearing. Even if she hadn't provided such a caution, the shrinelike atmosphere of Donovan's home would have convinced Edwin to keep his opinions to himself.

"A wise man doesn't make mistakes," Donovan replied.

"Not all of us possess the wisdom of Solomon, sir."

"Obviously not."

Rather than allow what she feared was fast becoming an increasingly hostile exchange to continue, Belle spoke before Edwin could reply. "Do you like to ride? I'm sure the countryside looks nothing like Virginia and I'd be happy to serve as a guide."

"Yes, I do ride, thank you. I'll look forward to it. I hope you're free tomorrow, as it might be the only time I'll have available."

Donovan listened to their conversation, but kept silent for the remainder of the meal. When Edwin pleaded fatigue from his journey and asked to be excused as soon as they had finished, he was relieved to be able to savor his brandy without him. "I don't have to ask what you thought of your cousin; it was plain that you liked each other," he stated rather gruffly.

"Isn't that what you wanted? He's very nice, but you seemed bent on driving him away rather than making him feel welcome. Perhaps you don't want me to find a husband after all."

"Of course I do. Every father wants what's best for his daughter and I'm no exception. Edwin has wit and charm, I'll give him that, but I still think he's a quitter who'll be repacking his bags before we're used to having him around."

"We'll have to wait and see."

"Mark my words, we won't have long to wait."

Early the next morning, Belle rode out to the butte before Edwin had awakened. She circled the cypress grove at the base searching for Coyote's horse, and when she found a handsome bay gelding grazing beneath the cover of the trees, she drew her mare to an abrupt halt. "Damn it all," she swore under her

24

breath. Not wanting the Apache to spoil another dawn, she had known better than to return before sunrise, but she quickly dismounted and climbed the butte eager to repeat her demand that he leave.

Coyote had seen her riding his way and met her at the summit. "Do you always dress like a man?" he asked.

"How I choose to dress is no concern of yours. I told you yesterday that it's much too dangerous for you to be here. Why aren't you gone?"

Coyote's glance swept over her with the warmth of a lover's caress. "I like the view."

His sly grin said something quite different and Belle couldn't stop a bright blush from flooding her cheeks. That her southern cousin liked to flirt was understandable, but it was the last thing she expected from an Apache brave and it was most disconcerting. "The magnificence of the view doesn't matter," she replied, attempting to ignore his suggestive comment. "You're trespassing, and I want you gone."

"You're wrong," Coyote argued. He gestured toward the red cliffs in the distance. "I came here because this land is sacred. Long before white men came here to raise cattle, the Yavapai believed this is where the world began. It is a very good place to admire the view."

Surrounded her entire life by some of the world's most hauntingly beautiful terrain, Belle followed his glance, not truly understanding that there was anything all that unusual about her home. She was openly skeptical. "Are you saying this is the Indians' version of the Garden of Eden?"

In hopes of convincing her to remain with him a while, Coyote gestured for her to follow him several steps away from the edge of the butte. He squatted down and, using a small stick, began to draw in the thin layer of sandy red soil that covered the rocky hilltop. "The Army confused the Yavapai with Apaches and put them on our reservations, so I have known some of them. They believe there were four worlds. During the first world came the first people from beneath the ground. They climbed up vines dangling below a gigantic pine tree. They all died in a flood.

"During the second world, the Goddess Komwida Pokwee

appeared. She was the first woman, and the Yavapai come from her. She was very lonely, and the rising sun gave her a daughter. When she was grown, she had a son, Skataamcha. When his mother was killed by an eagle, he was raised by his grandmother. She taught him how to make medicines and cure sickness.

"The third world ended in fire, but the Yavapai survived and say we are living in the fourth world now. Some say Komwida Pokwee is still seen in visions and dreams. She is supposed to be very beautiful. The Army took the Yavapai away, but their land is still sacred."

Coyote quickly erased his crude sketches of the goddess and her grandson, tossed away the stick, and rose to his full height. "Can you feel it?" he asked. "There is magic here."

The teasing light was gone from his gaze, and Belle realized his mood was now completely serious. "I've always felt something here, a presence, if you will." She paused, unwilling to reveal she believed it to be her mother's spirit rather than that of a Yavapai goddess.

"You don't think their story is foolish then?"

"Foolish? Why no, there's not that much difference between God creating life out of clay and Indians climbing up from underground. The flood that killed *everyone* is part of our religion, too, so it must have actually happened. There are Christian saints who saw visions, and other, just simple religious folk, too, so I'd certainly not dispute an Indian's word if he said he saw visions of a goddess."

"Is that why you stayed here?" she asked. "Do you hope to see a vision of Komwida Pokwee?"

Belle's tone was as serious as his own, but Coyote was still somewhat surprised she was not laughing at him. "No, I am looking only for myself, not an ancient goddess. Most whites will not even listen to the old tales, much less believe them. Why are you so different?"

His question hurt. Belle had never had a sense of belonging, a sense that she was part of a loving family, or any cohesive group, for that matter. Rather than blooming under the glow of love, her personality had been formed by her defiance against her father's narrow dictates of a young woman's role . . . and she knew as well as he did that she was not what she had been born to be. She lacked the softness a mother's love would have imparted. Feeling very different indeed, she had to swallow hard before she replied.

"I am 'different,' as you put it, in every possible way, but I consider it a source of pride."

Despite that boast, Coyote was touched by the hint of pain in her voice, and he reached out to caress her cheek lightly. Belle merely looked startled by the gentleness of his touch rather than offended he would take such a liberty. That pleased him. "I'm glad you are different whatever the cause, and I'm glad you came back to see me," he murmured softly.

Positive nothing she had said could have given him that impression, Belle was shocked that he would flatter himself with such a ridiculous notion. She quickly contradicted him. "I didn't come to see you. The exact opposite is true. I rode out here hoping that you'd be gone."

Coyote cocked his head to the side and again regarded her with a teasing gaze. "You don't have to lie about liking me," he advised. "I like *you.*"

"I'm not lying!" Belle swore, thoroughly exasperated with him. "Besides, whether I like you or not makes no difference. You're still trespassing on my father's property."

Coyote flashed a disarming grin. "You don't have to be *ashamed* to like me, either. Is that what I should have said?"

"No, it most assuredly isn't." But Belle found it impossible to return the Apache's level stare. He was handsome, and clearly bright, but she couldn't encourage his affection. "The only reason I'm talking to you is to tell you to leave. Don't imagine I have any other motive."

"I know how women behave," Coyote confided proudly. "I know you won't admit how much you like me this soon, but I'll be patient."

"Patient? What are you talking about? You can't stay here, and there's no reason for you to be stubborn about it, either."

Coyote shrugged slightly. "I'm not stubborn. *Determined* is a better word. I had to be determined to track Geronimo. Waiting for you to admit you like me will be no challenge."

Frightened by such open admiration from a man she ought

not even converse with, Belle began to back away. "You've made two grave errors," she warned, "first in remaining here, and second in believing I like you. Go now, and I won't tell anyone who comes looking for you that you were ever here, but that's all I'll do for you."

Coyote raised his hands as though she had again gotten the drop on him. "Please," he begged. "I didn't mean to frighten you. Most pretty girls like to be teased by young men. I didn't understand that you were so shy."

Having grown up in an almost exclusively male domain, Belle was indeed used to being teased, but not in the manner he had used. "I'm not shy," she denied. "I just don't want you making up excuses to remain here another minute."

"This land is sacred. It doesn't belong only to your father, but to everyone who believes."

"You've already told me you aren't on a religious pilgrimage, so I don't want to hear any more about sacred ground."

"But you said you could feel the spirits, too."

Belle put her hands on her hips. "Wait until the sun sets, then get out of here or your spirit is liable to end up dancing with all the other dead."

Coyote frowned. "I didn't say anything about spirits of the dead."

Realizing her mistake, Belle didn't explain. She just ran down the trail and hastened back to the pitiful island of safety she called home.

Disappointed that he had made such a poor impression on her, Coyote sat down and rested his elbows on his knees. He could feel the magic of the land and it had nothing to do with Yavapai legend. If Belle could feel that mystical force, too, he hoped it would bring her back to him.

Chapter Three

Edwin had assumed Belle would wear a riding habit for their tour of the ranch, but when she appeared in clothes apparently borrowed from one of the ranch hands, he found her boyish attire strangely stirring. She was tall and slim, and pants showed off the elegance of her limbs to every advantage. A leather belt cinched a waistline that clearly required no tightly laced corset to be spanned by a man's hands. She had rolled up her shirtsleeves, left the collar open and the top two buttons undone, tempting him to wonder if she had bothered with a camisole, or was simply bare underneath the pale-blue cotton garment. Twin pockets provided a modest covering for her breasts, but he couldn't help focusing his glance there.

No longer curled atop her head in a stylish coiffure, her glossy red tresses fell nearly to her waist, and he was sorry when she shoved them up under her hat rather than allow her hair to float on the gentle breeze as they rode. The previous evening, she had appeared to be as well mannered a young lady as any he had ever known, but now he felt as though he were truly seeing her for the first time. A creature born and raised in an untamed land, he now considered her to be a far more complex individual than he had first believed. He was astonished by how quickly he had become smitten with her, and hoped it didn't show.

Belle glanced toward the butte, then turned her mare in the opposite direction. "I'll take you down by the creek. It's the prettiest ride."

Edwin doubted that he would see much of the scenery, but

didn't embarrass either of them by saying so. "Fine, the countryside is magnificent every way I turn, but I'm sure you know what's best."

While Edwin freely admitted to being unused to a western saddle, he seemed comfortable enough, and after Belle had had a few minutes to observe how he handled his mount, she was pleased to see that he was a competent rider. "The land belongs to my father for as far as you can see. He works harder than any of our men, and they respect him for it. I just hope he doesn't make things too difficult for you."

"Believe me, so do I." He shook his head. "Does he always wear gray as he did last night?"

"Always, but his suits are several shades darker than his uniforms were. I know, because he still has one hanging in his wardrobe."

"That's rather sad really, although I doubt anyone who lived through the war will ever forget a minute of it."

"I don't mean to be impolite, but do you mind if we discuss something else? I'd like to hear about Harvard, or what your friends like to do back home. Just anything really, other than the war."

Edwin could readily understand her lack of interest in a subject that clearly obsessed her father. While he had chosen not to remain in medical school, he did have several amusing stories to relate about the year he had been enrolled and was delighted to share them. When Belle proved to be an attentive and appreciative audience, he told her about his friends back home. By the time they finally reached the creek, he feared he had exhausted his store of tales, but he was so interested in her, he hoped she would take a turn to entertain him.

The last sprinkling of wildflowers that had burst into bloom after the spring rains still covered the valley, but Belle chose to point out the plants she knew to be exclusive to the Southwest. There were agave cactus, which grew low to the ground in a starburst of triangular leaves, and tall yucca crowned with snowy white blossoms. She pointed out the graceful manzanita trees, the mesquite thickets, and the pickly pear cactus whose fruit made delicious candy.

"This country must all look very strange to you," she mused, "like touring the surface of the moon."

"Oh, it's not quite *that* strange," Edwin argued with a ready chuckle. "The pine and oak make me feel at home, even if nothing else does . . . No, that's not true. You're being very gracious. I'm sure I'll enjoy my stay here because of you."

When they reached the creek, Belle dismounted and waited for her mare to take a drink. Edwin came to her side. "Thank you," she said. "We've had company over the years, all friends of my father's from home. Usually they've been on their way to California and haven't stayed long."

"*I'm* going to stay," Edwin assured her. He bent down and let the swiftly flowing, icy cold creek water run over his hands. He scooped up a drink before standing, then wiped his mouth on his sleeve. "I realize I didn't make a good impression on your father, but I hope I've made a better one on you."

Edwin's eyes were as blue as the cloudless sky and filled with a warm glow of sincerity. Belle was flattered, but not certain how she was supposed to respond. She murmured another hasty word of thanks and then, leaving her mare to graze, she gestured toward the fallen trunk of a cypress bordering the water. "That makes a good place to sit. Would you like to stay here a while?"

"Sure," Edwin agreed. She took the place nearest the creek and he made himself comfortable at her side. He leaned down to pick up one of the smooth stones within easy reach and tossed it into the creek. A sophisticated young man, he couldn't recall the last time he had done something so simple as relax beside a creek, but he wasn't in the least bit bored.

"Tell me something about your mother," he asked.

Shocked by his question, Belle pretended a rapt interest in the peregrine falcon circling slowly overhead. "There's really nothing to tell," she finally replied. "I was only two when she died and I don't remember her."

"That's a shame, but surely you must know something about her. Tell me anything at all, even if it's silly."

Belle frowned slightly. "I don't know anything of that sort. If she had any especially endearing traits, I'm unaware of them. Her name was Isabel, and I was named for her. I do know I resemble her closely."

"Then she must have been very beautiful."

Unaware he had intended to pay her a compliment, Belle agreed. "Yes, she was."

Edwin waited for her to say more, and when she didn't, he prompted her again. "Forgive me, for I know this must be a painful subject, but I am family and have a right to know. Why did she take her life?"

For an instant, the rushing waters of the creek took on such a deafening roar that Belle doubted she had heard him correctly. Startled, she turned to look at him and his openly curious gaze assured her that she had. She glanced back toward the creek. Warmed by the soothing rhythm of the bubbling water, she found the courage to respond.

"I must have asked myself that same question a million times. My father speaks of her frequently, as he did last night when he mentioned their trip out here, but his comments are never of a personal nature. I only asked him about her suicide once, but his response was so horribly negative, as though it were none of my business, that I've never questioned him again. As you've had ample opportunity to observe, unlike a great many southern men, my father hasn't a bit of charm."

"You didn't know him before the war, or when your mother was alive."

"No, I didn't, but I think they must have been like sunshine and shadow. She had to have loved him once, but apparently not enough to go on living."

"Could she have been ill?"

"No. If she was ill enough to be bedridden, she wouldn't have been able to reach the top of the butte. It's a steep climb."

Edwin took her hand. She was wearing leather gloves, but he could still feel her warmth. "No, I don't mean physically ill," he explained hesitantly. "I mean, could she have suffered from some emotional problem, or simply been confused?"

Her cousin was taking care to be tactful, but Belle was still insulted and yanked her hand from his. "She wasn't crazy. No one even hints at that."

Belle started to rise, but Edwin again reached for her hand and pulled her back down beside him. "Please, I didn't mean to offend you. It's only that all we knew at home were the basic details of Isabel's death, and it's always been sort of the family mystery. Not that we pondered it endlessly, but every once in a while the subject would arise. It's only natural that we'd question her mental state. Suicide is scarcely the act of a rational mind."

"I won't have my mother called a lunatic," Belle vowed through clenched teeth.

Fearing he had made an enemy of his only friend on the ranch, Edwin immediately stood and pulled her to her feet. "Of course not, and that wasn't what I was saying. If the reason for your mother's death remains a mystery forever, it won't matter to me. You're the only one who concerns me."

Placated by the kindness of his manner and sweetness of his smile, Belle didn't struggle to break free when he inclined his head and kissed her. His lips were soft, his breath warm against her cheek, and, a stranger to affection, Belle responded with what she feared was unseemly enthusiasm. Mortified that he would think her completely lacking in moral fiber, she broke away from his embrace rather than cling to him forever. She hurried back to her mare, and swung herself up into the saddle.

"I think we better head back to the house," she called to him.

Edwin was as startled as Belle, for his first efforts to kiss the young ladies at home had always resulted in a hastily turned cheek. Belle hadn't let his kiss glance off her cheek, however, but had kissed him back with a wildness that matched her unconventional attire. He looked forward to their next kiss, and many more.

"Maybe there's still enough time for me to start work today," he responded with newfound ambition.

Grateful he had changed the subject, Belle promised him that there surely was. When they reached the corral, she signaled to their foreman, Kenneth MacKenzie, and quickly introduced the two men. "Win is anxious to learn whatever you can teach him about ranching. Do you have some time for him now?"

Kenneth tipped his hat toward the back of his head and regarded the young Virginian with a suspicious glance. "The major already told me to treat him like a new hand. Think you're up to that, young fella?"

Kenneth looked to be Donovan's age. A lifetime of working outdoors had given him a darkly tanned leathery skin and a permanent squint. Lean as a whip, he was obviously a hard man to please, but Edwin wanted to impress Belle too much to care. "Yes, sir, I most certainly am."

Belle left them to work out a routine and led her mare into the barn. As she curried her pet, she tried not to think about Edwin's questions, but they were the same ones that plagued her. "Why did you do it, Mama?" she whispered. "Why?"

Belle wore a ruffled Mexican blouse and tiered skirt to supper. In shades of rust and bronze, the outfit was as flattering as her yellow satin gown. She noted her father's raised eyebrow as she entered the parlor, but she had known he wouldn't approve of such colorful and casual attire. He had directed her to dress in whatever she and Aurelia could find, however, and that was precisely what she had done. As usual, his unfavorable opinion mattered not at all to her. She smiled as though his silent greeting had been full of loving praise.

Edwin leaped to his feet and hurried to Belle's side. He had again dressed in his new suit, but that night there was a touch of color in his cheeks from the hours he had spent in the sun and his fair skin was radiant with a healthy glow. "What a charming . . ." He hesitated as he searched his mind for an appropriate term. "Gown," he finally added. "You should always wear autumn colors. They're perfect with your coloring."

"The young women in Alexandria must miss you terribly," Belle teased in hopes of raising her own spirits as much as his. His curiosity about her mother's death had upset her far more than she had let him see, but Isabel's suicide was a wound that would never heal. Though her sunrise ritual had created a mystic bond with her mother, it hadn't filled in the blanks where her childhood memories of her parent should have been.

"I certainly hope so," he replied, "but I don't miss any of them."

Belle had caught her hair at her crown, allowing it to fall free that evening. Edwin couldn't resist reaching out to touch a curl, but before he could pay her another compliment, Donovan

34

brushed by him to lead the way into the dining room and he had to content himself with a wink and a smile. Because most men enjoyed talking about themselves, he encouraged his great-uncle to do so at his first opportunity.

"Last night, I was intrigued by your mention of your arrival to the Arizona Territory, sir. Could you tell me something more about your early days here?"

A perceptive man, Donovan knew precisely what Edwin was doing, but chose to ignore his blatant attempt to flatter him in favor of using the topic to his own advantage. "I had a partner then, Rick Vernon was his name. We'd served together during the war and, having gotten along well in the most difficult of times, decided to continue working together. My foreman, MacKenzie, had served with us, too. There were several other men in the early years who had fought with us, although, like Rick, they've all drifted away.

"Building a home, raising our first herd of cattle, fighting the Indians who defied the government's orders to relocate on reservations . . . We had more than enough work in those days. It was a constant battle either against the elements or thieving renegades, but, as you can see, we managed to build a ranch, and a fine one, out of nothing. This is a challenging land, Win. It's no place for a man who lacks the courage to carry out his vision. They belong back East where the towns, the homes—everything is already established and life is easy to the point of boredom."

With both his disdainful tone and piercing glance, Donovan was daring Edwin to claim he had the necessary strength of character to succeed in Arizona, but the young man refused to take the bait. Instead, he nodded and smiled. He was surprised Donovan had made no reference to his late wife, but after Belle's mention of the man's hostility on the subject, he dared not ask about her. Instead, he chose to inquire about his partner.

"After all the hard work you describe, I'm surprised your partner didn't remain with you to enjoy your success. Did he simply want a ranch of his own?"

Disappointed Edwin had missed his point, Donovan continued to stare at him coldly. "After the war, there were a great

35

many men like Rick who craved more excitement than ranching affords. Even with the occasional forays Apaches made onto our land, he was restless and moved on to California. I've no idea what he's doing there. He never bothered to write us any letters."

Belle had heard casual references to Rick Vernon her whole life, but she had never given him much thought until that evening. Her father was such an opinionated individual, it was difficult for her to imagine him sharing the responsibility for the ranch with another man without them coming to blows, and she wondered if that wasn't closer to the truth of what had happened.

"When did Rick leave?" she asked.

Donovan took another bite of his supper, chewed it slowly, and appeared to be searching his memories for the date while he swallowed. "We were only partners four years. He left here in 1869."

Belle directed her next comment to her cousin. "That was the year Mama died."

"Oh, no," Edwin murmured sympathetically. "That must have made the breakup of your partnership doubly difficult, sir."

Losing his appetite, Donovan shoved his plate aside. "That was so many years ago I scarcely remember it, but Rick Vernon was a lying snake and I didn't miss him at all. Now, if you'll excuse me, I've work to do. I'm positive you two can carry on a far more amusing conversation without me."

Startled by Donovan's resentment to what he had mistakenly assumed would be a safe comment, Edwin stared after him as he left the room. "I certainly didn't mean to upset him."

"You'll get used to it," Belle assured him.

Edwin nodded, but he doubted that he would. "Correct me if I'm wrong, but it seems odd your father would refer to Mr. Vernon as a man with whom he'd gotten along well during the war, then as someone who craved excitement, and, finally, as a lying snake. Doesn't it to you?"

"Not if he had grown disenchanted with him over the course of their partnership. Frankly, I can't imagine my father even having a partner, so it's no wonder they didn't stay together long."

Edwin wondered if anyone ever lived up to Donovan Cassidy's high expectations. From what he'd seen, it was simply an impossibility. The man still intrigued him, though.

"Your father's white hair and dark brows and lashes make for a dramatic contrast. He's a very attractive man," he confided. "Even if he hasn't remarried, is there a woman he sees?"

Belle was somewhat puzzled by his question, but answered as best she could. "He makes frequent trips to Prescott and Phoenix, but if he calls on women there, he doesn't care to discuss it with me."

Fearing he had embarrassed her, Edwin rephrased his question. "Those weren't the type of women I meant," he whispered discreetly. "I'm talking about a respectable woman, an attractive widow perhaps, with whom he keeps steady company."

"A woman he sits beside in church? That sort of thing?"

"Yes, exactly."

"No. I'm not aware of what he did when I was small, but for as long as I can remember, I've gotten the distinct impression that he barely tolerates women. He's not fond of most men, either. When he's not supervising the running of the ranch, he keeps to himself. Most evenings he just reads and sips brandy."

"Until he's drunk?" Edwin again inquired in a conspiratorial whisper.

"I don't stay up to watch, but I suppose so. Now please, could we talk about something else? I can understand your curiosity, but my father isn't a particularly interesting topic for me."

"I'm sorry. I've been very rude, haven't I?"

"I wouldn't go *that* far!"

"But my behavior has come very close, hasn't it?" Edwin was pleased she was smiling at him again.

When they finished eating, they returned to the parlor and he began to peruse the photographs on display. "This is your father here, isn't it? His hair is dark, but it certainly looks like him."

Belle came close enough to see. "Yes, that's him, and this is Kenneth MacKenzie here in the back."

"Oh, yes, of course it is. Is Rick Vernon in any of these pictures?"

"He must be, but no one has ever pointed him out to me."
Belle reached for the photograph they had been studying and
removed it from the wall. "Just as I thought, the names are written on the back. The ink's faded, but let's see. . . . Yes, Rick is
the third from the left." She handed the framed portrait to
Edwin, who quickly counted the men.

"His hat's pulled too low. I can't make him out clearly. Do you
suppose he's in any of the others?"

Belle was also growing curious about the man's looks and,
after checking several other photographs, they found one in
which Rick Vernon's face showed more clearly. He'd been fair-
haired like Edwin and extraordinarily handsome, but then, in
his twenties, her father had been very good-looking, too. "They
were a handsome pair," she mused absently.

"When did your mother and father marry? Was it before or
after the war?"

"It was during the war, actually. Why?"

Edwin replaced the last portrait they had taken down from
the wall to examine and turned toward her. "I was just wondering if your parents were newlyweds when they came to Arizona, that's all."

Belle licked her lips thoughtfully. Edwin's question wasn't
any more personal than any of the others he had asked that
night, but this one was particularly unsettling. There were all
sorts of implications which might be drawn about her parents
and Rick and, never having considered any of them, she began
to blush deeply. She took several steps away from her cousin,
and then gestured toward the bookcase.

"I doubt we have anything you haven't read, but perhaps
you'll find something to interest you. I hope you'll excuse me,
but I need to speak with our housekeeper before she goes to
bed. Good night."

Belle left the room before Edwin could open his mouth to
stop her and he was disappointed he had missed what he had
hoped would be another chance to kiss her. "Well, there's always
tomorrow," he quipped; thoughts of how hard Kenneth Mac-
Kenzie would undoubtedly make him work sent him off to bed,
too, but not without hopes he would dream of his lovely cousin.

Chapter Four

When Belle entered her bedroom, Aurelia was just turning down her quilt. "I'm glad I found you," she said, then hurried across the room, sat down on the end of the high iron bed and patted the place at her side. "Sit down with me a minute."

"It's early. Why are you neglecting your cousin?"

"I'm not neglecting him," Belle denied. "He's pestering me with questions and I need some answers."

Her work completed for the day, Aurelia eased down beside her. "You were the one who had tutors, *querida*. What answers could I possibly have?"

"This isn't about something we could look up in books. Tell me everything you remember about Rick Vernon."

Aurelia was in her forties and her once-jet-black hair was streaked with gray, but when she heard Rick's name, the weariness of the day vanished from her face and she giggled like a young girl. "I have not thought of him in years," she exclaimed.

"It's obvious you recall him quite fondly," Belle prompted, "or you wouldn't be smiling so widely."

Aurelia put her hands over her mouth momentarily, but wasn't able to erase her impish grin. "He was so handsome, *querida*. José and I were already married when we came here to work, but that did not mean I did not notice Rick. He was not merely good to look at, either, he was always laughing and teasing me about one thing or another."

Aurelia was still attractive and Belle could readily imagine how remarkably pretty she had been. "Flirting, you mean?"

"No, for flirting has a different purpose, *verdad?* He was just

39

having fun. He made everyone laugh. Not just women, but men, too."

"Could he actually amuse my father?"

Aurelia shrugged slightly. "Your father has always had a serious nature, but he was a different man then, and yes, he laughed with the others. That was such a happy time. Rick used to pluck you from your mother's arms and carry you around on his shoulders. You adored him. I'm sorry you don't remember him."

"Yes, so am I. Did my mother appreciate Rick's teasing as much as I did?"

At the mention of Isabel, Aurelia's expression lost its happy glow. She rose and spent a moment shaking out the folds of her skirt to cover her dismay before she took a step toward the door. "Yes, they were good friends. Now I must go or José will worry."

The housekeeper and her husband lived in a house that was so close by, Belle couldn't imagine her possibly getting home late. "Aurelia," she called out to stop her. "Wait a minute. If everyone was having such a wonderful time, why did Rick leave?"

"I don't know, *querida*, he just did."

Belle had seen that same troubled light come into Aurelia's dark eyes when she spoke about Isabel, and now, old enough to be aware of romantic possibilities, she couldn't help asking her next question. "Did my father object to the attention Rick gave my mother? Was he jealous? Is that why their partnership ended?"

Tears welled up in Aurelia's eyes. "Your mother was a good woman, and so full of love."

"I'm not denying that. I just asked if perhaps my father wasn't jealous. Rick was handsome, and you say he was charming, so it's not an unreasonable conclusion."

Aurelia gave her head an emphatic shake. "You must not even think such awful thoughts, *querida*. If your cousin has led you to them, then you must tell him to leave."

Her own curiosity far from satisfied, Belle didn't even consider such a request. "Edwin is very nice and I'll do no such thing. Try and remember all you can about Rick Vernon and we'll talk about him again soon."

Aurelia was already at the door. "There's nothing more to tell," she swore, hurrying out before Belle could delay her again.

When Belle awoke before dawn, thoughts of her mother still weighed so heavily on her mind that a trip to the butte was impossible to forgo. She dressed hurriedly, then rode along the trail her mare had worn into the rocky red soil. Seeking her former solitude, she was relieved to find Coyote's horse gone and climbed the butte grateful it would once again be her private domain. She sat down and awaited the dawn filled with the same longing that pierced her heart whenever she sought the reflection of her mother's love in the rising sun. A faint pinkish glow, the first sign of the coming dawn, had just begun to tint the sky when Coyote sat down beside her.

This time she had been unaware of his approach, and she reacted angrily. "I thought you'd finally had sense enough to leave," she whispered.

The hushed reverence of her tone convinced Coyote that she shared his respect for the mystical power he felt vibrating all around them. Indicating he wished to join her silent vigil, he raised a fingertip to his lips to beg her to be still. He then focused his attention on the rosy hue of the eastern sky. Gradually the first sliver of the sun's fiery bulk cleared the horizon and the goddess of the dawn opened her golden fan and sent shimmering rays of light through the heavens.

Coyote had watched many a sunrise, but never with such a lovely companion. He was far more aware of her than the beauty that lit the sky. Though she was sitting perfectly still, but he felt the restlessness of her spirit rather than the serenity her pose implied. He waited, silent, feeling her torment, and although anxious to learn its cause, he was unwilling to spoil the peace they shared by inquiring as to what troubled her.

Equally aware of him, rather than the joy she had sought in coming to the butte, Belle felt something primitive and deep. Closing her eyes, she tried to shut Coyote out, but the life force which coursed through him was too strong. The rising sun warmed her eyelids, but it didn't rival the heat of the young brave at her side. When she could stand no more of his intrusion into her life, she leaped to her feet.

Sensing how uncomfortable he had made her, Coyote remained seated. "Before you came, I led my horse to the creek. He is still so tired he leaned against me the whole way there and back. I cannot leave yet."

Belle had been about to threaten to notify the Army where he was hiding if he wasn't gone in thirty seconds, but his calmly spoken excuse defused her anger. She was grateful she had not made an ill-tempered demand before hearing it. "I'm sorry. From what I saw of him, he looked like a fine mount. I'd be willing to trade you one of our horses for him."

"No, he has been with me too long to give away. All he needs is another day or two of rest." Coyote looked up at her then. "What is it you need? Why do you come here?"

Belle shoved her hands into her back pockets and shook her head. "I have my reason, but I'd rather not share it."

"I told you why *I'm* here."

"That's different. You're trespassing and wanted to gain my sympathy. I belong here."

Taking care not to alarm her, Coyote rose slowly to his feet. "Tell me," he urged again. "I'll soon be gone and your secrets will be safe with me."

Belle responded with a nervous laugh. "I don't have any secrets."

"Every beautiful woman has secrets," Coyote assured her.

Belle looked at him askance. She was used to Aurelia fussing over her and calling her a beauty, but to have two young men in the space of a single week praise her appearance was a totally new experience. As for secrets, the only one that tortured her was the one her mother had taken to her grave.

"I told you the Yavapai legend," Coyote coaxed. "Now you tell me a story." He gestured for her to again be seated, and when, after a long hesitation she finally returned to her cross-legged pose, he squatted down beside her.

It was more in hopes of putting everything into place in her own mind than to enlighten him that Belle agreed to talk. As with a legend, she knew she ought to begin at the very beginning, but she wasn't certain just where that was. "One of my cousins has come for a visit and he's asked some troubling questions I can't answer."

"What sort of questions?"

Belle chose to be deliberately vague. "At one time, there was a

42

ranch that was owned by two men. One was fair-haired and full of laughter, the other was dark and more serious. The serious one had a wife and daughter, who liked the bachelor partner's teasing. Then everything changed. The wife died and the partner left, or . . . ," Confused, Belle paused.

"I'm sorry, I don't know which happened first," she explained. "Maybe the partnership ended, and then the wife died."

She looked so perplexed that Coyote reached out to give her back a comforting pat. Her muscles were tense and he massaged them gently. "Who is it who really wants the answers—you or your cousin?"

"I do," Belle admitted. While she often climbed the butte to watch the sunrise, she never stepped to the edge and looked down. Just coming too close to the rim of the hilltop filled her with panic, and while they were several feet away from that dangerous brink, she was suddenly overcome with the very same feelings of terror.

Coyote could see her distress; he didn't want her to leave. "Would you like a drink? I just filled my canteen."

"Yes, please." It took him only a few seconds to return with the water. Belle was grateful for the refreshing coolness, but like a swiftly passing summer rain shower, it only dampened the dust of her fright rather than washed it away. She removed her gloves, poured a little water in her palm, and splashed it on her cheeks. "I'm sorry. I didn't realize I don't know enough about this story to share it."

She looked so pained that Coyote knew the people involved had to be very important to her. When she handed him the canteen, he recapped it and set it aside. "Is there someone who knows the whole tale?"

Belle knew better than to ask her father, but she was positive Aurelia must know in what sequence the events had occurred. Kenneth MacKenzie had been on the ranch at that time, too. He might be willing to provide some insights if he didn't think her father would object, but that would still leave the most important question unanswered.

"There are people who know parts of it, at least. It's putting it all together that seems to be impossible."

Coyote nodded thoughtfully. "These people will know

what happened first?"

"Yes, but that won't explain why the partner left, or the wife died."

Readying himself for a lengthy discussion, Coyote adopted her cross-legged pose. "How many reasons are there for friends to end a partnership?" he asked.

"Probably as many as there are friends," Belle exclaimed. "They could have disagreed over so many things: buying more land, selling land, how many — or what kind of — cattle to raise, the price they got for them, who they employed, who did the most work, who spent the most money. Who knows? People can argue over anything, or nothing."

"But here there were two men and one woman," Coyote reminded her. "The source of the argument seems clear."

While Belle didn't want to believe her mother had been involved in a love triangle, it was obviously a possibility. "Yes, and if the woman died, the bachelor would have no reason to stay. Or if he left first, the woman might have had no reason to live."

Belle's voice had again dropped to a hoarse whisper and Coyote could almost feel her pain. "When did this happen?" he asked.

"A long time ago," Belle replied. "But the questions remain."

Coyote waited. The sun rose higher, but Belle's troubled expression did not lift. He had asked her to share secrets, but he had not expected her to become so sad as a result. Without considering the consequences, he reached out to tilt her chin, leaned over, and kissed her. When she didn't draw away, but instead relaxed, he rebelled against the awkwardness of their positions and pulled her across his lap. As her hat fell away, spilling her bright curls down over his arms, he wound his fingers in the colorful tresses to keep her mouth pressed to his. Her lips were soft, her taste delicious, and he didn't want their first kiss to ever end.

While caught off guard, Belle quickly recovered, but knowing she ought not to be allowing an Apache brave to kiss her and actually stopping him were two entirely different things. He had washed in the creek and his hair was still damp. She slid her fingers through his long ebony mane. Lost in the rapture of his affection, time ceased to exist.

Edwin's kiss had been pleasant, but Coyote's was magical and, afraid she would never ever recapture that same bliss, she sighed contentedly as their first kiss slid into a second, and then grew too numerous to count. The contours of their upper bodies fit together as comfortably as their lips, and while Belle felt the strength of Coyote's muscular arms and the broad planes of his chest, there was nothing unfamiliar in the sensation. Being wrapped in his embrace was like coming home. She clung to him, secure in the belief she was precisely where she belonged.

Unlike Belle, Coyote was no stranger to desire, but he had never found another woman whose kiss held such magical delights. She was no tease who gave only the hint of affection with a light brush of her lips. Nor was she so eager to possess him that her hasty kiss was a mere prelude to a release of animal instincts. No, Belle's kiss was flavored with love, and each one created a craving for the next. He would have kissed her all day had the rising sun not sent a painful, blinding ray across their faces.

At first, Belle shut her eyes more tightly, but then the realization that the dawn had become morning jarred her to her senses. She drew away so quickly that she knocked Coyote off balance, and they both had to scramble to keep from toppling over. "I'm not supposed to be late," Belle explained as she climbed out of his arms. She brushed the red dust off her pants and grabbed up her hat.

As agile as she, Coyote was on his feet before she had taken a step toward the trail. He reached out to stop her, and when she turned toward him, her gaze mirrored his own confusion. He was running for his freedom, perhaps his life. Why had he risked further danger by attempting to seduce a wealthy rancher's daughter? What madness had prompted him to steal more than a single kiss? Completely befuddled by the passion she had ignited within him, Coyote gestured toward the red cliffs in the distance.

"It's the magic of this land," he explained unconvincingly. "We were caught in its power."

The only power Belle had felt was that of a virile young Apache, and thinking his excuse absurd, she left him bathed in the warmth of her laughter.

Knowing she was unforgivably late for breakfast, Belle didn't bother entering the house, but instead rode around to the corral,

45

where Kenneth MacKenzie was giving several of the men their instructions for the day. She dismounted and waited until the foreman had sent them off to greet him. Because she spent so much time riding, they saw each other frequently and she attempted to phrase her question in the same relaxed manner their conversations usually took.

"I was looking at some of the photographs in the parlor last night and got to wondering about Rick Vernon," she began. "Can you tell me something about him? The ranch has done so well that I can't help but be curious about why he chose to leave. Do you know what his reason might have been?"

Apparently in the mood to reminisce, Kenneth tipped his hat back. Leaning against the corral, he hooked his arms over the top rail and propped the heel of his right boot on the bottom slat. "I know you were just a little bitty thing when Rick was here, but can you remember anything about him?"

"No, I'm sorry, I don't."

"Well, he was a natural-born clown, but a damn heroic man, too. He had a gift for making even the worst disaster appear to be no more than a minor setback. I don't mind admitting that I miss him to this very day."

With graceful nods and sweet smiles, Belle silently encouraged the foreman to continue his description of the man she wished she could recall. Extolling Rick's war record, Kenneth provided several examples of the type of courage that had kept the Confederacy alive long after all hope of victory had been lost. Then in a less dramatic, but no less interesting, fashion, he explained how Rick had been responsible for much of the ranch's early success.

Belle gradually came to understand that while Rick had possessed enormous charm, he did not merely give men hope but fulfilled all his promises in a dependable and resourceful manner. Kenneth complimented her father for having the determination to carve a ranch out of the wilderness, but credited Rick Vernon with making the long hours and exhausting work that effort required not only bearable but often *fun*. It sounded as though Rick and her father had possessed personality traits which had complemented each other perfectly, and she grew even more curious about why their partnership had ended.

"Why didn't he stay with us?" she asked.

Kenneth shook his head. "I'll be damned if I know. He and the major always had their differences, but none that ever seemed too serious. Then again, one day Rick was here and the next he was gone, so something had to have gone wrong. We were all hurt he didn't take the time to tell any of us goodbye."

"Wait a minute. You'd fought with him in the war and worked for him here for four years and he didn't speak to you before he left? Didn't that strike you as odd?"

"Oh, yes, ma'am, it most certainly did, but he left just before your dear mama died, and we were all heartbroken over that tragedy. That Rick had just up and left for California didn't seem to matter much after she died."

Kenneth straightened up, obviously thinking the conversation over, but Belle still had a couple of questions. "If Rick didn't tell anyone goodbye, how did you all know he'd gone to California?"

"The major told us the morning after he'd gone. There were several of the men who would have gone with Rick if he'd given them the chance, but, as I said, when your mother died, we were all needed here and no one tried to follow him."

Bracing herself for the same type of response she had received from Aurelia, Belle asked her last question. "This will be our secret, Ken, but was there anything more than friendship between my mother and Rick?"

"Oh, Jesus, honey!" Shocked, Kenneth turned his back on her for a moment, yanked off his hat, ran his fingers through his graying hair, and then replaced the hat with an angry shove. When he finally turned back to face Belle, he failed in his attempt to control his temper.

"There wasn't a man on this spread who didn't worship Isabel, and Rick was no exception, but there's absolutely no call for talk like that, young lady. Your mother was a fine woman, and nothing has ever been the same here since the day she died."

As the foreman turned away, tears were streaming down his face and Belle knew he had revealed an important secret after all: he had been in love with Isabel, and loved her still.

Chapter Five

Belle didn't want to see her father, or Win, or the damn Apache who tasted of love but claimed it was only the magic of the land, so, after speaking with Kenneth, she rode her mare on down to the creek. She let the horse graze while she took off her boots and socks and danced over the smooth wet stones bordering the boulder-strewn stream. The musical rhythms of the tumbling water buoyed her spirits and she began to imagine that her mother might have waded there on the first morning she had spent at the ranch.

Isabel had been nineteen when she married Donovan Cassidy, and twenty-one when they had come to the Arizona Territory. She'd been twenty-three when Belle was born, and only twenty-five when she had taken her own life. Belle chanted those ages as she hopped from stone to stone. Her mother's life had progressed in a predictable and orderly pattern, until its ghastly end.

What had her own life been? Belle asked herself. She counted out nineteen years. Like beads on a string, they slid back and forth blurring into a red haze that was indistinguishable from the iron-oxide-laden earth. The most significant event had been her mother's death, but that had taken place so long ago it was lost among the first beads on the string. Thinking the years of her life resembled the rushing waters of the creek that left no trace of their passing, Belle lost interest in wading and sat down on the fallen oak where she and Win had paused to chat.

Belle had come to the sad conclusion that her own life would never have any meaning if she couldn't make some sense of her mother's death. What frustrated her most was that it did not seem as though a conclusion could be reached from a mere sorting of the facts. What was sorely needed was wisdom gained through intuition, and she wasn't certain she wished to trust a heart that had never known love with such a difficult challenge.

She raised her fingertips to her lips and marveled at the fact that Kenneth hadn't noticed they were swollen from kisses. "But of course," she mused aloud, "he saw only what he expected to see." She had been dressed in her usual riding clothes. Her hair had been covered, although not all that neatly, by her hastily donned hat. Surely her skin had been flushed from her romantic escapade, but Kenneth would have assumed the early-morning air had imparted that pretty glow.

What had Kenneth missed seeing when her mother was alive? Certain she would learn nothing more from him, and reluctant to arouse his suspicions as to her motives, the next time she saw him she would simply pretend their last conversation hadn't taken place. Better still, she would avoid him for a couple of days; maybe he would forget all about it. From the passionate reactions she got whenever she asked about her mother, she knew she ought to choose her questions, and the people she consulted, with a great deal more care.

Growing hungry, she pulled on her socks and boots and returned home early for the midday meal, but when she saw Kenneth had set Edwin the task of riding a gray mustang that not even their best vaqueros would dare saddle, she forgot her plan to avoid him and shouted an objection. "You're supposed to be teaching him, Ken, not letting him get killed!"

Ignoring her protest, Kenneth hooted as Edwin landed in the dirt and had to roll out of the way of the mustang's flying hooves. "We've not lost a single man in this corral, Miss Belle, and your cousin won't be the first."

Sighting Belle, Edwin limped over to her side of the corral. "Morning. I don't suppose you've ever been bucked off a horse, but I'd no idea how much it hurt."

"I've been thrown plenty of times and the ground never gets any softer. If you've had enough, just say so."

Edwin looked surprised by her suggestion. "No, I intend to ride that horse. He might not understand yet, but I sure do." He tipped the hat, which had gotten trampled several times that morning even if he hadn't, and walked back toward the feisty little mustang. The horse bolted away, but Kenneth leaned over the top rail of the corral to grab his reins and Edwin pulled himself up into the saddle.

"Don't worry about him," Kenneth whispered to Belle. "He's a lot stronger than he looks."

"Are you talking about the mustang or Win?"

Always ready to appreciate a good joke, the foreman laughed again. "I'm talking about your cousin. He comes from good stock and he'll ride that horse if it takes him all day. You just go on in the house and leave him be. I won't let him get hurt."

In less than a minute, Edwin was again sitting in the dirt, but when he got up, dusted himself off, and waved to her, Belle realized Ken was right. Her cousin probably would have to devote the entire day to riding the foul-tempered horse, but he was equal to the challenge. She started toward the house pleased her father had been proven wrong: Edwin was no quitter.

Edwin was obviously tired and sore when he came inside to eat, but he winked at Belle and assured Donovan that he was enjoying his stay on the ranch immensely. Distracted by Edwin's questions about horses, the major forgot to reprimand Belle for missing breakfast and the meal was one of the most pleasant they had shared in a long while. At one point, Donovan even smiled at Edwin, and Belle was amazed by how dramatically the change in his usual stern demeanor altered his appearance. Because they had never gotten along, she didn't really think of him as being handsome, but on the rare occasions when he smiled, he most certainly was.

With Edwin occupied, and her father too busy to take notice of her, Belle chose to spend the afternoon looking through an old trunk in the sewing room that contained her mother's things. She had loved to dress up in the sachet-scented clothes when she had been small, but she had a different purpose for sorting through Isabel's belongings that day. She had no memories of her mother, and could not recall her wearing the beautiful gowns her father had saved, but she hoped there might be something else, something she had overlooked when she was a child just wanting to play.

The tray at the top of the trunk contained silk scarves and lace-trimmed lingerie, but no letters or diary that might have provided a clue as to what had driven Isabel to suicide. Belle set the tray aside and removed the first of the gowns. It was pale green and the waist looked impossibly tiny. Suddenly curious as to how similar she and her mother were in size, Belle stripped off her riding clothes and slipped the pretty gown on over her head. Much to her surprise, she found it to be too tight in the bust, nearly perfect in the waist, and a good three inches too short.

She walked over to the full-length mirror and turned slowly. "Well, Mama, it doesn't look as though I'll be getting much use out of this dress." She had never even considered wearing her mother's clothes once she had lost interest in playing at wearing them and hurriedly removed the green gown. She didn't try on another until she came to a white lace dress that she recognized as a wedding gown. Disappointed that it fit her no better than the green dress, she was about to remove it when Aurelia came to the door, peeked in, and gasped.

"For an instant," she explained, "I thought it was your dear mother standing there." The housekeeper came on in and circled Belle to admire the lovely gown. "With just a little work, I could alter it to fit you. Let me get the pins."

Belle studied her reflection. "This is Mama's wedding gown and I don't even have a fiancé. Isn't it a bit premature to bother with altering it?"

"Oh, no, *querida*. You will marry someday, and then the gown will be ready."

Unconvinced, Belle eventually let herself be talked into standing still long enough for Aurelia to place the pins marking where the seams would have to be adjusted. "I didn't realize I was so much taller than Mama. What about the hem?"

Aurelia quickly turned up the skirt of the gown. "See, there's plenty of fabric and I'll find some ribbon to cover the old hem if it shows after I've let this down. In fact, I ought to just remake the skirt so you'll have a bustle. We should have thought of doing this long before now."

Belle disagreed. "It has to be very bad luck to have fittings for a

51

wedding gown with no groom in sight."

"I've seen the way your cousin looks at you. You may have a husband sooner than you think."

Certain her parents' marriage must have had a disastrous flaw, Belle frowned slightly. "No, I'm going to take my time. When we were talking last night, why didn't you mention that Rick left here just a few days before my mother died?"

"I had forgotten." Aurelia mumbled her response between the pins in her mouth.

The housekeeper didn't look up at her, and Belle felt certain she was lying. She couldn't recall another occasion when Aurelia had been less than truthful and she was about to criticize her sharply for it when Edwin appeared at the partially open door. Embarrassed to have him find her trying on a wedding gown, she hoped his repeated falls from the mustang had left him too dizzy to notice her choice of attire.

All Edwin saw was a beautiful redhead in an old-fashioned gown, but thinking fashions might be considerably behind the times in Arizona, he tactfully did not mention it. "I didn't mean to bother you," he apologized, "but I actually think I've got that blasted horse ready to ride. I wanted you to go with me, but if you're busy—"

"Why, no," Belle assured him. "Ask one of the men to saddle my mare and wait for me at the corral. I'll be right there." Edwin hurried off and, thinking it a poor time to confront Aurelia about her faulty memory, Belle dismissed her and donned her riding clothes. She had not taken more than five minutes to join him, but Edwin greeted her as though he had waited hours.

"Good, you're ready. Let's go. I saddled your mare myself. I needed the practice."

While she trusted his good intentions, Belle took the precaution of checking the cinch before she mounted. Finding it was as snug as she herself would have made it, she swung herself up into the saddle and waited for Edwin to mount the mustang. The barely broken horse tensed slightly, but didn't buck Edwin off.

"I think he's begun to like you."

"It's about time." Edwin still looked a bit apprehensive, but the mustang fell in step beside Belle's mare and didn't give him any trouble as they started their ride. "I guess no one else was stubborn enough to outlast him."

"Don't belittle yourself. You put in a lot of effort and it paid off. He'll make a good horse for you."

"I hope so. Tell me something . . . Do you always wear a pistol when you ride?"

"Always," Belle replied. "It's more of a precaution against rattlesnakes than for any other reason."

"Rattlesnakes?" Edwin asked with an audible gulp.

"You needn't be so worried, Win. Snakes don't like us any better than we like them. Now, your horse looks fast, would you like to have a race?"

"All right, shall we make it to the butte?"

That was the last place Belle wanted to take him, so she quickly provided an excuse. "There's a gradual incline to that path and it would make it too strenuous for the horses. Let's just head south. The oaks in the distance can be the finish line."

Edwin agreed. They counted to three and then urged their mounts into a gallop. Belle kept her mare on a tight rein until they had covered half the course, then, relaxing her hold, she let the pinto set her own pace and they began to pull away from Edwin and the gray mustang. When the mare sprinted past the oaks, they had increased their lead to half a dozen lengths. Sorry the mustang wasn't nearly as swift as she had assumed, Belle turned her mare in a wide loop and looked back toward Edwin.

Desperately attempting to inspire the mustang to a speed approaching flight, Edwin was whipping his mount with the ends of his reins. He knew he had already lost the match to Belle, but he was frantically trying to escape the Indian who had come out of nowhere and was fast closing in on his left. He glanced over his shoulder, saw the snarling savage would overtake him in an instant, and let out a blood-curdling shriek as he tore past the oaks.

At first unable to believe her eyes, Belle watched in stunned horror as Coyote rode past. Riding bareback, leaning forward, his motions were perfectly synchronized to each lunge of the powerful bay. His long black hair whipped about his head with the dramatic flare of a war bonnet made of raven feathers, and, despite the danger he posed to her terrified cousin, she thought he presented the most magnificent sight she had ever seen. She could have watched him ride for hours, but knowing her cousin

53

deserved a quick rescue, she again nudged her mare's sides with her heels and took up the chase.

By the time she caught up with the men, Coyote had dragged Edwin from his mustang, thrown him to the ground, and stood over him with his knife drawn. He had waited for her, but he looked ready to slit Edwin's throat should she nod her consent.

The wind had been knocked out of him, and Edwin was struggling to catch his breath. "Shoot him!" Win gasped, his eyes wide with the terror that made his hands twitch as he reached out for her.

Confused by Edwin's hoarse plea, Coyote looked to Belle for some answers. "Do you know this man?" he asked.

Belle swung down off her horse. "Yes, I most certainly do. He's my cousin, Edwin Pierce. I told you he was visiting me, remember?" Belle brushed past Coyote, leaned down to offer Edwin her hand, and pulled him to his feet. "This Apache calls himself Coyote," she explained to complete the introductions. "But Lord knows what he thought he was doing just now."

Edwin's newly acquired tan had faded to a deathly pallor and Belle looped her arm through his to make certain he didn't slide to the ground if his knees felt weak. She then turned back toward the Apache. "Suppose you tell us why you chose to frighten Edwin half out of his wits. We're both eager to hear."

The proud mask of a warrior slipped from Coyote's face to be replaced by an expression of acute embarrassment. "Your cousin?" he asked. "¿Un primo?"

"Sí, un primo, but even if he were a complete stranger, you had no right to treat him as you have. This is my ranch, not yours, and my guests are free to come and go as they please."

Shaken to the very marrow, Edwin stared in fascinated disbelief as Belle scolded the tall Apache brave as though he were merely a naughty child. The Indian did look contrite, but he was still holding a wickedly sharp knife and Edwin felt no less threatened. "Belle?" he pleaded. "Let's just go."

"No, I want him to explain. Oh, by the way, Coyote, for an exhausted animal, your horse moves with astonishing speed."

No longer needing his weapon, Coyote slid his knife into its sheath. Unwilling to admit he had lied to her, he shrugged slightly. "He is stronger than I thought." When Belle continued to

54

glare at him, he gestured helplessly. "I thought he was chasing you. I had to stop him."

Amazed to learn he felt responsible for her safety, Belle wanted to hear more. "Did you just happen to notice us, or were you watching me?"

Coyote leaned close so Edwin would not overhear him. "What's the difference?" he asked.

"Let me put my question another way. Were you deliberately spying on me or did you just happen to glance up and think I was being pursued by a lone bandit?"

Before responding, Coyote made a face at Edwin, inspiring the Virginian to let go of Belle and leap back to avoid another attack. Amused, the Apache broke into a wide grin. "I have no time to spy on you," he scoffed. "I was caring for my horse. I saw you ride by, then him, and followed to help you. I thought you would thank me."

Their race had been over so quickly, Belle doubted that Coyote had had enough time to observe them from the butte, climb down, mount his horse, and overtake them. It seemed likely he was telling the truth. He may have yanked Edwin from his saddle unnecessarily, but when she viewed the incident from the Apache's standpoint, his actions were commendable, even heroic.

She began to blush for the second time that day. "I've never been rescued before. Thank you for trying, even if I didn't need it." She offered her hand. "Since your horse seems to be fit, I know you'll be leaving and I want to wish you good luck."

Coyote had shaken hands with white men, but never a woman, and her gesture surprised him. He took her hand in his, but then squeezed it to send a message other than a friendly farewell. "My horse was fit, but I have just exhausted him again rescuing you."

Belle would have argued that he had to leave whether or not his horse was up to carrying him, but the tenderness of his smile distracted her so completely she could not recall what it was she ought to say. She finally withdrew her hand from his, and anxious to be on their way, looked around for Edwin's mustang. Still more wild than tame, the horse had wandered some hundred yards away.

"I'll go and get your horse, Edwin," she offered. "It will only take me a minute."

Coyote winked at him, and, positive he did not want to spend even a second alone with the aggressive brave, Edwin promptly refused her help. "No, I'll get him," he said as he started toward the mustang with a stumbling, shaky gait.

When Belle sent Coyote an infuriated glance, he needed no further urging. He leaped upon his bay, caught the skiddish mustang with the skill of an accomplished vaquero, and led him back to Edwin. "I am sorry," he told him.

While the Apache sounded sincere, Edwin couldn't really believe that he was. He wanted to say something forceful and strong, in hopes of impressing Belle, but all he could manage was a strained nod. He watched the Apache ride off toward the butte, but he didn't feel any safer than when he had been pulled off his horse.

"I wish that you'd warned me you have Indians living here," he complained. "If you mentioned me to him, then I deserved the same courtesy."

Belle was watching Coyote with such an intense gaze that she barely heard her cousin. She feared she had handled the whole unfortunate incident poorly and felt torn between the conflicting desire to see the Apache again and the need to have him gone. Finally she realized Edwin was waiting for an answer.

"There *aren't* any Indians living here. Coyote is just passing through. He's been scouting for the Army, but with the last of the renegades being sent to Florida, there's no more work for him. Now let's get back home. I think what you need is a hot bath and a long nap before supper."

Edwin ignored her solicitous concern. "I can't believe your father would allow Apaches to even cross his land, let alone spend any time here."

"Coyote's had enough trouble without tangling with my father, so don't you dare tell him of his presence. You understand me, Edwin? I like you a lot, but I won't allow you to cause Coyote any more trouble than he's already got. Now come on, let's go."

If Edwin hadn't known better, he would have sworn that Belle cared for the brave, but that was just too outrageous a happenstance for a young southern gentleman to accept.

56

Chapter Six

Coyote came down off the butte at sundown. He stayed in the shadows as he approached the house and, hidden behind a mesquite thicket, kept watch on its occupants. He saw women passing between the kitchen and house with heavily laden trays that gave off delicious smells and tried to ignore his own hunger. He observed three figures moving from the parlor to the dining room. He assumed the slender woman was Belle and one of the men her cousin, but who was the other man? If he was her father, where was her mother?

Was she dead like the woman in her story? he wondered. He knew almost nothing about Belle other than how pretty she looked and how good she tasted. He knew she had a temper, that he had to admit, but he knew nothing about her people. She knew far more about him.

He had spent his life in the southeastern part of the territory and in Mexico. The legendary lands of the Yavapai were like a separate country to him. The deep red color of the earth, the majestic cliffs that rose up out of the desert floor, the strange rhythms he could feel if not hear, it was all foreign to him. As foreign as a pretty redhead who lived in the oddest looking house he had ever seen.

He had to wait hours for the house to grow dark. He saw a feminine shadow pass by the corner window upstairs and assumed Belle had gone to her room. A light shone briefly in another upstairs bedroom, but after the second story was dark, the lamps continued to burn in the parlor. Having seen no guards, Coyote inched toward the lighted window and keeping well to the side, peeked in. A gray-haired gentleman was asleep in a chair with his feet propped on a conveniently placed table. A book lay open on his lap, his fingers curled around an empty glass.

Coyote lingered a while to make certain the man was sleeping too soundly to hear the back door open and close. He was taking a risk in coming there, and well aware of the danger, he did not intend to be foolhardy. Remaining in the shadows, he passed by the now dark and silent kitchen and entered the back door. The lamps in the parlor provided faint illumination to the long hall and he kept to the shadows until he reached the bottom of the stairs. He waited there a long moment, and hearing nothing other than the heavy breathing of the man sleeping in the parlor, he put his foot on the first step.

Expecting creaks and groans from the stairs, he moved up them slowly, ready to lift his foot suddenly should his progress threaten to awaken any of the sleeping residents, but the stairs were as silent as the earth upon which the house was built. He paused at the landing, then, fearing he was moving so slowly he would not reach Belle before dawn, he quickened his pace. When he reached the top of the stairs, he went to the corner room where he thought he had seen her, turned the doorknob, and slipped through the door.

Outdoors, her perfume had had such a subtle fragrance he had scarcely noticed it, but now he recognized the tantalizing scent that filled the room as hers. His eyes were already accustomed to the darkness, and the soft glow of the moonlight filtered through the curtains lit his way to her bed. He stood at the foot for a long moment and watched her sleep. Her room was several times larger than an Apache *wickiup,* which sheltered an entire family, and thinking the distance between them was too vast ever to be bridged, he might have left without speaking had she not suddenly stirred.

Belle sensed Coyote's presence even in her dreams, and when she sat up and found him standing at the foot of her bed, she thought he must have spoken her name to awaken her. In truth, he had not uttered a word. "You have a rare talent for turning up where you're not expected. Do Apaches allow young men to visit their daughters in their bedrooms?"

58

Coyote chuckled softly, but did not explain a *wickiup* had but a single room. "No," he whispered.

"Well, neither do white men, and you must leave."

"That's what I'm doing," Coyote insisted softly. "I came to tell you goodbye."

That a handsome savage would bother to say farewell to someone he barely knew, while Rick Vernon had not bid his longtime friends goodbye struck such a jarring chord that Belle threw back the covers, got out of bed, and pulled on her robe. "Come with me, please," she said as she padded by him barefoot.

Coyote followed, but blocked her door with his shoulder before she could open it. "Where are we going?"

"Just down the hall to the sewing room. We can't talk here."

Coyote had not really come there to talk. He just wanted to see her one last time and he was afraid she was so angry with him for spoiling her ride with her cousin that she'd never come to the butte again. He stepped back so she could open the door and then followed her to a much smaller room. When she lit the lamp, he saw it contained a wardrobe, a chest of drawers, an old trunk, shelves filled with bolts of fabric, a long mirror, and several chairs. He had never seen such a large mirror and stepped in front of it.

The weary, thin man who looked back at him didn't please him, and with a surly grimace, he promptly turned away.

"What's the matter?" Belle asked. "I think you're handsome, don't you?"

"I look half dead." Disgusted, Coyote sat down on the trunk. "I came north because I knew if anyone did try to track me, they would think I went south to Mexico. They will have given up by now and I can go wherever I please."

His shoulders slumped in a dejected pose. It was difficult for Belle to recognize him as the valiant rider who had presented such a thrilling sight that afternoon. Her first impulse was to go to him, to wrap him in her arms and assure him everything would be all right, but she knew she ought not to comfort an Apache with an embrace, or make any promises she could not keep.

"Are you hungry?" she asked instead.

Coyote nodded. "Very."

"Then we'll talk in the kitchen. Come on." Belle extinguished the lamp, and this time took his hand to guide him down the stairs. She paused at the bottom, made certain they had not disturbed her father, and then led him out to the kitchen. Unfamiliar with the way it was organized, it took her a long while to locate and light a candle.

"I'm sorry to make you wait. The stove still has a little heat and I'll warm some tortillas. I know there's cheese, and there's usually a pot of beans. Here's some ham. Do you like that?"

Belle was dressed in a flowing white gown and pale-green silk robe. She had tied her hair at her nape with a green ribbon and reminded him of an illustration he'd seen of a princess in a book of fairy tales. She was as close to a princess as he would ever come.

He watched in amazement as she kept offering him food.

"A slice of ham, some cheese, a few tortillas, I don't need much."

"Surely a man who feels half dead can eat more."

"I don't feel nearly as bad as I look."

Belle laid out the tortillas to catch the heat remaining in the stove, sliced the ham and cheese, and put them on a plate. When the tortillas were warm, she handed the plate to Coyote. "There's just water here to drink. Will that do?"

"Yes, thank you." The Apache was so hungry he was nearly overcome by her kindness and, afraid he would choke on emotion, he ate without looking up at her or trying to speak. The tortillas had been made that evening and were as light and delicious as any he had ever eaten. The cheddar cheese had a good sharp flavor, and the ham was of a far superior quality than any they had ever seen on the reservation.

Belle tried not to stare, but Coyote was eating with such obvious gusto she was sorry she had not offered him some provisions earlier. "You told me you had food. But it wasn't nearly enough, was it?"

Coyote just shrugged and kept eating.

Belle pulled up a stool near the one he had chosen and, inspired by his effort to tell her goodbye, revealed what she had learned. "Do you remember the partners I told you about?"

When Coyote nodded, she continued. "The one partner left, and then the wife of the other died. That really doesn't prove anything—it could have merely been a coincidence—but there's one thing that troubles me."

Having eaten enough to take the edge off his hunger, Coyote looked up. "What?"

Belle explained how Rick had left without telling any of his old friends goodbye. "Doesn't that seem strange?" she asked. "It's almost as though he just disappeared, vanished."

Coyote swallowed and took a drink. "Our people don't just disappear. They gather their belongings and tell their friends and family where they are going before they leave."

"Yes, so do ours." Belle pursed her lips thoughtfully. "Something's not right, but I'm almost afraid to pursue it any further."

When she did not elaborate, Coyote sought to satisfy his own curiosity. "Is that your father sleeping downstairs?"

"Yes. He often stays up late reading."

Coyote doubted the empty glass in her father's hand had contained water, but he did not want to call the man a drunk and insult her. "Where's your mother?"

"She died when I was a baby." Having told him that much, Belle admitted the rest. "It's my father and his partner I've been talking about. I've known the story my whole life, and yet I don't really know it at all. That's what frightens me. I know so little, and if even that little bit is wrong, then . . ." Embarrassed, she quickly caught herself. "I shouldn't be burdening you with this. You've troubles enough of your own."

Coyote finished the last of the ham and cheese and set the plate aside. "I like listening to your problems. I think too much about my own. I could stay another day or two just to listen, if it's a help to you."

"I can't ask that of you," Belle responded shyly. "This mystery is nearly twenty years old. Another few days won't unravel it."

Coyote stood up, took her hands, and drew her to her feet. "If you need me, I'll stay," he whispered. She looked up at him, her brown eyes reflecting the golden glow of the lamp, and all he really wanted was to kiss her again and again. Warm and relaxed from sleep, she melted into his embrace even more readily than she had that morning. He didn't care what excuse he had to use, or how stupid it was for him to want a rich girl, he was going to stay.

Enchanted by the sweetness of his offer and thrilled by his passion, Belle slid her arms around his waist and leaned into his next kiss with her whole body. Her father was not a demonstrative man and their hired hands knew better than to touch her, but again Coyote's embrace was filled with a comfort and strength that echoed memories of a love she had forgotten. The wonderful sensation of belonging made no sense at all, so she sought only to enjoy rather than analyze it. When she remembered that he had attributed the joy they had shared earlier not to the magic they ignited by themselves but to the exotic terrain, she pulled away slightly.

Coyote looked as dazed as she felt and immediately tried to kiss her again, but Belle put her hands on his chest to force him away. "We're not up on the butte where the beauty of the surroundings can affect us, but in a crowded kitchen that smells of onions and chili peppers. Do you still believe we're merely under the spell of a magic land or is what I feel with you something far more rare?"

Having no ready answer, Coyote sighed softly and, after again pulling her close, pressed her cheek against his shoulder. He couldn't deny his desire or that a mere glimpse of her created a longing to possess her that was nearly pain, but to believe they had any hope of a shared future was lunacy and he would not lie to himself, or to her. He untied the ribbon in her hair and shoved it into his pocket before releasing her and stepping back.

"I'm a renegade now, no better than an outlaw. That we please each other is a cruel joke. It doesn't matter if it's the land or fate, nothing can come of it."

As before, his words did not match the honey-sweet promise of love that filled his kiss and rather than accepting his dismal view, Belle felt betrayed. "You're wrong," she swore angrily. "Love is too precious to throw away, no matter how absurd or unlikely it seems."

Before Coyote had time to respond, they heard someone slam the back door. "Get down!" Belle urged, and not wanting to be seen by anyone, the brave ducked out of sight behind the stove. Belle grabbed his plate and, licking her fingers, picked up the last of the crumbs.

Donovan Cassidy came to the door, looked in, and was shocked to find his daughter enjoying a midnight snack. "Didn't you have enough to eat at supper?" he asked.

"I guess not," Belle replied. "I woke up so hungry, or perhaps it was hunger that woke me, I don't know which, but I was sure I could find something good to eat and I did. Can I fix something for you?"

Donovan brushed his hair out of his eyes, and shook his head. "No, go on back to bed. You ought not to be out wandering around in the dead of night in a flimsy robe, child. It doesn't look right."

Grateful he had remained at the door, Belle snuffed the candle and followed him back into the house. Ordinarily she would have argued that there was no one around to see her so her choice of attire didn't matter, but this night she didn't want to delay his trip to bed and kept still. "Good night, Father."

Donovan was used to her defying him, and continued as though she had put up one of her feisty arguments. "I mean it, Belle," he stressed. "Keep some fruit in your room so you won't have to visit the kitchen to satisfy your late-night cravings. I don't want to find you out of the house after midnight ever again. It isn't safe and I'll not allow it."

"You needn't worry," Belle assured him. It was a comment that promised absolutely nothing, but Donovan failed to notice that was precisely her intention and went on to bed.

Belle closed her door and hurried to the window. Although she waited a long while, she didn't see Coyote make his way back to the butte. She felt certain he had the common sense to take some of the cheese and ham she had left by the stove, but thought it tragic he placed such little value on love.

Belle was deeply troubled by Coyote's visit as well as her inability to make sense of the part Rick Vernon might have played in her mother's suicide. It took her a long while to fall asleep a second time that night and when she finally did her dreams were plagued by darkly disturbing images in which her father leaped out at her from behind every shadow. He chased her through the house, up and down the stairs, then outside into the night where the brightness of the moonlight made it impossible for her to elude him. His face contorted with rage, he ran after her with his arms outstretched. Eager to choke the life out of her, he lunged time and again for her throat; although she slipped and fell repeatedly, she was too agile and quick to be caught.

When Belle awoke, she felt drained, as though she had actually been running all night. The sun was already up and her room was bathed in a brilliant yellow light. She sat up and brushed her tangled curls out of her eyes. She felt for the ribbon which ought to have been at her nape and dimly recalled Coyote taking it. Resting her elbows on her knees, she held her head in her hands and tried to separate her hideous dreams from what had actually happened.

Despite her ongoing verbal battle with her father, he had never struck her, or threatened her with bodily harm, or chased her through the house. Thinking her own guilt at being surprised in the kitchen with an Apache brave had inspired the disturbing dreams, she promptly dismissed them in favor of recalling Coyote's late-night visit. She understood that a rancher's daughter and an Apache renegade would not be anyone's idea of a good match, but she had a defiant streak that couldn't be tamed and didn't care in the least what anyone else, her father included, thought of Coyote.

She was not so foolish as to fail to note Coyote also had a voice in the matter. His choice seemed to be no, but he had offered to stay, and Belle considered that a good sign. But was it really? she agonized. Maybe he just felt sorry for her. Maybe he was just hungry and would have told her anything to secure another meal. Maybe he was simply using her to reach his own devious ends.

Frustrated that all she had were unanswerable questions, Belle left her bed fearing she had been an idiot to speak of love to a man she had known only three days. What had first seemed like a wonderfully romantic interlude now struck her as shameful. "How pathetic!" she cried. She had had such little affection in her life that she now feared she had thrown herself into Coyote's arms and called it love simply to justify their mutual lust. Tears of embarrassment filled her eyes. She owed the brave an apology, but maybe her mention of love had frightened Coyote away and he had left as he had originally planned.

She went to her window and looked up at the butte. She had greeted the dawn there for years, but Coyote's arrival had changed what had been a peaceful, joyous ritual into what she now feared was merely a ridiculously one-sided infatuation. As if that weren't problem enough, Edwin's ceaseless probing into her past had forced her to search for the answers a sudden disappearance and tragic death had apparently erased.

Hurt and confused, Belle reached the breakfast table ahead of her father for once, but she had never greeted a day with less enthusiasm.

Chapter Seven

While Donovan failed to note his daughter's downcast mood during breakfast, Edwin was keenly aware of it. Eager for another opportunity to spend some time with Belle, he followed her out to the barn after they finished eating. "I'd like to go riding with you again," he began. "If you're showing me around the ranch, and I'm riding the mustang, Kenneth will be sure to call it work."

Belle thought her cousin had made an amazing recovery after the physical abuse he'd suffered the previous day. "Are you sure you feel up to it? If I'd been thrown as many times as you were yesterday, I wouldn't have been able to get out of bed this morning."

Considering that a compliment to his endurance, Edwin's posture straightened noticeably, but he paid for that show of pride with a fresh burst of pain he barely managed to hide. "I'll admit it took me a little longer than usual to get up and dressed, but I'm afraid I'll just stiffen up if I don't get some exercise."

Belle would have preferred to wander off on her own, but fearing she spent too much of her time in solitary pursuits and was in deep trouble with Coyote as a result, she tried to smile and act as though she truly wanted his company. When they had saddled their horses, she again led the way toward the creek. The morning was cool and bright, perfect for riding, and she was sorry she couldn't be more cheerful for her cousin's sake.

Belle still looked far from happy and Edwin hated to think it might be his fault. "I won't tell your father about the

66

Indian. Is that what's got you so worried?"

Belle shook her head. "I trust you to keep still."

Edwin looked back over his shoulder toward the butte. "You said he was just passing through. Do you suppose he's gone?"

"I don't know. Maybe. Could we talk about something else?"

Edwin was trying so hard to get to know her, but she thwarted his every attempt to foster closeness between them. He was badly frustrated by her constant rebuffs. "You always change the subject," he complained. "Did you realize that? Every time our conversations begin to get interesting, you insist we talk about something else."

Belle was momentarily taken aback by his challenging tone, but she was so used to her father complaining about her behavior, it didn't really faze her. "Well, you're constantly pestering me for answers I don't have, so it's no wonder I don't enjoy your choice of topic."

"I'm asking about important things, Belle. I'm not trying to pry. Besides your father and me, how many members of your family do you know?"

"None, but the ones I do know might be two too many." Her point made, Belle dug her heels into her mare's ribs, and now confident the pinto had the speed to leave her cousin behind, she galloped off toward the creek.

Edwin swore angrily, but quickly followed in Belle's dusty wake. He couldn't overtake her, but kept up his pursuit until she finally drew to a halt. He tried to jump down from his horse the way he'd seen the vaqueros dismount but nearly fell. He was grateful Belle was too upset with him to have noticed.

She was tossing stones into the creek, and he took care to approach her slowly. "I'm sorry, Belle. Whenever the folks back home get together, someone always mentions you and your father, but I bet your father has never told you much about us, especially me. So here I am calling you family and you probably think of me as someone you've only known a few days. Maybe I'm simplifying the problem, but I hope I'm getting close to solving it."

Belle tossed the last of the smooth pebbles she'd picked up into the creek and shoved her hands into her hip pockets. Physically, she felt as though she were the one who had been thrown a dozen times, but the pain was deep inside, not anywhere a hot bath and rest would cure. When Edwin reached her side, she glanced at him only briefly, and then, ashamed of herself, looked away.

"Indians aren't the most predictable men in the world, Win, so there's no way of knowing whether or not Coyote's gone without riding out to the butte and looking for him, which I'd rather not do. If you're curious about his plans, you'll have to go out there and talk to him yourself."

Belle hadn't accepted his apology, but she was at least speaking to him, and Edwin decided that was perhaps the best he could hope for for the time being. "I'm really not that interested in the man," he hastened to explain. "I guess I was just jealous of him."

"Jealous?" Belle couldn't decide which was worse, that he thought he had any right to be jealous or that he suspected there was a romantic link between Coyote and her. Just pondering the question made her feel unbearably sad. "The Army's treated their scouts very badly. Coyote's bitter about it and I don't blame him." Unable to describe or deny how far their friendship went, she fell silent.

Edwin waited for her to add more, and was disappointed when he finally realized she never would. The Indian wasn't the only person he had expressed an interest in and he now feared he had been too forward in that area, too. "When I look at it your way," he tried again, "I guess my curiosity about your mother and Rick Vernon was too keen. Just because I'm family doesn't give me the right to ask you painful questions."

"Your questions were the ones I should have asked years ago," Belle assured him. "Everyone seems to have admired Rick and adored my mother, but he's gone and she's dead, so what's the use of trying to sort out what happened? It won't change anything. They'll still be gone."

"Wait a minute," Edwin cautioned. "Your father referred to Rick as a 'lying snake,' so he certainly didn't admire him."

Belle sighed unhappily. "In case you haven't noticed, my father has a bad temper. He walked out on us the other night when we questioned him about Rick and that's not a good indication that he'd like to be asked about him again."

"No, it certainly isn't." Edwin scooped up a stone and tossed it into the stream. "I suppose if there had been any question of foul play when Rick disappeared, or when your mother died, it would have been investigated."

Aghast at that comment, Belle turned to face her cousin squarely. His expression was completely innocent, as though he was merely stating the obvious, but what was fast becoming obvious to her was something entirely different. She tried to slam the mental door on the intrigues of the past, but like a chilling fog, the evil thoughts continued to seep through her mind. While there was no proof, she could no longer ignore the likely probability that her mother and Rick had been lovers, but she had no desire to discuss it with him.

"You're right," she said. "Shall we consider the matter of my mother and Rick Vernon closed?"

"Yes, let's. I'm afraid I've depressed you terribly with all my talk about your mother and Vernon and that was unforgivable. Would you like to walk up the stream a ways, or ride?"

Delighted he had been the one to change the subject for once, Belle suggested they walk, and distracted by bubbling water and rocky shore, his conversation remained pleasantly light and unthreatening for the rest of the morning.

That afternoon Belle was too restless to read, and she waited until Kenneth had put Edwin to work to go out for another ride. She took care to head north until she was out of sight and then swung southeast to make certain she arrived at the butte from the east without being seen. Coyote's bay was tethered among the cypress trees, but uncertain whether she had been wise to visit the handsome brave, she climbed the trail with a slow, reluctant step.

Coyote had seen her leave the ranch and was curious as to why she had taken such a circuitous route. "There was no one following you," he announced as she reached the top of the butte. When she looked up at him, her eyes were so full of pain, he reached out to pull her into his arms. "What's wrong? What's happened?"

Belle bit her lip to keep from crying while she searched for the words she had come there to say. It took all the courage she possessed to finally step out of the comfort of his embrace. "Edwin's the curious sort and I didn't want to give him any more reasons to be suspicious than he already has. I just came to tell you how sorry I am about last night. I never should have said what I did."

Coyote placed his fingers beneath her chin to tilt her head up so she would have to look at him with her beautiful, sad eyes. "I don't know what you mean," he replied. "You asked what I was doing in your room, said I'd have to go. Said I was handsome, asked if I wanted something to eat, told me about your mother and your father's partner. Oh, yes, you said love was too precious to throw away. Which of those things troubles you?"

A teasing smile played across Coyote's lips and his expression was so full of affection, Belle found it impossible to be insulted. Still, it was difficult to answer his question. "I've only known you a few days. I shouldn't have shouted about love when I don't even know what I'm talking about."

Coyote pulled her back into his arms, yanked off her hat, and rested his chin atop her curls. "No, you're right. Love is precious," he assured her, "but it shouldn't make you so sad."

It was easy to shut out her sorrow when she was with him, but she longed for him to speak of loving her. When the slow throb of his heartbeat was all that reached her ears, she felt like an even greater fool than she had the night before. She hurriedly slipped out of his embrace, reached for her hat, and plunked it down on her head.

"I've got to go," she murmured distractedly. "I'll probably not see you again."

With her long hair blowing about and the angle of her hat shielding her face, Coyote had to bend down to see her clearly. She looked so utterly miserable that he couldn't let her go. "Come with me," he coaxed. He took her hand and led her over to the blanket where he slept. "Sit down. Have a drink of water."

When he offered his canteen, Belle took a long sip and splashed a bit of water on her cheeks. "I must look a mess. I had such awful dreams last night, and nothing has gone right today."

Coyote squatted down beside her. His voice was low, as though they still had to speak in the hushed tones they had used in her bedroom. "I hope you didn't have bad dreams about me."

"No, they were about my father. He was furious with me, which he often is, but he's never chased me the way he did in my dreams," she recalled with a shudder. "It didn't make any sense, but it frightened me."

"Why does your father get mad at you?"

Belle had no ready answer. "We've never gotten along. Maybe he just didn't want the responsibility of a child after my mother died, but he's always been cold. Nothing I do ever pleases him. For as long as I can remember, he's barely tolerated me."

She was slender now, and Coyote could easily imagine her having been a skinny little girl with enormous brown eyes. How could her father not have loved her? Had he despised her mother, too? "Were you with your mother when she died?"

They were treading dangerous ground, but Coyote's question had been asked in such a sympathetic tone, Belle felt she had to answer. "No, she wasn't ill. She didn't die in bed with her loved ones gathered around her. She killed herself. She threw herself off this very butte and wasn't found until the next morning."

Having made that dreadful admission, Belle studied Coyote's reaction. She expected surprise, perhaps, or revulsion, but he looked merely puzzled. "Now that I know Rick Vernon had left the ranch a couple of days earlier, it's easy to imagine they were lovers. If so, then apparently my mother couldn't bear to live without him."

Coyote remembered how still Belle had been sitting the first time he'd seen her greet the dawn. "Do you come up here to be with your mother?" he asked.

"Yes. Does that seem morbid or foolish?"

"No, not at all." Coyote was silent a long while, then reached out to take Belle's hand and brought it to his lips. "Something isn't right," he confided. "If an Apache discovers his wife has been unfaithful to him, he cuts off her nose. What does a white man do?"

Horrified by that gruesome penalty, Belle pulled her hand from his. "Wait a minute. What if the husband is at fault? What if he's neglected his wife or treated her badly, and she's so lonely that she's driven to seek love in another man's arms?"

Coyote didn't want to be distracted with questions about his tribe when it was *her* family they were discussing. He answered her question quickly, then continued to pursue his own. "If an Apache woman is unhappy, she divorces her husband and takes another man as her mate. Now answer my question. What does a white man do if he discovers his wife has been unfaithful to him?"

Belle chewed her lower lip while she considered the possibilities. "Well, there would surely be an awful fight. Then I suppose he might leave her, or he might simply throw her out in the street and toss her belongings out after her."

"What would he do to the man?"

"He'd confront him, and there would probably be an even worse fight," Belle predicted darkly. "It would be seen as a matter of honor and there might even be a duel. Do you know what that is?"

Coyote nodded, and, again after thoughtful consideration, he pushed her thinking a little further. "Could a man be so angry that he might kill both his wife and her lover?"

Belle searched his face for some hint that his question was merely asked to satisfy his own curiosity, but the light in his dark eyes made the seriousness of his purpose clear. Stunned by his intention, she had to swallow hard before she answered. "A man would not simply ride away from the ranch he had worked four years to build without telling his friends goodbye, would he?"

"No, he would not, unless he was chased away, or—"

When Coyote left his sentence unfinished, Belle completed it for him. "Murdered."

She closed her eyes for a moment, but no matter how distasteful the prospect of murder was, she could not discount it. "My father was a hero during the Civil War. I don't know how many men he might have killed, ten, twenty, a hundred, but I'm certain he killed some. I don't like to think of him as being a murderer, but he's definitely capable of it."

"And if your mother knew?" Coyote whispered.

"I've always wished that I could ask her why she took her own life, why she left me," Belle revealed. "Perhaps she couldn't live

72

with the knowledge her husband had killed her lover, or—"

This time it was Coyote who had the courage to see the thought through. "Your father killed her, too."

Tears welled up in Belle's eyes as she realized she and a handsome renegade had found the answer for which she had searched her whole life, but it was like looking through the gates of hell and was much too horrible to accept. "We've no proof," she reminded him.

In that instant, Coyote finally saw Belle's life for the lonely existence it was. He had thought he had nothing to offer her but now knew anything was better than for her to go on living with a murderer who despised her. What good was a magnificent ranch if its success had been built on death and deceit? It was all lies, and the love he felt when he looked at her was the only truth they needed.

"Some things need no proof," he insisted. "Like faith, and love." He reached out to again remove her hat, and slipping his fingers through her hair, drew her mouth to his. No longer tentative or unsure, he unleashed all the passion in his soul and, with a searing kiss, branded her as his own.

To be presented with the most terrible of possibilities and the incredible sweetness of love almost in the same breath was too much for Belle. She clung to Coyote, relaxed in his arms, made no protest when he stretched out on his blanket and pulled her down beside him, but the turmoil of her thoughts and the tender assault on her senses lured her to the brink of madness rather than surrender. She clung to the brave she had come to adore, but she was still so frightened that her lips trembled beneath his.

Coyote wanted Belle so badly he ached all over, but her cheeks were wet with tears, and he knew if he made love to her now, all she would remember was the ugliness of their suspicions rather than the beauty he wanted them to share. He continued to kiss her, but more gently, and he shifted his position so that she lay snuggled in his arms rather than pinned beneath him. He had never cared enough about another woman to put her needs before his own, but Belle was precious to him and he did not want to frighten her with the strength of his desire when she had a far more real terror to confront.

Belle felt the change in Coyote's mood as his kisses went from feverish to slow and deep. She had not even known it was possible to kiss the way he preferred until the first time he had eased his tongue between her lips. Unwilling to admit her lack of experience, she had been afraid to draw away, and then, thrilled clear through, had not wanted to. Now she wound her fingers through his hair so he would not leave her and sent her tongue over his in a silent plea for more.

Now that Coyote had satisfied Belle's need for a safe haven, and she was at last responding solely to him, he gradually drew away. "I'll not take advantage of your sorrow," he whispered, "but I hope you'll come back to me soon."

Filled with disappointment, Belle would have cried out had she not understood Coyote's reasoning was sound. She slipped her hand under his shirt to feel the warmth of his bare skin and wondered if Rick Vernon's bare back had felt as good to her mother. She closed her eyes and soaked up the warmth of the sun. Its fiery heat as natural as Coyote's. While she accepted his reluctance to take their passion for each other any further, she could not help but regret his decision when she needed his love so badly.

Then she realized that was precisely why he had stopped. She needed him too desperately, and no mortal man could ease all her pain. She would only have destroyed him had he attempted to assuage her longing for love while the turmoil of her mother's past threatened her hopes for the future. He deserved a woman who could love him with her whole heart, and she knew that wasn't possible for her, yet. She gave him one last, lingering kiss and sat up.

"I'll come back, but not until I've found the proof I need."

Coyote reached out to catch her arm. "The proof of your love is in your kiss. What more do you need of me?"

"Nothing. This is something I must do myself." She leaned down to kiss him again, and memorized his face with a loving glance before she left him for what she prayed would not be the last time.

Chapter Eight

When Belle returned home, she lured Aurelia to the sewing room on the pretext of again discussing alterations to her mother's wedding gown. Once the housekeeper had followed her inside, Belle closed and locked the door. She pocketed the key and gestured for Aurelia to take a seat.

"Make yourself comfortable. We're going to have a long chat," Belle predicted.

"I'll let out the seams on the dress while we talk," Aurelia offered. She reached for her sewing basket to take out her scissors before she noticed how serious Belle's mood truly was. Puzzled, she put the basket aside and sat down. "What is it, *querida?*"

Belle did not wish to frighten the housekeeper unnecessarily, but she meant to do whatever it took to learn what she needed to know. "You've worked for my family since before I was born," she replied, "and I know you have an excellent memory. I'm nineteen, and that's certainly old enough to hear the truth. You needn't protect me from it another minute. Now I want you to drop the evasions and tell me whether or not I'm right."

Belle paused, but the fear that widened Aurelia's eyes didn't dissuade her from continuing. "My father is an attractive man from a fine family. I imagine when he was in his twenties, he was considered quite a catch. I think he and my mother were probably deeply in love when they married. Perhaps it was the suffering he'd seen during the war, or the hardships they faced when they came here, but something began to eat away at my father's spirit until he became the cold and bitter man he is today.

"At first, Rick Vernon might have tried merely to be a friend to my mother and to lift her spirits with his teasing banter, but gradually, they began to care for each other. My mother would have felt torn between the vows she made to my father and the love she began to feel for Rick. Rick's loyalties would have been equally divided, for in falling in love with my mother, he was betraying his best friend. Perhaps they fought the attraction that was growing between them, actively battled it until it became too strong to defeat. I believe finally they could no longer deny what they felt for each other and became lovers.

"My father was probably away from the house for most of the day like he is now. He might not have seen what was going on, but *you* would have been here. They couldn't have carried on a romance without your being aware of it, perhaps even participating by keeping it a secret from my father. You know exactly what happened, Aurelia, and we're not leaving this room until you describe it in detail."

Aurelia looked up at the young woman she had raised with the love she would have shown her own daughter, and remembered Isabel. She had kept Isabel's secrets for so many years, they now seemed almost to have been her own. She rose slowly and went to the window. The cloudless sky was a vivid blue, and wishing her memories were as pretty, she leaned against the sill as she agonized over what to do.

Belle waited several minutes, thinking the housekeeper needed time to organize her story, but she soon realized Aurelia was so lost in thought she had forgotten she was even there. "Aurelia," she urged. "Tell me. If what I described wasn't accurate, then what did happen? I must know."

Reluctantly, the housekeeper glanced over her shoulder. She had always feared this day might come, but now that it was here, she felt no relief in being able to set aside her longtime burden. "You look so much like her, and yet nothing about you is the same. She didn't have your strength, *querida*. You must forgive her for that."

"Don't forget I've spent nineteen years with my father. I don't blame my mother for anything."

Aurelia found it impossible to face the girl she had raised and again focused her attention on the vastness of the sky. "Your story was very romantic and sweet, but not even close to what really happened. Your mother never stopped loving your father. No, if anything, she loved him too much."

Startled, Belle straightened up. "What? How can that be?"

"If you can not appreciate a love that will drive a woman to risk eternal damnation to please her husband, then you are not ready to hear the truth. You may think that you are, but you'll not be able to understand how someone so dear as your mother could have gone so far astray."

Belle immediately thought of Coyote. He was a handsome devil who rode with the grace of the wind and whose kiss was flavored with a devotion she had never thought she would ever inspire, but would she risk her soul to please him? Instinctively she knew he would never put her love to such an awful test. "A man ought not to ask such a thing of a woman," she countered.

"Your father did not ask it of her, *querida*. He did not even know."

Losing patience with the housekeeper's riddles, Belle walked up behind her. "Nothing you can say will diminish my respect for my mother, so you needn't be afraid to tell me all you know. Just do it. The truth is long overdue."

Needing no further coaxing, Aurelia returned to her chair and folded her hands in her lap. She waited for Belle to take the chair opposite hers before she began. "Your parents wanted a child. They had been married for two years when they arrived here, and while I never heard your father mention anything more than that he hoped to someday have children, motherhood was an obsession with Isabel. The first year I knew her, she prayed, gathered good-luck charms, followed superstitions, and still she did not conceive.

"Then one day she pulled me into her bedroom and told me . . ." Aurelia paused, the memory obviously an excruciatingly painful one for her. Tears began to fill her eyes, and she wiped them away with the corner of her apron. "She told me that she had begun to fear she would never have a child with Donovan but that she hoped it would happen with another man."

"She meant to leave my father?" Belle asked.

Aurelia shook her head. "Oh, no, that was never her intention. She simply wanted another man to father a child Donovan would never even suspect wasn't his."

Feeling unwanted herself, Belle had found it so easy to believe her mother had longed for love, and she was shaken to learn that hadn't been the case at all. "Did you agree with her? Did you think such a deception was a good idea?"

"*¡Madre de Dios!* Of course not," Aurelia denied emphatically. "But she was not asking for my opinion. All she wanted was my help in fooling Donovan. At first I refused, but she cried, begged, and carried on so pitifully that finally I was forced to agree. You were born the next year."

Belle had always thought she had known Aurelia, but what she had heard that afternoon made her doubt that anyone ever truly knew another person. Her throat was so dry she wished she had thought to bring a pitcher of water and glasses with her. "Are you saying that Rick Vernon was my father, but rather than being in love with him, my mother simply seduced him in hopes he'd give her a child?"

Again overcome with tears, Aurelia needed a moment to compose herself before she replied. "I'm not certain who your father was, *querida*."

"You mean my mother had affairs with more than one man? My God, where did she find them all?"

The housekeeper sighed unhappily. "I knew no matter how I told the story, you would be ashamed of her. I didn't want that."

"I'm not ashamed, I'm astounded. Now the least you can do is give me some clues as to who my father might be."

"It may very well be Donovan," Aurelia insisted. "After all, she was with him most, or Kenneth MacKenzie."

"Kenneth?" Belle suddenly felt weak.

"Because you are the image of your dear mother *querida*, there's no way to know who your father was. You must simply believe as you always have, that he's the man who raised you."

Belle sat back in her chair. She had been prepared to excuse her mother for betraying her wedding vows for love, but to learn the woman had simply had a series of loveless affairs to become pregnant had hurt her badly. "What happened after I was born? Did she set out to have a second child in the same way?"

"No. Her prayers had been answered, and she was faithful to your father until the day she died. She was a good woman, *querida*. Perhaps I did not tell her story as well as it should be told, but she loved you and Donovan with all her heart and soul."

"Then why did she kill herself? Did my father, Donovan, discover I wasn't his?"

"The last time I saw her she was singing you a lullaby. I don't know why she chose death that same night."

But someone does, Belle thought to herself. Even if Aurelia's version of her mother's story had not been what she had expected, her father, or Donovan Cassidy, had still had an excellent motive for murdering both Isabel and Rick. "You told me you didn't know why Rick had left, but did he tell you goodbye before he set out for California?"

"No, *querida*. Your father just said he was gone, and because of what I knew, it didn't surprise me that Rick had chosen to leave quietly."

"Did Rick know about Kenneth, or the others?"

"No, I don't believe so."

It was possible that if Donovan had confronted Rick with accusations of adultery, he might have chosen to make a hasty exit, but there was a vast difference between being discreet and disappearing. Belle just couldn't accept the story that Rick had simply vanished one night, but she chose not to share her suspicions with Aurelia. "I shouldn't have kept you so long," Belle apologized. "You may go. I know I needn't warn you not to tell Donovan what you've told me."

"I beg you not to judge your mother too harshly," Aurelia pleaded. When Belle failed to reply, the housekeeper rose, patting Belle's arm lightly before leaving the room.

Belle closed her eyes, slumped down in her chair, and struggled to correct her naïve, and completely erroneous, view of her mother. From time to time her father had employed attractive young men, and while they had certainly caught her eye, nothing had ever come of it. She had been too shy to approach any of them, and while her father had never said anything to her, she thought it likely that in his usual forceful way he had discouraged the men from having any interest in her. None of those men had worked for the Cassidys for more than a few months and she could no longer recall their names.

Aurelia might cling to the slim hope that Donovan was her father, but never having felt close to him, Belle was certain he was not. Whether she was the product of some hasty union with a handsome drifter, or Kenneth, or Rick's daughter really didn't matter. Just knowing she wasn't related to Donovan Cassidy brought a stunning sense of release not even her mother's scandalous behavior could mar. She felt truly free for the first time in her life, and it was such an exhilarating feeling that she savored it until the time came to bathe and dress for supper.

Each time Donovan glanced toward her that evening, Belle managed a polite smile, but, as usual, he failed to respond with anything even hinting at warmth. Edwin was eager to learn more about the ranch, but rather than friendly advice, Donovan answered the young man's questions in a strictly professional tone. It wasn't until they returned to the parlor after supper that he made the reason for his sullen mood clear.

"You've been asking too many questions, Win, and while I find it merely personally annoying, I won't have you distracting my foreman or the hands from their work with incessant inquiries about things that don't concern you. And my wife's tragic death is first on the list. If you can't give me your word that you'll confine your curiosity to matters directly related to the running of the ranch, then I'll have to ask you to leave in the morning."

Horribly embarrassed, Edwin stammered out his reply. "It was never my intention to offend you, sir."

"No, of course not. You merely wanted whatever details you could ferret out to embellish your tales when you returned home. Isn't that closer to the truth? You planned to use Isabel's death to entertain the rest of the family whenever they gathered to trade malicious lies about anyone not present to defend themselves."

Aghast that his great-uncle would cast such an aspersion on the entire family, Edwin threw out his chest and began a bold defense. "Sir, I have never heard any gossip at a family gathering, and you may be assured that any reference to you and your

80

daughter has always been complimentary. My mother remembers you quite fondly, and my grandmother has always referred to you as her favorite brother."

"The other boys were all killed in the war," Donovan reminded him.

Belle felt a curious detachment as Edwin continued to describe the family members she had never met as the most charitable group imaginable. She doubted they could all be such good people or have such warm memories of Donovan, but he'd left home more than twenty years ago and she thought perhaps, as Aurelia had described, he had been a different man then.

When Donovan finally succeeded in wringing a promise from a mortified Edwin that he would confine his questions to those concerning cattle, he turned to Belle. "Don't think I don't know what part you've played in this, young lady. You've been feeding your cousin's unnatural curiosity about your mother's death and I won't allow it to continue another minute. Pray for her soul, and let the dear woman rest in peace."

No longer willing to give him the respect she had felt she owed him out of duty rather than love, Belle challenged him squarely. "I'll understand if you'd rather not speak in front of Win, but the time for secrets is past. You've kept everyone ignorant of what really happened to Rick Vernon and my mother, but sooner or later the truth will be told. You may have intimidated Win into dropping the subject, but I never will."

Donovan responded to Belle's ringing threat by striking her across the face with a savage, back-handed blow. Stunned, she would have fallen to the floor had Edwin not caught her, but the fire in her gaze continued to glow. They had always despised each other, and now that the hatred was out in the open, it could no longer be denied.

"If I still needed proof that you've never loved me, you would have just provided it," Belle cried. "How can you accuse your family of lying about us when you never speak the truth? Look at this house. Rather than a home, it's a damn monument to a cause that wasn't worth defending. You've wrapped the past around your heart so tightly there was never any room for me. Well, now I've no room in my heart for you. Something horrible happened to Rick Vernon and my mother, and no matter how loudly you protest and complain, I'm going to find out exactly what it was. Then you'll pay, and dearly, for all your lies."

Belle had to lean against her cousin, but Donovan saw in an instant that he would never be able to beat the defiance out of her and he turned on his heel and left them to deal with the result of his anger alone.

"Oh my God," Edwin moaned. "I can't believe that he struck you. Here, come lie down on the sofa. Rest, I'll go after him."

"No, don't bother. I've seen him settle disputes with his fists and he'd only hurt you much worse than he hurt me." Belle put her hands up to her face and gave her jaw a tentative wiggle. It was going to be sore for several days, but at least it wasn't broken. "I want you to leave, Win. Things are only going to get worse, and I don't want you caught up in the middle of it the way you were tonight."

Belle seemed not to notice the tears rolling down her cheeks, and Edwin pulled out his handkerchief to dry them. The right side of her face had already started to swell and she winced slightly as he wiped her cheek. "I'm sorry. Obviously I have more curiosity than sense, but I never dreamed something like this could happen. I can't leave you, not now when this is all my fault."

Touched by what she considered misplaced devotion, Belle reached out and took his hand. "Whatever ugly secrets Donovan is hiding, he's the one who's responsible for the trouble, not you, Win. That's why I want you to go. When I have everything straightened out, I'll write to you and explain."

His great-uncle had made a serious mistake in striking Belle in front of him, and Win refused to even consider leaving her alone with the hostile man. "No, I won't go," he insisted with the conviction he wished he had displayed in front of Donovan. "I don't understand what's going on, but I'll be damned if I'll walk away from it. This isn't like medical school, Belle. This is family, and I won't leave you."

When he leaned over to kiss her, Belle did not draw away, but no longer desperate for affection, her response was sweet rather than passionate. "When you started asking questions, you didn't expect to stir up a hornet's nest, did you?"

Edwin shook his head. "I just wanted to get to know you."

Belle studied his earnest expression and motioned for him to come closer still. "Donovan may not be my father, but he may well be a murderer. Perhaps there's no way to prove it, but I can no longer ignore the possibility. We may both be in very grave danger."

"No," Edwin swore. "If anything happened to us, it would look far too suspicious. Perhaps we can force him to leave. He wouldn't have to admit his guilt, but having to leave the ranch would be a severe punishment for him."

"Yes, it would, but it wouldn't be justice, and I won't settle for anything less for my mother and the man who may very well have been my father."

"You believe Rick Vernon was your father?"

Belle chose not to repeat Aurelia's colorful version of her conception. "I really don't know, but that's only one small piece of this puzzle. I don't want anything to happen to you, though, Win, so if you're determined to stay, keep out of Donovan's way. Just watch and wait. If he's as guilty as I think he is, then he'll betray himself."

"If he's lived with it for nearly twenty years, Belle, I doubt that it will destroy him now."

"There's always hope," she predicted darkly. "When I reveal my suspicions, Kenneth will help us. So will Aurelia, and there will be others who will take our side against him."

"Kenneth must have told him I was asking questions. I wouldn't count on him."

"You're right, but I doubt he understood the consequences. Let's not do anything for the next couple of days. Let's just wait to see what Donovan does."

Edwin kissed her again. "If you get up in the morning and Donovan tells you I took off during the night, you'll know he's lying, won't you?"

"Yes. Better lock your door."

"You, too." Edwin leaned close to give her another kiss. "To be safe, maybe I ought to sleep in your room."

Belle drew her fingertip along his cheek in a brief caress. "You might be safe then, but I doubt that I would."

Edwin had come to the Arizona Territory hoping for adventure, but he had never anticipated anything so exciting as his

83

beautiful cousin, or the chance to solve a murder mystery. "You know me better than I thought," he teased. He helped her up the stairs and bid her good night with another kiss, but filled with a heady mixture of fear and daring, he doubted he would sleep a wink.

Belle's door had a lock she had never used, but tonight she turned the key in it. As always, she remembered her mother in her prayers, but now she finally had the hope that Isabel hadn't deserted her, and it would be enough to keep her fighting for the truth in the dangerous days that lay ahead.

Chapter Nine

Donovan Cassidy paced his study with a long, fierce stride and cursed his ungrateful daughter with every foul expression he had ever heard. After several shots from the bottle of whiskey he kept in the bottom drawer of his desk, he became more creative and his epithets took on a maniacal flavor. Amused by his own cleverness, he laughed at the young woman who had dared to threaten him. His deep, rumbling chuckles echoed all around him in a haunting reminder of the way the sound of gunfire had hummed in his ears long after the last shots of a battle had been fired. Belle had declared war on him that night, but he was a seasoned veteran and wasn't afraid of a mere skirmish with the likes of her.

"Just who does she think she is?" he asked the ghosts of his former comrades in arms. Belle was nothing to him, and never had been. If she loathed him, he didn't care. It was a matter of absolutely no consequence to him, but he would not allow her to jeopardize all he had built with her wild accusations. No, she would have to be silenced, and soon.

He sank down into his chair, propped his feet up on the corner of his desk, and this time sipping his drink, savored his memories of Isabel. He had never loved another woman and never would, not even the daughter she had gone to such despicable lengths to bring to life. No, there was only Isabel, and as he had on every night since her death, he wallowed in grief and drank until, numbed by alcohol, he no longer felt the pain of her loss.

* * *

Belle climbed into bed intending to sleep, but when the turmoil of her thoughts made it impossible, she got up, dressed for riding, and went out to the barn to saddle her mare. That late the bunkhouse was dark, and although a light still shone in the window of Donovan's study, she was confident he was too drunk to notice she was gone, or care. She rode out to the butte, and tethered her pinto near Coyote's bay.

Bathed in moonlight, the Apache was stretched out on his blanket asleep. Belle took care not to wake him, sat down beside him, and for a long while simply watched him sleep. Rather than a strange pastime, to silently enjoy his company while he was totally unaware of her did not strike her as being in the least bit bizarre. In but a few days, she had come to trust him as she had never trusted the man who raised her. A renegade hunted by the Army he had once served, he had set aside his own anguish to become involved in hers. While she appreciated his help, she did not want to risk endangering his life.

She leaned down and kissed his cheek.

Coming awake in an instant, Coyote reached out to grab Belle and slammed her down onto his blanket before he recognized who she was. Immediately regretting his haste, he released her and sat up. "Don't ever do that again," he warned. "I could have hurt you."

It was too dark for him to see how badly the right side of her face was swollen, but Belle knew that, unlike Donovan, Coyote would never harm her intentionally. "How should I wake you if a kiss is too dangerous?" she asked.

Embarrassed, Coyote began to laugh. "I was asleep," he reminded her. "I didn't know it was a kiss. It could have been a tarantula out for a walk."

"What a charming thought." Belle reached out to grasp his hand and squeezed it tightly. "I want you to go," she said before she lost her courage.

"But why? If you haven't found the proof you need, I can stay a while longer."

"Thank you." Belle hesitated, scarcely knowing where to begin. "Since I last saw you, I've discovered I'm probably not related to the man I've always thought was my father. Rather than being hurt that I've been raised believing in a lie, I'm simply relieved to learn there's no blood tie between us. I'm convinced he murdered his partner and my mother, and I as much as told him so tonight."

Frightened for her, Coyote stretched out beside her, drew her close, and propped his head on his elbow. "I don't think that was wise."

"Probably not, but he had forbidden my cousin and me to question the circumstances of my mother's death and I couldn't agree. I've defied him my whole life, and with something so important, I just can't let him have his way, not when it may involve murder."

"You called him a murderer?"

"No, not in those exact words, but I let him know I didn't believe his version of what happened and wanted the truth."

Coyote leaned down to kiss her. "I can't leave you now. A man who has killed two people has no reason not to kill three."

"Or four," Belle pointed out. "That's why I want you gone."

Coyote sat up briefly and yanked his shirt off over his head. "No, you don't." He again lay down beside her and cuddled up close. "That's not why you came here, and you know it."

When his mouth covered hers, Belle did not break away to contradict him but instead welcomed his affection with an eagerness she again made no attempt to disguise. She slid her hands down his back, then wound them in his long ebony hair. Her fingertips brushed over the fine gold chain encircling his neck, and when he drew away to take a breath, she reached for the small crucifix dangling from it.

She had given no thought to his religion, but that he could be Christian was still a surprise. "Are you Catholic?" she asked.

In a single swipe, Coyote removed the gold necklace and dropped it over her head. "No. This was my mother's, but I want you to have it. She was from Mexico and when I'm certain I won't be followed, I'm going to my grandfather's ranch."

Belle had heard that Apaches frequently kidnapped Mexican women they kept as wives, but she couldn't imagine the father of such a victim welcoming his grandson. "Are you sure," she asked hesitantly, "that he'll want to see you?"

Amused by her fears for him, Coyote chuckled softly. "I know what you're thinking, but you're wrong. My mother was not a captive, but a woman my father courted for nearly a year. I've been to my grandfather's ranch many times, and he always begs me to stay. He'll be happy to see me."

"Good. I'm glad you have a place to go."

Belle had lost her hat when Coyote had first grabbed her; he brushed her curls away from her face with an adoring touch. "When an Apache wants a woman for his wife, he brings her a gift of horses and leaves them tied outside her *wickiup*. Even if she loves him, she doesn't water and feed them that first day. She'll make him suffer not knowing if she'll accept him or not, but if she hasn't cared for the horses by the fourth day, the man knows she's refused him and takes them away."

"My goodness, that sounds as though it's very hard not only on the man, but on his poor horses, too."

"Yes, especially if he's refused many times."

Belle began to giggle. "Surely that doesn't happen."

Charmed by her laughter, Coyote kissed her again. "There are some braves with more horses than brains and looks, so sadly, it does."

Belle considered that for a moment and decided Apaches were not all that different from white men, but she still felt sorry for the horses. "So what happened with your father and mother? Did he take her horses?"

"Yes, and he always swore it was more than he should have, while she argued it was not nearly enough. They're both dead now, but they loved each other very much."

Belle looked up at the star-filled heavens and tried to imagine her mother loving Donovan Cassidy as dearly as Aurelia had insisted she had. It had all been so long ago, and having no memories of a graceful southern belle and a dashing Confederate officer being together, she was forced to accept the housekeeper's word. "I wish I had known my mother," she whispered softly.

Coyote could feel Belle withdrawing into herself as she had the last time they had been together and he wanted her too badly to let her go again. He gave her an exuberant hug and kissed her soundly. "How many horses will I have to bring for you?" he asked.

Enchanted by his ardor, Belle wouldn't have cared if he had no more to offer than the bay gelding he rode but she did not want to make light of his people's customs by saying so. "Surprise me," she said instead, "and I hope you won't be disappointed if I don't keep you wondering and feed and water your horses the first day."

Pleased by her lack of guile, Coyote traced the outline of her lips with the tip of his tongue before kissing her again. "Now tell me how a white man asks a woman to become his wife," he suggested.

While Belle had no actual experience in the matter, she knew enough to explain. "First he must ask her father's permission, and if he says yes, then he asks the woman to become his wife."

"And if her father says no?"

"Well, I suppose it would depend on the man. He might simply give up, or he might continue to see the woman he loves secretly. Sometimes when parents object to a marriage, the couple elopes. That means they simply run off together and marry."

"Don't they ever come back?"

"Yes, they do, but once they're married it's too late for the bride's parents to object. My friend Janet got married last June. June is a popular month for weddings. Anyway, Janet's parents weren't fond of her young man, but she threatened to elope if they wouldn't give their permission for the marriage and when they realized that she meant it, they did."

"I think you and Janet must be a lot alike."

Belle also believed that to be true. "Yes, we've both been criticized for being headstrong and wild, but now that Janet's married, she's quite the proper lady."

"And you? Will you ever be a proper lady?"

Belle gave his hair a teasing yank. "You know I won't."

Coyote leaned down to kiss her, and this time he did not draw away. It was the wildness of her spirit that had first drawn him to her and he did not ever want her to change. He felt her pulse throbbing steadily at the base of her neck, then let his hand stray lower, at first only brushing lightly over the fullness of her bosom, but when she did not push him away, he began to tease her nipple with his thumb.

89

There were still several hours remaining before dawn and he wanted to spend them all making love. Rather than any resistance from Belle, he felt only a graceful compliance with his desires, and knowing what she wanted now was him rather than comfort, he deepened his kiss. For a moment, he longed for her big feather bed, but it didn't have a canopy of stars and that made his blanket infinitely superior. They were wild creatures who belonged out-of-doors where the only limits were their imaginations, and the gentle breeze that caressed his back felt as loving as Belle's touch.

For as long as he could remember, Apache women had worn flowing skirts like white women. It was easy to start at the ankle and slide his hand up their legs as far as he dared, but he had never tried making love to a woman dressed in pants and he wasn't certain how to go about removing the restrictive garment without appearing so clumsy Belle would only laugh and run away rather than beg him to hurry. He wanted to treat her tenderly, to be slow and sweet, but he could not reconcile that need with removing a gunbelt, belt, boots, and trousers.

Belle tasted Coyote's hesitance, but didn't understand its cause. "Am I doing something wrong?" she asked.

Coyote rested his forehead against hers for a moment. "No. I was just wishing you were wearing a skirt because I would know how to help you out of it."

While she was thrilled that he wished to make love with her, Belle was more than a little frightened. Having been raised on a ranch, she had seen enough animals mate to understand the basic process, but she was certain humans must do it with far more tenderness. At least she hoped so and gave a teasing response. "I could go home," she offered, "and see what I can find in my wardrobe."

"No, now that you're here, I won't let you go."

Belle wanted him, and not simply out of curiosity, but out of love. "I've been undressing myself for a long while," she said. "You needn't help me."

"But I want to help," Coyote insisted. "Very much."

Belle reached for his belt and unbuckled it. "My clothes aren't that different from yours. You know what to do."

Coyote gasped as her fingertips grazed the bare skin of his

90

belly. If she intended to undress him, then he would cease to worry about frightening her away. He sat up to pull off her boots and socks, and then lay her gunbelt aside. "Would you have shot me that first morning?" he asked. He had felt certain that she would at the time, but now he believed her to be far too kind-hearted a woman to shoot an unarmed man.

Not wanting to give the wrong answer, Belle licked her lips thoughtfully before she replied. "I couldn't have shot you, but another man, one who tried to harm me, yes, I would have."

"Good, I like a woman who can look after herself." He unbuckled her belt, then leaned forward to unbutton her shirt. She had on a lace-trimmed camisole underneath, and it pleased him to find she did not completely avoid wearing frilly, feminine attire. "I also like pretty women, and you are very, very pretty."

"Thank you." She knew she ought to compliment his appearance, too, but the words stuck in her throat. Her only consolation was that she had called him handsome before that night. He was more than merely attractive, though. He had a stirring masculine pride that was unrelated to arrogance. She knew if she lived to be one hundred, she would never forget how exciting it had been to watch him ride after her cousin. She truly liked poor Edwin, and had she not met Coyote first, she might have married him and never known what she had missed.

Coyote heard Belle's breath quicken and leaned down to kiss her. "The legend of the Yavapai may have brought me here, but I've stayed for you."

He began to speak to her in his own language then, but Belle heard the love in his voice and understood his meaning without needing to translate the words. She ran her hand over his chest, thrilled simply to be able to touch him, and when he pulled her into his arms, she was the one who now found their clothes in the way. She began to laugh with the sheer joy he brought her and, delighted with her enthusiasm, Coyote released her to yank off his moccasins and then stood to remove his pants.

His bronze skin gleamed with the moon's pale golden light, and rather than a handsome savage, Belle saw a young god whose masculine perfection embodied the very essence of love. He knelt to remove the last of her clothing and when they were both nude, she felt not the slightest sense of shyness, but only the heat of their mutual desire. In her mind, the butte became an altar to the pagan spirits who had sprung to life from the bloodred earth and, surrounded by the haunting pulse of their lingering power, she was a most willing sacrifice.

All Coyote felt was the love that flowed between them with such magical ease. He knew that after this night, they could never, ever, truly be parted. He slid his hands over Belle's supple body, praising the elegant proportions of her limbs, and then cupped her left breast in his palm. He flicked his tongue over the soft, sweet crest and felt it contract into a flavorful bud he had to savor. Her flesh tasted so good to him, but he was not so completely distracted that he forgot to continue pleasuring her with a deep and knowing touch.

They were sprawled across his blanket now, their arms and legs entwined in an ageless pose. With a smooth, seductive grace Coyote drew his lissome companion toward a wedding not merely of their vibrant young bodies but of their hearts and minds. He felt her shudder with the first waves of rapture he had taken such care to create. Confident he had pleased her, and unable to delay making her his own, he entered her with a deep thrust that tore away the last barrier to their total union and then, exulting in that ultimate possession, he lay still.

Coyote's kiss muffled Belle's cry. Knowing there was no escaping the initial burst of pain, rather than fight against it she relaxed and swam in its current until, spent, there was only the weight of Coyote's muscular body and the joy of his hot, moist kiss. When he began to move again, she timed the motion of her hips to his, and with every lunge drew him ever deeper into her spell. She felt his ecstasy build to a stunning climax that rocked them both and held him locked in her arms certain he was as much hers as she was his.

Coyote raised up slowly. Belle was smiling at him and he leaned down to kiss her again. "There are so many ways to make love. I'm sorry I can't teach you all of them tonight."

"You've taught me more than enough for one night," Belle assured him.

"No, not nearly enough," Coyote argued, and with teasing kisses and a sly, seductive caress, he made her want him again and again, until, exhausted, she finally fell asleep in his arms.

Donovan awoke with a start, his body stiff and sore from having spent so many hours pressed against the hard contours of his wooden chair. His legs felt numb, and he swung them off his desk with an ungainly lurch, rubbed his eyes, then turned up the flickering lamp. His head ached, but not so badly that he didn't recall his latest fight with Belle. Still disgusted with her, he rose and, ignoring the pain, stretched to dispel the cramps from his back, arms, and legs.

In peacetime, just as during the Civil War, he had not become the success he was by running from danger but rather by embracing it. Knowing precisely what he had to do, he climbed the stairs and went to his daughter's room. The door was unlocked and he pushed it open only to find her unmade bed empty.

He glanced toward the window and, seeing the first pale promise of dawn, he knew where she had gone. He leaned against the doorjamb for a moment, savoring the beauty of the fate she had brought on herself. Everyone on the ranch knew Belle liked to greet the dawn from the butte where her mother had died, and if in a sudden overwhelming burst of anguished grief she chose to follow Isabel in death, he would be the recipient of boundless sympathy, and not a bit of blame.

Chapter Ten

In the hushed stillness between darkness and dawn, Komwida Pokwee bent down to touch Coyote's shoulder. He opened his eyes, and then, awestruck by the shimmering white light surrounding the goddess, he sat up, mouth agape. She was exactly as she had been described, a being of such incredible beauty and purity that tears came to his eyes. Her voice was a clear soprano that sang like a silver bell on the crisp morning air, but her message frightened him badly.

He turned to shake Belle's shoulder, and when he looked back, Komwida Pokwee had vanished. "Wake up," he urged. "Someone's coming. We're in danger."

Clinging to her dreams, Belle awakened reluctantly. She sat up and clutched Coyote's blanket to her bare breasts. "I just had the most vivid dream," she related slowly. "It was my mother. She was dressed in white and all aglow like an angel. She was about to warn me of something, but you woke me and now I don't know what it is."

"That wasn't your mother," Coyote insisted. He yanked on his pants and pulled his shirt on over his head. "It was Komwida Pokwee and she said someone's coming."

"I know my own mother," Belle argued. "Besides, you didn't see her."

"I saw her," Coyote swore. He jammed his feet into his moccasins and brushed his hair out of his eyes. "Get dressed. It doesn't matter who gave us the warning; we've got to be ready." He picked up her gunbelt, withdrew the Colt .45, and checked to make sure it was loaded.

Inspired by his example, Belle donned her clothes with equal haste. It was still too dark to see anyone approaching, but she could think of only two possibilities. "It's either Donovan coming after me or the Army has caught up with you. What are we going to do?"

Coyote had been so certain it was Donovan who posed a threat to their lives that he had completely forgotten about the Army. "If it's soldiers, there will be no fight. I'll surrender. I escaped from them once and I can do it again. If it's Donovan, I won't let him harm you."

Belle folded up his blanket, took a sip from his canteen, and then passed it to him. He had used most of the water to wash away the evidence of their passion before they had gone to sleep, but there was enough left to dampen the dusty taste of fear. "Move your horse," she ordered suddenly. "If it's Donovan, we'll have the advantage if he thinks I'm alone."

Without asking her permission, Coyote strapped on her gunbelt. "If there's any killing to be done, I'll do it," he promised. "Sit down and wait for the sunrise." He tarried only long enough to give her a reassuring kiss and then disappeared down the trail.

Belle wound her hair atop her head and covered it with her hat. She moved Coyote's blanket and canteen out of the way and scanned what she could see of the top of the butte for any other telltale signs that she had had company. Because Coyote had taken care to disguise his presence, there was nothing more to conceal. She walked toward the eastern side of the butte, remaining well away from the edge. She sat down and rested her palms on her knees, but, rather than the dawn, this time she was waiting for something, or someone, far more sinister.

Edwin had slept only fitfully, and when he heard the sound of a solid masculine step pass by his room, he was certain his great-uncle was on the prowl. He left his bed and went to the door. He waited with his ear pressed against it, straining to hear, until he was certain Donovan had reached the first floor. Only then did he dare leave his room. Belle's door was open, and, alarmed, he rushed toward it. Terrified that she had disregarded his warning to lock her door and come to great harm, he called her name, but there was no answer.

With his principal ally missing, Edwin chose a decisive course of action. He pulled on the clothes he wore for riding and went out to the barn. Belle's pinto wasn't in her stall, and while he couldn't remember what sort of a horse had occupied the adjoining space, it was empty, too.

Grateful he had learned how to saddle a horse, he spoke in a reassuring tone, convincing his mustang, as well as himself, that they were equal to the task of rescuing Belle from the worst sort of danger. He could think of only one place she might have gone, and while he wasn't eager to see Coyote again, he hoped the Indian was still around to be on their side.

When he reached the butte, Donovan tethered his horse beside Belle's and climbed the steep trail with a cautious step. He had not been there since the night of Isabel's death but he shook off that bitter memory and concentrated solely on the distasteful job he had come to do. When he reached the summit, he saw Belle framed against the first faint glimmers of dawn and, thinking the deed as good as done, he started toward her with his arms outstretched.

The same sixth sense that had protected Belle from Coyote on the morning they met now warned her Donovan was near, but rather than merely being aware of another's presence, she felt his revulsion as a tangible force. The sickening waves of hatred emanating from him oozed across the rocky soil, pooled around her, and forced her to her feet. She had an oval stone clutched in her palm but kept it hidden at her side.

"Have you come to enjoy the view?" she challenged bravely.

Startled, Donovan drew to a halt. "No, I've come to put an end to a troublesome nuisance."

"That's all I've ever been to you, isn't it?" Without arousing his suspicions, Belle tried to see past him, but the top of the trail still lay in shadows and there was no sign of Coyote. She would have to stall for time and fortunately had a lifetime of anger for inspiration. "Why couldn't you have loved me? All we've ever had is each other and we should have been close. Did you hate my mother, too?"

With a bit of surprise, Donovan noted that Belle wasn't wearing her gunbelt. He had not known her to ever leave the house for a ride without it but took her sudden carelessness as a good omen that what he was doing was right. Because she was unarmed, he relaxed slightly.

"Your mother was the most beautiful creature ever born. You resemble her closely in appearance but you didn't inherit her sweetness. Her greatest joy was in pleasing me, and that's something you've never even tried to do."

Belle had never had any incentive to please the harshly critical man, but thought better of insulting him by saying so. "Tell me how she died," she coaxed. "You owe me that much. What really happened to her and Rick Vernon?"

His partner's name still bringing disgust, Donovan spit in the dirt and wiped his mouth on his shirtsleeve. "Vernon was a selfish bastard who never cared whom he hurt as long as he got what he wanted. He could have had any woman in the territory, but no, he set his sights on my wife. He was always doing little favors for her, bringing her presents and treats, reciting poetry, courting her right in front of me. He knew I loved Isabel more than life itself, but that didn't matter to him.

"We were in the study working late one night, long after Isabel had gone to bed, and I finally confronted him. I told him I was sick of watching him flirt with her and offered to buy him out. Rick denied I had any cause for jealousy but admitted being bored with ranching and said he'd be glad to sell. We decided on a price and drew up an agreement, but as soon as we'd both signed, he began to taunt me about Isabel. He said he would be happy to leave, but that he was taking her and you with him."

Donovan fell silent while his expression filled with the very same rage he had felt that night. "He laughed at me, said you were his daughter, not mine, and the time to set everything straight was long overdue. He told me to wake Isabel and let her choose between us, but I refused. I don't remember who threw the first punch, but when he grabbed the letter opener off the desk, I drew my knife. Rick was never any good with a knife."

When he failed to continue, Belle assumed the worst.

97

"So you killed him and hid the body?"

Donovan gestured over his shoulder. "He's buried right down below here. I had to kill his horse, too. That was a shame, but it had to be done to fit the story I'd concocted. I started a rock slide to cover the pit where I'd buried them both. It took me most of the night to erase all trace of Rick, but the next morning, when I told everyone he'd gotten restless and gone to California, they all believed me."

Knowing more than one man had killed his best friend over a woman, Belle almost felt sorry for him. "No one but my mother, you mean? Wasn't she suspicious that Rick hadn't told her goodbye?"

Donovan laughed. "No, she seemed as relieved as I was to have him gone, but I couldn't forget what Rick had said about her being unfaithful to me. It just ate away at me until nothing else mattered. I shouldn't have cared. After all, I'd won and she was with me rather than Rick, but I had to know the truth."

Belle could not recall the dawn ever arriving so slowly, but she still couldn't see Coyote and feared Donovan was fast coming to the end of his tale. Not eager to defend herself against the aggressive man armed only with a stone, she tried to keep him talking. "Tell me everything she said."

"She just wept and said she was heartbroken by my accusation. It was quite a performance, but I saw through it. I knew she was lying and I struck her across the face the same way I did you last night. It was the only time I'd ever hit her and she fell and struck her temple against the fireplace. In an instant she was gone, but I couldn't let people think I'd killed her, not when I'd loved her so. I had to make her death look like suicide, don't you see? Her body was still warm when I dropped her over the edge here. No one ever doubted my grief, because it's always been real."

Donovan Cassidy had never been a father to her, but Belle could see his pain and took a step toward him. "Rick was the first to grab for a weapon, so you were merely defending yourself. As for Mother's death, it was an accident. There's no reason for you to keep such horrible secrets any longer. We can go to the authorities this very morning and put everything right."

Thinking her daft, Donovan shook his head. "No one would

believe me now. It's been too long. I'd be charged with two murders and hanged."

"I believe you," Belle insisted.

"You're lying," Donovan replied. "You're just like your mother and you're lying to save your life."

For an instant, Belle thought he had simply made a poor choice of words, but then she understood he had foolishly revealed more than he had intended. Had her mother been struck only once and hit her head, he could have laid her body at the bottom of the stairs and called her death an accident. Knowing what a terrible temper he had, she thought it far more likely that her mother had been so badly battered by the time she fell and struck her head that a fall from the butte was the only way Donovan could cover the damage he'd done to her face and body.

As for Rick Vernon, she doubted the details of his death were accurate, either. While she still couldn't see Coyote, Belle trusted him to be close enough to come to her defense and chose to act with the bravado she had always seen Donovan display. "I want you to turn yourself in. Kenneth will swear to your devotion to my mother and so will Aurelia. You must still have that agreement Rick signed, and that will be proof of what led to your final argument. You're widely respected in the territory. Your innocence in both deaths will be believed. You're in absolutely no danger of hanging."

Again Donovan scoffed at her advice. "No, you're the only one who will ever hear that story, and you're not going to live long enough to tell anyone else."

"Someone else has already heard it," Belle warned. "There's an Apache brave standing behind you and he heard every word."

"An Apache?" Donovan sneered. "That's absurd."

"There's still time for you to decide to give yourself up," Belle pleaded. "Don't make him shoot you."

Convinced she was bluffing, Donovan didn't even glance over his shoulder before he started toward her. "I've waited a long time to wring your pretty little neck and—"

Coyote's first shot went over Donovan's head, but it was close enough to gain his full attention. He spun on his heel, and there in the pale morning light stood the Apache brave Belle had described. Donovan needed only one look at the Indian's knowing smirk to understand why he was there, but he again turned the full fury of his rage on Belle and yanked her in front of him to form a human shield.

"You bitch," he snarled in her ear. "You're just like your mother. But Rick couldn't save her and your lover won't be able to save you." He took a step backward, pulling them both closer to the rim of the butte. "What's the matter, chief?" he taunted Coyote. "Afraid you'll hit your pretty little squaw if you try to shoot me?"

"Let her go," Coyote shouted back.

Donovan laughed, and edged closer to the brink. "I'm not afraid of you. I never met an Indian who could shoot worth a damn." Belle struggled to break free, but Donovan tightened his grip and held her fast. "You see, Belle doesn't trust you, either."

Coyote took careful aim. "Release her, or you're a dead man," he promised.

Ignoring Coyote's threat, Donovan began to pivot, clearly intending to hurl Belle over the side of the butte. The stone she'd held fell useless to the ground, but, true to his word, Coyote put his next shot through Donovan's left eye. His blood splattered over Belle, but, his hold on her slackened and she broke away with a mighty shove that sent his body spiraling out over the edge of the butte and, like his beloved Isabel, he was long dead before he struck the rocks below.

Spurred by the sound of the first gunshot, Edwin had raced up the butte and arrived in time to see Coyote kill Donovan with his second shot. Sickened, he stumbled and fell to the ground, but he had seen enough to know the Indian had just saved Belle's life and was a hero rather than a murderer. "I saw it all," he called weakly.

Coyote shoved the Colt back into his holster and ran to embrace Belle. Not caring what else Edwin saw, he kissed her with all the passion that burned in his soul. Several minutes passed before he could bear to break away long enough to draw a deep breath. "I heard what he said," he assured her. "He admitted killing his partner and your mother.

Had I not been here, he might have killed you, too."

Savoring their last moment together, Belle clung to him tightly, but, knowing he was still being hunted, she had to let him go. "Thanks to your help, justice will finally be done here. We'll find Rick's body and that will prove what kind of a man Donovan Cassidy really was. You won't have to jeopardize your freedom by being involved. I want you to go now. Ride until you're safe and never look back."

"No," Coyote argued. "I won't let you take the blame for shooting him."

"I'm not taking the blame," Belle insisted. "I want the credit. I appreciate what you want to do, but all it will get you is a train ride to Florida, and neither of us wants that. Now give me back my pistol, and go on, get out of here. They've got to have heard the gunfire at the ranch and someone will be out to investigate soon."

"I don't want to leave you," Coyote repeated.

"You won't be," Belle promised. She reached up to kiss him, then hurriedly unbuckled her gunbelt and wrapped it around her own hips. "You've taken good care of me, Indian. Now take care of yourself."

Coyote knew she was right, but that did not make leaving her any easier. "I'll come back," he vowed, "with more horses than you can count."

He kissed her one last time and then disappeared in the mist of tears that filled Belle's eyes. The dawn which had taken so long in coming had now broken with unusual splendor and she turned to look up at the rising sun, finally confident of her mother's love. When Edwin walked up beside her, she wiped away her tears and tried to smile.

"We've got an awful mess to straighten out here, Win. Are you up to helping me?"

Edwin took her hand. "I sure am. What did Coyote mean about the horses? Is he really coming back?"

"I told you Indians aren't the predictable sort, so I doubt it, but it was enough that he was here when I needed him."

Edwin watched another tear escape Belle's lashes to trickle down her cheek and hoped for her sake that Coyote would keep his promise.

Just as Belle had predicted, once what was left of Rick Vernon's body was found, Donovan Cassidy's guilt in the man's death was accepted as fact. With Edwin serving as an eyewitness to corroborate her story of self-defense, her version of how Donovan had died also went unchallenged. No longer listed as a suicide, Isabel Cassidy's body was reburied in hallowed ground. What had clearly been a love triangle leading to murder provided months of delicious gossip, but now burdened with the responsibility of running the ranch, Belle simply chose to ignore it. After all, it had all been so long ago, and she had her own life to live.

Edwin stayed on and made up for what he lacked in experience in ranching with enthusiasm. Remembering the way Belle had kissed Coyote goodbye, he was patient and never offered more than friendship to his lovely cousin, but he prayed every night that Coyote had found himself an Indian girl and would never return. By tacit agreement, the pair never spoke of the Apache, but if Edwin could not forget him, then he was positive Belle could not, either.

It was a warm afternoon in June when Edwin knocked on the open study door. "Belle, there's a man here with some horses," he informed her in a lazy drawl.

Belle didn't look up from her ledger. "We've all the stock we need, Win. Send him on his way."

While Win would have loved to do precisely that, he couldn't. He wanted Belle, but by choice, not default. "No, he insists upon talking with you."

Belle threw down her pen. "I'm going to make you add up these figures next month, Win. This is just too big a headache for me."

"I'll be happy to do it, you know that. Now come on out and talk to the man. He seems nice enough."

Belle rubbed her neck and stood up slowly. "All right, but the next time some peddler comes calling, I'm going to expect you to say you're the boss here and send him on his way."

"Yes, ma'am, I'll be happy to take a turn at running the place anytime you're tired."

Belle tickled his ribs as she walked by. "I'm already tired, Win."

Expecting a stranger with a few mustangs, she opened the front door completely unprepared for the sight that greeted her. "My God," she whispered. She had not dared hope that Coyote would really come back for her, but there he sat astride the most magnificent black stallion she had ever seen. That alone would have been astonishing, but he was surrounded by enough horses to claim a princess. There were pintos and bays, roans, dapple grays, a few snowy white mares, and half a dozen sleek colts with coats as dark as midnight.

Having known only abandonment and loss, Belle needed a moment to catch her breath and to appreciate the fact that not only had Coyote come for her, but the love they had shared was real. No matter what Apache protocol dictated, her choice was made in an instant. She returned to the house, dashed up the stairs, and changed into the lace wedding gown, that despite her protests, Aurelia had insisted upon altering.

Her preparations for a June wedding as complete as they were likely to get with an Apache groom, Belle returned to the front porch and gave Win an enthusiastic kiss. "Please call some men to take care of the horses and, until we get back, you've got your chance to run the ranch." Before Win could offer more than a brief hope for her happiness, she left him and ran to Coyote.

His stallion danced in place as the handsome brave swung her up in front of him and, once she was nestled securely in his arms, he kissed her with all the love his heart could hold. Then he whispered in her ear, "Let's find a new place to watch the sunrise."

"I don't need the sunrise anymore," Belle replied with a seductive laugh. "All I need is you."

Thrilled by her love, Coyote carried his beautiful red-haired bride into the enchanted land where the spirits watch over lovers and make all their dreams come true.

Mail-Order Maiden

by

Kathleen Drymon

Prologue

Clarksburg, West Virginia, 1863

Time was a precious commodity at the Clarksburg Inn. Leaning against the closed door to her chamber, which was furnished only with a small cot and a wardrobe, Heather Collins stole a moment alone. Eagerly she pulled from her apron pocket the rumpled envelope she had stuffed there after finding the packet of mail on a table in the inn's front common room. Her name was written in bold script on the face of the envelope, and a prickling of fear overtook Heather at the thought of her punishment if she were caught with the letter in her possession. Clarence Bosworth, her stepfather, ruled the Clarksburg Inn with an iron fist, and with an image of his large, meaty fist making contact with the side of her head, Heather hurriedly tore open the envelope.

Quickly she scanned the contents. The writer had wasted few words; the instructions were clear. When she finished, she ran a finger over the sheaf of bills and the stagecoach ticket that had been included.

Hearing her name shouted from downstairs, Heather hurried across the bare floor of her chamber, pulled the tapestry valise from under the narrow cot, and tucked the envelope under with the clothes she had packed earlier that week. Then she pushed the valise back out of sight.

Hurrying to the door, she straightened her apron and drew a deep breath before placing her hand upon the knob. Her stepfather would demand an explanation for this unrequested break in her routine of cleaning tables and serving the inn's customers, particularly at this busy dinner hour. Feeling a light flush upon her pale cheeks, she knew she would have to claim her monthly womanly ailment for her need of a moment's privacy. She could easily envision the leer that would cross Clarence Bosworth's hard features, and with that image, she told herself once again that she had little choice but to go through with the plan she had already set into motion.

A mail-order bride; how could becoming the wife of a complete stranger be any worse than having to endure her stepfather's abuse as an unpaid servant, always wondering when he would make good his threat and send men up to her room to bring in added coins to his purse? Heather felt her flesh crawl at the thought of Clarence Bosworth's solicitor and best friend, Samuel Tate. Of late the overly thin, balding, middle-aged man had been coming to the inn and sitting alone through the dinner hour. Heather had felt the heat of interest in his small, beady eyes as he followed her every movement. She knew for a certainty that Samuel Tate would be the first man her stepfather would send up to her chamber. Heather shuddered at the thought.

The signature on the letter, now safely hidden in her valise, was "Bret Saber." Surely this unknown man could not be as unsavory as what her stepfather had planned for her!

Chapter One

Miles City, Montana
June 6, 1863

A safe haven was all Heather Collins had ever wanted, but as the bouncing stagecoach pulled into Miles City, Montana, she once again wondered what her future would hold. The closer the stage had come to Miles City, the more she worried that she had made a terrible mistake. Perhaps she should have found some other way to get away from her stepfather and the Clarksburg Inn. She knew nothing about this man, Bret Saber, whom she had traveled so far to wed. But what other choice could she have made? With no family besides her stepfather and no money of her own, becoming a mail-order bride had been her only available option. She had known it from the moment she had read the advertisement in the monthly gazette she'd found in one of the guest chambers at the inn.

At least she would be marrying the man whom she would bed, she told herself once again. She would not become coarse and hard like Nell and Emily who worked at the inn and each evening, after the dinner hour, traveled up and down the stairs to their chambers with different men. She would be a proper wife, and with any kind of luck, she would not be treated too unkindly.

The letter she had received from Bret Saber had instructed her to remain in front of the general store, where the stagecoach would leave her off, until someone arrived for her. Now, standing on the wooden sidewalk that ran in front of Bailey's General Store, she tried to brush away some of the dust that seemed to have settled permanently over her dark, serviceable gown. The threadbare valise, which had seen better days in her mother's time, remained at her feet as she pushed the dark tendrils of her escaping hair back beneath her bonnet. She was worried Bret Saber would find her haggard from her days of travel and would deem her less than attractive at first sight.

Travel-worn and dirty, Heather stood alone on the sidewalk and waited for Bret Saber to come and take her to the church where she would repeat the vows that would forever bind her to him. She felt her unease increasing by the moment as several women passed her on the sidewalk. After a tentative smile, they quickly looked the other way. Perhaps they knew that she was Bret Saber's mail-order bride. Did the whole town know that she had traveled all the way from West Virginia to marry a man whom no other woman in Miles City would have? She felt as though all eyes were upon her, silently appraising the woman who was brave enough to answer an ad for a wife!

She began to pace as the moments slowly drew into an hour and still there was no sign of Bret Saber. Surely he must have known what time the stage would arrive. Had he forgotten that she would arrive today? Had he changed his mind about wanting a mail-order bride?

Gazing around at the small, quiet town, Heather wondered what she should do if Bret Saber did not come for her. There was little money left from the funds he had sent her, and even with all possible thrift, what she carried in her small reticule would not last a week. Of course she could always find some sort of job. She was not afraid of hard work, and she could read and write passably well. But even if she could find work, could she stay in Miles City and be known to all as the woman who was jilted by a would-be husband she had never even met? Where would she go and what would she do?

Feeling more alone than ever before in her life, Heather picked up her valise and started toward the front door of the general store. The first thing she should do, she told herself, was to question someone in the store. Perhaps Bret Saber had left word that he would be late for some reason or another and she was just being silly to worry.

"Miss Collins?" A masculine voice called from the seat of an open carriage, just as Heather was about to take a step through the doorway of the general store.

Swinging around with some relief that she had not been completely forgotten, Heather looked toward the man who had called out her name. "Yes," she answered as she was met by a pair of appraising, ebony-black eyes set in a darkly tanned, handsome face.

"Get in then, the preacher's waiting for us." The husky tremor of his voice settled over her and, at the same time, his words left her feeling rather chilled.

"Are you . . . are you Mr. Saber?" Heather asked, not believing that this could be the man who had advertised for a mail-order bride.

"Who else would be here to fetch you to the church?" At first glance at the woman who had replied to his advertisement, Bret Saber was somewhat surprised by what he saw. She appeared to be in her early twenties, and though she was plainly travel-worn, she was certainly not unpleasant to look at. This was much more than he had expected from a woman answering an advertisement for a husband, and with that thought, some unbidden spark of anger ignited in the pit of his belly.

Heather nervously stepped across the sidewalk in front of the store. Approaching the carriage, she placed her valise on the floor before the seat and looked around, as though searching for a handhold on the carriage to pull herself up into the seat.

Seeming to come to his senses, Bret jumped down from the carriage seat and hurried around to give Heather a hand up. "Excuse me, ma'am, I'm afraid I wasn't thinking," he said.

Heather settled her dusty skirts as he reclaimed his seat and took up the buggy reins to direct his horse down the street. Neither he nor Heather spoke as they made their way to the church, both lost in their inner reflections on their first meeting.

Glancing sideways at the large, darkly attractive man sitting next to her, Heather was at a loss to understand why such a man would have to resort to advertising for a wife. Surely any number of women would jump at the chance to become this man's bride! His hands, holding the reins loosely in their grip, appeared strong and capable, the nails clean and trim. He was dressed entirely in black, western boots and silk suit, except for the white shirt which sported a bit of a ruffle at the throat beneath his vest. He reminded her of a gentleman gambler, the type she had read about in the penny magazines which portrayed life in the West as glamorous and adventurous. Even the carriage they rode in, with its red-leather-upholstered cushioned seat and the tasseled awning overhead, was much more lavish than Heather had expected.

The drive to the church lasted only a few minutes. When the carriage stopped in front of a small, wood-framed building on the outskirts of town, Bret Saber jumped to the ground and in seconds was helping Heather down from the carriage seat. She had no more time to ponder his reasons for wanting a mail-order bride.

"Reverend Waters is waiting for us. We are already late." He took her arm and began to lead her up the front steps to the church as he offered his explanation for his hurried manners.

Well, it certainly was not her fault that he had arrived so late to pick her up, Heather thought to herself as she stood close at his side, surrounded by the faint masculine scent of sandalwood cologne.

Once inside the small church, the reverend's plump, energetic wife Beth hurried to Heather's side. "Why, my dear, you must be simply exhausted! Bret told us that you would be arriving by stagecoach this afternoon. Come with me now and I will show you where you can freshen up before the ceremony." Wearing a bright yellow print dress, her graying brown hair pulled back in a tight bun at the back of her head, Beth Waters took charge of Heather immediately and directed a withering eye in Bret's direction. Miles City was a small town and she, like everyone else in town, knew what time the stagecoach arrived in front of Bailey's General Store. It was obvious that Bret Saber had left this young woman standing alone for well over an hour!

Heather was more than a little relieved when Beth Waters handed her a damp cloth to wipe away the dust and grime from her face and neck. With efficient movements, the full-figured preacher's wife pulled the bonnet from Heather's head and began to gently brush out the tangles from her glistening black curls.

Within minutes the elder woman had most of the dust brushed off Heather's gown. Standing back to look at the young woman who was soon to become Bret Saber's bride, she smiled kindly upon her. "There, that is so much better. I only wish you could have a proper wedding gown. I always thought if I had a daughter, I would one day see her in a beautiful gown for her June wedding. But I reckon that some things can't be helped. Reverend Waters and I only had boys, and the three of them are all married now and living elsewhere."

Heather smiled fondly at the kind woman. It was nice to have a woman fussing over her once again. Since her mother died two years ago, there had been little womanly affection directed her way.

"Well, we had best not keep that young man of yours waiting any longer than necessary. It seems as though he and everyone else in Miles City are in such a hurry these days." Beth Waters could well remember when this had not been the way of things and Bret Saber had been as easygoing as the next man, but now, with all the rustling going on and ranchers pointing the finger at the nesters and Indians and the nesters pointing their finger in the direction of the ranchers, there appeared to be little peace. Bret Saber had had it harder than the rest with the death of his first wife, and nowadays he always appeared hard and restless. Perhaps this young woman would be able to soften the shell he had built up around himself, Beth hoped.

With the two women returned to the front of the church, Reverend Waters and Bret Saber halted their conversation. A warm smile settled over the tall, lanky preacher's friendly face, but Bret Saber's features were unreadable as he viewed the woman who was to be his wife.

Heather Collins was not in the least what he had expected in a mail-order bride. Her creamy, smooth features were framed in a cloud of soft curls that lay down her back, and as her violet-blue eyes caught his regard, long, thick, dark lashes feathered against her pink cheeks as she delicately lowered her glance.

Clearing his throat, Reverend Waters looked to Bret and, reading the confusion on his face, quickly took charge of the situation. "Let us get on with the ceremony, if everyone is ready." He took hold of Bret's arm and led the group toward the front of the church and before the altar.

The wedding ceremony was a hurried affair, and seemed to pass quickly in a blur of words and repeated vows as Heather stood nervously next to the tall, solid frame of Bret Saber. Beth Waters stood on Heather's other side, and it was the kindly woman who kissed Heather's cheek in a motherly fashion at the completion of the vows.

"I have made a wonderful plum spice cake for this special occasion," Beth offered generously as she beamed at the young, handsome couple.

Heather would have gladly accepted the invitation and was more than willing to stay in her company and prolong the moment. Now that the vows that bound her to this man had been spoken, she was not quite sure what was expected of her.

It was her husband, standing at her side, who replied to the preacher's wife's kind offer. "I'm afraid there is no time for cake, Mrs. Waters." Bret took hold of Heather's forearm and began to lead her away from the altar. "Molly's out at the ranch with Cam, and I don't like being away too long." Heather felt her life careening crazily out of control.

Why would this man, her new husband, not allow her a piece of cake on her wedding day? And who were this Molly and Cam that he worried so about?

Once again Heather found herself next to Bret Saber on the buggy seat, and as she toyed with the slim band of gold he had placed upon her finger, she stole a glance at him. He appeared to be in a bleak mood and did not seem in the least to want her company. Glancing at him, she noticed that a dark lock of hair had fallen over his right eye. Absently, he pushed it aside, as though not welcoming even this small disruption upon the sanctuary of his thoughts.

Heather had to admit that he was very handsome in a darkly brooding sort of way. She wondered what he would expect from her as his wife, and with the thought her gaze was drawn to his sensual, full lips, and a tingling of goose flesh traveled over her arms. Perhaps she should say something. She tried to pull her mind away from such dangerous thoughts as the carriage ride seemed to last an uncomfortably long period of time. Finally, clearing her throat, Heather ventured, "You told the reverend's wife that you had to get back to the ranch? Is it a large ranch?" She hoped he would tell her something about his life before they arrived. Bret nodded his head, but that was the only response he made to her question.

Damn. Bret swore silently as he directed his horse down the dusty road. He should have thought to make some kind of inquiries about this woman before he sent her the money and the ticket to come to Miles City! He should have at least asked her age and something about her appearance; two of the things she had not volunteered when she had replied to his advertisement for a bride. Now here he was once again taking a hell of a good-looking woman out to his ranch! Only this time, he swore to himself, things would be different! He would not be taken in by an attractive figure and a sweet smile.

It was easy for Heather to see that he was a man of few words. As the late afternoon drew on into lengthy shadows, and still he had not answered her questions to her satisfac-

115

tion, she forced herself to try and draw him out, hoping to learn something about him that would put her at ease. But the farther the horse and carriage took her out of Miles City, the more inscrutable he became! Could she have gotten herself into an even worse situation than the one she had fled from? "Who are Molly and Cam? You spoke of them at the church," she reminded him, hoping he would not take offense and think her prying. But she had never been one to sit and quietly await what would happen next.

Expelling a deep sigh, Bret at last relented. "I guess there are a few things you should know, Miss Collins."

Had he forgotten so quickly that he had given her his last name? Heather felt her unease growing, but she dared not remind him of his slip, for at last he had decided to share *something* with her!

"First, I guess you should know something about my home. My ranch is north of Miles City. We mostly raise cattle, but we also have some fine horseflesh."

Heather was interested in all he had to say, and as she held her gaze upon him, he became more direct. "I don't know what you expected when you answered my advertisement in the gazette, but my needs for a woman on my ranch are a little complicated. Your duties as my wife will be very limited." He tried to explain.

"Just what are you trying to tell me, Mr. Saber?" Heather asked, more than a little confused.

He liked her directness, and only to himself would Bret admit that he also liked the sound of her soft, lilting voice. "I was married once before, Miss Collins. My wife died a little over a year ago."

There he was, calling her Miss Collins again! Silently she nodded her head at his confession. How could she have expected to arrive in Montana and find the man of her dreams—the one who had been waiting his entire life just for her?

"You see, the reason I took out the ad for a bride, is that I am in need of a mother for Molly, my daughter."

Chapter Two

"Molly is your daughter?" Whatever Heather had expected out of this venture, she had never even considered that she would be forced into becoming a mother so quickly, nor had she thought that she would be tied to a man who was still in love with his dead wife! Trying to bring a measure of calm to her racing heart, she took a deep breath before asking, "Why did you not say something in the advertisement or in your letter about your need for a mother for your child?" From the start she had expected it to be difficult to adjust to being the wife of a total stranger, but being told that their marriage was to be one in name only because her husband was still in love with his first wife, and then in the next breath to be told that she was also expected to be an instant mother! This was a bit too much!

Bret had been watching his bride closely to gain her reaction to all he had to tell her, and he easily read the surprise on her face. "This whole affair was Cam's idea." He now regretted that he had ever listened to his uncle!

"And who is this Cam that you keep speaking about?" Heather's head was swimming and she wondered if there were more children besides the girl called Molly.

"Cam is my uncle. He was the one who told me to put the advertisement in the gazette. He swore that there wasn't a woman in all of Montana fit to become Molly's mother. He said that I would be just as well off to get myself a mail-order bride!"

"So you took your uncle's advice in this matter?" Heather could not believe her ears! Who would so cal-

117

lously get themselves a wife in this manner?

Bret was feeling more than a little uncomfortable. Cam had told him that he needn't bother telling about Molly, and that any woman answering the ad would be more than glad to become his daughter's mother. "It does sound rather foolish now, but the fact is, I didn't really care about getting myself a wife again. All I want is a mother for Molly!"

"So it did not matter to you where you got one?"

"Truthfully? No!" His dark stare held upon her for a full moment before he turned his gaze away. "Molly's all that matters, and once I figured that Cam was right and she needed a woman with her at the ranch, I did what I had to. I got her a mother."

And I'm it, Heather thought to herself.

"I guess if it doesn't work out, with Molly and all, I mean, I can always pay your fare back to Virginia." Bret had thought this whole affair would be nice and simple. He would get Molly a mother, and his bride would get herself a home. But who could have expected that she would be so damn pretty, and probably not in the least interested in being a mother to some stranger's child?

His words held the effect of dashing her with ice water. She could never go back to Virginia! The thought of the gloating look in her stepfather's eyes if she returned to him and begged to be allowed to remain at the inn caused a shiver to course over her. Though she knew virtually nothing about children, she would do her best to be a fitting mother to his daughter. Drawing a deep breath, she looked him straight in the eye. "Unlike you, Mr. Saber, the vows that were spoken in church were not mere words to me. I will do my best to be a mother to your child." Whether she liked the situation she had been thrust into or not, she would be a mother! And if it were true that all Bret desired was a mother for his daughter, she should be pleased. Had she not fled Virginia because of her stepfather's desire to force men upon her? If her

118

only duty in this marriage would be to play the part of mother, she should be happy! But some small nagging feeling of disappointment filled her thoughts.

Bret would have answered her that he had had first-hand knowledge of how women honored their wedding vows, but instead he satisfied himself with her promise of trying to be a mother to Molly. After all, that was all he had wanted, wasn't it? he asked himself, even as he tried to push away the feelings of guilt he was experiencing.

Just as the sun was lowering, the buggy pulled down the long drive to the Saber-Bar ranch. The ranch house itself was a sprawling two-story wooden structure, built upon a low hill that overlooked a wide, fertile valley on one side and the Powder River on the other. The oil lamps were just being lit by Jasper, the Sabers' cook and housekeeper, as Bret led his new bride through the front door of her new home.

It was also Jasper who greeted them. With a nod of his gray head, he spoke through the side of his mouth. "Howdy, ma'am, Bret. Cam and the little gal are in the study. They been waiting fur ya." His sparkling blue eyes gave Heather a quick onceover, taking everything in for the boys out in the bunkhouse. Jasper had promised he would tell them everything about the new missus just as soon as the house settled down for the evening.

Heather smiled at the small-framed man who wore jeans, a red plaid shirt, boots, and an apron tied around his waist.

Bret Saber appeared not to notice his new bride's nervousness as he set the worn valise down in the foyer and started through the large, open front portion of the house.

Not knowing what else to do, Heather followed her husband, her sapphire eyes taking in the central great room and the massive fireplace with brass-trimmed, oak mantel running the length of one wall. Family portraits hung on the opposite wall, and dark leather overstuffed furniture and plush-embroidered rugs were placed comfortably about.

Seemingly unaware of his wife's interest in her new home, Bret went straight down the hall to the study. As Heather entered the oak door, she instantly glimpsed pale-blue petticoats as a tiny, dark-haired child jumped off the knee of a large-framed, middle-aged man and hurled herself against Bret's long legs. A squeal of happiness filled the room as the little girl cried in a loud voice, "Daddy, Daddy, I want a horsey ride!"

"I tried to entertain her while you were away, boy, but I'm afraid that she near tuckered me out. This old knee ain't what it used to be."

This must be her husband's uncle, Heather thought to herself as she looked around Bret's shoulder and glimpsed the same dark eyes as his looking in her direction. And the child must be Molly.

"Let's wait a few minutes for that horsey ride, sweetheart." Bret lifted the child into his arms and turned toward Heather. "Molly, I want you to meet someone."

There was a warmth in his tone that Heather had not heard until this moment. In that instant, as she looked at the little girl held tenderly against Bret Saber's chest, she knew that he adored the dimpled-faced, dark-haired child.

"Miss Collins, this is Molly." Bret looked directly at her as he began to make the introductions.

"What do you mean, Bret? Didn't you two get hitched up before you brought her out here to the ranch? I thought that was the plan?" Cam Saber drew the attention of both Heather and Bret.

"Sure we got married, Cam." Bret looked confused.

"Then what's all this Miss Collins business? Ain't she Mrs. Saber now?" Cam knew how hard all of this was for his nephew, but the moment the couple had entered the study, he had taken a good look at Bret's bride, and finding her more than passable to look upon, he had instantly decided that perhaps with a little time this marriage would prove the right thing, not only for Molly but also for Bret. Cam Saber believed that once you're thrown by a wild mustang, you get right back on his back as quickly as possible. And to his way of thinking there wasn't much difference in being thrown by a woman or thrown by a horse!

Heather felt her face flush with embarrassment over her husband's insistence on calling her by her maiden name, and as Bret looked from his uncle and then back to her, he also seemed somewhat embarrassed.

"I'm sorry . . . I meant Mrs. Saber, of course."

"Why don't you call her by her first name, boy?" It was his uncle who spoke up once again.

"Heather will be fine," Heather choked out as she felt her face flaming now as both men stared at her. Lord, she had expected that her arrival at her husband's home would be rather uncomfortable, but this was a bit more than she had expected. She wished that she could just vanish!

Bret must have sensed her discomfort, for he quickly amended, "Yes . . . Heather." And, turning back to Molly, he said softly, "Honey, I want you to meet someone very special."

"Mommy?" the little girl shyly questioned and then turned her head in her father's shoulder, her blue eyes peeking over at the woman who had accompanied her father into the study.

Both Bret and Heather were surprised by what she said, and once again Cam spoke up. "I guess I sort of gave away the surprise. I told her that you were bringing her home a mommy."

Looking at the little girl, Heather felt her heart melting. "Yes, Molly, I am going to be your mommy." A tender smile came over her lips as Heather reached her arms out for the child to come to her.

For a few seconds the little girl hung back, secure in

her father's arms, but not given to a timid nature, she was slowly drawn to the pretty lady with the bright blue eyes. Her chubby arms reached out to Heather.

Taking the child into her arms, Heather softly sighed as though an important step had been taken by them both. Being a mother would not be as hard as she had expected, she thought as she felt the soft weight of the little girl in her arms and her hand gently brushed back a wayward dark curl as it fell over her eye. Her hair was just like her father's, Heather thought, and in that moment she looked up and was met by Bret's dark regard.

Bret Saber felt a lump in his throat and had to swallow hard in order to get his wits about him. What had he thought would happen when he brought home a woman to be Molly's mother? Wasn't this how he wanted things to turn out? Molly was taking to Heather as though she really *was* her mother. So why was he the one feeling so empty inside? As he looked at the two of them together, he knew that by his own words he had forced a wedge between himself and his new bride, and in so doing had taken himself out of the picture of a happy family.

"Well, I'll be danged if'n she ain't taking to you right off, Heather." Cam grinned and nodded his head as though he had known this would be the way of things right from the start.

Bret's look grew darker with his uncle's words. "I had best take Molly up to her room. It's time for her to go to bed." Bret took his daughter from Heather's arms, even as the little girl pleaded.

"I want to stay with Mommy, Daddy."

Heather was more confused than ever. If Bret Saber's intention had been to gain his daughter a mother, why was he acting so strangely now that his plan was succeeding? As he pulled the child from her arms, Heather felt a strange emptiness settle over her. "I will come and tell you good night in a few minutes, Molly," she promised.

122

Bret left the study with Molly in his arms without another word spoken, and as Heather turned about, not quite sure what she should do, Cam broke the silence that hung in the air.

"Just call me Cam, Heather, everyone around here does, including my hard-headed nephew. And don't think too hard on the boy. It might take him some time, but he'll come around. I'll have Jasper show you to your room, and you can freshen up some before dinner."

Heather felt her head swimming from everything that had happened since she arrived in Miles City. First, Bret Saber had been late picking her up, and then when he *had* arrived, he looked nothing like she had expected, and then the rushed wedding ceremony. Now, after he had plainly told her that he did not really want a wife but only a mother for his daughter, he was acting as though he wanted her nowhere near Molly. Perhaps she had only imagined the dark look her husband had directed at her as Molly had snuggled against her breast. Maybe all she needed was some rest. After all, these past couple of weeks had worn her nerves pretty thin. Though she had only had breakfast when the stagecoach had stopped at a station to change horses, she was not feeling very hungry. "I think I will skip dinner tonight, if that is all right."

Cam Saber's dark eyes held concern as he nodded his head. "A good night's rest might do us all some good," he muttered under his breath. "Jasper!" he shouted, and within seconds, the little man was standing in the doorway of the study. "Take Mrs. Saber up to her room and send a dinner tray up." He turned to Heather. "You might decide that you're a little hungry after a while," he said.

"Thank you," Heather said softly. Her husband's uncle had proven to be a friend of sorts, and something told her that she would be needing all the friends she could muster here on the Saber-Bar.

123

Chapter Three

Heather sat nervously on the edge of the comfortable bed centered in the chamber to which Jasper had shown her. The tray of food he had brought up to her still sat with its covered lid across the room. She was much too anxious to eat anything this evening. Having gone earlier into Molly's adjoining chamber and bid the little girl good night, she had returned to her own room. Feeling as nervous as a cat, she had paced about, as though waiting for something to happen that would send her fleeing from her husband's house.

Though Bret Saber had stated that he did not desire a wife for his own needs, Heather was still reluctant to believe him. If her stepfather's inn had taught her anything, it was that she could not trust men. She had been pinched and pawed enough to know that most men had but one thing on their minds, and that was to see how quickly they could tumble a woman!

As the hour grew late and the house seemed to quiet down for the night, exhaustion finally forced Heather to pull out her nightgown from her valise. After quickly washing at the washstand, she pulled on the gown and climbed into bed.

For some time she forced her eyes to remain wide, as the sound of her heartbeat sounded dully in her ears. Soon, though, sleep overcame her, but the darkly brooding visage of Bret Saber haunted her in her sleep.

Sometime during the late hours of the night a soft,

crying noise wound its way into Heather's consciousness. She fought the clutches of sleep and pulled herself upright in the bed. Shaking her head to clear it, Heather at first imagined that it was her mother calling to her from her sickbed. For three years, she alone had tended to her mother's needs, day and night, until she had at last succumbed to her lingering illness. As Heather groggily wiped at her eyes with the back of her hands, she thought herself back at the Clarksburg Inn.

It took only a moment or two for her to recognize that the sounds coming from the next room were those of a small child. Pushing back the covers, she made her way barefoot over the varnished wooden floors and quietly reached out and opened the adjoining chamber door.

A small tallow candle had been left lit upon a table across the room, and Heather could barely make out the slight form of Molly sitting up in bed and crying softly.

Going to the child's side to lend her the comfort she needed to go back to sleep, Heather gently sat down on the edge of the bed. "What is it, darling?" she asked as she reached out to brush the dark strands of wayward curls back from the child's eyes. Without a second thought, Molly climbed into Heather's lap.

At first Heather felt a little shy with this child who seemed to accept her with no reservations. Soon, though, she was singing softly in her ear, remembering an old lullaby she had heard her mother singing one day, and gently rocking the little girl back and forth.

Bret Saber halted in his tracks where he stood in the doorway that connected his bedchamber with his daughter's. He stood holding the cup of water he had gone downstairs to get when he had first heard Molly crying. The sounds now coming to his ears were not those of a crying child, but the softly lilting singsong voice of a woman.

With the candlelight behind her, Heather and Molly

were silhouetted before the golden cast of light, and Bret was held immobile by the sight before him, not able to break away from the vision. Then, as Heather laid Molly back down upon her bed and bent over her to tuck the covers tightly around her, Bret felt his heart skip a beat. He drew in a deep, ragged breath.

Hearing the slight noise from the opposite doorway, Heather turned her head. The dark form of a man standing beneath the portal forced her to gasp aloud in surprise as her hand rose to her throat.

Bret's gaze lingered upon the cloud of dark hair in wild disarray from sleep. It fell over her shoulders and down her back, and with her gown thin enough for him to see each curve of her shapely body, he devoured her with his hungry eyes. He heard her gasp of surprise at seeing him standing in the doorway. As her hand rose to her throat, his gaze followed it, the dark tips of her breasts drawing his eyes with a hungry stare.

"I didn't mean to frighten you. I brought Molly a cup of water." He forced himself to speak as the silence lengthened and they could but look at each other, unable to move.

The husky tremor of her husband's voice settled over Heather in a heated flush. Unable to respond, for her own throat seemed closed up at the moment, she spun around and, feeling her legs trembling beneath her, hurried toward her chamber door.

Bret stared after her, the outline of her buttocks and shapely, long legs holding him fast near the doorway. With the closing of her chamber door, he at last recovered his wits. Stepping to the side of his daughter's bed he looked down at her sleeping visage. Then, slowly, his gaze went back to the connecting door.

Heather would have gladly locked the door that joined her chamber to Molly's, but there was no lock. She could content herself with only pulling the soft coverlet of her

126

bedding up beneath her chin as she lay in bed, every inch of her body trembling.

She lay there for some time, hardly daring to draw a breath as she imagined that her husband would come through the doorway and seek her out. Would she submit to him? She felt her entire body flush with the heat that her thoughts evoked as she recalled the masculine strength she had glimpsed beneath his clothes and the power of those obsidian eyes when they touched upon her. Though he was her husband, he was also a stranger. She tried to force him from her mind as she drew the covers tighter around her, as though this would afford her protection from his sexual power. As the minutes slowly passed, Heather felt herself beginning to relax. She heard no noise coming from Molly's chamber, so after a time, she told herself that he must have gone back to his own room. Though Heather had prayed for this, for some strange reason she felt disappointed.

It was some time before Heather could find sleep. Every time she shut her eyes, she saw again the dark image of Bret Saber standing in the doorway and staring at her. She could feel the heat of his eyes as they had traveled with leisure over her, and even in her imaginings, where his sable eyes touched, she felt her flesh seared.

The next morning Heather awoke to the sounds of a working ranch, hearing the shouts of men and the whinnying of horses coming from her open chamber window. Wiping the sleep from her eyes, she stifled a yawn as she sat up in bed. Instantly she was reminded of the encounter with her husband the night before, and as quickly, she felt her face beginning to flush crimson.

Taking her time with her dressing, for she dreaded coming face-to-face with Bret Saber this morning, she made up her bed and straightened her chamber after she had hung up her skimpy wardrobe in the cherrywood wardrobe. Wearing another dark gown, made of the same heavy, serviceable material as the one she had arrived in Montana wearing, she brushed out her hair and tied it back with a piece of bright red ribbon.

Having waited as long as she dared, Heather slowly made her way downstairs. The smell of food drew her through the central part of the house and toward the back portion of the downstairs.

Cam Saber was sitting at the large, intricately carved oak dining-room table. "Come on in, Heather, and sit yourself down. Jasper will bring you out a plate directly."

Taking a seat, Heather looked around the large, formal dining room. It had a fireplace with a marble mantel; on the opposite wall was the buffet and server. This room, like the rest of the house, was lavishly furnished, but in the morning light Heather could see that a woman's hand could be used here and there.

"Bret's already left with some of the hands to round up some steers from one of the western pastures." Cam spoke between bites of scrambled eggs and smoked ham.

Jasper placed a plate heaping with food and a cup of steaming coffee before her. All Heather could do was nod her head at her husband's uncle, relieved that there would be more time before she would once again have to face Bret Saber. "Where is Molly this morning?" she asked.

A wide grin split the older man's craggy features. "Every morning after breakfast Molly rides her pony, Taffy. If you want to eat with that young'un of a morning, you have to get up mighty early."

"I usually do rise early," Heather replied, remembering her days of work at the inn when she would have to get up long before daybreak to start the kitchen fires and begin cooking breakfast for the guests. "I guess I was just overly tired last night." She did not mention running into Bret in the middle of the night in Molly's chamber and how she had lain awake for a long time, not knowing what to expect of the man who was now her husband.

"Well, don't fret none about that. There will be plenty of mornings to have breakfast with Molly." Cam pushed his plate away and sipped his coffee as he eyed the young woman sitting across from him with a more leisurely regard than he had been allowed the night before. She was even more beautiful in the light of morning, he told himself. His nephew sure was blessed with a stroke of luck! Who would have guessed that a mail-order bride could be so fetching? For a few seconds he speculated over what could have made her so tired last night, and though he hoped that Bret would have taken advantage of his luck, he rather doubted it. His nephew still didn't trust women, and it would probably take him a while to realize what fortune had brought to his very doorstep.

Heather sampled the fare upon her plate, then, sipping the strong, brewed coffee, she grimaced at its harsh taste.

Cam chuckled aloud. "I reckon that old Jasper ain't used to having a woman around the ranch as yet. I'll call for him to bring you some honey to sweeten your coffee."

"Oh, no, don't bother." Heather put the cup back down. "I think I have had enough anyway." Heather had never wanted much to eat in the morning.

"Bret said that you're from Virginia. Do you mind my asking why you answered his advertisement in the gazette?" Cam had never been one to beat around the bush, and there was something about this young woman that brought out his softer nature. He hadn't liked Bret's first wife, Carrie, and he would never have bothered asking her any personal questions, but he was curious to know what would make a beautiful young woman travel across the country to marry a man she had never met.

Heather swallowed hard and tried to appear calm. She

129

had hoped no one would come right out and question her about her reasons for becoming a mail-order bride, but now, faced with the question, she felt a blush stain her cheeks as she looked away from the elder man's dark, questioning eyes. "My mother passed away after being ill for some time, and there was nothing to keep me in Clarksburg any longer." She could not tell him that she had fled in the dark of the night in order to escape her stepfather's horrible threats!

Cam Saber said nothing more, only nodded his head as he wondered what more there was to her story. He had not lived as long as he had without being a good judge of human character, and he could tell that she was leaving something out. He hoped the time would come when she would feel free to trust him. Then perhaps she would be able to confide her true reasons for being in Montana.

Pushing back her chair, Heather rose to her feet. "I think I will go and watch Molly take her riding lessons." Heather hoped that Cam Saber would understand that she had no desire to be questioned. She should let him know right from the start that she valued her privacy, she told herself.

"Go right ahead, Heather. The girl's already taken to you. I heard her asking her father this morning where you were." Cam watched her features pinken with mention of his nephew and he kept his small smile to himself. "I'll be spending most of the morning in the study going over the books. These damn rustlers are making it harder and harder to tally up our inventory! If you need anything, just tell Jasper," he added as an afterthought.

Heather and Molly spent the morning together, getting to know each other. Heather was entranced with the warm, entertaining little girl, and Molly quickly appeared to welcome the new woman in her life—the lady she now called Mommy.

While watching Molly taking her riding lesson, Heather decided that she also would learn to ride a horse. The following morning, she told herself, she would join Molly in the corral for a lesson. After Molly's lesson, Heather followed the child around the grounds of the ranch house, looking with much interest at the place she could now call home.

Before lunchtime, Heather took Molly upstairs and helped her change into a fresh dress. It was a lively threesome that sat around the dining-room table as Molly entertained Heather and Cam with animated stories about the litter of puppies out in the barn. Magpie, one of the dogs that ran free on the ranch, had had a litter of nine puppies and Molly was the only one the mother dog did not growl at when she approached. The child, if allowed, would spend hours playing with the tiny pups.

Heather smiled with delight as the little girl laughed aloud as she told them about the puppy she called Spike. He was brindle in color like the rest of the puppies but sported a white ring around one eye, and Molly claimed him the most wonderful of the group.

Molly refused to take a nap that afternoon when Jasper sought her out for this daily ritual. She insisted that she be allowed to help Heather with the cleaning of the downstairs portion of the house. With Cam locked up in his study and Heather more than willing to have the child remain at her side, Jasper gave the little girl a wink for her stubbornness and headed back to the kitchen where he was baking fresh bread for dinner.

Heather tied her hair back in a kerchief, and looking down at Molly with a grin, she pulled the child's dark hair back and tied a bright red kerchief over her wayward locks. "This is so our hair won't get in the way." She laughed as she went out into the kitchen, Molly following closely, and found them both aprons to tie around their waists.

Heather knew it would take a few days to get the house in order, and she threw herself into the job. Her stepfather's inn and the work she had done there, scrubbing and cleaning, had given Heather a critical eye where housework was concerned. With Molly as her shadow, she soon had the foyer scrubbed down and was ready to tackle the central great room.

Sometime later in the afternoon, sounds of laughter drew Bret Saber through the now-sparkling front foyer and toward the entrance of the great room. For a few minutes he allowed himself to enjoy the sight of Molly cupping her hands in a bucket of water and splashing the front of Heather's dress. Laughter bubbled out of the little girl's mouth as she tried to scamper out of Heather's reach.

"Why, you little minx!" Heather laughed, and grabbing hold of her plump arm before Molly could get far, she splashed her with a handful of water. Then, catching her up within her arms, she swung her about, causing the childish laughter to fill the lower portion of the house. "How are we to get our work finished if we play all day?" Her soft, feminine laughter mingled with Molly's as she set her back down and brushed the dampened droplets from the front of her gown. "I fear that we will never . . ." She did not finish; for some reason her gaze went to the entranceway and her blue eyes met and locked with those of midnight black.

Following her gaze, Molly screeched with glee, "Daddy, Daddy! Me and Mommy are cleaning." With all her childish nature she ran to her father's side.

"I can see that, sweetheart." Bret hefted his daughter up into his arms and placed a kiss on her soft cheek, but his gaze never left Heather's.

Heather felt herself blushing profusely as his glance slowly roamed from her face to her breasts, which were

132

outlined fully by the damp material clinging to them, and then back up to her face. "I . . . I . . . had best clean this up," she stammered as she bent down to the bucket of water to avoid those warm sable eyes.

For a few lingering seconds, Bret looked down at his bride before mumbling, "I guess I should go and clean up, too."

"Aren't you going to kiss Mommy, too?" Molly questioned before her father could leave the room.

Heather felt her face flush crimson, the heat traveling down to the points of her breasts as she heard the child's words.

"Mommy has work to do," Bret tried to dodge.

"But mommies need kisses, too." Molly was determined that her father would not leave until he kissed Heather.

"All right, Molly, Mommy gets kisses, too." Bret could do naught but relent. He didn't want Molly to know there was anything other than peace and security here in her home, and at the moment the only way to prove this was by kissing his wife! Still holding Molly in his arms, he stepped across the dampened wood floor to Heather's side.

Feeling more than a little uncomfortable, Heather was forced to rise slowly from her position on her knees beside the bucket of water. Turning her cheek to him, she only prayed that he would get the kiss over with as quickly as possible.

For some strange reason that Bret at the moment could not understand, his dark eyes sought out the rosy lips that seemed to move out of his reach. Without a word his large, workhewn hand tenderly reached out and he turned her chin a bit, his dark head lowering, and as gently as a butterfly's caress, he placed a soft kiss upon her lips.

Molly squirmed within his arms, the action forcing Bret back to his senses. Standing to his full height, the warmth within his eyes was instantly replaced with the anger he felt at himself. Was he so weak he could not last a day around a beautiful woman without wanting to sample her charms, even with his daughter held against his chest? Turning around, he stomped out of the room, leaving Heather standing breathlessly alone in the center of the great room with her bucket and rags.

It was a few minutes before Heather could regain her heartbeat. She had expected him only to kiss her on the cheek for the child's sake; she had never expected that he would kiss her on the lips! Her hand rose up and tenderly traced the outline of her trembling lips. Though the kiss had not been long and had been given with the tenderest care, its power was such that Heather had begun to feel her limbs trembling beneath her. Thank God he had not tarried in the great room but had turned and left, as though her touch was just as unwanted to him as he seemed to believe his was to her. As she lowered her hand, she was not as sure of herself as she had been the day before!

Cleaning up the mess she and Molly had made, Heather took up the bucket and rags and made her way out into the kitchen. Relieved to see that the room was empty, she hurried to put the things away, wanting only to escape to her chamber and try to pull her frayed nerves into some semblance of order before she saw her husband again.

As she turned away from the cabinet where she put the bucket, her attention was drawn by the sound of Molly's voice outside the back screen door.

"I like my mommy, Daddy. She watched me ride Taffy this morning."

"That's good, sweeting." Bret was washing up on the back porch, and as he heard the happiness in Molly's voice and saw her animation, he once again could feel the softness of his wife's mouth beneath his own. He was

134

certainly not happy with the thought. There was something about Heather that left Bret feeling more than a little unsettled. He again saw her as he had the night before, as she stood over his daughter's bed and the candlelight outlined her shapely curves through her nightgown. With that thought he felt his insides begin to tighten. Why had he allowed himself the pleasure of kissing that sweet mouth? he stormed at himself. As he dashed water on his face and it ran down the length of his naked torso he inwardly railed, that all women were created out of the same mold. They were treacherous vipers at heart, he would never again be taken in by their lovely looks and sweet voice! His body's needs were well taken care of by Ginger, the redheaded young woman who worked for Sal Canfield. A whore was all he needed, he told himself. He had no need for a relationship with a woman. He was not a man who had to be taught a lesson twice!

At that moment Heather had no idea of her husband's thoughts as she gazed out of the window over the sink and caught a glimpse of the rush of water cascading over the bronzed, muscular planes of his shoulders and back. The wide breadth of his glistening chest forced Heather's heart to skip a beat as her hands whitened from her grip upon the sink. What was this man doing to her emotions? she wondered as she made herself turn around and hurry to the safety of her chamber.

Chapter Four

Over the past six months the Saber-Bar ranch, as well as its neighboring ranches, had been plagued with rustlers. The Saber-Bar had been losing seventy to seventy-five head of cattle every month. Some claimed it was the group of nesters that had settled near Miles City who were stealing the cattle, while others swore it was Cut Finger's band of Sioux warriors that were plaguing them with thievery.

Against all of Bret's objections, Cam Saber had declared the Sunday after Heather's arrival as a day for relaxing and socializing and a chance for the ranch hands to get to know the new Mrs. Saber. Bret warned his uncle that they should not slacken their guard and should hold their men posted around the ranch on the lookout for the rustlers, but Cam would not be put off, believing Bret's words just a ploy to keep him away from the ranch as he had been doing over the past few days. He sent Jasper out with invitations to their neighbors, as well as one to Reverend and Mrs. Waters.

Cam had set two cowboys to turning a steer on a barbeque spit since before daybreak, and the rest of the hands were scrambling in and out of the house all morning. He had them setting out comfortable chairs beneath shade trees, making pitchers of lemonade, and readying their instruments for the music and dancing that would come later in the day. Cam smiled with satisfaction as he made one last check to make sure everything would run smoothly. He didn't want his nephew and his wife to worry about anything but each other on this day. Good food, a little dancing, and who knew what would happen?

Heather wore the only gown she owned that was not made of sturdy, dark material. It was light blue with darker shades of tiny flowers printed all over. The bodice, which was a bit too tight because of the fact that her mother had bought her the gown a few years ago, had cream lace running in a V to the trim waist. Looking in her dressing-table mirror, Heather wished the dress were not so tight across her breasts, but that could not be helped, she told herself. She had no other gown. The color brought out the brilliant blue of her eyes, and pulling her hair back with a dark-blue ribbon and allowing it to fall freely down her back, she knew she was as fetching as a spring day.

Bret was unusually quiet throughout the morning, keeping himself locked within the study. As the guests began to arrive, manners demanded that he greet them, but he swore once again that the whole affair was a waste of a day.

Trying to avoid any contact with his young bride, Bret lingered with the men as the guests gathered around the long tables of food that had been set up outside under the trees.

Heather and Molly filled their plates and made their way back to the group of women. Heather felt comfortable in their presence as she sat down next to Beth Waters and Amy Farnsworth.

The men also filled their plates and took seats near the women. Bret sat opposite his daughter and his wife.

Heather's tinkling laughter filled his ears as Molly made a sour face after taking a sip of lemonade. Without willing it, Bret's dark gaze was drawn to his wife's smiling face as she teased his daughter. For the past week he had intentionally tried to keep himself busy and away from the house. There was something about this woman that was getting under his skin, and each time he glimpsed her it became harder to escape her charms, especially when she was in Molly's presence. The two of them together seemed to tug upon his insides.

"It ain't likely that you're having any regrets about that pretty little bride you got yourself, Bret. You sure are one lucky man. Who would have thought a mail-order bride could be so pretty?" Amos Butler spoke between bites of food from his plate, his eyes resting on the woman sitting across from him and Bret.

Cam was the one who answered Amos Butler. "Bret isn't any man's fool, and everyone knows it. He knows when he's got himself a good thing, don't ya, boy?"

Bret had to smile and nod his head in agreement, even as he damned his uncle under his breath. From the moment Heather had come to the ranch, it had been his uncle Cam who had played the part of her champion, calling out her praises whenever possible, always reminding Bret what a lucky man he was. "If you gentlemen will excuse me for a few minutes," Bret said, then set his plate down next to his chair and rose to his feet. "I need to speak with a couple of the hands. It's time for them to relieve the men riding the south pastures."

"The boy can't take a single afternoon off." Cam grinned, knowing how irritable his nephew was since he brought his lovely young bride out to the ranch. It wouldn't be too much longer, he figured, before everything would come to a full head, and Bret would have to face the fact that Heather was his for the taking.

"You can't be blaming Bret much these days." Clyde

Farnsworth, a heavy-set man with an easy smile beneath his bushy mustache, spoke up. "Even the nesters are complaining that they're missing a few cattle. They're claiming that their fences have been cut twice in the past month."

"If you can be believing any of them no-account nesters!" Harry Doud stated loudly and drew several heads nodding in agreement. "They might just be claiming to have problems with the rustlers in order to try and throw the guilt away from themselves."

"Did you all hear that Ben Avery and Bill Peters got into a fight just the other day outside of Bailey's General Store? Avery, who everyone knows is the spokesman for them nesters, came right out and confronted old Bill with every inch of that temper of his! The result was that several of Ben's ranch hands were in town and they quickly came to his aid. You can be sure that Bill sports two black eyes and a few broken ribs!"

"Things are getting out of control," Reverend Waters spoke up. "I know that the ranchers are against the nesters, but Bill Peters is a God-fearing man who loves his family just the same as the ranchers do. It's a shame when men fight out in the street like criminals and call one another vile names!"

"Some say that it is Cut Finger's braves who are stealing the cattle." Cam tried to smooth over the conversation. He liked the reverend well enough, as preachers went, but he and the men sitting around him were in no mood for a lecture on how to treat the nesters.

"We all know that it ain't no Injuns doing this rustling, Cam," Harry Doud grunted, not caring if the preacher liked hearing what he had to say or not. "It's them nesters, and I'll bet my boots on it!"

Heather was hearing much of the same from the

139

ranchers' wives. The conversation centered around the rustlers and the nesters who, the ranchers supposed, were the outlaws! The wives of the ranchers had taken up a crusade to snub every nester's wife they came into contact with.

It was with some pleasure to Heather when their attention was drawn toward a group of the ranch hands who began to play a lively tune with fiddle and harmonica.

As several weather-hewn cattlemen and ranch hands alike stood around clapping their hands and tapping their feet to the tune, Cam Saber pulled Heather from her chair.

"I reckon as how I ain't a man to allow good music to go to waste. Come on, gal, let's show these good folk how to kick up our heels!"

Heather felt her face blushing as she was pulled to her feet before the other women, but unable to beg off, Cam pulled her along behind him. "I am not much of a dancer," she stammered.

"Don't be worrying about that none. Pretty soon they'll all be joining in and none will be the wiser if you know the steps or not." His wide grin was contagious and soon he had Heather lifting her heels as her pretty blue-flowered skirt flew out around her ankles.

For the first time in days, Heather was truly enjoying herself. Cam had become her friend since her arrival at the ranch, and as much as her husband seemed distant and withdrawn, his uncle was kind and gracious.

Leaning against the base of a tall oak, Bret watched as his wife left his uncle's hands and then danced in turn with each one of the ranchers. He studied her easy smile, the way her tight gown seemed to cling to her shapely curves, and the flash of an ankle when her skirt flew high. Each time he heard her soft laughter,

140

he felt the blade of a sharp knife twist a bit deeper in his gut.

To Bret his wife seemed to welcome the attentions of other men all too easily, and though inwardly he knew he was not being fair, he could not help but compare Heather to Carrie, his first wife. Her unfaithfulness had left him distrustful and hard where women were concerned, and at this moment Heather seemed just as conniving and dangerous as she had been.

"It's my turn to dance with the little lady!" Corry Jessup, one of the newest ranch hands on the Saber-Bar shouted, and grabbed hold of Heather by one hand and positioned the other around her slim waist. With a loud whoop of joy he began to swing her to the music amidst the smiles and calls of the other ranch hands standing around. His friend Seth Mansfield was the loudest of the group, whooping as he watched his friend swinging the boss's wife around.

Bret had just about had all he could take of his wife being the center of such attention, and given by his own men! With a hard glint in his black eyes and a determined tilt to his stubborn jaw, he stomped over to where the music was playing and almost everyone was dancing. With his eyes on his bride, he pushed his way through the small group and without a word took hold of Heather's arm.

Relief instantly filled her at having been taken away from the tight pressure of Corry Jessup's hand upon the rise of her hip, and at first Heather smiled at her husband, thinking that at last he had decided to dance with her. But his chilling stare made her think differently.

Without a word spoken, Bret pulled her away from the dance floor.

Stumbling behind him, Heather tried to pull away from his hard grasp upon her arm. What in the world was wrong with him? she asked herself as she fought to keep from falling to the ground.

Once inside the foyer of the house, Bret swung Heather around to face him, his hand still biting into her flesh.

"How dare you embarrass me before your friends!" Heather lashed out at him before he could say a word. "Who do you think you are to treat me in such a manner?" Her face was flushed to flame, her blue eyes sparkling with anger as she remembered feeling the stares of all their guests upon her and her husband as he dragged her away from the dancing. She had had enough of this man, and at the moment she was more than willing to tell him just what she thought!

"I am your husband, in case you have forgotten!" Bret could not forget the image of her in the arms of every man on the ranch except him! Even knowing at that moment that he wasn't thinking rationally, he pulled her up tight against his chest.

Heather would have lashed out at him since he had not acted like a husband from their first meeting, but being held so tightly against his broad chest, she could only gasp for breath. At last she got out on a strangled breath, "You don't want to be a husband, remember? You only want a mother for Molly!"

Knowing that she was right and hating her that moment for making him feel so out of control, all Bret could do was kiss her! At first his mouth covered her soft pink lips in a hard, cruel manner, making Heather push against him with fear. All too quickly, though, his lips softened of their own accord and the pressure on her mouth relaxed, as well as the hands upon her forearms as they stole within the softness of her midnight locks and roamed over her back. He pressed her fully into him with a slight pressure against the slim curve of her back.

With his mouth covering hers, Heather tried to draw away, but something strange quickly took over. His hands stole over her body, his sensual lips winning a soft sigh as his warm, moist tongue slipped between her teeth and sought out the heat that awaited him there. Never had she been kissed in such a manner, and she could only cling to the broad shoulders that seemed to surround her!

As abruptly as Bret had grabbed her against him and kissed her, just as suddenly he took his hands away and let her go. For a moment he appeared to struggle for his own breath, but as his obsidian eyes gazed down into her flushed face, he took a step away from her before he spoke. "Be forewarned, Heather, I will never be made a fool of again by any woman!" And so saying he turned toward the door and stomped out of the house.

Heather had to clutch the hall tree to keep herself upright. Stunned, she stared at her husband's retreating back and then at the stout oak door. Her hand rose up and pressed against her kiss-swollen lips. *How on earth had she made a fool of him?* she asked herself in a daze. *What kind of devils rode this man she called Husband?*

Bret had known the second his lips had covered hers that he was lost. He knew as well, that if he did not force himself to take his hands from her and step away, he would fall too far into her charms to ever turn away!

He slowly made his way back out into the yard and to his guests. He had shown his wife that he would not be trifled with, he told himself. As long as she wanted to stay on his ranch and be treated with the respect that a wife of his was due, she must refrain from flirting and attracting other men! Keeping his mind on thoughts of how he had set Heather straight, Bret could not forget how her body had molded itself per-

143

fectly against his, nor could he banish the taste of her honey-sweet mouth!

By the time Heather returned to their guests, she had pulled herself together and straightened out her gown and hair. Without allowing herself to glance in the direction where she knew her husband would be standing with the other men, she made her way to the chairs under the shade tree where Beth Waters was watching Molly. Picking up the child and setting her on her lap, she tried to ignore the memory of her husband's powerful body held tightly against hers and the feel of his lips against her own. She silently observed the antics of the ranch hands and the ranchers and their wives as they entertained themselves with the dancing and singing.

Watching from the sidelines as he chatted with his neighbors, Bret appeared at ease as his glance went frequently to his bride and daughter. It was just as dark descended that he noticed Molly had fallen asleep in Heather's lap. It had been a long day for the child, and with bold strides, he silently made his way to Heather and gathered the sleeping child into his arms. For a lingering moment, his hand seemed to caress the tender flesh of his wife's arm where Molly rested her head, but, seeming to recover quickly, Bret stood to his full height and turned, with the child in his arms, toward the house.

Heather felt her breathing coming in short, ragged gasps from the contact of his hand upon her bare flesh. As she looked around to see if anyone had noticed the bright stain of crimson she knew must be covering her cheeks, she was thankful that the evening shadows were settling over the ranch as her husband walked away from her.

By the time Bret returned from putting Molly to bed, the ladies were making their way inside the house

144

toward the front parlor. Clyde Farnsworth pulled Bret toward the cover of a large oak, out of sight of the ladies and the reverend, before he pulled a bottle of whiskey out of his jacket and pressed it into Bret's hands. "I have been waiting for the ladies to retire into the house so we gentlemen could have a moment to congratulate you, Bret."

"Drink up, lad, and pass that bottle around. Here's to your fine-looking little lady!" Amos Butler added, and a low-voiced chorus of ranchers and cowboys alike agreed as Bret turned the bottle up to his lips.

Chapter Five

Readying herself for bed that evening, Heather could still feel those warm, dark eyes upon her as she had earlier, after the men had entered the house and retired to Cam's study. Standing in the doorway opposite the parlor where the ladies were conversing, Bret had periodically appraised Heather as she sat as though on pins and needles in a parlor chair. She once again felt gooseflesh coursing over her arms, just as she had when she looked up to find Bret boldly staring at her over the rim of the glass pressed to his lips.

After the guests had left the ranch and the house was quiet, Bret had remained quietly contemplative in the study. After Cam bid the couple a good night, Heather escaped her husband's heated gaze and fled upstairs, upon trembling legs, to the safety of her bedchamber.

Now, feeling relatively secure, Heather glanced at her reflection in the dressing-table mirror where she sat brushing out her long hair.

Her fingers rose up to brush against her lips, those lips that her husband had ravished so thoroughly. Her eyes closed dreamily as though she allowed herself only in privacy to remember the feel of his muscular length pressed so tightly against her and his arms holding her so securely yet so tenderly. She had never experienced such feelings before in her entire twenty-two years. She had not even imagined a kiss so wonderfully all-consuming! And though she fought off her feelings by telling herself that she was not a wanton, that she was not a woman of easy virtue, as her stepfather had told her time and again she was, she still could not force herself to forget.

The side of her nature that had always rebelled against Clarence Bosworth while she was growing up and that had aided her in fleeing the inn now stood her in good stead. *Do not forget, my girl, Bret Saber is your husband! Why can you not enjoy a kiss shared between husband and wife? What matters the strange manner in which you two met, the fact that he still loves his first wife and only desires a mother for his daughter? He is still your husband, after all, and you must admit that he is all man!*

Lost in thought, Heather did not hear the adjoining chamber door ease open and softly shut, nor did she notice the dark image of Bret Saber leaning against the doorjamb.

It was some small noise that finally pulled her from her daydreams. Looking into the mirror, she noticed her husband standing behind her. Unable to turn around and face him, Heather stared as he silently crossed the room.

The war that raged within Bret Saber's soul had brought him to his wife's room. All evening he had fought off the urge to take her away from their guests and bring her to these chambers to press his mouth over hers once again and find out if this afternoon had been but an illusion! Since the moment he had met her, he had told himself to keep a distance, but now with the aid of the alcohol he had consumed throughout the evening, he told himself that he would take no more. She was his wife! He recalled now how she had smiled so sweetly at all their guests, her soft voice filling his soul with a hunger that was growing unbearable.

He could not say the words that would explain his

147

presence, for, in truth, he did not understand himself what it was that drew him to this woman. From the moment of their first meeting he had forced himself to appear hard and unyielding, but even through the depths of this self-imposed hardened shell, every time he looked at her, there was a need that he could not deny. His strong hands reached out and gently touched her shoulders, turning her away from the mirror to face him.

Heather was lost to the inner sanctums of tender despair that she glimpsed within his black eyes. In one fluid motion she rose to her feet, aided by the slight pressure of his hands as she turned to him.

For a full moment Bret Saber traced the image of her beautiful features in his mind. The liquid blue eyes framed with thick lashes, the high cheekbones that were flushed rosy against the alabaster creaminess of her skin, and the soft, tempting, pink bow-shaped lips. The fingers of one hand twined within the silken soft texture of her lustrous hair, and as he drew the back of her head toward him, the fire within his gaze ignited into lost dimensions of searing flame.

Heather felt her heart beat within her; her breath caught in her throat. His mouth lowered, and as each sensitive fiber of her being cried aloud, the manly scent of him surrounded her. She felt his breath warm against her cheek for that fleeting second before his full, sensual lips slanted softly against hers.

His kiss was everything she remembered from this afternoon, and more! The hunger of his mouth scorched to the very depths of her soul and ran a heated avenue to the farthest points of her toes. She clung to him on trembling legs, so overcome by the leaping fires of passion he evoked, she forgot all but the feelings of need that swept over her.

His tongue slipped between her teeth even as he pulled her up tightly against his broad, muscular chest and explored the inner caverns of her mouth. The softness of her curves filled his arms, the sweet nectar of her essence wrapping around his senses and leaving him mindless in the grasp of passion's boundless realm. His lips stole across the small jut of her chin and, with a sensual path that was devastating, burned down her slim throat and caressed the soft indentation above her collarbone. From deep within his chest an animallike groan escaped him and reverberated in the silent room.

Heather was powerless to push his hands away as he began to unbutton the tiny row of buttons running down the bodice of her nightgown. Even through the material of the gown, where his fingers touched, she felt rapture's potent power. She welcomed the feel of his lips upon her as his moist tongue toyed daringly with the pulsebeat at the base of her throat and then seductively ran a wet path toward the valley of her breasts as the soft flesh was slowly revealed with each tiny button that was freed.

With the last button Bret's head rose once again, and for a second his sparkling dark eyes locked with Heather's deep passion-laced violet ones, before once again his mouth lowered and they shared a tantalizing kiss. Without a word, as though the intrusion would surely spoil the spell that had woven around them, Bret's head lowered to the soft flesh of her breasts. Pushing back the material of the gown with a gentle hand, he sought one full, pale globe with a thrilling assault of tiny kisses and then, with a movement that left Heather clutching at him to hold herself upright, his lips parted as his tongue circled the pink tip and he began to suckle there.

Heather knew for a certainty that she was being

149

drawn into the outer boundaries of no return. The things his mouth and tongue were doing to her left her panting for breath. At the same time, her hands clutched his shoulders for support as leaping flames licked upward from the very center of her womanhood. She ached for something she could only guess at, and as Bret's mouth went to her other breast and favored it with the same searing love play, she was driven all but mindless as his hands roamed over her body.

"God, I want you. I need you so much, Heather." The words were torn from Bret on a beating pulse of despair that was not lost on his bride. Need! His body cried with the need he had for this woman. He had thought that, once within her chamber, a kiss would sustain him. With a kiss he would find that she was like all other women, and he would be able to take her or leave her! But that one kiss had drawn forth another. The feel of her satin flesh beneath his hand was catapulting him onward, and now he knew that there could be no stopping! He could feel her body's wanting as much as he felt his own. The soft moans escaping her lips as he caressed her breasts whispered to him of her raging desires, and at the same time the blood boiled within his loins, rushing within his manhood and pounding with every heartbeat.

Heather could not answer him; she dared not try. She fought to draw a breath as his lips flamed across the upper portion of her body, and as he drew her gown over her head and let it fall in a pool at her feet, she was all but lost to the heated seduction of his gaze. Then, for a few lingering seconds, he drew back and, in an all-consuming branding, his eyes traveled over her length and took in every inch of her perfection.

Full, high, pouting breasts strained toward Bret as though in welcome, the flesh over her rib cage as creamy smooth as the rest of her alabaster skin. The tiny indent of her navel caught his heated attention before going over her slim waist and shapely hips. The junction of her womanhood shimmered with a dark, silken triangle which forced his glance downward. He took in her long, slender legs and small, perfect feet. *Breathtakingly beautiful!* Those were the only words that came to Bret Saber's mind.

The feasting of his heated glance lasted but a spare few seconds, but to Heather time stood still as she found herself the subject of his adoring gaze. For a fleeting moment she thought to turn away, to find something to cover herself with, but as that thought entered her mind, another followed: Why should she turn from the warm favor she saw in her husband's regard? For the first time in her life she felt proud of her naked beauty.

As his hands reached back out to gather her to him, Heather pushed the thought aside that this man was still in love with his dead wife. *She* was his wife now, and though he had sworn he did not need her to share his life, she knew that this prelude to loving was right. Right or wrong, Heather admitted, if only to herself, that she cared not the reason; she could not bear for him to leave her now!

Half expecting some resistance, Bret sighed softly against her throat as he carried her to the bed. Laying her upon the silken coverlet, his lips regained hers and plied her with a burning fervor of kisses, raining down her throat and over her breasts. "You are so beautiful. I have never desired any woman as I do you at this moment." The words were pulled from his heart as he kissed the delicate flesh beneath her breasts and languorously roamed over her ribs and across her belly, pausing only for a brief moment over her navel.

151

His titillating seduction of her body left Heather gasping, her fingers clutching the coverlet at her side. His lips seared her with a consuming, branding heat and Heather writhed beneath his thrilling assault, knowing at that moment that they were both wildly out of control.

His heated lips and moist tongue scorched a trail over her rounded hips, and as his hand boldly touched the crest of her woman's jewel, rioting sensations shot throughout her body. His touch was so intense as he made contact with the nub of her very essence, Heather had to clamp her teeth tightly together to keep from crying aloud.

But with the heated contact of his lips, she could not help the cry torn from her lips as she rose up and clutched Bret's dark hair. What was he doing to her? She was consumed with igniting flame, becoming a mass of trembling desire! She had not the strength to pull him away, could only ride out this incredible journey of ecstasy, her mind void of all but the rippling waves that filled her body and erupted into scalding pleasure. As shudder after shudder left her trembling and writhing, fulfillment came . . . and Heather no longer fought to regain her sanity.

Bret rose up to stand at the side of the bed. Looking into Heather's passion-laced features, he began to take off his shirt and pants.

Heather never imagined that such sensations as she was now feeling were possible. Though her trembling had quieted somewhat, her body still tingled with anticipation. Her eyes broke away from contact with his as he allowed his shirt to fall to the floor, her gaze lowering to the wide breadth of his shoulders. The sheen of perspiration over his upper torso drew her eyes to the glistening expanse of his muscular chest and arms as he slowly unbuckled his belt and began to slip his trousers off his hips. The crisp, curling dark hair that matted his chest lowered to a thin line beneath his navel, and as his breeches lowered even further, down his narrow hips to his powerfully muscular thighs, Heather's eyes widened as he kicked his legs free and stood to his full six-foot-two-inch height.

He stood before her curious gaze only a few seconds longer, but the time was more than enough for Heather to glimpse the jutting image of his large, throbbing manhood. Her breath caught in her chest as he bent toward the bed. She had heard many stories about what took place between a man and a woman there, but at this moment, as his mouth covered hers once more and his hands gently roamed over her body, she forgot everything she had ever heard. This was her first experience with a man. She alone felt these incredible feelings. No other woman could ever have shared such a rapturous experience!

As his mouth played over her breasts, his hand seductively roamed over her body and lingered between her legs. Gently he eased back the soft, dark ringlets, and savoring Heather's heated response as her body moved against his hand, he eased a finger into her warmth. Feeling her moistness, he slowly eased her thighs apart; his body poised above hers as the tip of his pulsing length gently pushed against her velvet warmth.

Too far caught up in the moment to pull away, Heather felt the heated tip of his manhood touching her and easing into her tightness. A gasp of surprised pain escaped her lips as he pushed through the slim barrier of her maidenhead; her hands clutched at his firm flesh as her nails raked over him.

Hearing her cry from the initial intrusion of his entrance, Bret stilled atop her for a moment and looked down into her face with question. Never had he expected that he would find his wife still a virgin. How could he have known? He had imagined her becoming a mail-order bride to escape some jaded past! At last he spoke softly. "I did not mean to hurt you, Heather. It will get better, I promise." And for some reason that Bret did not wish to explore at the moment, he felt some inner joy over finding her untouched by any other man.

The pain that had come to her had as quickly fled, and now Heather remembered the time one of her stepfather's serving girls had taunted her about the pain she would one day have when she first lay with a man. The fullness in her lower body made her move her hips somewhat as she adjusted herself to her position beneath her husband.

Her slight movement made Bret's breath catch; his passions were inflamed to unbearable heights. There was no help now for the fact that his bride had been an innocent until he touched her; he was ensnared by the feel of her enticing body. As his lips lowered to hers, he moved further into her depths, and at the same time rained kisses over her eyelids, down along her cheek, to the softness of her throat. She was his wife! Even if he had known her to be chaste, would that have made any difference to him while these raging feelings of need claimed him? This past week had been little more to him than a living hell! Each time he looked upon her had been torture, knowing that she belonged to him but keeping himself in check and at a distance! He would not stop now, nor could he if he tried!

Heather pressed her lower body closer to him. Her hands eased their grip upon his sides and traced a tempting path over the expanse of his muscled back, in-

154

creasing his wild desire to fulfill his body's need for release. Keeping in mind that this was her first time with a man, he gently moved in and out of her warm depths, holding himself back to keep from harming her unnecessarily.

All pain had flown, and in its place an incredible pulsing swelled within her, sending rapturous delight spiraling within her core as he slowly moved in and out. As though with a will of its own her body began to undulate, her hips rising with his and keeping a steady movement that was breathtakingly pleasurable. Within the depths of her womanhood a spark ignited, and as the currents shimmered throughout her entire body, the flames grew into a towering blaze that skyrocketed and burst into an overwhelming intensity throughout every portion of her being. Her hands clutched his back tightly, her legs rising about his hips to receive all of him and to taste the full measure of this unbelievable feeling. Her eyes grew wide and moans of passion escaped her lips as wave after wave of ecstasy's pleasure claimed her.

Bret was caught up in her passion as he looked down into her beautiful face. As her body shuddered and trembled beneath him, he was lost to all but the raging within his own depths that drove him onward. He thought not of caution or gentleness as her legs rose up above his hips and tempted him beyond endurance to sample all that she possessed. With a deep moan, he was held upon the brink of a towering climax. Another plunge and wildfire shot through his loins, leaving him shuddering without control atop her, his fluid racing up and showering her very depths, as he clutched her tightly to him and rode out the crest of his passion.

Heather's mind was in a whirl as she fought to recapture her breath as well as her senses. Bret's arms held her tightly to his chest, his heartbeat sounding as a drum against her ear.

No words would come to Bret's lips to tell her what this moment meant to him; he was unable to speak. He had tried so hard to convince himself that he could live without the softer elements a woman could bring to him that at this moment it was hard to admit he had made a terrible mistake where she was concerned.

Chapter Six

Awakening the following morning, Heather found herself alone in her large bed. A small smile settled over her lips as she stretched. With the movement, she was reminded of what had taken place between her and her husband the night before and a tender ache filled her body. Clutching the pillow next to her up closely to her breasts, she thought she could still smell the masculine scent that Bret Saber had left behind.

Dreamily she pulled herself out of bed and dressed, remembering vividly how she had fallen asleep in his arms, his heartbeat sounding in her ear and lulling her into a sense of security she had never known.

Paying special attention to her toilette this morning, Heather left her chamber with a feeling of well-being. When she entered the dining room her mood was not lost on those sitting around the table. Unfortunately Bret Saber was not one of those looking toward her as she entered the room.

"Well, it seems that the shindig yesterday agreed with you, Heather. You're as pretty as a wild mountain bloom this morning." Cam eased out a chair for his nephew's wife and, settling himself back in his own, he wondered just what had taken place the night before. Bret's mood had been broodingly quiet this morning before he left the house, and Cam had not missed the look of disappointment that swept over Heather's face after a quick look around the dining room.

When Jasper entered the side door with Heather's breakfast plate, Cam noticed the way her eyes jumped across the room in his direction, then quickly turned away. "Bret left early this morning to go out on the range," Cam told her. "He mentioned that he might not be back for a couple of days, because of the trouble there with the rustlers." He hated to be the one to tell her this, but it couldn't be helped. He only hoped she wouldn't take it too hard.

Heather could only nod her head stiffly at Cam's words as she tried to swallow the bit of biscuit she had in her mouth. She felt Cam watching her and tried to force herself to act normally, though her stomach was tied in knots. How could Bret treat her in such a heartless manner? After what they had shared last night, he could at least have told her he was leaving! He could at least have told her that what they did last night had meant nothing to him, that she had been merely another conquest, nothing more! Feeling the sting of unshed tears, she took a deep breath and forced back the tears. If last night had meant nothing to Bret Saber, then so be it! She cloaked herself in growing anger in order not to feel the hurt so stingingly. She had not expected to find a great love here in Montana, she reasoned. She had desired only a home and perhaps a small bit of contentment. She would not pin her dreams upon a man who cared so little about her. She would go on as though last night had never happened, and that would be even easier with him gone.

Over the course of the next few days Heather was indeed almost able to make herself believe those hours spent in Bret's arms had never happened. She threw

158

herself into her housework after spending each morning riding the sorrel mare Cam had picked out for her. All the affection she would have given to a loving husband, she now showered upon Molly.

Though she could force her memories to the back of her mind during the daylight hours, her nights were another story. At every turn she was reminded of the man she had given herself to so completely. Sitting at her dressing table and looking into the mirror, she would suddenly find herself lost to the seduction of her daydreams and envision her husband standing close behind her as he had done that night. She could feel his strong hands on her shoulders, the brush of his sensual lips against the nape of her neck, and she could almost convince herself that his scent still lingered on the night breeze that swept through the open windows of her chamber.

Her bed was a place of tortured dreams! She could no longer shut her eyes and fall into a dreamless slumber. Now she would fall asleep only under the power of ebony eyes. She would fitfully pound her pillow until at last exhaustion overcame her and she was pulled into the realm of a dream-filled sleep which held her until the early hours of the morning.

Her body ached for the fulfillment that Bret Saber had given her. As he came to her in her sleep, she welcomed the touch of his hard flesh against her soft contours. His mouth ravished hers with a plundering that stirred her to the depths of her very soul. The touch of his hands roaming at will over all her secret places left her heart pounding and her own body yearning for the surging power of him, caring only that she once again know the ultimate feelings that she now knew could be had with a man!

Moaning aloud, Heather would awaken with only her pillow for comfort, reminded once again that her husband did not care for her, but still cared for a wife who was long gone from his life!

Once again Bret and his ranch foreman, Cal Hart, had been unable to catch the rustlers who'd been plaguing the Saber-Bar ranch, but today they had come close. They had set out early in the morning to head back to the ranch house, and were just coming over a rise when they caught sight of a group of men cutting a fence . . . and directing about fifty head of cattle away from the Saber-Bar.

As soon as Bret and Cal caught sight of the rustlers, the rustlers also caught sight of them. With a shout, the outlaws turned their horses and fled, the dust flying beneath their mounts' hooves as they left the Saber-Bar cattle, along with the tools they had used to cut the fence.

Bret and Cal gave chase, but the outlaws had too much of a lead. Vanishing over another ridge, they disappeared through a portion of thick woods near the Powder River. Once again they had gotten away, but this time they had been in sight and it was easy enough to see that they were not Cut Finger's braves. Venting much of his anger then and there as he repaired the cut fence, Bret seethed over the fact that he and Cal had not caught up with the desperadoes. Since he had ridden away from the ranch house, he had been spoiling for a good fight. Deprived of even that, he used all his built-up energies on the work at hand.

"I can't shake the feeling that I have seen the leader of that gang before," Bret stated as he drew the strand of wire tight and tacked it back on the wood fencepost.

"You mean the rustler in black?" Cal questioned, recalling the horseman who appeared to be the first to notice them riding down from the ridge—and also one of the first to hightail it away from the cattle and the cut fence.

"Yeah, that one. I got this odd feeling that I should know him from somewhere."

"Well, I'm sure it will come back to you, Bret. I reckon we are both a bit worn out. Maybe after some rest, you'll be able to recall something."

Cal was right, of course, Bret told himself as he searched his mind over and over to recall where he had seen the rustler before. No wonder he couldn't think straight, he told himself as they finished with the fence. He had been pushing himself and his foreman pretty hard these past few days. They had covered virtually all of the fence line of the entire Saber-Bar. There had been little sleep and only a small amount of time taken for meals. Every time Bret seemed to have a moment's respite, he was plagued by the image of a dark-haired beauty with deep-indigo eyes, and with the image, he pushed himself all the harder, not wanting to be confronted with what he had shared with her the night he had gone to her room. He did not want to let himself feel these softer emotions toward another woman. He did not want to let down his defenses and take a chance at being hurt again.

"What say we head on back to the ranch house now? It's for sure them wranglers won't be coming back on the Saber-Bar at least for the next few days." Cal was as used to the life of the open range as any of the other cowboys on the Saber-Bar, but this pace Bret had set for them had worn him a little thin. He hoped that, whatever devil was riding Bret's back, he would be able to throw him in the dust pretty darn soon.

"I guess you're right," Bret admitted as they began to mount their horses. "I only hope that I will be able to remember where I have seen that demon before." Something about the outlaw dressed all in black bothered him. It could be the clue they had been looking for for months. Bret tried to keep his mind on business, but as the afternoon wore on and the two men silently directed their horses toward the ranch house, there was little else for him to do but think about the woman who would be awaiting him.

Once again Heather lay upon her empty bed and tossed and turned. She had pushed herself harder than ever today, scrubbing the upstairs floors, hoping that by the time she retired to her room she would be exhausted enough to find a peaceful night's sleep. She found instead that no matter how tired she was, she could not avoid the sensual dreams that persisted in interrupting her sleep. Her husband's darkly handsome face and powerful form tormented her without release.

It was just as one of these unwelcome dreams had her calling out loud for Bret Saber that Heather felt the gentle touch of a lover's caress easing back a wayward curl from her soft cheek. She sighed deeply in her sleep, as though she could not fight off the invasion of her dream lover another minute.

Bret had returned to the ranch to find everyone abed. Silently he climbed the stairs and went to his own room. The first thing he always did when returning to the house, day or night, was to check on his daughter. With a light step, he went into the adjoining room and, for a few minutes, he looked down at Molly's sleeping face.

There was little of her mother in the smooth, innocent features, and for this Bret was thankful. Carrie Saber had been fair of feature, her hair a pale blond, with creamy white skin and a faint spattering of freckles across the bridge of her small nose. Looking down at Molly, Bret wondered how he had ever been taken in by

162

Carrie's faithless charms. She had been flamboyant and loud, and completely different from the other young women he had known in Miles City. Maybe that had been the reason for his great attraction to her.

Bret could hardly remember his courtship of Carrie now. It had taken place so fast; before he knew what was happening, they were married and he had brought her as his bride to the Saber-Bar.

Cam had been against the marriage from the start, but Bret had not listened to anyone who had anything bad to say about his Carrie. While courting her, Bret had shot and wounded a man just for mentioning that he had seen Carrie in the arms of Sam Bennett, another rancher. He had also gotten into a fight with one of his own ranch hands who made a coarse remark about something he had been told about Carrie Saber. That very day, Bret had kicked the cowboy off the ranch.

Bret now wished that he had not been so blinded by Carrie's flirting ways, and that he had listened to his friends when they tried to warn him about the grave mistake they thought he was making. Shaking his head, Bret stepped away from his daughter's bed. Molly would never have to be told about her mother. He didn't want her fresh innocence to be tainted with the knowledge of what her mother had been!

As Bret started to turn back to the door of his own chamber, a noise drew him across the room. Instant black fury coursed over him as he thought he heard his wife crying aloud as though in the clutches of passion. He had known he could not trust her! He swore as he quietly eased the chamber door open. He would catch her with her lover and he would deal with them both, this very minute!

With his eyes already well adjusted to the dark, Bret silently approached the bed. He would kill the man who was with her, with his bare hands! He swore again as he heard the sound of someone thrashing around on the bed.

Caught in stunned disbelief, Bret stilled as he heard his own name being cried aloud as though his bride were fighting off some troubled dream. Without will to stop himself as he stood looking down at her, his hand brushed aside the curl that lay across her cheek and prevented his full viewing of her lovely face.

The soft sigh of unrestrained passion that this simple touch evoked left Bret feeling the swift racing of his heart.

No longer able to fight off his desire for his bride, he forgot his days on the range, when he had sworn to resist her charms. Standing shirtless and barefoot beside the bed, he silently shed his breeches, and in a single motion stretched out his large frame next to her. His strong hands reached out and pulled her slim, curvaceous body up against him, his mouth covering hers as though his thirst were driving him and she alone held the secret to the fountain of eternal life.

At first Heather thought herself caught up in another dream. The hard contact of a man's body, the pressure of his mouth over hers, drew an instant response as she wrapped her hands around his broad shoulders and pressed herself closer. "Oh love me . . . please don't leave again," she whispered as her lips were released for a single second, and she tried to appeal to her dream lover to have mercy on her this night.

Her plea went straight to Bret's heart. His lips hungrily kissed her mouth, her chin, the slim column of her throat. They traveled then to her breasts, and there he feasted as his swollen manhood pressed against the heat of her precious jewel.

As a cry was torn from Heather's lips, her legs widened and her body opened to receive the pulsing lance that begged entrance into her moist sheath. And as she felt the fullness she had sought so desperately these past few nights, her eyes flew open and the hands that had been holding the broad shoulders began to push against the powerful chest above her.

Realizing that she had at last awakened from her dream, Bret stilled, his lips tenderly feathering kisses as he worked his way back to her lips. "Do not be frightened, Heather, I would share your bed this night." For a moment his dark gaze looked down into her face as though begging that she not send him from her.

A soft sigh escaped Heather. *This was not a dream!* Bret had returned and he had come to her! "Yes . . . yes," she cried aloud, and drew his lips back to hers. She knew that she should refuse him for his treatment of her, but she could not. Nothing mattered but these feelings that she held for him. She had fought them off long enough, but no more!

Bret's feelings were much the same, but at the moment he did not allow himself to dwell upon them. He would sort everything out tomorrow! For now all he wanted was to feel himself deep within this woman, to hear her cries of boundless passion, to lose himself in the raging currents of his own desire. His manhood stirred deep within her and, as though both had been starving for the sensations that lay in wait, their bodies strained together, their lips meshing. Heather's legs rose up in order for her body to accept all he would give her.

Bret's large hand filled with her buttocks as he pulled her ever closer, the surging hardness of his length moving in and out as rapture filled his soul and the tightness of her moist, heated passage furthered him to breathless strokes of storming desire.

Heather's passion knew no bounds, her body moving in rhythm with each stroke of his manhood as the very depth of her core was gently plundered. A searing heat of such pleasurable intensity stirred into existence and gushed forth and upward. She was left trembling and quaking upon the fire of his hard, throbbing shaft.

The contraction of her muscles, clasped so tightly around his manhood, sent Bret spinning over the boundaries of coherent thought. Clasping her tightly against him, his strokes intensified as his body labored for an added few seconds before he, too, scaled the portals of divine rapture and was hurled forth into a shuddering climax.

It was some time before they resumed their natural breathing. Bret held Heather tightly in his arms as though fearing that releasing her would somehow return them to reality and he would have to face at last those feelings that held him without control where this woman was concerned.

As Heather started to speak, Bret pressed his lips softly over hers. "Tomorrow we will talk and settle this thing between us. For tonight, let me hold you." He whispered against the side of her mouth as his lips left hers, and, unable to resist him, Heather snuggled against his chest, for the time willing to feel herself surrounded by his large body. Tomorrow would be soon enough, she told herself, to come to some kind of understanding about this strange marriage they had created.

Chapter Seven

In the back of Heather's sleep-fogged brain she heard the soft sound of a door closing. Pulling herself upright in bed, she found that her husband had once again left her side while she was still sleeping. He was doing exactly what he had done after the first time they had made love. More than likely he would be gone by breakfasttime, and she would not see him again for days . . . until she would find him in her bed again!

By God, she would not sit back and allow him to treat her in such a fashion, she railed inwardly as she left the warmth of the bed and began to pull on the breeches and shirt that Jasper had given her for her riding lessons. If Bret Saber was leaving the ranch, she would, too! He had promised last night that they would talk today, and that was exactly what they were going to do!

If she had wanted to be treated as though she were nothing more than some man's plaything she could have stayed at the Clarksburg Inn and obliged her stepfather's wishes! Bret Saber was her husband and she was more than willing to meet him halfway, but she would not go along with him holding free rein over her body at night when it suited his mood and then, in the daylight hours, appear not to have any use for her.

The words he had spoken to her on their wedding day during the carriage ride out to the ranch instantly came back to her: *"I guess if it doesn't work out, with Molly and all, I mean, I can always pay your fare back to Virginia."* Well, things were working out with Molly just fine; it was Molly's *father* who was driving Heather to distraction! Whether Bret Saber wanted to hear what she had to say or not, he was going to get an earful, just as soon as she could find him! She stormed out of her room and downstairs. Finding the lower portion of the house still empty, she headed outside toward the back of the house and straight to the stables.

Her anger spurred her as she caught a glimpse of a rider off in the distance to the east of the stables. Finding Bret's large black stallion gone from the stables, Heather hurried to the stall of her own mare. She was in the process of saddling the horse when Corry Jessup, one of the new ranch hands, silently approached her.

"Let me do that fur ya, ma'am." He startled Heather as he reached from behind her, took the saddle, and threw it over the animal's back. "Ain't it a bit early fur yer riding lessons?" His pale-blue eyes freely roamed her figure in the tight-fitting breeches, and, with a gleam in his eye, he noticed the way her full breasts pressed against the fabric of her red plaid shirt. The best part of his day was watching the lovely Mrs. Saber during her riding lessons. And it was a rare treat to find her all alone out here in the stables.

Pulling the cinch tight, he straightened to his full height. Heather found him standing far too close to her for comfort. There was something about Corry Jessup and his friend Seth Mansfield that made Heather uncomfortable. Taking a step backward as he reached next to her to take up the reins, Heather felt the brush of his forearm upon her breast. She tried not to allow herself to blush. "I am riding with my husband this morning, Mr. Jessup," she said quickly, trying to keep her voice calm. For the first time she realized that she was very much alone with this man in the stables, and with the mention of her husband, she reminded him who she was.

"Yeah, I saw Bret leave the stables a few minutes ago. It didn't appear as though he was waiting fur ya, though." Corry led the mare out of the stall and stood holding the reins loosely in his hand. "Maybe I should ride out with ya. To make sure, that is, that yu're safe and all. Never can tell these days with them Injuns rustling the Saber-Bar cattle." His washed-out green eyes hungrily drank in the beauty of her creamy-fresh features.

Willing herself to remain calm, Heather took a deep breath to steady her nerves. "That is quite unnecessary, Mr. Jessup. Regardless of how it appears, my husband knows that I will be following him and he will soon turn back to meet me."

"Whatever suits ya, ma'am." Jessup walked the mare out of the stall, his gaze now mocking.

Heather was more than a little irritated by his manners, but, trying to ignore his rudeness, she took the reins from him and mounted her mare without his help. Not giving a backward glance, she kicked the horse's sides and directed her out of the stableyard and in the direction she had seen her husband take.

For a few lingering minutes Corry Jessup stood in the stable doorway, and as his buddy Seth Mansfield strolled up beside him, he nodded his head in Heather's direction. "It sure be a shame that such a right pretty-looking woman is pining away over a cold-blooded bastard like Bret Saber."

"I been thinking the same thing lately." Seth grinned widely. "In fact, every morning while I'm watching her and the kid taking their riding lessons, I wonder if it feels any different bedding a woman that needs to find a man through an article in a paper."

"Maybe it's time fur us to be finding out." Corry's voice held his excitement as he turned about and looked toward his companion.

"Yeah, I think it's time for Saber to find out that his days of playing boss man are about up, too." Seth nodded his head in full agreement.

"I'll saddle the horses, you go and send the signal on to the others that we're ready to meet up with 'em." Corry turned into the stable as Seth started around the back of the corral. A piece of reflecting glass had been hidden there to signal their cohorts in crime, who were camped just far enough away from the ranch to avoid detection.

Leaving the stables, Heather tried to forget how uncomfortable Corry Jessup had made her feel. All she could think about right now was what she intended to say to her husband when she met up with him. Then, as she made her way through a small band of trees on the outer edge of a rise leading into a fertile valley, she glimpsed her husband sitting on his stallion and conversing with another cowboy. As she drew closer to the pair, she saw that the other man was Cal Hart, the ranch's foreman.

The two men seemed deep in conversation and did not notice Heather's approach at first. When Bret did, his last words to Cal were: "See if you can't find them around the ranch, and send one of the hands into town for Marshal Bryan. Maybe one of the two will talk and tell us where the rest of the group has been staying."

With a nod of his head, Cal Hart turned his horse away from his boss and his wife.

Turning his full regard on Heather, Bret questioned if something was wrong. He instantly noticed the heated look of anger in her azure eyes. He had left the ranch this morning intending only to be gone long enough to find Cal and tell him where he remembered seeing the rustler dressed in black. Having found the ranch foreman already gone from the bunkhouse and the stables, he had saddled up and gone in search of him. Thank God, Cal had left the ranch only a few minutes earlier, and he had not been hard to find.

"You are asking me if there is something wrong? I think I should be the one asking you that, don't you?" Heather tried to keep herself from remembering the way his hands had roamed over her body the night before as she looked at his strong, sun-bronzed hands lightly holding his stallion's reins. They had to get this thing settled between them, she told herself. She could not go on living this way, even though she had already fallen in love with Molly. She wanted *more!* She wanted a husband who cared for her, not a man who only wanted a mother for his child!

At first Bret was confused, thinking she wanted him to explain what he and Cal Hart had been doing, but understanding quickly settled over him. "Listen, Heather, I'm sorry I left you this morning, but there was something I had to talk to Cal about."

"And what about your promise to me last night, that we would talk this morning?" Heather still believed that Bret had been about to leave her again for a few days.

"I didn't forget that. I know we have to talk." Bret pushed his black hat to the back of his forehead and wiped at the sweat that was beading on his brow. He had hoped for more time to pull his thoughts together. He had never thought she would follow him! Why wouldn't she, though? he questioned himself. She probably thought he was once again going to run away from her. "I know a place along the river that's pretty quiet. If you want to come with me, we can talk there." His voice held a soft, masculine tremor; his black eyes

171

seemed to plead with her not to deny him.

Heather knew in that moment that she would follow this man anywhere. All he had to do was ask. Trying to keep some slim shred of her pride, she lifted her chin a notch before slowly nodding her head. She had decided earlier to tell him she would take him up on his offer for her to leave the Saber-Bar if he was not willing to give their marriage a fair chance. She could hardly bear to return to Virginia, but she knew deep in her heart that what she felt for this man would not allow her to remain at his ranch and be treated improperly.

Bret turned his horse's head and began to lead her in the opposite direction from the one they had been heading. They circled the ranch house and rode a small distance north toward the Powder River.

Heather followed silently, her heart hammering wildly in her chest as each look at her husband's wide expanse of muscular back reminded her of what they had shared the night before. Her flesh felt heated even at this early hour of the morning, and she unbuttoned the collar of her shirt as she fought to keep her emotions under control. She had to take a stand and ask for what she wanted, she told herself. She could not back down now, or she knew she would lose all.

It took a little less than an hour's ride before they at last pulled their horses into a small wooded section of land running down to the side of the river. Still Bret had not spoken, but as he helped Heather to dismount, his hands remained on her waist as his gaze filled with the image of her shapely figure in tight trousers and shirt. He drew in a ragged breath. "Do you purposefully do these things just to drive me mad with passion?" He spoke the words as though he were drowning from the very sight of her.

172

"Of course I don't," Heather stammered, and pulled herself away from his hold. She had seen his heated black eyes held on her breasts and realized in that moment, the magnetism that flared between them was such a physical thing it could be aroused with the simplest glance. She could not allow herself to be swept away by her desire for this man! She had to be strong if she was to gain anything out of this so-called talk they were to have, she told herself as she stepped away from him and turned toward the riverbank. This could be her last and only chance to force Bret Saber to look at her as an equal — as his wife!

Watching her walk away from him, Bret could not help lowering his eyes to the swaying of her shapely hips. Even in men's clothing, she was still more woman than he had ever known before. Pulling his blanket from the back of his horse's saddle, he followed her to the edge of the river. He slowly spread out the blanket over the thick meadow grass that grew along the river, and at last sat down upon a corner of the cover, then looked toward her where she stood staring at the slowly flowing water. "I guess we should have had this talk days ago, Heather, but I admit, I was at a loss then as to my feelings."

Heather felt a shiver of something akin to desire sweep over her as she heard his softly spoken statement. Turning back toward him at that moment, she feared that she had made a terrible mistake. Did she truly want to know what this man felt for her? Did she wish to hear that he still loved his first wife and be reminded once again that her purpose was only that of a mother to his daughter? Perhaps it would have been best if she had just gone into Miles City and gotten on the first stagecoach leaving Montana! Looking at him now, she knew that her feelings for this man were far too strong, and she was not sure that she could take any more rejection. "Perhaps this is not a good idea," she at last managed to say. "Molly will be waking soon and she will wonder where I am. I think I should be getting back to the house." She started to turn, thinking to regain her horse and act as though this morning had never happened.

In a single lithe motion, Bret was instantly off the blanket and standing next to her, his arms tenderly drawing her against his wide chest as he whispered next to her ear. "Don't leave me, Heather." The words were a heartfelt plea before his mouth covered hers. "I need you as I have never needed anyone." He sighed as the kiss ended.

"Is your need more than that of your memory of your first wife?" The question came out of Heather's mouth before she could stop the words. She had to know this very minute if he was telling the truth. Was his need for her real, or was it just the natural need that a man had for any woman?

Still holding his arms around her, Bret looked deeply into his wife's face. What was going on in that mind of hers? he wondered, more than a little surprised at her question. At last he spoke. "Heather, my memories of Carrie are filled with bitterness," he stated truthfully, not holding back any of his deep feelings about his first wife.

His words surprised Heather. "Bitterness?" she questioned in confusion. "I thought you loved your first wife!" Wasn't that why he had treated her in the fashion he had since she arrived in Montana? She had believed him so in love with his first wife that there was no room in his heart for another woman!

"At one time perhaps I did love Carrie, Heather, but it was only a few months into the marriage that all the softer feelings I had held for her were gone." Bret knew it was time for him to be truthful with his young bride.

174

He would leave nothing out of his story about Carrie Saber.

Heather shook her head in confusion and tried to clear her wits as she looked up into her husband's handsome face. "I thought it was your love for your first wife that you could not forget. That is the reason I believed you did not care for me, why you did not want me as your real wife!" She felt the sting of tears filling her eyes as she softly confessed how deeply hurt she had been by his treatment of her.

Bret Saber felt his heart wrench with pain as he looked down at his wife and realized fully with her statement how terrible he had been to her since she arrived at his ranch. "The only good thing that Carrie could ever lay claim to was Molly. I have been afraid to care for another woman with the fear that she, too, would be as unfaithful as Carrie was." He knew in that moment that he had to confess all. He had to explain to Heather why he had kept her at a distance, and with the telling, he prayed that somehow she would be able to forgive him. He knew now that he wanted this woman to share his life, his future, whether good or bad!

"Unfaithful?" Heather had picked up on this one word and was stunned by what it implied. Did Bret truly mean that Carrie Saber had been unfaithful to him? Why would any woman with Bret Saber to claim as her husband, wish to be unfaithful with another man?

Bret knew that Heather was totally in the dark about his relationship with his first wife. He had made his uncle swear to keep quiet about Carrie, and it appeared that for once in his life Cam Saber had stayed out of his business. He took a deep breath, glad at last to have it all out in the open. "The day of Carrie's death," he began, "she had been running away to meet her lover, a no-account drifter she had met in Miles City. She was

175

still on Saber-Bar property when her horse stumbled in a rabbit hole. She was thrown and her neck was broken. A couple of the ranch hands found her later that day and brought the body home."

"I am so sorry," Heather whispered after hearing the terrible story. Her sympathy was with the man who had been forced to endure an unfaithful wife, not with Carrie Saber, who had had all that Heather would ever want—a handsome man and an adorable child—and still she had not been satisfied, and had tried to run away with another man.

"Don't be sorry, Heather. By the time the accident happened there was no longer any love between Carrie and myself. We were living separate lives. The only thing we had in common was Molly."

Understanding more of his reasons for keeping her at a distance, Heather wondered if there could be any future for the two of them. Could he forget what he had gone through with Carrie Saber, or would he at every turn mistrust her, and always be on the defensive?

"I guess I have been the one to make a mess of things between the two of us, Heather, but I was hoping you would consider giving me another chance. Let me try to make everything up to you." His dark eyes glimmered with a flicker of warmth that Heather had only seen before when he was talking to his daughter.

Heather could not speak. She had not expected him to say any of this to her. Oh, she realized that he was not making a bold declaration of undying love, but he *was* asking her for another chance. As she looked into his ebony eyes, she wondered how she could deny him anything. Slowly she shook her head, and with the slight movement, his arms were again around her and his lips plundered hers with a consuming intensity.

Bret had not fully realized until this moment how much he had wanted to take back those words he had

176

spoken on the carriage ride to the ranch, when he had claimed his only reason for marrying was to obtain a mother for his child. He now could not remember how many sleepless nights he'd had since that afternoon, when he had tossed and turned, lying awake, wishing he could somehow take back those words and bring Heather to his home as a real bride should be taken to her husband's home on her wedding day.

With his arms still wrapped about her waist, Bret felt his heartbeat accelerate, and with a bold movement, he swung her up into his arms and carried her over to the blanket. The sound of the gentle rushing river filling their ears, he laid her down, and leaning upon an elbow above her, he looked down into her sparkling blue eyes. Lightly he brushed away a strand of silken black hair from her soft cheek as he asked, "Are you sure you can be happy here on the Saber-Bar? You will not regret staying here with me in a year or two?" Though Bret wanted this woman more than anything in his life, he knew he had to offer her this one last opportunity to change her mind about him and his family.

Heather could not believe this was happening to her, that her husband was so close and yet was asking her these questions. "You know so little about me, Bret Saber." Heather sighed softly as she felt herself drowning within his tender regard. "You will learn with time that I am not a woman who changes her mind on a whim. I told you the day of our marriage that our wedding vows meant much to me, and I tell you now that they mean even more after what we have shared together." For the first time Heather was able to give a small part of herself to her husband, even as she realized that only a short time ago she had questioned if she should forget the vows they had repeated in the church.

Bret realized all the time he had wasted with his fear of allowing himself to care for this woman. "Why did

177

you answer my advertisement in the gazette, Heather?" His finger still caressed her cheek. He felt he had all the time in the world to wile away the morning at the side of his beautiful wife, and because he knew so little about her, he was curious about her past and about her reasons for wedding a man she knew so little about.

Heather was unsure how much she should tell Bret. Though she knew that she had done nothing wrong by replying to his advertisement and leaving her stepfather's inn, she still felt uncomfortable with the thought of telling anyone about her past. In her entire life she had shared things only with her mother. She had never had a friend to confide in, so it was difficult now to open up to this man.

"You can tell me anything, Heather," Bret softly prompted as he noticed her withdrawal over his question. From the first moment he had seen her standing before Bailey's General Store, he had wondered what had made her reply to his advertisement, and though he no longer believed she had been running away from some unsavory past, he still was curious about her life before she came to Montana.

For a full minute Heather turned her head away from her husband's seeking regard, as though she still dared not trust him with the portion of her life that had brought her so much pain. "I was living with my stepfather, Clarence Bosworth, at his inn in Clarksburg, West Virginia, when I found your advertisement while cleaning one of the guest chambers."

She fell silent for a moment, and Bret tried to draw her out. "Was your life so hard, then, that it would force you to seek out a husband in a man you had never met?" Bret knew his bride to be a hard worker, and knew that this surely was not her reason, but he wanted to hear her tell him so herself.

"I was used to the hard work. From the age of ten,

178

when my mother married Clarence Bosworth, I worked every day for my keep."

Bret heard the hard edge to her tone that told him what he already knew to be the truth. "Then what was it, Heather?"

"My mother died two years ago, from a long, drawn-out illness, and I was left alone."

Bret knew there was more, and patiently he probed, "You were not alone, though, Heather. You still had your stepfather."

It was plain to Heather that this man had never suffered from abuse at the hands of someone who was supposed to protect and love him. "I could have stayed on at the inn, but without my mother around to intercede, my stepfather bullied and threatened me almost daily. What made up my mind about answering your advertisement was his constant threat of sending men up to my room at night, to increase the coins in his own purse." There, she had said it. She could not even look into her husband's face to determine his reaction as she felt her own face flushing with humiliation at having to tell such a story. He must wonder why her stepfather had acted so basely in his treatment of his stepdaughter. Suppose Bret believed that she had brought such treatment on herself!

Whatever Bret had expected, it had not been this confession. How could anyone treat this lovely woman so cruelly? He could only guess at the depths of the suffering she had endured at the hands of this man she called her stepfather. All of his fatherly instincts welled up inside him, and he began to feel a tight fist of anger knotting within his belly over the threats Clarence Bosworth had made. Tenderly Bret wrapped his arms around her, and drew her up against his chest.

Heather pressed her face into the hollow of his throat, the masculine smells of horse, leather, and sandalwood

179

assailing her senses as his husky words came to her ears. "No man, no matter who he is, will ever threaten you again, my heart, and if I could, I would confront Clarence Bosworth this very day and make him pay for the suffering you have endured through his harsh treatment." At the thought of his own child suffering such abuse at the hands of a stepfather, Bret's anger increased.

Heather could feel the tension in the muscles beneath her hand as they flexed with his passion for justice, and at that moment her heart swelled with feelings of tenderness for him. He was capable of such strong emotions, from anger to tenderness, that he overwhelmed her. She felt tears come to her eyes with his claim of becoming her protector, and she softly placed kisses along the broad column of his throat, feathering them downward to the V in his shirt that revealed the dark fur matting his powerful chest.

Realizing that this was the first time his wife had ever kissed him of her own accord, Bret's heart sang with joy as he gathered her closer to him. His sensual lips slanted over hers. "I will make everything up to you, I swear. We will start over from the beginning." Bret leaned over her as he drew his lips away, and with his words he looked deeply into her sapphire eyes and hoped that after what had taken place between them, she could trust him enough to give him the chance to prove himself capable of being a good husband to her.

"If only it were not impossible to start over." Heather's tone was softly reflective, even though she knew at the moment that her husband meant every word he was saying.

"You think it not possible?" With a wide grin, he pulled her up so that she stood on the blanket, and with a single movement he was on his knees before her. One of his large hands clutched both of hers, and his midnight eyes glimmered with a passionate light in their depths as the husky tremor of his deep voice seemed to fill her to the depths of her soul with their plea. "Heather Saber, you have fully captured my heart. I did not know what the words love and adoration were until I met you. Neither did I know the meaning of the suffering that a man can feel when he tries to fight off the attraction of his own wife. You say we cannot start over, but I ask you now, no I beg you, Heather, please marry me. Please be my wife."

Chapter Eight

Heather was overwhelmed by the warm sensations that his words evoked. He was declaring his love to her, her mind kept repeating over and over. Now that he knew her, he was asking her to become his bride! She felt giddy with excitement as she looked down on him. "But we are already married," she finally got out on a single breath, as she was held by the dark magnetism of his glowing eyes.

"Then we will repeat our vows for all to witness how much you mean to me!" Bret declared, rising to his feet and, with a single movement, catching her about the waist and swinging her high in the air.

Heather laughed in gay abandon at his antics. She had never known Bret to be so carefree, and she delighted in the moment. "But I have always wanted to be a June bride, and June is now almost over," she cried as he at last put her on her feet.

"Whatever you wish, my sweet, it shall be granted to you. You are definitely the most beautiful June bride I have ever seen." His mouth covered hers in a hungry possession that blotted out all conversation and stole Heather's breath away.

Opening her mouth to him, Heather's tongue danced with his in a mating ritual that left her pressing her shapely length hungrily against the solid wall of his body. Her slim hands wrapped around his neck and tangled within the strands of dark hair that lay against his broad shoulders. This is what she had escaped her stepfather's inn to find! This is what she had been waiting an entire lifetime to feel! Somehow, at that moment, she knew that all the feelings she had harbored for this man, all the anger, resentment, sorrow, and passion, all had brought her to this moment of realization. She truly loved him! She was in love with Bret Saber, in love with her own husband!

Nothing else mattered to this young couple as they came together in a wordless fusion of their minds, bodies, and souls. As they lay naked next to each other, Bret rose above his bride, his searing gaze devouring her beauty with a bold glance that left nothing untouched and caused Heather's heartbeat to flutter out of control. "Heart's love . . ." He spoke softly. "I pledge to give unto you all that I have. My heart, my life, my very breath I place before you, and pray you only consider my plight tenderly. Do not forsake me without cause."

His words went straight to Heather's heart. She felt her own salty tears upon her cheeks as she looked into the depths of the consuming gaze that held her, and she drew his mouth to hers with a hand pressed behind his neck before she spoke her promise. "Never will I forsake you. I love you, Bret," she whispered softly.

No more words were needed. Bret took her softly spoken vow as a promise to be his, throughout this life and all eternity. Tenderly he cradled her against his length as his mouth and tongue plied their magic over her body and left her gasping aloud as he seared a path from her lips down to her breasts. He worshipped the twin globes of pale flesh, taking one by one the rosy-hued nipples into his mouth to suckle.

The canopy of trees overhead, the noises of the river, and the sounds of the morning songbirds combined to heighten the couple's passions as the earth smells encircled them and inflamed their ardor to fever pitch.

Heather could not get enough of the taste of his body as her hands reached out and caressed any part of him that she could reach, and her body writhed beneath the onslaught of his wild seduction. As he leaned over her and feasted upon her breasts, her own mouth met his muscular shoulder and her lips made a bold pattern of tiny kisses down toward the upper portion of his chest. At the same time her hands glided over the strong planes of his muscled body, outlining the broadness of his sculpted back, down to his narrow hips, and over his firm buttocks. An indrawn breath caught and held for a breathless time as one hand brushed against the length of his shaft.

With the slight touch of her hand, the size of him seemed to enlarge, expanding to mighty proportions as the blood rushed through his loins, and a deep groan started in the depths of his chest and rumbled upward.

Feeling the woman's power that she held at this moment, Heather wrapped her slim fingers around his swollen member and slowly drew them up the length until she touched the heart-shaped head, then slowly, tantalizingly she traveled back down the thick, throbbing measure of him, inch by inch.

Bret felt a shudder travel over him from her play. Dragging his mouth from her breasts to hungrily settle over her lips, he gasped aloud, "I can take little more of your gentle touch, my heart. Your simplest caress brings home fully to me my great need for you." And with these words, his hand gently drew hers away from his manhood. He pressed her thighs apart, and settled the yearning fullness of his length against the heated portal of her womanhood.

With the movement of him rubbing against her moist cleft, she moaned aloud as she undulated beneath him, seeking out the fullness she knew he would soon be giving her. Not willing to wait another moment for the rapture that awaited her, she placed her hands upon his firm buttocks and pulled him closer, rising up to meet him.

Sweet pleasure flamed between them, their bodies seeking, thrusting, striving to claim that moment's splendor within the vortex of incredible oneness. Caught up in a wild frenzy of emotion, Heather barely noticed when her husband drew her slim body over him, his passion-filled eyes blazing as his hands roamed freely over her shapely curves and brought her to passion's edge. She rose above him, her body writhing to a primal rhythm.

She felt a craving through her entire being as her hands splayed across the broad, fur-matted chest, her lips seeking his and her silken tresses surrounding them both within a shimmering curtain. Her body moving and seeking, her breath was ragged and gasping as a shuddering caught hold of her and her body came up and down, up and down, in the same motion, until she was lost to all reason, so caught up was she in the overwhelming feelings within her. The rapturous sensations of his thick, pulsing length moving in and out of her added fuel to the raging fire within her depths and skyrocketed toward the outer bounds of no return, then shattered around her, leaving her breathless and perspiring atop him, her womanhood tightening with trembling contractions that caused Bret to moan aloud.

Fighting to maintain a strong will over his erection, Bret pulled his bride back beneath his powerful body. "The pleasure that you have just given me is incomparable, but now it is my turn, my sweet." His voice was low and husky, his sable eyes devouring as his lips caught hers in a tender hold.

As he again looked into her passion-blue eyes, he held her spellbound for a time. As he moved his length within her, she called out his name with a gasp. "Bret!" It was a breathless caress, more of a plea.

"Hush, my love, do not move. Take this pleasure that I give you to the fullest." As he slowly began to move his lower body, his lips and hands began to wander to the sensitive areas of her body. Chills of pleasure danced along her spine as she forced herself to try to remain still as he had instructed.

Bending over her in order for his mouth to close over one rose-tipped nipple, his tongue teased the ripe peak, his teeth gently tugging as he suckled. She cried aloud from the sheer ecstasy of it. His mouth charted a damp path from one breast to the other as his fingers roamed freely over her belly and ribs and his body moved to a timeless beat of sensual pleasure.

"Bret!" The shout came from deep in her throat. "Bret, please!" She did not know at that moment whether she was begging him to stop or to continue with his divine torture. Her head was thrown back and moving from side to side, her lips parted, her entire body aflame, as at last she was consumed by the powerful riot of passion blooming deep within.

Held in the throes of blinding ecstasy, spasms still quaking over her entire body, Heather cried aloud with the total force of her pleasure, and Bret also sought his release. Their rapture rose higher and higher, until Heather felt a towering surge rippling, growing, as if a gigantic tidal wave were washing over her, drowning her in its power as she pulled Bret into its glowing center with her and they spun into its maelstrom together.

Adrift at last upon the fleecy clouds of sated passion, Heather sighed happily in her husband's strong embrace. His arms still encircled her as Bret fought for his breath, his sensual lips tenderly running kisses along the outline of her delicate collarbone.

"I do love you," Heather at last whispered. "I think I fell in love with you the first time I saw Molly in your arms," she softly confessed, unable to keep herself from proclaiming the words aloud.

Rising on an elbow above her for a timeless moment, Bret stared down into her beautiful features. "In the past I have claimed myself a man not given to the softer nature of being able to love a woman, but you have changed all of that. You have turned my very life upside down since your arrival in Miles City. I have been unable to work without thoughts of you distracting me. I cannot find rest at night without your sapphire eyes boring into my soul. I thought I had no need for the affection and tenderness a woman brings to a man, but there, too, you have proven me wrong. I confess I would die for your tender smile, and my heart leaps with the sound of your soft, lilting voice. You have totally captured my heart, Heather, and I confess that I do love you also."

Stinging tears filled her eyes from these words that Heather knew had cost him much to speak. He was a man who had been mistreated terribly in the name of love, and now here he was admitting to her that he had at last opened his heart once again, and she was the full recipient of his affections. Joy surged through her as she realized that she would never be alone again. She was loved! With this realization the tears came, and as her husband tenderly cradled her against his chest, she could not still them. She had traveled so far, and suffered so much, but it had all been worth it!

"I did not mean to make you weep so, Heather." Bret tried to soothe away the crystal drops upon her cheeks as he brushed away dark strands of curling hair.

"I only weep with joy that you feel as I do," Heather at last got out.

"Then I had better be more careful of what I say to

you. I surely would not want you to fall to weeping each time I declare my love for you." Bret laughed aloud as he pulled her out of her reflective mood. Knowing now the hardship of a past lived with her stepfather, Bret wanted her to know only joy from this day forth.

"Oh, no, I love hearing you talk to me like this." Heather pulled herself upright and dashed the tears away with the back of her hand.

"I was only jesting, my heart. I could not stop myself from speaking my love aloud for you, even if I tried. These past days have been a torture that I do not wish to know again." Bret also rose, and pulling her to her feet, their naked bodies clutched tightly for a long moment as he covered her lips with his own and drank of the sweet essence of her charms. "We had best dress and return to the ranch. Molly and Cam will be up and about, and it's time that I showed them both that I might be slow in realizing my feelings for my wife, but at least I am not totally stupid!" Bret grinned down at her, his dark eyes holding that tantalizing sparkle that told Heather of his love for her.

Some minutes later Bret helped Heather to mount her mare, and his large hand ran down the outside of her thigh. "One of the first things that we shall do," he stated softly, "is to see about having some new clothes fashioned for you. That too-small dress you wore the day of the barbeque near drove me to distraction, but these tight trousers and that shirt of Jasper's are more than I can handle . . . even after a bout of lovemaking." He felt the stirring of his manhood within his own trousers as he witnessed the way the shirt clung to her breasts and the pants molded to her shapely form.

Heather was more than enjoying the female power that she experienced under her husband's gaze. She had never felt herself as attractive as she did while in his presence. "Whatever you say, Bret," she purred, and wiggled her tightly outlined bottom just a bit to keep the sparkle in his eyes.

Bret inwardly moaned as he tied the blanket to the back of his saddle and mounted up. It was certain that his bewitching bride planned to lead him a merry chase, and he guessed he deserved all the sweet, sensual pain she could give him! A small grin settled over his lips as he looked over to her. "Are you ready, sweet? I find myself a little tired after this morning's exertions and long for us to find our bed."

Tired, indeed! Heather thought as she felt her face beginning to flush with the meaning of his words. Without saying anything more, she began to follow him away from the riverbed, her heart leaping within her breast with anticipation of what the rest of the day would hold for the two of them.

Just as the couple broke through the group of trees that they had earlier traveled through to gain the river, they were approached by a group of men who drew their horses up tightly in a circle around them.

"Hold up there, boss man, and you, too, little lady." It was Corry Jessup's voice.

Instantly Bret reached for his rifle, which was in the sheath in his saddle, but before he could draw it forth, Seth Mansfield grabbed hold of his arm, his pistol pointed at his heart. "I wouldn't be doing nothing like that, Saber," he drawled in a dangerous tone that left Heather feeling chilled even as the morning sunlight gleamed down upon her.

Bret could have kicked himself for being taken by surprise. He should have been more cautious, he should have been paying closer attention! His dark eyes held a cold stare as he looked at Seth Mansfield. "What do you want from us?" He would have reached out to comfort Heather in that moment, but he knew

189

that he dared not move while the gun was pointed at him.

"Why, you and your wife here are coming along with us," Seth replied as though it was a usual thing for his band to approach people and demand that they go along with them to an unspecified destination.

"Like hell we will!" Bret declared, and in that instant he lunged off the back of his stallion and knocked Seth Mansfield to the ground. *If he could just overpower him and get hold of his pistol* was the only thought on Bret's mind. He could not allow himself and Heather to be taken by this band of rustlers!

It was Sam Holt, the rustler whom Bret and Cal Hart had chased the day before, who leaped to his feet and, without a second thought, brought the butt of his rifle down upon Bret's head.

"What'd ya do that fur?" Seth cried as Bret fell to the ground in a semiconscious state. "I could have taken care of him myself!"

A gasp of shock left Heather's lips as she jumped from her horse to gain her husband's side, just as Sam replied. "We ain't got time for you to roll around on the ground and get your ass kicked! Another minute and he would have had your gun!"

"Bret, Bret!" Heather cried as she wiped at the trickling line of blood on her husband's forehead.

"I'm all right, Heather." He tried to soothe her fear as he drew a ragged breath and forced himself, despite the aching in his head, to sit up.

"Get the girl, and get him on his horse!" Again it was the tall, thin outlaw dressed entirely in black who gave the order.

As Seth reached down and caught hold of Heather's arm, she glared her hatred of him. "I will go nowhere with you, nor will my husband!" she cried.

"I don't be thinking ye have much choice, little lady."

190

Corry Jessup and another man dismounted and offered Seth their much-needed help.

Heather's tamper flared as she looked at the two men to whom her husband had given jobs on his ranch. "You are all a band of worthless, despicable outlaws!" she cried as she was held by the arms by Seth Mansfield and Bret was grabbed by the other two men.

"You are right there, lady. We *are* outlaws, and you will get the chance to see just how far we will go when we reach the lion shake in the hills north of the Saber-Bar. And by the time we are through with you, you'll know exactly what an outlaw is!" Sam Holt's pale-blue eyes raked her from head to foot. As she struggled as valiantly as her husband against those who held him, the outlaw stated coldly, "If you got to use your fists to control her, do it, but get her and Saber on their horses, and let's get out of here before someone comes riding up!"

"It's just like me pappy always said, a woman, a dog, and a walnut tree, the more you beat 'em, the better they be!" Corry Jessup laughed aloud as he goaded his friend on.

Heather's anger knew no bounds as she listened to these men. More than likely they would beat her, and there was no telling what other vile things they had in mind for her once they reached the lion shake! Without a thought to her own welfare, she kicked Seth Mansfield in the shin, her small fists doubled up and striking out at any portion of him she could reach.

Hearing what these men said and knowing what their plans for his wife were, Bret felt a towering rage that threatened to strangle him. With an animallike growl coming from deep within his chest as he witnessed his slim wife fighting off the man holding her prisoner, he broke free of the two men holding his arms, his hamlike fists smashing into one face and then the other!

At just that moment a shot was fired in the air, and a familiar voice shouted over the commotion, "That's enough, boys. Take your hands off of Mrs. Saber!"

Still clinging to Heather's forearm, even under her heated attack, Seth Mansfield looked up to find they were completely surrounded by Cam Saber and the Saber-Bar hands, all holding rifles pointed in the direction of the rustlers.

"I was wondering when you would arrive!" Bret looked from his uncle to Cal Hart. "I hope you sent for the marshal like I told you."

"Yep, I sure did, Bret. He should be arriving most anytime now."

Heather pulled herself away from Seth Mansfield's stunned grasp. "You mean you were expecting them, Bret?" she asked.

Bret drew her up tightly to his side, and after looking her over from head to foot to make sure that she was unharmed, he answered her question. "Cal and I chased these bandits yesterday. That one in black," he nodded toward the rustler who now sat gunless in his saddle with his head lowered, "I knew I had seen him somewhere before, but I didn't remember until early this morning where. I left the ranch to find Cal and to tell him to send for the sheriff and to keep an eye on Seth and Corry, for I had seen them talking in town to their friend in black."

Heather could only thank God that the morning had turned out as it had. If Cam and Cal had arrived any later, they might have missed them, for surely the outlaws would have eventually "subdued" her and her husband and they would have been on their way to the lion shake . . . and more than likely to their deaths!

"Well, it 'pears to me like this day has turned out mighty good after all!" Cam winked down at Heather as he noticed the attention his nephew was giving her

192

and the way his arm was wrapped protectively around her slim waist.

Heather could not help grinning up at her husband's uncle, but it was Bret who replied, "Well I reckon you're right, Cam, so why don't you and the boys here make sure that these no-accounts are taken care of while Heather and I relieve Jasper from watching Molly."

"That's a good idea, boy. It's about time you started using your heart instead of your head!" And with a last grin, he turned toward the rustlers. "All right, you worthless good-for-nothings," he said. "Let's get mounted and moving slow-like right toward the ranch!"

Once again Bret helped his bride to mount her mare. "Are you sure you are unhurt?" he questioned for the third time, his hand resting upon her thigh as she sat in the saddle, his dark eyes holding her with all the tenderness he felt for her in his heart. She had fought like a tigress at his side and he was proud that she was his woman, but it had been in that moment she had rushed to his side, thinking nothing of her own safety at these outlaws' hands, when she had brushed back his hair from the wound on his head and had called out his name, that any doubts he might have had about her love for him had vanished.

Heather reached down and lightly brushed away the lock of dark hair that always seemed to fall against Bret's forehead, her eyes taking in the sharp gash. With the remembrance of what she had felt when she saw the dark-clad bandit hit him with the rifle, tears filled her eyes. "I am fine now, Bret. As long as I have you, I will be just fine!"

"Well, Mrs. Saber, you will have me for a long, long time, so don't be making no mistake. When I love, Heather, I love deeply." He wished he had not placed her upon her horse, for at that moment he desired nothing more than to hold her in his arms and kiss her soft pink mouth. "Let's not linger around here any longer, Heather," he said instead. "I have a yearning for that nap we spoke of earlier. I'm sure Jasper will watch Molly for just a little while longer."

Epilogue

June 1, 1864

The bride was dressed in a white gown boasting layers and layers of snowy lace, with a tight-fitting bodice trimmed with hundreds of painstakingly hand-stitched tiny, perfect pearls. Her handsome husband had insisted that this day be as special as though it were their first wedding ceremony.

The entire town of Miles City had been invited for the occasion of the marriage, as well as all the ranchers and nesters. Now that the rustlers were a thing of the past, there seemed less tension around town, and occasionally the feuding ranchers and nesters were seen sharing a draft of beer or a shot of whiskey in the saloon.

Standing at the back of the church with Beth Waters at her side fussing like a mother hen, Heather smiled softly as her gaze took in the rows of chairs filled to capacity. Her attention was drawn by a small, chubby hand tugging at the skirt of her gown.

"Mommy, Mommy, can I be your best girl? Cal is Daddy's best man, and I want to be your best girl!"

Heather's heart filled with the love that she had for this child. Looking down into the features so much like those of the man she loved, she smiled tenderly. "Of course, darling, you can be Mommy's best girl." She bent to the child's side, not caring that she was mussing her gown. "You will always be Mommy's best girl, Molly."

A large grin split the chubby features with Heather's words. The little girl's happiness was now complete.

"It's time, Heather; the music has begun." Beth Waters kissed her on the cheek as Cam Saber stepped to her side and they awaited the moment to step down the aisle.

Grabbing hold of Molly's hand, Heather kept the child at her side. As they started the walk from the back of the church, Cam's dark eyes twinkled with happiness. "The boy has made me proud this day. He's one lucky man, Heather."

"I am the lucky one, Cam." Heather spoke softly as she held tightly to his strong forearm, her blue eyes going to the end of the aisle where Bret and Cal Hart stood in front of Reverend Waters. "I was going to tell Bret my news this evening, but I would like you to know first, Cam. You are going to be an uncle again."

As Cam's free hand grabbed the hand upon his forearm and squeezed tightly, Heather knew that Cam was ecstatic with the news that she and Bret were going to have a baby. And she also knew that he would be hard pressed to walk her up the aisle without giving a yelp of excitement. He had been her first friend in Montana, and she felt as close to him as she would to an uncle of her own. She felt no guilt in telling him her news before she told her husband.

Bret Saber's dark eyes glowed with dancing lights of happiness as they filled with the vision of his bride, his daughter, and his uncle coming down the aisle toward him. These people were his life, his heart and his soul. He glimpsed the joy upon their features, and once again he silently thanked God that He had sent him this woman for his own. When he thought how differently things could have turned out if any other woman had answered his advertisement for a mail-order bride, his heart shuddered with dread. God had surely been watching over him, he told himself once again.

As the three gained his side at the front of the church and Cam silently kissed Heather's cheek and took his seat in the front row of chairs, Molly remained at Heather's side.

"Dearly beloved, we are gathered here in the presence of God to join this man and this woman once again together within the bonds of matrimony." The preacher's words filled the silence of the small church.

Heather slipped her hand into her husband's, her world complete, her heart filled to bursting with this new life she had found for herself in the mountains of Montana.

A Captive Bride

by

Susan Sackett

Chapter One

"Your father should have taken the offer I made to him two years ago, Samantha. She was still in fair shape then. I'm sorry, but I can't pay you much for her now. Nothing worse for a ship than neglect. She'll cost more than she's worth just to make her seaworthy. In fact, I'm only making an offer at all out of the respect I bore your father and the affection I feel for you."

Samantha Waverly looked down at the bonnet she'd removed and now held in her lap. It was black, as was the ill-fitting dress she wore. Not that she cared, but it was hardly becoming even if it was appropriate for the task of burying her father.

What was not appropriate, she thought, was having this conversation, at least on this particular day. If John Prescott had had an ounce of decency, he'd have waited before coming to make an offer for the *Lady Alyssa*. And when he came, he wouldn't be foolish enough to blather on about the respect he bore her father. John Prescott hadn't respected her father. In fact, she doubted there was a person on the island who hadn't lost all respect for David Waverly years before.

Not that waiting a few days before coming to see her would have done Prescott much good. After all, he wasn't a sailor, he was a shipping broker, and her father had hated brokers and bankers and anyone else of their ilk. And he'd hated John Prescott in particular, hated him so much that he'd made her promise that when the time came, she'd starve before she'd sell the *Lady Alyssa* to the man.

She fingered the dull ribbon of her bonnet before she could force herself to look up at him.

"You needn't apologize, Mr. Prescott," she replied. "I've no interest in an offer for the *Lady Alyssa* just now."

"You can't mean to tell me you intend to go on living in this rotting hulk?" Prescott asked.

It really wasn't an unfair question under the circumstances, but Sam took exception to Prescott's disapproving expression as he looked around the deck.

"I don't know what I intend to do," she said curtly. "At least, not yet."

"I thought you'd be glad of the offer," Prescott huffed. "If you sell the *Lady Alyssa,* you could at least live decently. It's not that your father had anything else to leave you."

"No," she agreed. It was true, and there was no use denying what the whole of Martha's Vineyard Island knew. "He didn't. All the more reason for me not to just turn my back on her."

Her manner seemed to fluster Prescott. Apparently he'd thought she'd jump at an offer of hard cash, however little of it, in return for washing her hands of the decrepit-looking clipper ship. He sat for a moment in strained thought, rubbing his fingers against the gold handle of his cane and staring at it with myopic preoccupation. Realizing himself unable to find anything further to add to his argument and aware that she was in no mood for the exchange of pleasantries, he pushed himself to his feet.

"I'll give you a few days to consider the matter, Samantha," he told her. "Perhaps you'll change your mind."

Sam looked up at him and smiled almost sweetly.

"I won't," she said.

He scowled and turned away, making his way uneasily

across the *Lady Alyssa*'s deck. Sam watched him climb clumsily down to the wharf, not really thinking about him any longer now that the conversation was at an end. Once he was safely on firm ground, she dismissed him from her thoughts entirely, and turned up to look at the dark outlines of the ship's masts, like stark sculpture against the flawless backdrop of the fading blue late April sky.

It wasn't only Prescott who seemed incapable of believing that she didn't want to wash her hands of her father's ship. It seemed as though everyone wanted her to leave the *Lady Alyssa*. That afternoon, after the funeral, her aunt Elinore had told her quite clearly how unfitting it was for her to remain there.

"Are you sure you won't come back to the house with us, Samantha dear?" Elinore had begun in that wheedling tone that Sam hated. "I never did like the idea of your staying on that dirty old boat, and now that you're alone, I like it even less."

Sam hadn't needed to look at her aunt's face to know that Elinore's expression had been pinched with distaste. Elinore had never approved of her younger sister Alyssa marrying a sea captain when her own husband's younger brother, a respectable banker, had been quite open about his interest in making a match. Her disapproval of David Waverly had grown when Alyssa had died in childbirth shortly after Sam's ninth birthday. And it had continued to grow and flower after that, continuously being fed by David Waverly's descent into dissolution during the four years prior to his death. Sam couldn't say that she exactly blamed her aunt for the antipathy she'd borne David, but she knew she heartily disliked her for it.

"The *Lady Alyssa* isn't a dirty old boat, Aunt Elinore," Sam had replied wearily, "and I shall be perfectly fine there."

Sam had looked up then, and for an instant had trouble keeping from smiling slightly as she noted her uncle Matthew's exhalation of relief. She knew her uncle wanted her to move into his already crowded house almost as little as she wanted to become part of such a noisy, quarrelsome household.

Elinore had been either oblivious or unconcerned about the wants of either Sam or her own husband. She was a woman on a mission, and she hadn't liked being thwarted.

"I don't consider it appropriate for you to remain alone on that boat," she had insisted.

"All I want to do at the moment, Aunt Elinore, is to be by myself for a little while and spend some time thinking."

"Well, I suggest you spend the time thinking about selling that boat, if you can find someone fool enough to buy it, and moving in with us. No decent man would think of marrying a woman who lives as you do."

Sam fingered the ribbons of the ugly black bonnet in her lap as she recalled that part of the conversation. It hadn't been the possibility of finding a husband that had really been on her aunt's mind, she thought. It was the prospect of having a free nursemaid to help with the nine children and the housework that had really interested Elinore.

The thought of spending the rest of her life humbly begging crumbs at her aunt's table had been enough to make Sam shudder. The thought was still so unpleasant it was able to send a chill finger of dread along her spine.

"No decent man would think of marrying me anyway, Aunt Elinore," she'd replied, her impatience making her tone sharper and more bitter-sounding than she had intended. "Men want pretty wives, or plain wives with money. I am neither."

Elinore had wagged a scolding finger. "I don't want to hear you talk that way. You'd be pretty enough if you took some effort with yourself. Wearing those old dresses and horrible spectacles," and Elinore had scowled and shaken her head, "well, what do you expect?"

The truth was, Sam didn't really need the spectacles, at least not when she wasn't reading. But still, she'd taken to wearing them all the time. Partly, she supposed, she did it to annoy her aunt. But mostly she wore them because they were a kind of armor for her, a way of proclaiming to anyone who might be the least bit interested that she didn't care what they thought of her appearance or her clothing, the cut-down dresses she took from the old trunk of her mother's belongings. The spectacles were her way of saying that she was indifferent to the fact that they thought her ugly, that she had more important things to consider than trying to make herself into someone else's image of what she ought to be.

"New dresses cost money," Sam had muttered, then bit her lip. The mention of money would only lead Elinore to make mention of her father's inability to provide properly for his family, and that was not a subject she'd wanted to explore at the moment. Moreover, she knew there was no use trying to argue with Elinore. There never was. And she hadn't had the heart for it, anyway. "I really am tired, Aunt," she'd murmured, hoping to change the subject before Elinore could pounce on it. "Please don't worry yourself about me. I'll be fine. I just want to get some rest."

Then, before Elinore could protest, Sam had pushed open the door of the carriage and climbed quickly out. She'd smiled and nodded to her aunt and uncle, then hurried down the stone steps leading to the rotting wharf where the *Lady Alyssa* had been tied for the previous four years.

It had been good to sit on the deck of the ship after that, taking off the ugly bonnet and letting her hair be blown loose of its pins by a pleasant April wind. It had been good to allow her mind to empty itself and then simply wander. But John Prescott's visit had ruined the mood, and now she realized the wind had grown cold and biting. She shivered as she tugged her shawl around her shoulders. She ought to go below to the galley and fix herself some dinner, she told herself. And after that, she should sleep.

It would be good to be able to *really* sleep, she thought, to let herself drift off without having to worry about her father stumbling in the dark, perhaps even falling into the water and drowning. It occurred to her that she'd never again have to climb up to the deck in the middle of the night and help him down to the captain's cabin despite his drunken protestations that he could take care of himself. All those nights when she'd worried he'd drink so much that he would harm himself . . . they were gone now, she realized, gone forever. She had no need to worry any more about a dead man.

It seemed a bit ironic to her now, realizing that it hadn't been a serious fall from the deck or the wharf, the sort of fall she'd feared so much, that had finally killed her father. He'd simply passed out and fallen on the smooth sand of the beach just beyond town. Perhaps if he hadn't been so drunk, he might have noticed the tide change and the water climbing up onto the sand. Or perhaps he'd simply lain there and watched it come closer. In the end, he'd drowned in less than six inches of water.

Perhaps, Sam thought, it was what he had really wanted.

At the thought, her throat suddenly grew tight and thick-feeling. A wrenching hurt washed through her and settled with a sharp ache inside her. She hated the thought that he had simply given up. She remembered a time when there had been so much life in him that it would have been inconceivable to think of him turning his back on it.

But then, in many ways, he'd given up the day Sam's mother had died.

She let her head fall forward into her hands and finally released the tears that she'd managed to keep hidden all that day. They'd been there, just beneath the surface, but she'd refused to shed them where her aunt could chide her for them. She hadn't allowed herself a single one, not even when she'd thrown her handful of dirt on her father's casket and heard the dull thud as it landed on the thin wood.

"I miss you, Papa," she whispered, her tone ragged and raw with the hurt.

It didn't seem strange to her that she was talking to a dead man. He was there, she knew, his spirit so close to her she could feel it touching her. She knew it would always be on the *Lady Alyssa* and that, more than her promise even, was what kept her from selling the ship to John Prescott.

That spirit wasn't the sick, drunken invalid her father had been for the previous four years. He was a different man altogether from that, the determined young captain who had brought her on board the *Lady Alyssa* for the first time when she'd been just a child. He'd been the strongest and the handsomest man in the world then, and she'd been weak with pride of him. All the horrible things that had happened after that day, all the things he'd done, they faded and grew indistinct in her memory until they were finally washed away. She closed her eyes and saw her father again as she remembered him, tall and strong and proud.

It was the spirit of that Captain Waverly who helped

her now, leading her down to the mate's cabin and guiding her climb into the narrow bed.

When Sam awoke she felt as though she'd slept for a year. She lay on the bunk for a long time, her muscles feeling almost as if they were unable to lift her. The gentle rocking of the *Lady Alyssa* on the waves beneath her was a pleasant sensation, surprisingly comforting, the way a baby must feel when it is rocked in a cradle.

But she didn't stay in bed long. She'd never eaten dinner the previous evening, never eaten anything at all the day before, and now her stomach was groaning with hunger.

She pushed herself out of the narrow bunk bed, washed herself quickly with the chilly water in her pitcher, and ran her comb through the tumult of her auburn curls. This cursory toilette completed, she took an old dress from a peg on the wall and pulled it on over her head. Its fabric had once been a cheery print, but the background had long since faded to a dull gray and the flower springs of the pattern now resembled tiny blemishes. She took a thin piece of ribbon of indeterminate color and left her cabin, heading forward, to the *Lady Alyssa*'s galley, her mind occupied with the limited possibilities of what she might find there for her breakfast.

She was just finishing tying her hair back at the nape of her neck with the piece of ribbon when she reached the galley. She stopped at its entrance, and stood, shaking and staring wide-eyed at the sight of a dark shadow at the far side of the room, leaning over the stove.

For an instant, she almost believed that the ghost she'd imagined the night before had come to life.

"Papa?" she murmured as she stood and stared at the figure as it slowly straightened.

208

But when he turned to face her, she realized it wasn't her father, not even her father's ghost.

"What are you doing here?" she snapped.

"Fine greeting, Miss Waverly."

"What are you doing here?" she demanded again, this time her tone stating clearly that she wanted an immediate answer.

"I came to tell you how sorry I was about your father's death—" he began.

"You did that yesterday at the funeral," she interrupted.

He went on as though she hadn't said a word.

"And as it was apparent you were still asleep, I thought I'd do you the favor of preparing something for you to eat."

"I don't need your favors," she said.

He cocked a brow. "It looks to me as though you damn well need someone's favors," he told her. "There's damn little food in your larder, Sam. I don't suppose you have money to buy more?"

"I have everything I need," she snapped. "And I'll thank you, Mr. Stone, to mind your own business."

Jason Stone sighed audibly as he turned back to the stove, lifted a battered coffeepot, and filled two mugs from it. He hadn't assumed this would be easy, but he really hadn't expected she would make this meeting as difficult as she seemed determined to do. He brought the mugs to the thick slab of oak that served as a table and set them down beside a pan of lumpy-looking biscuits.

"Maybe your humor will improve after you've had something to eat," he said as he seated himself on a narrow bench. He lifted one of the cups of coffee and stared up at her as he sipped from it.

There seemed to be nothing else to do but eat. And she *was* hungry.

Sam seated herself across the table from him, still staring angrily at him as she tore off one of the warm biscuits and began to chew hungrily at it.

"You're a terrible cook," she sputtered, her mouth still filled with biscuit.

Jason shrugged. "I suppose I am. But then, captains don't usually do the cooking."

"As far as I can see, you aren't a captain," Sam mumbled through the crumbs of a second bite of biscuit. "A captain needs a ship and, from the looks of it, Jason Stone, you have none."

She smiled. It rather pleased her to watch him scowl at her and know it was because she'd said something he didn't like.

Jason stared at her for a moment. Were she any other woman he'd know what to do to get what he wanted from her, how to charm her with a boyish smile and the sort of words she wanted to hear a man say. But this wasn't any other woman. Samantha Waverly didn't expect a man to charm her, and she would dismiss any attempt as exactly what it was—outrightly insincere flattery. Thin and sharp-featured, with those wide brown eyes staring owlishly out at him through her round metal spectacles, she looked a bit like a street urchin in her old hand-me-down dress. No, she'd be as likely to accept flattery as she would to give him the *Lady Alyssa* straight out.

"You know your father wanted me to have her, Samantha," he said finally. "As much as he didn't want to see her go to the likes of John Prescott."

Sam dropped the half-eaten biscuit and lifted the mug of coffee. She stared at the dark line of a hairline crack in its side before she took a sip of the strong, hot coffee.

"Don't tell me what he wanted," she said finally. "I've heard it more times than I can count. 'Sell her to a real

210

sailor when I'm gone, Sam, not to a lousy broker who'll syndicate her and turn her into a piece of merchandise rather than a ship.' You can't imagine how many times he repeated that litany in the last year."

"Then you know he wanted me to have her, to take her back to sea," Jason said, suddenly hopeful that she might actually be reasonable for once.

Sam stared straight into his dark-blue eyes.

"My father was a drunkard," she said sharply. "From the day he lost his leg and his ability to captain this ship, he lost his self-respect. And mine. Why should I care what he wanted?"

Jason stared at her for a moment. He'd never heard her talk like this before, never really expected her to say anything against David.

"You don't mean that," he told her. "You don't mean a word of it."

"You don't know what I mean," she snapped. "For the last four years you've been back here . . . what, a half dozen times? For a month at the most between berths. You don't even know me, Jason Stone. And you don't know how I think."

Jason swallowed uncomfortably. He should have known it would be like this from the way she'd been so withdrawn the day before at the funeral. She'd bottled up a good deal of pain inside her, and he could only begin to guess at its cause.

There was only one thing of which he was entirely sure, and that was how much he wanted the *Lady Alyssa*. And whether she knew it or not, that was the best thing for Sam as well.

"I do know he would have wanted the *Lady* to be sailed again," he said softly.

Sam shrugged, as though his words were as meaningless to her as if they'd been in some foreign language.

"My father was a ruin," she said through tight lips.

211

"He gambled away our house and just about everything of value he ever had—everything except this ship. That was all that was really important to him, the *Lady Alyssa*. And the rum. And that he let kill him."

With each word, Sam felt as though she were tearing herself apart inside. Not that it wasn't all true. But she'd loved her father, still loved him, and it was only because Jason was sitting there telling her *he* knew what her father thought that set her anger churning inside her. It was the anger that was making her say all those things she'd never otherwise have thought to utter.

"He had his reasons, Sam," Jason murmured.

She nodded. "I know. And he let them kill him. But I'm still alive, and I have no intention of letting them kill me. All he left me was the *Lady Alyssa*, and I intend to do with her what's best for me."

She couldn't believe she was saying these things, couldn't believe she was even capable of thinking about her father and the *Lady Alyssa* so coldly. And she really had no idea why every conversation with Jason Stone seemed to end in a shouting match between the two of them.

Or maybe she did. Maybe it was because she knew there wasn't a woman on Martha's Vineyard who he wasn't able to charm, or maybe it was because she knew that he knew it as well. Tall and good-looking, with those melting blue eyes and dark hair, he had only to look at a woman and smile to get what he wanted. Any other woman, that was, besides herself.

And it pleased her inordinately to know she had something he wanted so much.

She could see him staring at her over the rim of his mug of coffee, could see the way his eyes were weighing her mood as he tried to decide how best to convince her. She felt a sudden flush of power over him, a feeling that was entirely alien to her. It left her nearly giddy

212

with the realization of what that strength could do for her.

He put his coffee mug down and leaned across the table to her.

"Look, Sam," he said, "you know you can't sell her to Prescott. You'll hate yourself for the rest of your life if you do that."

"Will I?" she asked.

He scowled, but went on, pretending he hadn't heard.

"I can't pay you as much as Prescott can, but I can do better than that. I can give you eight hundred, everything I have, plus a quarter share of the *Lady*'s profits. It was your father's idea. That way, you'll never be in want."

Sam shrugged, unimpressed.

"Assuming, that is, you don't run her aground or sink her in a storm, or do any of a hundred other things that would make a quarter share of her profits a quarter share of nothing. I have no intention of sitting here in Edgartown waiting for the *Lady* to come home while you're out sinking her."

"For God's sake," Jason shouted, finally giving vent to his own growing anger with her. "You know I'm a damn good captain."

"So was my father," she shouted back. "Until he lost his leg. He could have kept sailing with her. But he didn't. Instead, he had her tied up to this wharf and drank himself to death."

Her words startled him, but they mollified him as well.

"We both know it wasn't the leg, Sam," he said softly. "He started to die a little bit every day after your mother's death. The leg was just an excuse."

She put her hand to her mouth and gasped softly. For a moment, Jason thought she might start to cry. He almost hoped she would. He could comfort her, and then,

213

perhaps, she might be more open to persuasion. In any case, he could understand a woman in tears a lot more easily than the calculating, unfeeling creature sitting across the table from him.

But she didn't cry. Instead, she took two long, deep breaths, and settled herself.

"I know all that," she said. "But it really doesn't change anything, does it? He's still dead, and I'm still here, with the *Lady* and nothing else."

"Then you're going to sell to Prescott?" he asked her.

Sam considered his expression. The truth was, until that moment she really had had no idea what she ought to do. She knew she couldn't go on indefinitely as she was, living alone on the *Lady Alyssa*. She had almost no money, and she had to eat, after all. Still, she knew she'd sooner starve than sell her father's ship.

But as she sat staring at Jason she realized she really didn't have to leave the ship. The *Lady Alyssa* had, after all, been one of the fastest clippers to cross the Atlantic. Her father had once earned a very handsome livelihood with her. And with a little help, she might be able to do the same thing.

She shook her head. "No, I won't sell to Prescott, not if you want her."

He furrowed his brow. "But I thought you just said you weren't interested in my offer."

"I'm not," she agreed. "But I'll make you a counteroffer, and it's the only one you get. You keep your eight hundred; you'll need it for repairs in any event. She needs all new sails, and there's some rot in the stern. You see, I'm being perfectly honest with you."

"If you don't want my money, what *do* you want?" he asked, his tone guarded, as though he weren't quite sure what to expect from her.

"In return for making her seaworthy," Sam replied, "I will deed over to you forty-nine percent of the *Lady* and make you her captain."

Jason's eyes narrowed. He wouldn't own the ship as he wanted, but it wouldn't bankrupt him either, to buy the *Lady*, and he'd still be her captain. And with any luck, forty-nine percent of her profits could enable him to buy her outright in a few years' time, far sooner than he'd be able to save enough for another ship were he to go on taking berths as a mate. It sounded too good to be true.

"Those are your terms?" he asked, bewildered as to why she was suddenly being so reasonable.

She nodded. "With one other stipulation," she said.

Jason groaned internally. He'd been right. It really *was* too good to be true.

"Which is?" he asked.

Sam shrugged as though what she were about to add was simply a minor addendum.

"I sail with you to keep an eye on my fifty-one percent of the *Lady*," she said.

"You can't be serious."

"I am completely serious," she told him. "After all, the *Lady* is my home."

Jason waved a hand in a gesture of dismissal.

"It's impossible," he told her. "An unmarried woman on board a trading vessel. Impossible."

She shrugged, unruffled by his objection.

"Then I suppose I will be forced to marry you," she said. "After all, business is business."

She ignored his startled gasp of disbelief.

"That wasn't amusing, Sam," Jason hissed at her. "I'd never thought you the sort to make tasteless jokes."

"I wasn't joking," she replied evenly.

"We can't so much as carry on a civil conversation for longer than half an hour."

215

"I said this is business, Jason," Sam interrupted as she picked up her dropped biscuit and tore off a piece, "not romance. If you refuse to have an unwed woman on board, then I'll simply become a married woman. In name, at least. I have no intention of becoming a wife to you, nor need you expect to change your present manner of living to accommodate one." She put the piece of biscuit into her mouth and chewed it slowly. Once she had swallowed, she smiled at him, pleased to see how completely unprepared he was for her offer, delighting in his look of confusion. "Those are my terms. You may accept them or not, as you like."

"I'll need a while to think," he told her.

"Take as long as you like," she agreed. "Five minutes, even ten."

She smiled sweetly at him, her eyes wide with child-like innocence, as though she had suggested nothing more momentous than inviting him to a second cup of coffee. She lifted her mug and sipped the hot liquid, concentrating on the warmth as it slowly drifted into her stomach.

"I don't have much choice, do I?" he asked. "You know as well as I do that if you won't sell me the *Lady*, it would take me years working as a mate to save enough money to buy my own ship."

"That is assuming you can continue to find unsuspecting captains willing to take you on," Sam interjected. "How many different berths have you had since you sailed with my father, Jason? Four? Five? It would seem you have a problem dealing with authority."

Jason scowled. It was true and he knew it. He hated following orders he knew were wrong. And he also knew that sooner or later he would get into real trouble if he didn't have his own ship.

"So it would seem that it is my name for your clipper," he mused softly.

Sam sipped her coffee. "You made the condition, Jason. I merely suggested a way to meet it."

He pushed the bench back and stood. "All right, Sam. You have a bargain. I'll arrange for the repairs to be started as soon as possible."

Sam grinned. "And I'll have my uncle Matthew draw up the papers," she said. "We want everything all legal and proper."

Jason grunted. "Legal and proper, is it?" he asked. He stood looking down at her. "Despite all appearances to the contrary, it would seem that you've grown up lately, Sam. And I never even noticed it."

Sam only looked up at him and grinned.

Chapter Two

Jason was as good as his word. Two days later, they met in front of the law office of Sam's uncle Matthew on Water Street, shook hands, and went inside. There, under Matthew's watchful eye, they signed partnership papers and a marriage contract.

During the short meeting, Sam thought she caught an admiring glance from Matthew. She took that to mean her uncle thought she'd made a shrewd bargain, and she found herself feeling, for a few moments at least, very smug and pleased with herself for having come to an arrangement that even her money-grasping uncle could appreciate. After a bit of reflection, however, she realized that Matthew was probably simply relieved to find he no longer had to fear that his wife would insist he maintain a niece who was, from all indications, doomed to lifelong spinsterhood.

Jason left immediately after the formalities were completed to oversee the start of the repairs he'd ordered begun on the *Lady Alyssa*. As much as she would have liked to have joined him, Sam found herself commandeered by her aunt instead. Elinore was determined to make the most of this opportunity to celebrate her niece's marriage, and nothing Sam could say would dissuade her. In less than an hour Elinore had laid out the plans for the ceremony and the small celebration that would follow before the newlyweds were to leave on the *Lady Alyssa*'s first voyage in more than four years. Matters settled to her satisfaction, she then had Sam don her mother's wedding dress and began pinning it so that it might be altered.

"I could do this myself," Sam tried uselessly to protest as Elinore pinned the pale ivory silk bodice so that it hugged her midriff and waist.

"No, you can't," Elinore told her tartly through a mouthful of pins. "I won't have you appearing at your own wedding looking like a street urchin with a dress that doesn't fit."

Elinore went back to work, and Sam found herself staring at her reflection in the mirror. It was a beautiful dress, she decided, and when Elinore had done pinning it, she even found herself wondering for just a moment what Jason would think when he saw her in it.

"You see," Elinore said when she stood back to take in the effect, "I told you you'd be pretty if you took some pains with yourself. Now all we have to do is get rid of those spectacles and do something reasonable with that hair of yours."

But when Elinore reached for the pins that held Sam's hair in a tight bun at the nape of her neck, Sam backed away.

"This marriage is a business arrangement, Aunt," she said quickly. "Jason Stone and I will be partners, not lovers."

Despite her words, what Sam was thinking was something altogether different. *Better not to try too hard,* she told herself. *Better not to want to please him. Then it won't hurt when I discover that I can't.*

"A wedding is still a wedding," Elinore told her. "But I suppose I'm wasting my breath. You'll do just as you like, no matter what I say."

By the time Alyssa had extricated herself from her aunt's house, the morning was long past. When she returned to the wharf, she found there were already half a dozen workmen, Jason among them, busily prowling the *Lady Alyssa*'s deck.

For the next six weeks Sam woke every morning shortly

after dawn to the sounds of sawing and scraping and hammering, noise that continued each day until nearly sunset. Rotted planking was removed and repaired, the deck and hull scraped, repainted, and revarnished, and heaps of moldering canvas and cordage carted away to be replaced by fresh new sails and lines.

Once the repairs had begun, Sam found herself unable to stand idly by and watch the *Lady* being transformed without her help. She polished brass that hadn't been cleaned since money for polish had disappeared two years before, delighting each time she discovered the bright shine of golden metal beneath the dark stains. She carefully cleaned and polished every inch of the captain's cabin, preparing it for the *Lady*'s new captain and removing those few remaining items of her father's personal belongings that hadn't been sold long before to pay his gambling debts or for bottles of rum. And she personally disposed of the battered old galley furnishings, feeling every bit as much delight with the new pots, pans, and dishes Jason had purchased as might the most domesticated housewife.

The repairs progressed surprisingly quickly, and soon the odor of fresh spar varnish mixed with the scents of brass polish, new hemp, and canvas. Jason was anxious to make the ship fit and seaworthy, for he'd contracted to transport a cargo of Virginia tobacco from Williamsburg to Liverpool and he didn't want to lose his contract. When Sam protested the need to finish the repairs in less than six weeks and the fact that he'd agreed to the run without first consulting her, he countered by telling her how much they stood to earn for the trip. She quickly demurred. Even after paying a crew and deducting the cost of supplies, they would recoup the cost of all the repairs to the *Lady Alyssa* from the one trip alone.

And so it was with a pleasant sense of anticipation that on the first day of June, when the sun had nearly set and the workmen gone, Sam stood on the edge of the *Lady Alyssa*'s wharf at Jason's side. She stared up at the mermaid whose carved features, freshly painted and resembling the Alyssa for whom the ship had been named, supported the *Lady*'s bowsprit. She felt herself suddenly awash with a flush of sheer delight. She was dirty and exhausted, but she realized she was happy, happier than she'd been in more years than she could remember. She even found herself feeling a wave of fondness for Jason, thankful to him for making it all possible.

"You've transformed her, Jason," she murmured. "She looks the way she did the first time I laid eyes on her. She's beautiful."

Jason turned and glanced at Sam. Her cheek was smudged with dirt, her hair was wrapped haphazardly with a dingy scarf, her sleeves were rolled up to her elbows, and her hands and arms were undeniably filthy.

"More than I can say for you," he muttered.

She looked up at him and scowled. Any warmth she'd felt for him the moment before vanished. She knew what he was thinking, knew he was wondering, now that the time was getting close, how he had allowed himself to be convinced to accept her along with his captaincy and half share of the *Lady Alyssa*. Not that she could blame him altogether. He could have had his pick of any woman he wanted. She knew it must be hard for him to accept the fact that he was about to find himself tied to a plain, mousy little person rather than the beauty he no doubt would have expected to be his wife one day.

"I suppose that's because I don't care to be transformed," she told him in her most waspish tone. "Even if that were possible. But you needn't worry. I promise to be thoroughly clean and respectable Saturday morning. I won't completely disgrace you in front of your friends, assuming you've chosen to invite them to our wedding. Unless, that is, you care to back out?"

Jason gritted his teeth. "Meaning, I assume, you'd release me from our contract if I give up my share of the *Lady* after all I've put into her?" he asked.

221

She nodded. "Certainly," she told him.

"Now that she's seaworthy again, I suppose you could get a fine price for her from Prescott," he accused.

"I have no intention of leaving her," she snapped.

"Nor do I," he retorted. "I agreed to the bargain, and I intend to live by it. I'll go through with the wedding."

She considered his tone as he spoke the last sentence. There was something about it that made her think he considered the prospect about as appealing as walking a pirate's plank.

"However painful it may be?" she asked.

She wondered why it hurt her so much to realize that he considered that particular aspect of their near future with so much obvious distaste. She told herself she ought not to care what he thought. After all, the whole arrangement was nothing more than business. But she did.

"You were the one who made the stipulation that you sail with the *Lady*," he reminded her.

"And you agreed," she replied.

"Business is business," he said, aping the tone she'd used to him six weeks before.

And now it was his callousness that hurt her. She turned away from him, not wanting him to know what she felt. She told herself she ought not to feel as she did, that she'd inured herself over the years not to expect anything else, especially not from a man. Still, she couldn't keep away the hurt his disdain caused her, and that troubled her almost as much as his coldness pained her.

She nodded and murmured, "Yes, and this is strictly business."

"Then you'll realize it is strictly a matter of business when I tell you it's time you moved your belongings out of the mate's cabin and into mine," Jason went on.

She looked back at him, entirely perplexed and feeling just the smallest hint of pleasure that he might actually be suggesting they become husband and wife in fact as well as name.

222

"We both agreed—" she began.

"You needn't worry," Jason interrupted. "Your virtue will remain unsullied as far as I'm concerned. But the mate's cabin is for the ship's mate."

Whatever small rise of pleasure she'd had was squashed only too completely.

"I thought because I'd be serving as cook, and there would be one less crew . . ."

He shook his head. "You can't expect the mate to live with the rest of the crew, Sam. He needs his own cabin. It's a matter of discipline, if nothing else. A man can't be expected to unquestioningly obey a mate he sees in nothing but his socks every morning."

He was right, and Sam was ashamed she hadn't thought of all that herself. His cool logic, however, and his vehement assurances that he had no interest in her, left her once again feeling a stab of hurt and a rising wave of unexpected anger.

"Yes," she muttered. "I'll move my belongings first thing in the morning."

"You needn't worry about the sleeping arrangements," he went on. "I've already installed hooks for a hammock. I'll use that and leave you the bed. I'll try to give you as much privacy as possible."

His continued assurances of how safe she was with him only served to fuel that first spark of anger. It was bad enough knowing he found her unattractive, but the more he dwelled on the subject, the more she realized that he considered her with little more than contempt.

"Your thoughtfulness is overwhelming, Jason," she snapped.

He seemed bewildered by her sudden display of anger.

"You'll be done by tomorrow afternoon?" he asked. "Argus will want to bring his belongings on board tomorrow. After all, we sail Saturday with the afternoon tide."

They were to be married Saturday morning, Sam mused, but that was not what most occupied his thoughts.

It was the fear of losing his cargo that interested him, and nothing more.

"I know," she snapped as she stalked back toward the gangway to the *Lady Alyssa*'s deck. "The cargo of tobacco in Williamsburg won't wait forever." She stopped for a moment at the top of the gangway and stared down at him. "And business is business," she called back before she turned away once again and disappeared.

Jason didn't try to stop her or ask what was wrong. Women were curious creatures at best, he told himself. And Samantha Waverly was surely the most curious of them all.

Sam sat in her father's cabin, at her father's desk, with her father's pen in her hand. Only none of it was her father's any longer, she told herself firmly. Jason was captain of the *Lady Alyssa* now, and it was Jason's cabin, Jason's desk, and Jason's pen. There was only a minor amount of comfort in the fact that the diary sitting on the desk in front of her was entirely her own.

For the first time since that morning six weeks before when she'd awakened to find Jason in the galley, she felt overwhelmed by doubts. It was wrong, she told herself, wrong to have forced him into this marriage, wrong for her to think she could live her life with a man who so obviously cared nothing more about her than the fact that she brought as a dowry the captaincy he coveted. He'd made that fact only too clear to her that morning, going through the wedding ceremony with a stoic, determined expression on his face and then immediately leaving to return to the *Lady Alyssa* to oversee the final preparations for departure. He hadn't even so much as accompanied her to her aunt's house to eat a piece of their wedding cake.

She ought to have expected nothing else, she told herself as she dropped the pen and turned away from the diary, looking instead at the cabin that had once been so familiar

224

to her and that now seemed so entirely alien.

Jason's books filled the small shelf on the far wall by the bed, and it was Jason's shirt that hung on the peg on the back of the door. She told herself that this was her cabin as well as his, her home, but she found she couldn't quite believe it, no matter how many times she repeated the words. It had been her father's cabin for her whole life prior to that moment, and now it was suddenly Jason's. And she was nothing more than an interloper, someone who did not belong and whose presence was tolerated only because it could not be avoided.

She turned back to her diary, but the page was blurred and she realized her eyes were filled with tears. She removed the spectacles and let them fall to the surface of the desk.

"Oh, Papa," she murmured. "What have I done?"

There was no answer to her question, for the ghost she'd thought would always be there seemed to have disappeared, his place usurped, perhaps, like the cabin, by the *Lady's* new captain. But even if he had been there, even if she'd felt a comforting presence or thought she'd heard a friendly word murmured on the wind that blew through the porthole, Sam knew it could not change the fact that she and Jason were tied to each other until death parted them. They'd both gotten what they had wanted, she reminded herself, he his captaincy, while she had saved the *Lady Alyssa*. But at that moment the bargain suddenly seemed to have cost her far more than she could ever have imagined she would have to pay.

"We're about to sail, Sam. Don't you want to come out on deck?"

She turned around, startled. She hadn't even heard Jason open the door or enter the cabin. Seeing him standing in the doorway, she felt oddly guilty, as though she'd been caught doing something she ought not to be doing . . . although she couldn't imagine what that might be. She could feel her cheeks grow flushed and warm.

As startled as Sam was, Jason was even more bewildered as he stood looking down at her. He realized he hadn't seen her without the huge, ugly spectacles since she'd been a child. Without them, her eyes were large and warm, not even remotely owlish. And dressed as she was now, in her mother's wedding gown, which her aunt had altered to fit her, rather than one of the washed-out, worn, too-large dresses he was accustomed to seeing her wear, she looked small and delicate rather than skinny and unpleasantly angular. He found himself thinking she was actually pretty, and he even began to wonder what it would be like to remove the pins that held her hair in that tight little knot at the nape of her neck.

He smiled suddenly, although he wasn't quite sure why.

Sam reached hastily for her spectacles and put them on, relieved that once she had, she felt more settled, as if they afforded her some manner of safety. The blush faded from her cheeks and she stared up at him with a look he took to be thinly veiled dislike. The look, combined with the fact that she was once again staring owlishly up at him through the ugly spectacles, transformed her back into the Samantha Waverly he had expected to find. For an instant he wondered what illusion he could possibly have seen to make him think her attractive. And then he simply dismissed the matter altogether.

"I'll be along as soon as I've changed," she said.

"Change later," he told her. "The tide won't wait."

She nodded. "I'll be right there," she said, then watched him turn and leave. When he was gone, she picked up the pen, turned to a fresh page in the diary, and wrote in her neat, tight script:

June 6, 1804 Today, in the presence of Aunt Elinore and Uncle Matthew, I stood in front of the Reverend Merriweather and became the bride of Jason Stone.

226

If the wedding was a disappointment to Sam, sailing out of Edgartown Harbor was not. The *Lady Alyssa's* new white sails filled slowly with wind, and as they did, the clipper ship seemed to glide out of the harbor. The rows of neat white houses with their well-tended gardens and widow's walks grew slowly smaller until they looked like dollhouses clinging to the side of a small green rise at the water's edge. And then they were nothing more than pale dots, their features lost amidst the greenery that surrounded them and the blue of the water at their feet.

Sam closed her eyes, pressing the memory into her mind, wanting this to be the way she thought of the island, idyllic and welcoming in the afternoon sunshine, and not as it really had been for her the previous four years.

And then she turned her back on it, and looked out to sea.

Her heart leaped into her throat as she felt the wind rise and heard the new cordage straining against the weight of the wind-taut sails. This was what she'd really wanted, she told herself, to feel free as she did at that moment, to feel the wind tugging at her skirts and pulling her hair free of its pins. She began to laugh out loud with the sheer joy of it. Whatever it had cost her, it had been worth the price after all.

Within the hour Edgartown was nothing more than a memory, and the *Lady Alyssa* was skimming over the waves. It was like dancing, Sam thought, the feeling of the movement beneath her, like dancing or maybe taking flight. She knew only that she was in love with the sense of movement, in love with the realization that, for the first time in her life, she was free to make her own choices and live her own life.

"Not seasick, are you?"

She turned to find Jason standing behind her. He was staring at her oddly, the way he had for that single moment when they'd been below, and just as the look had then, once again it made her feel flustered and embarrassed. She turned away from him, looking back to the endless rows of waves.

"Certainly not," she told him. "I've sailed before."

Jason laughed. "I remember. It was my first berth and the last thing I expected was for the captain to bring his wife and daughter along. You were eight years old and a monster. I almost threw you overboard half a dozen times."

Sam couldn't help but smile at the memory. That trip had been the happiest time in her life. Shortly after they'd returned, her mother had died. After that, everything had changed, most especially her father.

"I don't remember it that way," she told him. "I remember you were almost nice to me at times."

He nodded. "I was trying to impress a new captain. I suppose I thought that if I was kind to you, he'd keep me on."

"It must have worked. He kept you on until he stopped sailing."

"And all these years I've deluded myself by thinking that was because I was good at my job."

He'd walked up close to her, Sam realized. She could feel the warmth of his body just behind her and a hint of what must be his breath against the back of her neck. For an instant that closeness startled her, and she would have given anything to have him put his arms around her. But then she reminded herself of what he'd done that morning, how he'd expended all his interest on the *Lady*'s sailing and hadn't enough left over for her to even spend a moment sharing a piece of their wedding cake. He'd made a point of telling her he thought their wedding not worth celebrating. She had received the message only too clearly.

She stepped away from him and turned back to face him.

"And I suppose now it's time for me to prove I'm capable of performing my job," she said. "I'll go below and start dinner. It'll be suppertime soon."

Jason nodded. "That's what I came to remind you of," he

said.

Sam told herself she might have known. The *Lady Alyssa*'s captain was getting hungry and he wanted the cook to prepare his supper.

She nodded. "With your leave, Captain Stone," she muttered as she edged past him.

She marched forward to the hatchway to the galley, not quite understanding the anger with him that was churning inside her. As she turned into the hatchway, she bumped into Michael Argus, the mate, coming up onto deck.

"Pardon, Mrs. Stone," the burly mate murmured in apology.

"It was my fault entirely, Mr. Argus," she replied as she slid past him.

But although she dismissed the small mishap, she could not quite forget the mate's words. He'd called her Mrs. Stone, and she realized that that was the first time she'd been called by her new name. Odd, she thought as she tied an apron around her waist, that it hadn't startled her or even seemed strange.

And odder still, she mused, that she was beginning her honeymoon by preparing dinner for eight men, all of them strangers to her, including, it seemed, her new husband.

It was dark when Jason finally left the *Lady*'s deck. He knocked softly on the door to his cabin before he opened the door. There was no response to his knock, and he pushed the door open a few inches to stare inside. It was dark save for one lantern that had been turned low. Its pale light picked out the white of the hammock hanging in the center of the cabin. Obviously Sam had strung it up for him before she'd retired.

"Sam?" he whispered as he moved inside, wondering if she might still be awake.

Again he was met with only silence. He pulled the door closed behind him and began to undress silently in the near darkness. Before he climbed into the hammock, however, he moved to the bedside and stood staring down at his new wife's sleeping features.

For the third time that day he was startled by what he saw. The first time had been when he'd come upon her writing in her diary and the second when he'd approached her earlier on the deck and gazed at her, feeling a surge of surprise when he saw the wind blowing her hair free of its pins and a strangely evocative glow lighting her dark eyes, a glow that hadn't even been muted by the spectacles. Now, even shrouded as she was by the blanket that was pulled up to her neck, she seemed oddly vulnerable. A surprisingly lush mass of auburn hair lay spread out on the pillow, framing her face, and the lamplight softened her skin, giving it a pale, golden glow. Dark-auburn lashes just touched her cheeks beneath her eyes. Funny, he thought, that he'd never noticed how long and thick they were.

His hand seemed to reach out of its own volition, his fingers lightly caressing her cheek and brushing against the thick mass of curls on her pillow. He didn't know why he did it, and he drew his hand back quickly, afraid he might awaken her.

He backed away from the bed, wondering how she could seem so appealing to him when he knew she was anything *but* appealing, when he knew she had one interest in her life and one interest only—the ship her father had left to her. He blew out the lamp, then climbed into the hammock she'd hung for him, murmuring the words she had used more times than he cared to think about: "Business is business." It wasn't hard to remind himself just what sort of bargain they had made with each other.

Sam didn't move until she heard the regular sound of breathing and was sure he was asleep. Then she turned and looked toward the shadow that she knew was him, staring into the darkness and wondering what he had been thinking when he'd stood over her, when he'd touched her cheek. For she hadn't been asleep as she'd pretended then, nor had she been oblivious to the sight of his body as he'd stripped off his clothing. She closed her eyes and the sight of his naked torso filled her mind, intriguing, frighteningly arousing, the memory of the way she'd pretended to sleep as she'd watched him making her squirm with guilt and a sure feeling of having sinned.

It was no good, she told herself, and reminded herself of what he'd murmured when he'd climbed into his hammock. She'd heard regret in those words. She told herself he had one thing to regret and one thing only. Everything about their arrangement pleased him save for their marriage and her presence.

She turned round, facing the wall, telling herself she didn't care what he thought. But as much as she tried to force herself to sleep, she remained uncomfortably awake the whole of the night, fighting with the demons that told her she had sold her happiness for the fresh sails and sound planking that now enabled the *Lady Alyssa* to slide through the Atlantic's dark waves.

Each time they accused her and told her that one day soon she would regret the bargain, she swore to herself they were wrong. Still, she knew otherwise, knew she already regretted what she'd done even as she knew there was no way to change any of it.

Chapter Three

Sam's first look of Liverpool was a decided disappointment. She stood on the *Lady Alyssa*'s deck as the cargo of tobacco was being unloaded and stared up at the wealth of small, dirty buildings clinging to the sides of the winding streets near the wharves. It was only too obvious that more of them than she could count housed brothels and drinking establishments. Most of the rest looked like warehouses, dingy, charmless structures that only made the rows of brothels and alehouses seem even more depressing.

Whatever civilized part of the city lay beyond, she quickly decided, could hardly impress her after the introduction that met her eye at the harbor. She assumed that the houses were cleaner where the respectable people of the city lived, that there would be some shops and churches, but she lacked any great desire to see them. She'd spent the whole of her life in a harbor town, and this one, she told herself, could not possibly offer any enticements she could not easily deny herself.

At least that was what she told herself as she politely refused Jason's invitation to join him on an excursion the following afternoon once the cargo had been offloaded.

"I have the accounts to attend to," she told him by way of excuse.

"You'll have two weeks to ponder over the pennies, Sam," he told her. "That shipment of crystal Carmichael promised us isn't ready. We'll have to sit here and wait for it if I can't find anything else."

For a moment, Sam was tempted. The possibility that Jason might actually want to spend time away from the *Lady Alyssa* with her, time he was not strictly obliged to spend in her presence, was more than a little flattering. She wavered, part of her wanting very much to accept his invitation.

Before she did, however, the part of her that had grown wary of men over the years told her she ought not let herself assume things she had no right to assume. He was probably only trying to be polite. Besides, if she accepted his invitation to join him, she'd only succeed in making the two of them uncomfortable. After all, he was at liberty after nearly two weeks at sea. He doubtless would be better amused by any one of the wealth of whores who roamed the wharf area than he could possibly be in her company.

She shook her head. "I think I'd better tend to the accounts," she said.

"Suit yourself, then," he told her as he shrugged and left.

Samantha sat at the desk once he'd gone, telling herself she'd done the right thing, that he certainly hadn't shown any great regret that she wasn't joining him. Still, she couldn't keep herself from thinking how pleasant it might have been, from thinking that he might really want to show her the city.

She ended her internal battle by telling herself that thinking the worst only made her miserable and that she ought to have taken his invitation at face value. If they were to go on as they were, they should at least become friends. Perhaps an afternoon roaming the city might ease the tension that had been growing between them since they'd left Edgartown.

She snatched up her coat and darted after him, taking the stairs up to the *Lady*'s deck two at a time. Once there, she stood and pulled on her coat, scanning the waterfront for Jason and finding him and Argus amongst the crowd on the busy street that fronted the wharves.

But before she had the chance to call out to him, she saw two women leave a doorway where they had been loitering in the hopes of finding a willing sailor and approach Jason and the mate. She didn't need to hear what was being said as the women draped themselves on Jason and Argus's arms. Their movements were more explicit than words could possibly be

233

and even Samantha was not so naive as to mistake them.

She turned her back on the foursome and returned below, running away from what she'd seen. She told herself she'd fled because she didn't want Jason to see her or to think she'd been spying on him. But all the while, even when she told herself she ought to have expected nothing else, still she knew she was fleeing from the sight of him going off with the whores.

Jason put his mug down on the table, pushed his chair back, and stood.

"I'll be wishing you and the lovelies a good day, Mr. Argus," he said with a grin.

"What's this, Captain?" Michael Argus asked. "You're not leaving?"

"I'm afraid so, Mr. Argus," Jason told him. "I don't relish the thought of waiting around for Carmichael's shipment. I think I'll see if there isn't something else to be found."

"But you can't go now, ducks," one of the women said, smiling up at him. "We're just all gettin' to be friends."

"The ladies will be heartbroken if you leave, Captain," Argus said. He put one arm around the waist of each whore and the three stared up at Jason.

"I'm sure you're man enough to be able to salve their loss," Jason told the mate with a wide grin as he reached into his pocket, withdrew some coins, and dropped them onto the table. "Have a few more rounds on me, Mr. Argus, and enjoy your evening."

Jason exited the alehouse, mildly surprised that he didn't feel so much as a pang of regret at the thought of leaving his mate and the two women. Ordinarily he enjoyed his first hours of freedom after a voyage as much as any sailor, but on this particular afternoon he couldn't find the right mood to enter into the games Argus and the women would soon be playing. And that fact quite bewildered him.

It was the weight of his responsibility as the *Lady Alyssa's* captain, he told himself. There was too much he could be doing to think of wasting the afternoon in an alehouse. There were at least two dozen exporters he could see to try to find a cargo ready to leave.

But as he walked along the crowded streets, he realized his mind wasn't entirely on business. For no reason he could explain to himself, his thoughts kept drifting to Sam. He couldn't keep himself from thinking about the way she'd looked in her wedding dress, about the way she looked when she slept. The resentment he'd felt toward her for the bargain that tied their marriage to his captaincy had begun to fade. As bewildering as the situation seemed to him, he realized he'd even begun to think of her in an entirely unbusinesslike fashion.

He found his eye being drawn to the goods displayed in the shop windows, to the displays of kidskin gloves and fine leather shoes, to the signs proclaiming the availability of the best silk and sheerest lawn available to be made into fashionable ladies garments. It would be worth the investment, he told himself, to see what a new wardrobe might do to transform his ragamuffin of a wife. At worst, it would mean he wouldn't have to look at her in those unbecoming and worn old things she wore.

And at best, he mused, but then quickly drew back, not letting himself make any assumptions. Perhaps, he told himself, it wasn't yet quite time to think of what the best might be.

"Are you still worrying over the accounts, Sam?" Jason asked as he walked into the cabin and found her just as he had left her nearly six hours before, leaning over the desk with the account book open in front of her.

She looked up, startled to see him there. She'd thought he'd stay away that night, thought he'd take advantage of the freedom of a night in port. But when her eyes met his, she found she couldn't continue to look up at him. He seemed so pleased with himself, so smugly satisfied.

"I do own fifty-one percent of the *Lady*," she reminded him as she returned her attention to the rows of figures in front of her. "That means fifty-one percent of her profits are mine. It seems only reasonable that I keep an eye on my investment."

He put his hand down in the middle of the page, forcing her attention back to him, and leaned forward to her.

"Are you suggesting I'm trying to cheat you, Sam?" he asked with a crooked smile.

He was close enough for her to realize there was a hint of rum on his breath. Sam knew the scent well enough to recognize it, too well in fact. Its presence only confirmed what she'd suspected.

She pulled back.

"No, I don't think you're trying to cheat me," she told him. "I just think that one of us ought to be reasonable and businesslike if we're to make our arrangement a profitable one."

"Is that what you are," he asked her thoughtfully, "reasonable and businesslike?"

"I'd like to think so," she replied.

He shook his head. "I think otherwise, Sam," he told her. "I think what you are is afraid."

"Don't be ridiculous," she retorted. "What would I have to be afraid of?"

"Of enjoying yourself," he told her. "Of being human."

She pushed her chair back, stood, and crossed to the far side of the cabin. "I don't think this conversation warrants being continued," she said. "We can talk tomorrow, when you're sober."

"I'm sober now," he told her.

"Are you?" she hissed. "Do you really mean to tell me you haven't been drinking?"

"As you ask so politely, I'll admit that I've had a drink," he said. "That doesn't mean I'm drunk."

But Sam wasn't interested in explanations. She told herself she'd already heard a lifetime of explanations, already heard all the excuses she ever wanted to hear. She'd had to listen to them from her father, but there was no need for her to listen to them from Jason.

"I've heard it all before, Jason," she snapped, then turned

away, not wanting to look at him, not wanting to be faced with the lies she knew she ought to expect to follow. That was the procedure—first excuses, then lies. Maybe her aunt Elinore was right, maybe all sailors really were the same. "A hundred times. A thousand times. It never changed anything, no matter what he said."

"He?" Jason asked. "Just who are we talking about now, Sam?"

She swallowed. He was right. What her father had done should have no bearing on Jason.

"Papa," she admitted. "That's how it was with Papa."

He followed her, crossing the cabin in a few long strides and stopping just behind her.

"I'm not your father, Sam," he told her firmly. He put his hands on her arms and turned her back to face him. "And you *are* afraid."

"Don't be a fool," she said.

"It's true and you know it."

He didn't release his hold on her, and they stood for a moment, his hands on her arms keeping her still, their eyes meeting. Sam wasn't sure whether she was angry with him or if she was simply miserable, aching with the hurt he'd done her by going off with a whore and now returning to her with his belly full of rum. All she knew was that there was a thick, aching ball of grief inside her. It had begun to form the morning of their wedding, and it had been growing larger and more painful ever since.

"Let me go," she said finally in a ragged whisper.

He nodded. "In a minute," he replied.

Then he pulled her to him, wrapped his arms around her, and pressed his lips to hers.

His lips were firm and warm against hers, and tasted slightly of the rum he'd drunk. But what Sam noticed most about them wasn't the taste or even the feel of them, but rather the fact that they seemed capable of sending a thick ripple of liquid fire through her. It slipped through her veins, leaving her feeling as though she was melting inside. Nothing had ever made her feel like that before, nothing had ever

237

seemed so overwhelmingly powerful in the effect it had on her.

It occurred to her that he had been right. She was afraid. She was afraid of him.

When finally he released her she was no longer quite sure that that was what she wanted him to do.

She looked up at him, and found he was smiling. For an instant she felt a wave of intense anger, for she realized that he knew precisely what he'd done to her. But it seeped away quickly. She couldn't deny that what she really wanted was for him to do it again, to make her feel that way again.

"I almost forgot," he said as he put his hand into his jacket pocket.

"Forgot?" she asked.

He pulled out a small bottle and held it out to her. "All that money we earned was burning a hole in my pocket," he told her.

She took the bottle. "For me?" she asked, bewildered now and not quite sure what to think. Was this some sort of peace offering? she wondered. Or was it just a polite thank-you, an exchange for not making a fuss about his spending the day in the company of a whore?

He nodded. "Open it."

She pulled the small cork and sniffed at the contents. "Perfume?" she asked. "I've never had any perfume."

He grinned, surprised to realize how delighted he was that she seemed pleased with his offering. "Just lavender water, Sam. I'm not good at this sort of thing."

"Thank you," she murmured. She was blushing, and she knew it. "It was very kind of you."

And at that moment he remembered again how pretty she'd seemed dressed in her wedding dress. It might have been just a mirage, he told himself. Or it might have been something else. He glanced at her ill-fitting dress.

"Why don't we spend a little more of those profits you've been carefully accounting?" he suggested. "We could visit a dressmaker tomorrow. It's about time you had a new dress or two."

Sam felt a glow of pleasure seeping into her. It didn't really matter what he'd done that afternoon, she told herself. He'd kissed her. And he wanted to buy her something pretty. Perhaps he really did care something for her after all.

But the glow faded as quickly as it had come.

"There won't be time," she murmured.

"Unfortunately, the only thing we have for the next two weeks is time," he replied. "Carmichael's cargo is all there is to be had, and that means we have nothing to do but wait."

She shook her head.

"We have a cargo, and we leave in two days' time."

He shook his head. "I've been to every exporter in town this afternoon," he told her. "There's nothing."

That surprised her. How, she wondered, could he have seen exporters if he'd been with the whore she'd seen him meet on the street? But that mystery would have to wait to be considered. She had to tell him what she'd done, had to show him that her presence on the *Lady Alyssa* wasn't a useless waste of space.

"Apparently you missed one," she said. "A Mr. Palmer. Cecil Palmer."

Jason shook his head. "I never heard of him."

"I'm sure there are at least a score or two individuals in Liverpool you've never met, Jason," she said in a slightly sarcastic tone.

"How did you find him?" he asked.

She shrugged. "He found me. He arrived this afternoon and offered us the shipment."

"What is it?" He was more than a little bewildered, unable to understand how he'd managed to miss a shipment ready and begging for transport.

She returned to the side of the desk, lifted a sheet of paper from beneath the account book and handed it to him. "Farming implements," she told him, relieving him of the necessity of reading the list. "Shovels, hoes, pick axes."

"Looks fine," he said as he glanced down the list. "But what about Carmichael's crystal? We stood to make a good profit on it."

"That's the best part," she told him with a wide grin, delighted now, sure he would be pleased with what she'd done. "We'll be back here with more than enough time to take on Carmichael's shipment. Mr. Palmer's shovels go to Alexandria. Three or four days there, three or four back, and we'll still be back in plenty of time for Carmichael. And we'll be earning a hundred and fifty pounds." She smiled up at him smugly, sure he'd be pleased.

He wasn't. He shook his head. "No," he said. Nothing more, just the single word.

Sam couldn't believe what she'd heard. The warmth that had lingered following his kiss suddenly vanished, washed away by a wave of anger.

"What do you mean, no?"

"Just what I said. No. We don't take your Mr. Palmer's shipment."

Sam couldn't believe he was being so dictatorial. There was no reason for it that she could see, other than the fact that he didn't like her taking an active part in a business where she had every right to do just that.

"I'm afraid we do," she replied in a sharp, waspish tone. "I've already agreed."

"Then you'll just have to unagree," he told her. "I'm not taking the *Lady* anywhere near the Barbary Coast, and that's all there is to it."

"You're being absurd," she accused.

"No, I'm being practical," he countered. "Or haven't you read a newspaper in the last two years? Those waters aren't exactly safe, especially for ships flying the American flag."

"Of course I've heard of the pirates," she snapped.

"They aren't really pirates," he said. "Not the way you think of them. They aren't a few bands of sea-roving brigands who are hunted by every country's authorities. They are, in effect, the navy of those nations that harbor them, operating with the full cooperation of their bashaw, or whatever it is they call their damned kings."

"But President Jefferson has sent the Navy to patrol the area, to ensure the safety of ships like the *Lady Alyssa*."

"All the more reason for us to stay away," he said. "Or haven't you heard that waters where ships are flinging cannon balls at one another aren't quite safe?"

"You said yourself that the *Lady Alyssa* is one of the fastest clippers you've ever sailed on," she countered. "If we see any trouble, all we have to do is get out of the way."

Jason took a deep breath, forcing himself to remain reasonably calm. Why was it, he wondered, they always ended in battles of this sort? Why couldn't she simply accept his word?

"Yes, the *Lady*'s fast, Sam," he said, pronouncing the words very carefully, as though he were teaching a lesson to a very slow pupil, a lesson that he ought not to have been obliged to teach. "She's fast if she has winds with her and plenty of open water. The Mediterranean doesn't always afford that. I'm not risking my ship by taking her anywhere near the Barbary Coast. We are definitely not taking this cargo!"

"We're not giving up a hundred and fifty pounds sterling because you're afraid of a few North African bullies," Sam retorted. "And she's not your ship. She's *ours*."

"Damn it, you don't know what you're doing," he shouted. "I'm the *Lady*'s captain. I determine where she sails and what cargo she takes on. You can't make those decisions."

"Oh yes I can," Sam shouted back at him. "I can and I have." She slapped her hand down on the open account book. "You forget, Mr. Stone, that I own fifty-one percent of this ship. Fifty-one percent. That means I am the controlling owner, and *that* means I decide where we go and where we don't go. We're taking this cargo of Mr. Palmer's to Alexandria. And if you don't like it, then I'm afraid I'll have to find the *Lady* another captain."

"You can't do that!"

Sam straightened her back, standing as tall as she could, refusing to be bullied by him. She should have known it would come to this, should have known he'd want to take complete control of the *Lady* and relegate her to the role of cook or mere passenger. Well, she wasn't going to sit by and meekly become some submissive, agreeable female because

241

that would suit him. That was why she'd agreed to sell him only forty-nine percent of the *Lady*. It was still her ship, and she intended to hold on to it no matter what he thought.

"I can and I will," she shouted back. "The *Lady* will be perfectly safe. I will not lose a hundred and fifty pounds without a rational reason."

"Doesn't anything have any meaning to you but business?" he demanded. "Does everything have to be weighed in dollars and cents for you?"

She turned her back on him. It was no good going on with the argument. He would simply have to come around or she would make good on her threat to find another captain, and that was that.

"I've made my decision," she said. "You can choose to continue to sail as the *Lady*'s captain or not, as you see fit. The discussion is over, Jason."

"Damn it," he hissed. "Let it be on your head, then."

He stalked from the cabin, slamming the door closed behind him.

Chapter Four

Sam wiped her still-soapy hands on a towel, then hung it on a peg to dry. She'd finished washing the dishes from the crew's dinner and cleaning up the galley. No matter how hard she tried, she couldn't think of any further excuse to remain below, especially when what she really wanted to do was go up on deck, look at the scenery, and watch the sun set.

It was no use trying to avoid Jason any longer, she told herself as she climbed the aft ladder to the *Lady*'s deck. They each knew how the other felt about this trip, and each knew they couldn't budge the other's attitude. It was a standoff between them, tense and uncomfortable.

Once they'd delivered the cargo and collected their hundred and fifty pounds, he'd come around, she told herself. So she might just as well enjoy the last of what appeared to be a glorious spring evening, even if it meant ignoring, or at least pretending to ignore, Jason's foul mood.

He'd been extremely conservative from the moment the *Lady* had entered the Mediterranean, staying fairly close to the northern coast even though it meant it would take them a good deal longer to reach Alexandria than it might otherwise have done. Still, she'd made no complaint. They had time to spare, and she wasn't about to challenge his right as captain to determine the *Lady*'s course. Her share of the *Lady* might buy her the determining vote as to what cargo they take on, but she was just as aware as any sailor that once a ship had left port, her captain was as near to God as

243

those sailing with him were ever likely to know. She was in no position to challenge that authority even if Jason had given the slightest indication that he was of a mind to listen, something he most decidedly had not done.

Besides which, the detour had afforded her the opportunity to catch a glimpse of the Spanish, Italian, and Greek coasts. She had to admit she was charmed by the constantly changing scenery. It was all so different from Edgartown, different from anything she'd ever seen before. She told herself she would never tire of standing on the *Lady*'s deck and watching the world slowly drift past her. Given the opportunity, she'd gladly spend her life doing nothing else.

When she reached the deck, however, she discovered that there was no longer any hint of land in view. There was little to see but the azure blue of the Mediterranean and the steadily deepening blue of the sky.

"Come to share the lookout, have you? I suppose you wouldn't want to miss a glimpse of any pirates we might stumble across."

Sam only needed to hear his voice to know that Jason was behind her. And she needed nothing more than his terse and baiting tone to tell her he still hadn't forgiven her.

She decided to ignore his mood, to pretend they were on perfectly normal terms.

"We're no longer skirting the Greek coast?" she asked.

"We turned our back to the last of Greece more than six hours ago," he told her. "Much as I would like to stay to safer waters, we can't afford to be roaming around the islands of the Aegean for the next two or three weeks. We're headed due south, to Egypt."

And he isn't at all happy about that fact, Sam told herself.

"How long will it take to reach Egypt?" she asked.

She finally turned to face him, smiling, hoping to avoid any unpleasantness by showing she was willing to be agreeable if he was, willing to make up their differences if he had any inclination to as well.

He shrugged, ignoring the smile or any invitation it might imply.

"It depends on the winds," he replied. "They're tricky here this time of the year. If we're lucky we'll make landfall by tomorrow noon. Assuming, that is, that storm holds off."

Sam looked up. There were a few clouds scuttling across the sky and the western horizon was streaked with deep purple, not red as it had been the previous nights at sunset, but there was no sign, as far as she could see, of a pending storm.

"It looks clear enough," she murmured.

He shook his head. "It tastes like rain."

She didn't argue. She'd come to realize that he had an uncanny ability to sense the weather. Even if he hadn't, however, she would have let the assertion pass. It struck her that she quite simply did not want to fight with him anymore.

Over the preceding few days she'd realized that she was not quite as independent as she would have liked to think herself. Her threat to find a new captain for the *Lady* might have angered Jason, but it had frightened her far more. And at that moment, she realized she needed him, and not just to captain the *Lady Alyssa*. Without him, she was quite literally completely alone, and like it or not, she had to admit she was terrified by that thought. It had been easy to tell him in a heated moment that neither she nor the *Lady Alyssa* needed him, but the prospect was far from easy to accept once the anger had passed. However little the fact pleased her, she was completely dependent upon him and she knew it.

Part of her was willing to admit it to him, even if the admission seemed to her like complete surrender. She wished she could think of some way of telling him how she felt without giving up everything, most especially her pride, to him.

But it was more than that, she admitted to herself, more

than the fear of being alone. As much as she would have liked to forget the way she'd felt when he'd kissed her, she found her thoughts continually returning to those brief moments when he'd held her in his arms. And each time she remembered, she knew she wanted to feel that way again. Whether Jason knew it or not, he held a power over her, and that realization terrified Sam more than anything she had ever imagined, for it meant she was falling in love with him. It was the worst thing she could do, she realized, and it meant she was nothing more than a silly fool. But still she could not change it however much she might wish to.

At that moment, all she could think to say was, "It seems a nice enough evening now."

He lifted his brow, his expression superior. A glance at his expression made Sam realize that he had already mentally dismissed her. She felt herself cringe inwardly when she saw it, for it only made her realize that much more clearly how unimportant she was to him. She felt a wave of sick dread inside her. She was falling in love with him, and he quite clearly wanted nothing more than to be rid of her.

"For those who think themselves safe, I suppose it is," he told her. "I'll leave you your solitude to enjoy it."

With that, he turned and left her standing, staring after him.

When Sam awoke, the cabin was absolutely pitch-black. The *Lady Alyssa* was heaving beneath her, and when she sat up, she found she had to hold on to the side of the narrow bed to keep herself steady until she got her bearings.

She assumed it was the storm Jason had promised that had awakened her, the clash of thunder, or perhaps just the erratic movement of pounding waves beneath the *Lady*'s hull.

"Jason?" she murmured into the darkness.

She really didn't expect him to answer. He'd be on deck in a storm, she told herself. Probably he'd never left it, expecting rough weather to arrive as he had. She carefully felt along the shelf at the foot of the bed for the box of matches she knew was there, then, when she found it, withdrew a match and lit it. The flare seemed blinding after the inky darkness, and she let it burn too long before her eyes adjusted. She had to shake out the flame and strike a second in order to light the wick of the lantern hanging from the ceiling.

She found, much as she expected, that Jason's hammock was empty. For a moment she sat on the edge of her bed, staring at it as it swayed back and forth from the pegs on which it was hung. It was almost hypnotic, that rhythmic swaying motion, and for a while she sat as though she were incapable of doing anything more than watching it.

But a deafening noise startled her out of the trance. The *Lady* shook with the force of it, and Sam was compelled to cling to the beam that supported the bed.

"That wasn't thunder," she whispered aloud.

Finding her own voice was less than steady only made her realize she was afraid.

She edged her way to the side of the cabin and put her face close to the cool glass of the porthole. Staring out did little but tell her that Jason had been right the previous evening. A storm *had* been brewing. She could see nothing except an endless stream of falling rain.

It was no good, she realized, for her to think she could sit where she was, not knowing what that horrible boom had been. Her mind filled with all sorts of gruesome possibilities, and the most gruesome of all was that the *Lady* had been set upon by pirates.

She'd never heard cannon fire, but now she found herself wondering if the noise she'd heard meant they were being fired on. Was it possible that Jason had been right about the possibility of meeting pirates in these waters? The vision sprang up in her mind of a band of dirty, mustached, and bearded men, coarse and leering, brandishing bloody knives and swords. She shuddered.

This is insane, she told herself as she firmly pulled herself together. *I can't just sit here, alone, quivering in the darkness, frightened by my own fantasies.*

In all probability, what she'd heard had been the sounds of the storm. Thunder. Wind in the *Lady*'s cordage. An angry wave beating against the hull. She'd let Jason's talk of pirates make her imagination run wild.

And that was probably just what he'd intended, she told herself. He probably thought that if he frightened her enough, she'd give up her share of control of the *Lady* and leave it all to him. That was, after all, what he'd wanted from the start, his own ship, free and unencumbered, and that meant without her. He'd married her for the *Lady Alyssa*. He wouldn't stop at frightening her a bit if he thought it meant she might agree to staying in Edgartown at the end of this voyage while he ran his little kingdom just as he pleased. And what he pleased was without her.

Well, she wasn't going to sit in the cabin cringing like a frightened little mouse. And she'd be damned if she was going to give up the *Lady Alyssa*.

She got her father's old slicker out of a cupboard and pulled it on over her nightdress as she started out of the cabin and up to the deck.

Once on deck, Sam began to wonder if she hadn't taken some horribly wrong turn somewhere and fallen into a nightmare. The deck was heaving beneath her feet, dropping away so suddenly and sharply that she seemed suspended in midair momentarily before she joined it, falling to her hands and knees, scrambling wildly to pull herself upright. Rain was falling in thick enough torrents to make seeing more than a foot or two in front of her nearly impossible. It washed along the smooth deck, rushing from side to side with the *Lady*'s movements until it finally reached the scuppers. Sam felt as though she were trying to wade upstream as she started to move aft in search of Jason.

She heard him before she saw him, his shouted orders loud and clear even in the clamor of the wind tearing through the rigging and the pounding of the rain against the *Lady*'s deck.

"Mr. Argus, unfurl the foremast!"

"Aye, Captain."

There was some sort of movement not far from her, and Sam assumed it was one or two of the crew, carrying out Jason's orders. She continued forward, holding on to any available handhold as she moved toward the wheel. She was completely bewildered, wondering why Jason would want to increase the sail when it seemed far more logical to reef it in a storm. It made no sense to her at all.

"Jason!" she cried out when she finally could make out his form standing at the wheel, fighting to keep the *Lady*'s bearing.

He darted a glance toward her.

"Get back below," he shouted. "You're only in the way here."

Sam didn't so much as stop her advance.

"Why are you unfurling more sail?" she demanded. "That's madness in a storm."

Whatever answer he might have been about to offer her was drowned out by the sound of another boom like the one she'd heard when she had been below. This time Sam knew she hadn't been imagining anything the first time. This time she saw the flash that accompanied the sound, a momentary gleam of light from a short distance behind the *Lady Alyssa*'s stern.

She had no doubt what the noise meant. The boom had been the sound of a cannon being fired.

The ball fell just in front of the clipper's bow, tearing the jib and ripping away a piece of the bowsprit as it fell. The torn sail began flapping wildly in the wind.

When she turned back to him, all Sam could see were Jason's eyes, angry and blazing as they returned her

249

glance. She knew what he was thinking, that this was all her fault. She couldn't even blame him.

"Does that answer your questions?" he hissed angrily at her. "Now go below." With that he dismissed her, turning his attention back to the business at hand. "Mr. Argus," he called. "Prepare to jibe. We'll see if we can't outrun her."

"Aye, Captain," the mate responded, and he called to his men to man the mast lines.

Sam stood, frozen to the rail, watching as the *Lady Alyssa* began to come about just as the shape of the pirate ship appeared out of the darkness of the night and the storm. It loomed frighteningly close, appearing as it did seemingly out of the nothingness.

This was madness, Sam told herself. The *Lady Alyssa* ought to be perfectly safe. Mr. Palmer had assured her when he'd offered her the cargo to Alexandria that they'd have no trouble, that the Egyptian coast was safe, that the American warships President Jefferson had sent were keeping the pirates at bay.

All of which, from what little she could see at that moment, had been either outright lie or deluded and wishful thinking. In either case, she could only curse herself for having believed a stranger rather than Jason.

Her regrets were momentarily pushed aside in the necessity to cling to the *Lady*'s rail as the forward mast swung and the ship listed to the side. For an instant the *Lady* seemed to flounder lifelessly in the water, pounded on all sides by angry waves. Then the sails filled again with wind and the *Lady* started to move, turning her back to the ship that had fired on her and fleeing into the murky darkness of the storm.

Sam darted a glance back to where Jason stood at the wheel. He wouldn't let the *Lady* be taken, she told herself. The *Lady* was fast, certainly faster than some filthy pirate ship. They'd outrun those brigands and that would be the end of it. But even as Samantha assured herself they'd be safe, she felt her heart beating with fear. She had no real idea of what it would mean were they to be captured by pirates, but she was sure it would not be pleasant, not for any of them.

But when she looked back she found the ship had once again disappeared into the oblivion of the night and the storm. *We're getting away,* she whispered to herself, half a prayer, half a hopeful wish.

As if to prove that she was right, the pirate ship fired another cannon shot. This time the brief flare of light was a good deal further distant than it had been the first time she'd seen it. The ball landed far to the *Lady's* rear. They would be safe, she told herself. The *Lady* had already pulled away from the pirate ship. There was no doubt that she could easily outrun any chase they might care to give.

Sam let the slicker's hood fall away from her head. The rain pelted her, and her hair was soon completely drenched, but she didn't even notice. For those few moments she had been frightened, more frightened than she'd ever been in her life. But now the fear was gone and she felt herself fill with a thick wash of delighted relief. There had been danger, but now it was safely passed, and nothing seemed more wonderful than the elation she felt at their escape.

She pushed herself away from the rail and back toward Jason. He was intent, all his attention riveted on holding the *Lady's* course in the rough water and the gusting winds, and he didn't notice her until she was beside him.

"I thought I told you to go below," he shouted at her above the sound of the wind.

But this time there wasn't any anger in his eyes, Sam saw. He was feeling the same elation she felt, the same intoxicating wave of relief.

"I told you the *Lady* was fast," she said. "She's a wonderful ship."

"Yes, she's wonderful," Jason replied.

But he wasn't really thinking about the *Lady Alyssa* when he spoke. He was staring at her, her thick auburn curls ly-

251

ing in wet tendrils around her face and on her shoulders, her eyes, naked of the ugly spectacles, glowing with delight. Rain poured down on her, slid down her cheeks in rivulets, drenched the small V of her white cotton nightdress that showed at the neck of the too-large slicker she was wearing. There was an air of abandon about her that he'd never thought to see in her, an air of freedom that had nothing in common with the woman who had argued with him in Liverpool over who had the right to determine the business of running the *Lady Alyssa*. This was a creature of feeling and whim, not plodding reason. And she was beautiful.

It came as a shock to him. *My God,* he thought. *She's beautiful. Not just pretty, but absolutely beautiful.*

But the sudden fascination was dispelled by the realization that they weren't as safe as she seemed to think they were. They might be pulling steadily away from the pirate ship, but something told him that escape could not be so easy.

And the need for flight, he reminded himself, was entirely due to her insistence that the *Lady Alyssa* take this particular cargo despite the fact that he'd been against it from the start. She'd bartered the ship and the crew's safety for a hundred and fifty pounds, and now they'd be lucky if they came out of the little escapade even. At best, the *Lady* had lost an expensive new sail and needed repair to her bowsprit, and that would probably cost them all they stood to make on the delivery of their cargo.

At worst, they might still not have seen the last of the pirates. And that could cost them a good deal more.

Sam needed only a glance at his expression to know that whatever he was thinking, he'd reminded himself he was angry with her. The spark she'd seen in his eyes was gone and the pained look she'd come to see too often in his expression when he glanced her way had returned.

"What is it?" she murmured, wondering what had happened, how she'd lost that moment of shared elation.

252

He didn't answer her question. Instead, he barked, "Go below. It isn't safe on deck."

She shook her head, refusing to leave.

"But we've left that ship far behind us," she protested.

"Have we?" he mused. Then his jaw suddenly clenched sharply and his expression grew dark as though he'd suddenly become aware of some new danger lurking in their path. "Mr. Argus," he called out. "What does your lookout spy?"

Sam heard the muffled sound of voices, and then the mate's response, "No signs, sir."

There had been a satisfied, assured note to the mate's voice, and it calmed whatever fears Sam had begun to feel when she'd seen Jason's worried expression.

But the mate's report obviously did not satisfy Jason.

"Prepare to jibe again, Mr. Argus," he shouted.

"Aye, sir."

Sam had no idea what Jason intended, and from the hint of confusion she'd heard in Argus's response, she realized that the mate had none, either.

"What are you doing?" she demanded. "You'll just slow us down by changing course now. They'll be able to gain on us."

Jason darted a glance at her, and from his distracted expression, Sam realized he'd nearly forgotten about her.

"I thought I ordered you below," he growled.

Before either of them had the chance to dispute her presence on deck, the sound of rifle fire filled the air. Sam turned. Not two hundred feet off the *Lady Alyssa*'s bow, a second ship had appeared out of the murky darkness.

And it was headed straight for them.

Jason groaned. They had been maneuvered into a trap, caught between the ship they'd outrun and a second that had been lying in wait for them.

He shouted the order to come about, but he knew that it was too late. There was no room for the clipper to turn, and no time.

The *Lady Alyssa* was about to be boarded, and there was nothing he could do to save her.

Sam was frozen by the sound of the rifle shot. She understood now what Jason had realized a few minutes before, that the only reason the first ship had fired on them while it was still so far away was to scare them into the arms of the second pirate ship. And they'd done just what had been expected of them, gone running directly along the path they'd been expected to take.

Jason's voice seemed to be coming from a great distance, the sound muffled by her own guilty thoughts. This was all her fault, she told herself. She could only wonder why he wasn't shouting those very words at her.

But he wasn't. He was telling her to go below, to hide.

Her legs felt soft and uncertain as she started forward, and she wondered how they managed to hold her erect. The sound of rifle and pistol shot continued, and when she looked up, she saw that the second pirate ship was getting closer. She could see the crew now, could see the dark puffs of powder rising from their weapons as they fired.

And then she saw one of the *Lady*'s crew falling to the deck, grasping his thigh, and heard his shout of pain. She froze, unable to move another step, unable even to flee to the comparative safety of the cabin below.

The second ship was only a few feet away now, and her crew were standing on her rail, grappling hooks at the ready, set to fasten the *Lady* to their own ship so they could leap across to the *Lady*'s deck as soon as they were close enough. They held knives grasped in their teeth and swords in their hands, and a look of cold disdain for the half dozen weapons that were raised against them filled their eyes.

It didn't take any great leap of thought for her to realize that the *Lady*'s crew stood no chance against them. Outnumbered ten to one, Jason and his men were doomed.

And suddenly the noise seemed to fade. Only a sharp, biting hurt in her arm seemed real, and Sam looked down at it to see a bright-red blossom of blood begin to leak from a hole in the slicker. She could almost hear the sound of her own heartbeat, and knew that with each dull thud a bit more of her life was slipping out through that ragged gash in her forearm.

She looked up, dazed by the hurt, to see what seemed like an endless swarm of those wild-looking men leap over the *Lady*'s side, brandishing their swords, shouting loud, indecipherable words.

The rifle fire had ended, but there was fighting all around her now, hand to hand, pirate swords pitted against the sailors' knives. Everywhere she looked there were more of these strange, frightening men. Even had she been able to move, there was no longer anyplace for her to go.

She hardly noticed the first hand that grasped her, but when the second seized her, pressing down against the wound in her arm, she cried out. The hurt galvanized her, startling her out of the frozen daze that had held her. She struggled against the two men who had put hands on her, kicking and scratching, but without any success. They laughed, and pushed her roughly toward the side.

At first she thought they were simply going to throw her overboard, and she told herself it was better to drown than to be captured by men of this sort. She looked around, wildly searching for Jason in the melee, wanting to call out to him, to tell him how sorry she was, to tell him she loved him. If she was about to die, a voice inside her told her, at least she ought to tell him she loved him.

But as she had been so many times in the previous hour, she soon found she was again wrong. The pirates didn't push her overboard, but into the waiting arms of their captain.

He was their superior, that was made obvious if by nothing else than the fact that he was dressed in silks and not the thick, coarse linen as were the rest. He smiled when he saw what his men had brought him.

"I think the fight is over," he told her in perfect, only slightly accented English. "I think I now have a weapon not even these foolhardy American sailors will be unwilling to face."

With that, he grabbed her, turning her roughly and pulling her close to him, holding her around the waist. She struggled for a moment, kicking back at him and trying to wrench herself free, but he seemed oblivious to her attempts to free herself. He moved forward, forcing her along with him.

She darted a look at the deck and soon realized that Jason and those remaining members of the crew who had not been wounded were being forced aft. They were vastly outnumbered and completely surrounded, and the pirate crew was pushing them together, forcing them to either surrender or make a last stand.

But the crowd of the invaders parted as their captain, with Sam in tow, made his way along the deck. Within a moment he was standing in front of the small group of the *Lady*'s crew.

"Put down your arms," he shouted to them. "Surrender and your lives will be spared."

"Better to die fighting than live as your slave," Jason shouted back.

"A noble sentiment," the pirate captain called back. "But perhaps you might wish to reconsider if I assure you that further resistance will mean the lady will be the next to die."

Jason stopped fighting and turned to see him unsheathe a knife and put it to Sam's neck.

"Leave her be!" Jason shouted.

"As soon as you and your men lay down your arms," the captain replied.

"Don't, Jason," Sam cried. "Don't give him the satisfaction."

He pressed the knife closer. It bit into her neck, and she

could feel a slight nick and then the warm seep of blood it released. She couldn't help but wince.

Jason's face paled.

"All right," he shouted. "You win. Just let her be."

He dropped his knife and his pistol, and motioned to his men to do the same.

The captain smiled. He nodded to his men to retrieve the fallen weapons. Only when Jason and his crew were disarmed and firmly held by his own men did he once again sheathe his knife.

"Lock them in the hold," he directed.

His men started to push Jason forward, but he balked.

"You promised to release my wife," he hissed at the captain.

The pirate shook his head. "Did I?" he asked. "I seem to have changed my mind. The lady stays with me, Captain Stone. She will ensure your cooperation." He brushed his hand slowly against Sam's cheek. "You are a lucky man, Captain, to have such a wife," he said. "A pretty woman has great value in Tripoli." Then he nodded to his men. "Into the hold," he directed. "Leave a crew of ten to man her."

With that, he pulled Sam back toward the rail.

Sam looked back in time to see Jason staring at her just before he was forced below deck. Then she found herself being lifted and carried over the rail, taken from the *Lady Alyssa* to the pirate ship and whatever fate she'd managed to bring down upon herself and the *Lady*'s crew.

Chapter Five

Jason sat on a wooden crate and stared dully at his hands.

"What now, Captain?"

He looked up at Argus's hopeful expression. It pained him. He could think of nothing about their situation that seemed to be even the least bit hopeful. The mate's apparent expectation that he would be able to provide a logical course of action to improve it only made that fact even more painful.

"Damned if I know, Mr. Argus," he muttered angrily.

"We can't just sit here, Captain," Argus insisted.

Jason scowled. "I'm willing to entertain suggestions, Mr. Argus," he said.

The mate glanced up at the thick metal grate covering the hatch to the hold. Even if they had some way of reaching it, which they didn't, for the pirates had drawn up the ladder once their prisoners had been placed in the hold, he knew the grate had been securely locked. They were trapped, and there was no way he could ignore the fact.

"I'm afraid I have none, Captain," he murmured.

Jason saw the hope leak out of the mate's expression, and he realized that its loss was more painful to him than the expectation that he would be able to devise some magical means of escape.

"Just give me some time to think, Mr. Argus," he told the mate. "Maybe I can think of something."

He looked around at his crew. Three had been wounded,

one seriously—Peters, the man who had taken a bullet in his thigh. Jason had done what little he could for them, bandaging the wounds with torn strips of clothing, but there was little else he could do without the box of medical supplies he kept in his cabin. Three wounded, he mused. That left five of them, including himself, able-bodied and capable of fighting. Assuming, that was, they could find some way to get out of the hold.

It galled him to realize that he was just sitting there, a prisoner on his own ship. Still, he knew he couldn't have done otherwise. The sight of that knife held to Sam's throat had been enough to turn his belly to ice. He knew he could not have changed what had happened, knew there was no way he could have stood there and watched Sam die.

Not that death might not have been preferable for her. When he closed his eyes he could see her again as he'd last seen her, held in the pirate captain's arms, the thin drip of red washed by the rain down her throat from the prick of the knife, staining the white of her cotton nightgown, the thick line of blood seeping down her arm. And her bare feet, pale against the dark of the *Lady*'s rail. Somehow he couldn't keep himself from thinking about her bare feet and wondering how he hadn't noticed until then that she'd come up on deck without any shoes.

He ought to curse her, he thought, to blame her as the cause of what had happened to all of them. But he couldn't. All he could think of was the way she'd looked when he'd last seen her, frightened, hurt, and unaccountably beautiful. He told himself he ought to hate her, but his body and his heart were telling him something entirely different.

"It was like they was lyin' in wait for us," Argus muttered. "Like they knew we was comin'."

Jason looked up sharply.

"What?"

"I said it was like they knew we was comin'," Argus repeated.

Jason considered the possibility, and suddenly realized the mate might be right. Their capture had been too carefully arranged for it to have been mere chance. And then he remembered something that had, until that moment, escaped his notice.

"They *were* waiting for us, Mr. Argus," he said. "Not just any merchant ship, but us, just us." The mate looked up at him with an expression that suggested he might have become slightly deranged. Jason couldn't blame him. "Think back," he said. "The captain of that ship called me by name. They were waiting for the *Lady*, just the *Lady*."

Argus looked bewildered for a moment as he thought, and then he nodded. "You're right, Captain," he said. "I recall it now."

"Which leads me to wonder what makes the *Lady Alyssa* so important as to warrant such notoriety," Jason went on, musing aloud now as he thought. "As far as I can see, the only thing about us that could make us that special is our cargo."

Argus shook his head. "Shovels and hoes?" he asked. "What's special about shovels and hoes?"

"I never saw any shovels," Jason replied. "Just because the manifest said that our cargo was shovels doesn't mean that that's what we're carrying."

He jumped to his feet, then stood for a moment, considering the crate on which he'd been seated. A quick inspection proved to him that it was nailed securely shut. Even in the dim light cast by the single lantern, he could see that the side had been neatly stenciled with a maker's mark and a small drawing of a crossed pair, a shovel and a hoe.

"Bring that lantern here," he directed one of the sailors.

"We've no way to open it, Captain," Argus murmured as he put his hand to the place on his belt where a knife was ordinarily sheathed. It was empty, and none of the others had any weapons, either. The pirates had removed anything they might use as a weapon before they had locked them in the hold.

Jason nodded. "We could use one of those shovels or hoes just now," he agreed.

Then he unbuckled his belt and pulled it free of his trousers.

"What do you think, Mr. Argus?" he asked as he fingered the ornate silver buckle.

"Worth a try, Captain," the mate agreed.

Jason slid the edge of the buckle under the corner edge of the top of the crate, then slowly pushed, working it forward until he felt he had it firmly wedged. Then he pulled it upward, prying the wooden top away from the body of the crate.

The silver wasn't nearly strong enough to use as pry, and it quickly bent, but not before the top of the crate had been opened enough for Jason to slip his fingers beneath it. It took several minutes more with both him and Argus working at it, but finally they pulled the top free.

The two of them stared down at the contents lying in a bed of wood shavings.

"Fancy shovels, wouldn't you say, Mr. Argus?" Jason asked.

"Aye, Captain," the mate agreed. "Fancy shovels, indeed."

Jason reached in, pulled out one of the rifles, and held it up to the light. The metal barrel and the polished stock shone dully in the flickering light of the lantern.

"I'd say the upstanding Mr. Palmer has played us for fools, Mr. Argus," he muttered angrily. "I'd say he sold these weapons illegally to the bashaw of Tripoli, and then used us to make his delivery. All he'd have to do would get word to Tripoli, and the rest would be easy enough for them. They would just have to patrol the waters approaching Alexandria."

"So they *were* waitin' for us," Argus murmured.

"Thanks to friend Palmer," Jason agreed.

"I think I'd like to find him and let him know what I think of his manners," Argus muttered.

"So would I, Mr. Argus," Jason said. "I just hope we live

long enough to get the opportunity to return to Liverpool and express the sentiment personally."

Argus motioned to the heaps of crates lashed to the sides of the hold.

"But with all this, Captain, surely we can fight back," he said.

"Set the men to opening the crates, Mr. Argus," Jason ordered, "and have them search for ammunition. I doubt they'll find any, though." He sighed. "I suppose that would be making it too easy," he muttered. "But it'll keep them busy while I try to think of some other way to get us out of here."

Sam found herself being unceremoniously thrown onto the bed in the far side of the pirate captain's cabin. She stumbled and landed on her hurt arm. She heard a gasp of pain, and realized it had been hers.

She pushed herself up and turned to find her captor staring down at her. He was smiling as he stripped off his wet shirt and dropped it to the floor. Tall, well muscled, his bare torso shone with the wet. He stood over her, his dark eyes bright with sardonic amusement at the fear in her expression.

He reached forward, putting his hand to the front of her wet slicker, and pulled it, tearing the top open. Startled out of her fear, Sam pulled away from him and slapped angrily at his hand.

As much as her fear, her anger seemed to amuse him. He withdrew his hand, and considered the abrupt change in her attitude.

"Barbarian," she hissed at him.

He seemed unruffled by the slur.

"Believe me, I've been called far worse," he told her. "British schoolboys are perhaps the cruelest creatures on earth."

Sam stared at him in confusion for a moment.

"British schoolboys?" she murmured.

A boy entered the cabin carrying a robe which he handed to his captain. Sam's captor took it from him without so much as offering him a glance, continuing with his conversation as he shrugged into it.

"Didn't it strike you as odd that I speak the king's English?" he asked.

She hadn't really thought about it, she realized. But now that he mentioned the fact, she found it did. He spoke with an upper-class British accent.

"You were educated in England?" she asked.

He nodded. "A common enough practice. Younger royal sons are routinely sent off, hopefully to keep them out of mischief. As the youngest of eight royal princes, it was assumed, I suppose, that I'd manage to lose myself in the British brothels and leave Tripoli to my older brothers." He backed away from her, settling himself into a cushioned chair across from her. He sat, smiling again as he stared at her. He seemed to be warming to his story, even more to the surprise it seemed to rouse in her. "But I wasn't about to be cheated out of a throne by a few uninspired siblings. I returned to Tripoli better educated and far fitter to rule than any of the others. It was a lesson they found painful to learn."

Sam couldn't believe what he was telling her.

"You killed your own brothers?" she asked in a hoarse whisper.

"Shall we say I helped them find the eternal peace of Allah," he suggested.

"You *are* a barbarian," she hissed.

He shrugged, and his smile disappeared. He seemed to have reached the end of the amused tolerance he had shown her to that point, and was beginning to be put off by her show of disdain.

"Perhaps I should introduce myself to you, Mrs. Stone," he said. "I am Muhammad Ali Mousef, bashaw of Tripoli. I hope it is not necessary to instruct you in good manners.

Let me warn you, it is not healthy to insult a pasha." He glanced around at the rather large cabin. "Especially when you are held captive in his lair."

Sam swallowed, nearly choking on the thick ball that suddenly filled her throat. If she'd momentarily forgotten her fear of him, she was sharply reminded of the fact.

"How do you know my name?" she murmured, suddenly aware that he had used it without her having given it to him.

He arched a brow, the sardonic smile once again turning up the corners of his lips.

"Because I've been waiting for you, Mrs. Stone," he told her. "Mr. Palmer sent word, mentioning you specifically. He said you drove a hard bargain."

Sam was more confused by his answer than she had been before she'd asked the question.

"Why would Mr. Palmer send you word of our arrangement to ship his farm supplies?" she asked.

Mousef's smile grew just a bit broader.

"Because he had no customer in Alexandria," he told her. "Nor was his shipment farm tools. In point of fact, I am his customer and his shipment was rifles. You were hired to bring them to me." His expression grew smug and superior. "We thought it wise not to worry you with unpleasant details."

"Rifles?" Sam repeated, her tone dull with surprise. "Jason was right. I was a fool to accept the charter."

"But a charming fool, Mrs. Stone," Mousef assured her. "In fact, I'm surprised Palmer didn't mention that you were quite pretty. It was, no doubt, an oversight. Or perhaps poor Mr. Palmer was simply more impressed with your lack of business acumen than your other, more physical, assets. He strikes me as that sort of man." He smiled again, and this time there was more lechery in his look than anything else. "I assure you, I am not."

Sam drew up her legs, covering them with the heavy slicker. She pulled the neck closed and tried, uselessly, to draw away from him. His suggestion that she was pretty bewildered her, for she'd grown accustomed to thinking of herself as plain, used to expecting men to ignore her. But what she saw when she looked at him told her he was decidedly not ignoring her.

"What do you intend to do?" she asked.

He seemed amused by her movement, by the way she huddled into the rain-soaked slicker.

"I haven't quite decided," he told her as he pushed himself to his feet once again and started toward her.

He was standing over her when the boy returned, this time bearing a tray with food—bread, cheese, and fruit—and a ewer and two cups. He put the tray down on a table without so much as glancing at either Sam or his master, then turned to leave. Before he reached the door, Mousef called out an order to him. He nodded and bowed, then disappeared.

Mousef continued to stand over Sam for a moment longer, then he suddenly grabbed the slicker and pulled it. This time he had no intention of letting go. Sam tried to hold on to it, but he pulled sharply and the thick material pressed painfully against her hurt arm. She was forced to release her hold. He tore the slicker away.

She looked up at him, shivering more with fright than with cold, and saw her own image in his dark eyes as he stared down at her. He dropped the slicker, then leaned forward to her, touching his finger first to the nick on her neck, then to the open, bloody weal on her arm. She tried to pull back from his touch, but there was no place to go.

"So this is how the wife of an American captain dresses," he said, his amusement only too obvious as he glanced at her torn and bloodied cotton nightgown. He lifted the hem, then dropped it as though the feel of the thick cotton insulted his fingers.

"I—I was asleep," she murmured, only wondering why she was trying to explain herself to him after she'd uttered the words.

265

"Remove it," he told her, disinterested in whatever she had to say.

She edged away from him. "I will not," she told him.

When he reached out to her again, Sam jabbed at his hand, pushing it away. She lunged forward, darting past him and running to the table where the servant boy had left the tray of food. She grabbed the small knife that had been lying on the plate with the cheese and held it out threateningly at Mousef.

He looked at her a moment in silence, apparently not quite believing what he saw. Then he laughed.

"You can't be serious," he said. "Put that down."

"You stay away from me," she cried.

He put his hand to the sheathed knife he'd held to her neck while they'd still been on the *Lady*'s deck and slowly withdrew it, watching her eyes as he held the blade up to the light.

"*This* is a knife, Mrs. Stone," he told her. "Now put down that toy, and do as you're told."

Sam swallowed. She was under no delusions that she would be able to stop him with the small paring knife she held in her hand. But she also knew she was not about to submit to him. Better a clean death by the blade he held threateningly out to her than that.

"You can go to hell," she hissed in angry defiance.

"You were right, Captain. No ammunition." Argus's expression was decidedly depressed as he made the announcement.

"I didn't suppose there would be, Mr. Argus," Jason told him. "But I don't remember a good fight ever bothering you, even if you were outarmed."

Argus smiled slyly. "You have an idea, Captain?" he asked, but he already knew from Jason's expression that his captain had reached some decision.

"Hardly an idea, Mr. Argus," Jason replied. "Just a way

to get out of here. Once we're on deck, we'll still have to face those damned pirates unarmed."

"Sounds fine to me, Captain," Argus replied. "Give me the chance to put my bare hands to their necks and I won't ask for anything more." Behind him, the others murmured in agreement.

"Good," Jason said as he reached into the opened crate and withdrew one of the rifles. He held it by the barrel. "We'll have these," he said. "If nothing else, they'll make fair clubs."

"Better than fair, Captain," one of the seamen agreed.

"Let's move a few of these crates, boys," Jason directed, and the men hurried to help, pushing a half dozen crates and stacking them where Jason directed, directly beneath the hatch to the deck.

"I'll still need a lift," Jason muttered when he'd climbed onto the pile and was still more than four feet beneath the overhead opening.

Argus and one of the men hastily climbed up beside him. The stack wasn't all that steady with the three of them on it, and it shifted with the *Lady*'s movement in the storm, but they managed to keep their balance as Jason climbed onto their shoulders.

He peered up through the open grate of the hatch first, well aware that his field of vision was limited, but still feeling better when he found at least the portion of the deck he could see was unguarded. Then he slipped the barrel of the rifle through the grate, maneuvering it carefully, slowly edging the lock that held the hatch until it fell forward directly on the grate, where he could grasp it with his fingers. He lowered the rifle, handing it down to Argus.

"How goes it, Captain?" the mate asked.

"So far, so good," Jason muttered as he reached up and found he had the padlock firmly in his grasp.

He pulled it down through one of the holes in the grate, moving it slowly as the fit was tight, making the lock scrape against the metal bars. He didn't want to make enough noise to draw any attention from their captors. Luckily the noise of the storm muffled whatever sounds he made.

Once the thick lock was hanging down, he took the rifle back from Argus, pushing the barrel through the thick loop of the hasp. It was a tight fit, too, but he managed to push it far enough to get a fair amount of leverage.

He put his weight against the butt and began to turn the rifle. At first it seemed a useless effort, for the hasp didn't give in the least. Jason began to wonder if he'd made a mistake thinking he would be able to break the lock, to wonder if there was absolutely nothing he could do to get him and his men out of the hold. The thought of having been outwitted, of being trapped, ate at him like a canker.

But he reminded himself of the age of the lock and of the fact that he hadn't bothered to replace it when he'd had the *Lady Alyssa* refitted. It was more than fifteen years old, and had spent most of those years exposed to the elements. It had to break. It was their only chance.

He strained and pushed against the rifle butt with all his might, telling himself that the metal could not still be strong enough to long sustain the pressure he was exerting on it.

Sweat was streaming from his forehead and into his eyes, but he didn't release his hold. And finally he was rewarded with a small cracking sound. His arms felt numb, and he knew he had to rest.

He released his hold of the rifle, leaving it wedged where it was as he climbed off the men's shoulders and onto the heap of crates.

"Well, Captain?" Argus asked expectantly.

Jason rubbed his aching shoulders, waiting for the stiffness to ebb. He looked at his mate and he smiled.

"It'll go, Mr. Argus," he said with a wide grin. "Get yourself ready for that fight you were so anxious to find. You're about to get it."

268

Chapter Six

Sam's eyes never left the blade in Mousef's hand.

"You are lucky my beliefs preclude the existence of your Christian hell, Mrs. Stone," he said after a protracted silence. "Otherwise, I might be inclined to be angry with you."

"I meant it," she hissed. "You can translate it into whatever sort of damnation you do believe in."

"In my country a woman would be stoned for daring to speak such things to a shaikh," he said.

Sam lifted her eyes from the knife to his eyes. "We are not in your country," she hissed in reply. "And you are not *my* lord and master."

A wash of anger filled his expression, and for a moment Sam thought she had pushed him to use the knife. But it passed quickly, the sardonic smile replaced his angry scowl, and he erupted in a burst of laughter.

"I will say this for you, Mrs. Stone," he told her. "You are not quite what I expect a woman to be."

No, Sam thought bitterly, *I'm not what a man expects a woman to be.* At that moment she wished more than anything that she had been more of what Jason had wanted, wished they might have had at least the past few weeks to find in each other the happiness other couples shared. She had no doubt there would ever be another chance for that. Mousef's humor would not long outweigh his anger with her, of that she was only too sure.

Before she had the chance to think of some words of reply, Sam heard the door open behind her. She watched as

269

Mousef's eyes strayed to whoever had entered the cabin. She told herself not to drop her guard, not to let herself look, but one glance at Mousef's smile loosened her resolve. She couldn't keep herself from turning so that she, too, could see.

As soon as her eyes shifted, Mousef darted forward, grabbing her arm and wrenching the knife away. He dropped the blade along with his own, letting them both clatter to the floor, and grabbed her hands, roughly jerking them behind her back. Sam winced with the hurt it caused her injured arm and with the pressure he exerted on her flesh as he dug his fingers angrily into her wrists.

"You do test my patience, Mrs. Stone," he told her. "You seem determined to push me to do something that would prove pleasant for neither of us." He put the back of his hand against her cheek, stroking it slowly, the feel of his flesh warm and damp against her skin. He lowered his face until it was close to hers. "My own inclination is to propose an entirely different alternative."

She threw her head back and tried to push him away, giving up only when she realized his hold on her was unshakable.

"I'd sooner embrace your knife than you," she hissed.

His grasp tightened, and he pulled her closer to him, ignoring the whimper of hurt that escaped her. She realized as she looked up at him that the insult was probably the greatest she might have offered him. The amusement was completely gone from his expression and his eyes blazed with anger.

"You're lucky you're useful to me just now," he told her. "Your presence keeps your husband and his crew docile. As I choose not to disturb that circumstance, at least not until I have those rifles you so kindly brought me in my men's hands, you may consider yourself, for the time being, inviolate. But I warn you, my patience wears thin. Push me too far and I may choose to overlook your value as hostage in favor of other, more intrinsic worth."

He released his hold of her wrists, and she backed a step away from him, rubbing her wrists.

She was confused by his words, not understanding what he intended. "But you told me . . ." she murmured, stopping when she saw the anger begin to fade a bit and the sardonic smile return to his lips.

"To remove that bloody rag," he finished the sentence for her. "It offends me. Besides, I would rather you not bleed all over my cabin." He pointed to the boy who had entered the cabin and now stood behind her. He was holding an armful of clothing and a roll of bandages. "He will bandage your arm and help you into clean clothing." He took a step back from her. "I hope I can assume you will not attack the boy with that," he said, and nodded toward the small knife.

Sam felt slightly numb. "No," she murmured, agreeing. "I won't attack the boy."

"Good," Mousef said as he took his own weapon, which the boy hurriedly retrieved for him and replaced in its sheath. "I suggest you eat once you've changed your clothing. And then perhaps rest. I may need you to persuade your husband to continue to be docile, and it wouldn't do for you to appear anything but at your best."

With that he spoke a few sharp words to the boy, then turned and left.

This time, when Jason exerted pressure against the lever he'd made of the rifle, the hasp of the lock first cried out as though it were in pain, and then shattered. Jason removed it, then lifted the grate, testing to be sure it was free, and then slowly let it drop, taking care to make no sound.

He could hear the murmur of anticipation from his men and he turned back to them, motioning them to silence.

"The injured stay here," he told Argus once he'd climbed back down, this time with the broken lock and the rifle in his hand. "Everyone else takes a rifle to use as a club. Hopefully we'll get more useful weapons from our friends on deck."

Argus nodded, indicating that he understood.

"I'll go first," Jason continued. "If it's clear, I'll motion to you to follow. If I'm spotted as I climb out, I have an odd feeling we'll all be dead rather sooner than we expected."

"The storm's still blowing," Argus reminded him. "We've got that on our side."

Jason nodded. "Little enough," he replied. "Hopefully it will keep us out of sight, at least at the start. Once on deck we work our way aft taking out any men on deck before they can call an alarm. With any luck, they'll have let a few men go below, out of the storm, and we'll find two or three of them snug in their bunks, fast asleep."

"Snug in *our* bunks, Captain," one of the sailors corrected him.

Jason grinned. "An unacceptable liberty, I think," he said. "One they ought to be dissuaded from ever taking again." His smile faded as he turned back to Argus. "We want to take as many captive as possible, Mr. Argus. They may prove to be useful."

Argus nodded. "Aye, Captain."

With that, Jason grasped the rifle, and for the third time climbed onto his mate's shoulders. He edged the grate off the hatch, and then reached up to the edge of the hatch. He slid the rifle onto the deck, got a firm grip to pull himself up, then swung himself out of the hole and onto the deck. Instinct told him to keep low, and he immediately rolled away from the open expanse of deck to the small amount of shelter offered by the shadows near the rail.

His instincts were right, keeping him from standing up and making a clear target of himself. As soon as he was on his feet, crouching by the rail, he realized he was only fifteen feet from where one of the pirates was posted near the bow. The man, presumably serving as both guard and lookout, hardly seemed delighted with his job. He was hunkered down, his rough jacket pulled over his ears, miserable in the seemingly endless downpour.

Jason told himself that circumstances gave him the right to make the pirate a bit more miserable.

Jason lunged forward, holding the rifle by its barrel and swinging it like a club as he moved, striking a clean blow to the side of the man's head before he'd even realized that he was not alone on the deck. He fell backward, and lay motion-less and senseless.

Jason crept back to the hatch and looked down. Argus was already reaching up to the rim of the hatchway, waiting for him. The others were standing either on the pile of crates or nearby it, staring up, waiting for his order to climb up on deck.

"Hunting good, Captain?" Argus asked.

Jason nodded, and he gave the mate a hand up. "They left just one guard. I don't think they're expecting any trouble from us."

"A smug lot of monkeys," Argus growled.

"Keep low," Jason whispered.

While Argus helped the others out of the hold, Jason re-turned to where he'd left the unconscious pirate lying on the deck. He confiscated the man's weapons—a long knife, a sword, and a pistol—then tied him securely with line. By the time he'd finished, Argus and the others were standing beside him.

"A full complement, Captain," Argus whispered, nodding toward the small pile of weapons.

Jason nodded. "Here," he whispered as he handed the mate the sword and hefted the knife, getting the feel of its balance. He considered the pistol before he handed it to a second sailor. "Try not to use that," he instructed. "If there's a choice, a blade is preferable. They make less noise, and I don't think we want our friends' friends to come calling again if we can help it." He nodded toward a light that seemed to float in the distance, a few hundred feet off the *Lady*'s bow.

"Our escort, Captain?" asked the mate.

"It would seem they consider us important, Mr. Argus."

Argus nodded. "Us, or our cargo," the mate replied.

"You two come aft with me," Jason went on, nodding to Argus and one other of his men. "The rest fan out. Keep to the shadows. And remember, try not to make any noise. We don't want to alert our friends that we aren't still safe and snug below."

Jason started first, and the others followed, dividing into

two groups that moved slowly aft on either side of the deck.

Jason saw the group of three pirates first, and he motioned the men behind him to crouch into the shadows. The three were probably supposed to be on watch, but they weren't well disciplined and had given in to the desire to try to shield themselves from the storm. They huddled near the rail, trying to salve the misery the pounding rain caused them by sharing the contents of what looked to Jason suspiciously like his decanter of whiskey.

When Jason and his two men appeared out of the darkness, brandishing the weapons they'd taken from the forward guard, the three were too drunk and too surprised to react logically or call out. Only one managed to withdraw a weapon before the Americans were on them, and Argus was forced to kill him for his effort, using the sword Jason had given him with a cool and frighteningly expert precision. The other two were quickly subdued, stunned by their comrade's death. In a matter of moments, the Americans had disarmed them. They were left lying unconscious on the deck with the sailor busily going about the business of tying and gagging them.

There were two more at the helm. Jason prepared himself for a fight when he saw them, knowing that they must be the more senior men and probably still sober. Much to his surprise, they simply surrendered without offering any resistance when they saw the armed Americans appear out of the darkness. It was obvious that they were not ready to take on a fight where they did not have the advantage of numbers and surprise.

The remaining four were, as Jason had hoped, below decks, in the crew's quarters. They were soon rousted from their sleep and brought up onto the deck to join their fellows.

With their prisoners herded forward and securely tied, Jason once again took possession of the *Lady Alyssa*.

"Orders, Captain?" Argus asked with a pleased grin.

"Now we see how well the *Lady* can run, Mr. Argus," Jason told him.

"Run?" the mate asked. He was obviously surprised that

Jason thought there was any need to run now that they were once more in control of the ship.

Jason nodded and motioned to the faint floating light beyond the *Lady*'s prow. It flashed occasionally, disappearing altogether for an instant when the downpour increased, and then reappeared eerily out of the murk.

Argus stared in the gloom. "I only see one of them, Captain," he murmured. "There were two before."

"The other is probably running home under full sail with the news that they've captured a hold full of rifles," Jason replied. "Let's try to make that report a lie, Mr. Argus. We don't have long before dawn, and I think it expedient that we put as much distance between ourselves and that ship as we can before full light."

"Aye, Captain," Argus agreed. "Let's show that Barbary scow what a good American clipper can do."

"I'd rather save the lesson for some other time, Mr. Argus," Jason said. "Let's do it on cat's feet. Have our lanterns extinguished. We want them to think we've just disappeared." He looked up at the *Lady*'s sails. Most of them had been haphazardly secured by the pirates who hadn't wanted to fight the storm by continuing on under full sail. "Let's get that canvas unfurled, Mr. Argus," Jason ordered. "And then prepare to come about."

As Jason turned the *Lady Alyssa* east, away from the pirate ship, he could see the first fingers of dawn's light creeping into the sky. Under full sail, the *Lady* began to pull steadily away from the pirate ship. Almost effortlessly, they were leaving the pirate ship far behind in their wake.

After what they'd been through in the previous hours, it seemed almost anticlimactic to Jason that they were sailing away from the Barbary craft completely unchallenged. It wasn't long before it was little more than a dark smudge on the rain-obscured horizon.

"I'd say we've done it," Argus told him. "Shall we bring up the wounded from the hold now?"

"Aye, Mr. Argus," Jason agreed. "See they're made as comfortable as possible."

Argus turned away to oversee the removal of the wounded men from the hold. He was, like the rest of the men, Jason noticed, buoyant with their escape. All of them went about performing their tasks with wide smiles on their faces. But Jason realized he wasn't quite ready to share their exhilaration.

Sam, he knew, was either on the ship they were leaving behind them, or else on the one that had left the small convoy, presumably to return to Tripoli. He was in no position to attack the pirate ship and board it to see if she was there. Nor was he in any better position to sail into Tripoli to claim her.

A nagging part of him, the logical part, told him that her capture was all her own fault, that she'd made her own uncomfortable bed and ought to be left to lie in it. He told himself he wanted to forget about her, to let her face alone the fate to which she'd almost condemned them all. And he told himself that were he to leave her, the *Lady Alyssa* would be completely his.

But despite all that, he knew he was as capable of leaving her as he was of storming the bashaw's castle single-handedly.

He'd question the pirates they'd taken captive, learn where they had taken her. But even before he heard their answers, he was already sure where she'd be taken. He was under no delusion about the existence of white slavery in North Africa. And he knew the pirates would not waste a valuable commodity, especially after they'd been cheated out of the rifles they'd expected to be their booty.

He had to go back for her, that he knew. There was nothing else he could do. The image of her as he'd last seen her, being dragged off the *Lady Alyssa*'s deck, was haunting him. He knew it would haunt him for the rest of his life were he to turn his back on her and accept her loss.

He knew he had to save her. What he didn't know, was *how*.

"It's a palace!"

"What did you expect, Mrs. Stone?" Mousef asked. "Did

you really think the bashaw would live in a filthy tent, like some Bedouin sheep herder?"

Now that he voiced the possibility, Sam realized that that was precisely what she'd expected. But this structure his carriage was approaching was hardly a nomad's tent. They'd left the last of the storm behind them on the water, and as the carriage drew closer to Mousef's palace, Sam stared at its outline, crisp and sharp in the fine morning air. Situated high on a ridge overlooking the port, surrounded by stone walls, it was half fortress, half palace. It was a decidedly imposing structure, dark and looming, framed by the rising sun behind it.

And it might just as well be a prison, she thought as the carriage passed through the gates and came to a halt in front of a pair of wide doors. Behind her, soldiers pushed the gates to the wall closed. A quick glance told her that there were more, many more, stationed along the top of the thick fortification. Mousef's palace was impregnable, she thought. And there was no way she, Jason, or the others would ever be able to escape.

Mousef climbed out of the carriage and started for the door that had been pulled open at his approach to admit him. Sam shrank down into the seat of the carriage and watched his back, wondering hopefully if he might have forgotten her.

He hadn't. He stopped at the portal, turning to find she hadn't moved.

He motioned to one of the servants who stood by the door. The man nodded, crossed to the carriage, and reached in, grasping Sam's wounded arm and urging her forcefully forward.

Sam was thoroughly dissuaded from any thought of trying to fight him by the searing pain that shot through her arm at the touch. Mousef's boy had cleaned the wound and bandaged it, showing her that the bullet had only passed through the fleshy part, exiting without causing any permanent damage. Still, the wound was growing steadily more and more tender. The servant's touch was more than enough to bring her quickly out of the carriage. He released his hold, but quite obviously was ready to repeat the inducement if necessary. Sam decided the wisest path was to go docilely where he wanted her to go.

Mousef quite clearly saw her pain reflected in her expression.

"You will find you will save yourself a good deal of discomfort if you do as you are told, Mrs. Stone," he told her when she'd reached him.

"You didn't tell me what you wanted me to do," she countered.

"I didn't, did I?" he mused. He didn't seem at all upset by his omission or by the hurt she'd suffered as a result of it.

He started forward again, entering a huge, marble-floored entrance hall. Sam hesitated only a moment. One look at the servant was sufficient to send her scurrying after him.

He started up a wide marble stairway, and Sam hurried after him even as she glanced quickly around. Under other circumstances she would have stood and simply gaped. She couldn't quite believe the magnificence of the place, the wealth of shiny marble that gleamed at floors and walls, the thick, dark-colored carpets under her feet. There had certainly never been anything like this in Edgartown. Even her all too precarious situation could not dim the awe she felt at what she saw.

Mousef stopped when he'd climbed only a half dozen steps.

"As soon as the American ship reaches port, I am to be notified," he ordered the servant.

"Iywa, ya shaikh," the servant replied and bowed his head.

Mousef seemed about to start up the stairs again, but he stopped and glanced back at Sam, his stare evaluating, weighing.

"Take her to the women's quarters," he directed. "I do not appreciate the sight of a woman dressed in sailor's clothes."

"Iywa, ya shaikh," the servant repeated as he put his hand once more to Sam's arm, using just enough pressure to warn her not to disobey.

Mousef turned away and quickly climbed the stairs. The

278

servant allowed Sam only a minute to watch him go. Then he tightened his hold on her arm, nudging her away from the stairs and toward a long corridor to the rear of the hall. Bewildered as to what was to become of her, and thinking now of all the trouble she'd brought down on Jason and the *Lady's* crew, she told herself she had no right for self-pity.

Whatever Mousef decided to do with her, she knew she deserved it.

Consul William Eaton leaned his head back against the dark-green leather of his chair and closed his eyes. He put the fingers of his hands together and pressed them in and out, apparently lost in his own thoughts.

Jason's stomach churned with angry impatience, but he controlled it and kept his silence.

He opened his eyes finally and leaned forward to Jason.

"Yours is a very interesting story, Captain Stone," he said. He spoke very slowly, as though he was taking pains that his words be understood. "I appreciate all you and your men have been through. But frankly, I'm afraid I don't know what I can do for you," he said.

"You can help me get my wife out of Tripoli," Jason told him.

Eaton shook his head in mournful commiseration.

"Believe me," he said, "I understand how painful this is for you, and I do grieve for the pain you no doubt are suffering at the loss of your wife. But what you do not understand is the complexity of our situation with Tripoli. The bashaw has trampled on those treaties that existed with his predecessors. Mousef is more than intelligent enough to realize that Napoleon's exploits in Europe have left England and anyone else who would reasonably be expected to oppose him with their hands full. They can't afford to waste the effort it would take to deal with a minor potentate stirring up trouble with shipping in the Mediterranean, especially as it seems his victim of choice is American. So we are left to deal with an arrogant enemy who knows we have limited resources here. And to make matters worse, diplomatic relations with him have been severed entirely, which is why you find me here, in Alexandria, rather than in Tripoli."

Jason held up a hand, hoping to halt Eaton before he became so immersed in his lecture that he'd forgotten entirely what he'd been told about Sam.

"I understand all that," Jason told him. "I recognize that diplomatic protests are useless, and I'm not looking for them. What I want is some military help in freeing my wife."

"I'm afraid, Captain Stone, that is, under the current circumstances, entirely impossible," Eaton told him. "Even were we officially at war with Tripoli, which we are not, I could not condone sending military people into a foreign country without strict authorization from the President. If you insist, I can convey your request with my next dispatch. If such intervention is deemed acceptable to the President and Congress, then I would, of course, offer you every assistance."

"Damn it, that would take too long," Jason cried angrily.

"There is absolutely nothing else I can do for you, Captain," Eaton insisted.

"Nothing else you can do, or nothing else you're *willing* to do?" Jason demanded. "What kind of a man are you? How can you be willing to leave a defenseless woman in Mousef's hands?"

It was only when he'd uttered the words that Jason realized how he'd described Sam. Certainly, he'd never before thought of her as defenseless. Until that moment, he'd considered her the one woman he'd ever known who was entirely capable of protecting herself. But that was wrong, and he knew it now. Her sharp tongue, like her insistence on wearing those dowdily ill-fitting clothes, was really a way of hiding, of trying to keep herself from hurt. In many ways, he realized, she was less able to defend herself than a woman who knew how to use her beauty to her own advantage.

"Believe me, this is not what I want," Eaton was saying. "Admiral Preble has recently received authorization from the President to shell Tripoli if he feels it justified. The admiral has determined that bombardment of the city is the only way to make Mousef reasonable. Any unauthorized American shipping in the area would only complicate the issue."

Jason leaned forward to Eaton's desk, putting his hands on it as he rose.

"I don't like what I'm hearing," he said. "My wife's life is not a complication."

Eaton backed away from him, clearly unsettled by the threat he heard in Jason's tone.

"I understand what you're feeling at this moment, Captain Stone. Believe me, if there was anything I could do . . ."

Jason slammed his hand down on the desk.

"You mean if there was something you *wanted* to do," he shouted.

"Please, Captain, calm yourself," Eaton chided in a pedantic tone. "This does no good."

Jason swallowed the angry lump in his throat and straightened. As much as he hated to admit it, Eaton was right. Anger wasn't going to help him.

He stared down at the consul.

"I have a hold full of rifles," he said slowly. "I was going to offer them to the American Navy in return for their help. It seems I will be forced to use them as currency to buy my wife's freedom instead."

"I warn you, what you are suggesting could be construed as treason, Captain," Eaton told him. "Providing weapons to an enemy in time of war is not something the government takes lightly."

Jason stared coolly down at him. "You've just told me that there had been no declaration of war," he said. "Even if there were, I wouldn't shrink from it. In my place, would you do otherwise?" he asked.

Eaton considered the question for a long moment, then he shrugged. He leaned forward, and, unseen by Jason, pressed a button on the floor beneath his desk with his foot.

"What I might or might not do is begging the question, Captain," he said. "The simple fact is, I cannot allow those arms to fall into Mousef's hands. I'm afraid that means I shall be forced to have you and your crew restrained until the

Navy removes the cargo from your hold."

"You can't do that!" Jason shouted.

"Oh, but I can, Captain Stone," Eaton replied. "The rifles are contraband, and therefore subject to seizure. As I can feel only compassion for your situation, I will see that neither you nor your crew will be charged. And I believe I can convince the naval attaché to compensate you for the loss of your cargo. But I'm sure you understand that I cannot allow you to place those weapons into Mousef's hands."

The truth was, Jason realized, he *could* understand, at least his mind could. But his heart was telling him something entirely different, something that said it was madness to leave a woman to a horrible fate, and that in the event she escaped injury or death from Preble's bombardment of the city.

But he didn't have the opportunity to tell the consul what he thought of diplomatic logic. Three soldiers had silently entered Eaton's office through the door to the rear, and now they stole up behind him and restrained him, firmly grasping both his arms and giving no sign that they would release him.

"You can't do this," Jason cried in frustrated anger.

Eaton ignored him.

"See that Captain Stone remains here until further notice," the consul instructed the soldiers. "And send for the naval attaché."

"Damn you, Eaton," Jason shouted at him as he was being marshaled from the room. "You're signing my wife's death warrant."

Eaton didn't reply. He knew what he was doing, and as necessary as he knew it to be, he found he didn't like it in the least.

Chapter Seven

Sam knew that the feeling wouldn't last long, but for the moment, she felt almost safe.

Much to her surprise, Mousef's women were treating her with courtesy. Although she didn't understand a word they spoke, she did understand their gestures of hospitality. She was frightened enough and tired enough to accept it all gratefully.

One woman particularly, a strikingly beautiful dark-haired woman who walked with a decided limp, was being very kind to her, giving orders to have a bath and fresh clothing prepared for the stranger and then hurrying off to herself oversee that all was done properly.

When Sam had installed herself in a gleaming copper tub of steaming water, she once again approached, smiling shyly as though she wanted to be assured that all was acceptable.

Sam obliged, smiling and nodding as she lounged back in the large tub. She noticed the way the woman stared at the bloody bandage on her arm, and the dark clot of blood left by the nick on her neck. She fingered the hardened scab on her neck, then began to wash it away, sure it must look frighteningly hideous.

The dark-haired woman seated herself beside Sam on a chair set beside the tub. She gave every indication that she wanted to be friends.

"Ayesha," she said, pointing to herself.

"Samantha," Sam replied with a ready smile, completing the introduction.

That seemed to be the extent of Ayesha's need for verbal

communication, but she continued to stare at the wound in Sam's arm.

Self-conscious now, Sam scrubbed away the last of the dark clot on her neck. Once it was gone, she gingerly unwrapped and began to wash the inflamed wound in her arm.

"Mousef?"

Sam looked up, startled by Ayesha's frightened and hushed tone. She nodded slowly.

Ayesha looked around, apparently to assure herself that no one was watching or was close enough to see what she was about to do. Satisfied, she lifted her own skirts to reveal a long, ugly scar running the length of her left leg from knee to ankle.

Sam looked at the scar with horror. She came abruptly to the shocked realization of what it was Ayesha was trying to tell her.

"Mousef?" she asked in a halting whisper.

Ayesha nodded, her dark eyes wide with meaning as she returned Sam's stare.

Sam wanted to talk to her, to ask her why Mousef would have done such a horrible thing, to ask what sin required maiming and disfigurement as payment. But she had no way to ask, and in the end decided it was probably best that she not know.

The two sat silently staring at each other for a moment, each feeling pity for the other. Then Ayesha stood and wordlessly left, leaving Sam alone to consider what she'd just learned.

There was nothing, she told herself as she idly washed away the grime that clung to her, that could warrant the sort of treatment Ayesha had been given, no sin she might have committed that would justify such violence being done to her. Still, the scar and the limp were more evidence than she needed that Mousef had done this thing and then kept Ayesha among his other women, perhaps as a warning of what might be done to them should they fail to please him.

And the warning was clear enough, at least to Sam. She knew now what could happen to her, knew that the women

Mousef kept were as much his prisoners as she was, and equally as powerless to escape from him. The two huge men who stood guard outside the doors to the women's quarters weren't there to keep the world out, she realized. They were there to keep the women trapped within.

The illusion of safety she'd fleetingly felt was completely gone. There was nothing she could do to protect herself from Mousef, she realized. She was in no better position among his women than she had been alone as his prisoner on his pirate ship.

She climbed out of the tub, dizzy suddenly with the heat of the water and the knowledge of her situation. She began to dry herself with a thick cloth, her mind dully blank save for the guilt she felt at what she'd done to herself and to Jason and the *Lady Alyssa*'s crew. They were all prisoners of a ruthless man, one who seemed to have no compunction about the spilling of blood.

And the more she thought about the situation she'd put Jason in, the more she realized he would not remain a model prisoner for very long. He hated being ordered about, hated being under another man's thumb. She knew that perhaps better than anyone else could. Jason would, sooner or later, strike out at one of his jailers. And when he did, he would certainly be killed.

The thought left her feeling weak and sick. He'd be killed, she told herself, and it was all her fault. She felt dizzy, and needed to grab hold of the side of the copper tub to keep herself from falling. She'd killed Jason, she told herself. It was no different than if she'd plunged a knife into his heart.

She felt a hand on her arm, and turned to find her unexpected friend had returned.

Ayesha set down a large bowl she'd brought, then offered Sam a steady arm, helping her to sit in the chair she'd vacated not long before.

"I'm really all right," Sam protested, but she found she was more than willing to sit for a moment until the dizziness subsided.

Ayesha lifted the bowl she'd set on the floor and held it out to Sam. It was half filled with a cloudy liquid in which tiny bits of green floated. Sam sniffed it, then drew back at the acrid odor. She fervently hoped she wasn't expected to drink any of the stuff.

But Ayesha quickly made it clear that the potion was to wash the wound in her arm, and this she helped Sam do. After only a few moments Sam found the dull ache beginning to fade. When Ayesha deemed the process finished, Sam realized a good deal of the redness surrounding the wound had lessened and her arm felt much less painful. Ayesha patted the wound dry, proceeded to coat the wound with ointment, and then wrapped it with soft, clean linen bandages.

"I wish I could say thank you to you so that you could understand," Sam murmured as she pulled on the gown Ayesha handed her, more a draping of thin, gossamer soft silk really than any gown that Sam had ever seen before.

But the woman only shrugged and murmured, *"Ana mush fahem,"*—I don't understand.

Ayesha didn't need words, however, to tell Sam that Mousef had sent for her. Her expression as she led Sam to the large doors was warning enough. The doors were pulled open as they approached, and Sam saw that the servant who had brought her to the women's quarters was there, waiting for her.

Sam stepped out, into the corridor, and as she did, her stomach filled with a thick feeling of dread. She looked back to see Ayesha still there watching her being led away.

Sam was haunted by the compassion that she'd seen in Ayesha's dark eyes as the doors were closed and barred between them. More than anything else, those dark, soulful eyes told her that she was about to confront a fate that was far worse than any she might have imagined.

"They can't get away with that, can they, Captain?"
Jason shrugged.
"It would seem they already have, Mr. Argus," he replied.
"But stealing our cargo?" Argus insisted.

286

"A cargo of contraband, Mr. Argus," Jason told him. "According to the good consul, they can do just about whatever they want to do with it."

"But you had nothing to do with contraband. It was supposed to have been farm implements, like the manifest said. Can't you make him believe that?"

Jason scowled. "Oh, he believed me," he replied. "And in consideration of that fact, he told me I ought to be grateful he isn't having us all held and charges pressed against us into the bargain."

The two men were standing by the *Lady Alyssa*'s rail and watching as a half dozen sailors wearing the insignia of the USS *Constitution* on their sleeves carried the last of the crates of rifles off the wharf and placed them into the rear of the wagons that had been brought for that purpose.

A small fortune in weapons, Jason thought, and no one to whom he was either morally or legally bound to deliver them. How Sam would regret their loss.

The thought of her was like a sudden, dull stab in his chest. He could have changed her if he'd tried, he thought. If he'd cared as much for her as he had for her ship, he could have shown her that there were things far more important than money. But he hadn't even bothered, and now there might never be another chance.

There will, he told himself angrily, striking his fist against the rail. He couldn't allow himself to give up on her. After all, she had no one else.

Once the crates were all stowed, a lieutenant stepped forward, saluting smartly as he approached Jason.

"Admiral Preble sincerely regrets the inconvenience you've been caused, Captain Stone," he said. "I'm instructed to tell you that the purser of the *Constitution* will have a draft ready for you in five days' time. If you present yourself to the *Constitution*, it will be presented to you with the admiral's compliments."

Jason ignored the salute.

"Admiral Preble can go to hell," he replied through tight lips. "He's about to go off and kill my wife, and he's just stolen the only coin I might have used to buy her freedom. I don't give a damn for his compliments."

Jason's words seemed to confuse the young lieutenant. His own world was carefully circumscribed by naval regulations, regulations that clearly excluded the freedom to curse a superior officer.

He stepped back and away from Jason, apparently hoping to reach the gangway before any further unpleasantness might ensue.

But Jason wasn't about to let him escape all that easily. He went after him and halted him, blocking his way.

"You might at least let me know when he's going to bombard Tripoli," Jason hissed. "At least that way I know how long I have to get her out."

The lieutenant swallowed, trying to rid himself both of the uncomfortable lump that had formed itself in his throat and of the guilt he felt at being a part of the way Jason had been treated.

"I'm afraid that's classified information, Captain Stone," he said. "Consul Eaton was gravely mistaken in telling you as much as he did."

"For God's sake, man," Jason growled. "Do you really think I'm going to run to Mousef and warn him? He hijacked my ship and stole my wife. I assure you I want to see him dead more than you or Preble or the whole of the US Navy."

"I can appreciate your problem, sir," the lieutenant murmured.

"Then tell me when, Lieutenant," Jason prodded. "You people owe me that. At least tell me how much time I have to find my wife and to get her out of Tripoli."

"I'm only a lowly lieutenant, Captain," he muttered. "I'm not privy to that information."

"Damn it, man. Isn't there anything beneath that uniform but hot air and a book of regulations?"

The lieutenant swallowed again, this time with discomfort as he realized he was about to do something that his conscience told him he ought to do, but that he knew was strictly against regulations. He cleared his throat.

288

"I only know that I have orders to make ready to sail at dawn tomorrow," he said in a hoarse whisper. "That would put us off Tripoli sometime near sunset."

Jason nodded.

"Thank you," he said. "I hope I'll be able to repay you."

The lieutenant shook his head.

"Forgetting where you heard it is all the thanks I want," he muttered. "Now, with your permission, Captain Stone." He nodded toward the gangway.

Jason stepped aside.

The lieutenant saluted one last time, and this time Jason returned the courtesy.

"Now what, Captain?" Argus asked as he and Jason watched the lanky young lieutenant cross the wharf and approach the wagons filled with the crates of rifles.

"We make the *Lady* ready to sail," Jason told him. "We leave within the hour."

"For Tripoli, Captain?" Argus asked, his tone suggesting that perhaps Jason might not be quite sane to even consider such a move.

"There isn't much time, Mr. Argus," Jason told him. "Let's not waste any in idle chatter."

"But without the rifles, Captain, what use is it?"

"I don't know what good it will be," Jason admitted. "I just know I haven't any choice."

"Ya shaikh."

Mousef turned away from the window at the servant's murmured words and looked at Sam. He didn't shift his gaze for even an instant as he dismissed the servant with a movement of his hands.

Sam found herself growing unpleasantly uncomfortable under his stare. She was not accustomed to evaluating looks from men, certainly not openly hungry stares such as the one she saw now in the bashaw's eyes. She wished she had armor, or someplace to hide. More than anything else, at that moment she wanted her too-large, washed-out dress and her spectacles, the camouflage that had always made her virtually invisible to the opposite sex in the past.

"You are much improved, Mrs. Stone," Mousef said when the servant had left the room. "Turn around so that I may enjoy the view."

Sam didn't move. She told herself she couldn't afford to show him just how afraid she was of him, that if he knew, she would be left as cowed and compliant as the women of his harem. She hoped that a small show of rebellion would not warrant repercussions she would regret.

"What do you want?" she demanded.

Mousef smiled, the same sort of knowing smile he'd offered her while they were still on board his ship.

"We'll discuss that later," he told her. "In fact, I have every expectation that we will soon be free to share a deeply intimate conversation on the subject. For now, however, I have the small matter of your husband's ship and my rifles to consider." He turned back to the window where he'd been standing when she'd entered. "Come here," he ordered.

Sam hesitated, then slowly approached the window. Mousef, apparently not satisfied with her progress, turned, grabbed her arm, and pulled her close. He pointed out to the sparkling blue waters of the harbor spread out beneath them. The sunlight glinted off the waves. A fair number of small vessels, fishing boats and the like, Sam assumed, bobbed gently on the waves. And far to the side of the bay, floating peacefully at the sides of two long wharves, were two large vessels. One Sam recognized as the ship on which she and Mousef had arrived early that morning. The second was a bit smaller, but a similarly fitted three-masted ship, square-rigged fore and aft.

It was to these two that Mousef directed her attention.

"You see that ship, the one tied to the wharf beside mine?" he asked.

"Another of your private fleet of thieving pirates?" she asked.

"They are part of my navy, Mrs. Stone," he told her, his tone sharp. "You will refer to them as such."

"Very well," she replied, trying without much success to

hide the sarcasm in her voice, "another of your private navy?"

"Precisely, Mrs. Stone," he told her, apparently pleased with the content and not the intent of her words. "In fact, it is the very ship from which you were fleeing when you so thoughtfully ran into my waiting embrace last evening. Surely you remember?"

Sam nodded. She'd never forget the terror she'd felt at that moment, seeing all those armed men leaping aboard the *Lady Alyssa*, their swords and knives flashing.

"Yes," she murmured, "I remember."

"Then you will understand my perplexity," he went on, "when I tell you that it arrived about an hour ago. It was to have escorted your ship back here to port. And yet it seems to have returned alone."

Sam felt an undeniable wash of sheer joy at his words, felt her heart leap with a burst of hope she'd never thought she'd feel.

"Jason's escaped," she fairly crowed, not thinking before she spoke, too delighted with the possibility to realize that she would anger him. "He's taken back the *Lady* and escaped with your damned rifles."

Her words chased away what little remained of Mousef's superior smile. He grabbed her arm, pulling her sharply so that she faced him and held her.

"You're hurting me," she cried as a stab of pain ran through her arm and shoulder.

Her admission seemed to please him. He tightened his hold on her arm.

"I suggest you offer up prayers to your Christian god, and beg that you are wrong, Mrs. Stone," he hissed angrily before he released her.

Sam backed away, putting her right hand uselessly to her arm, trying to still the throbbing hurt.

"I do not like being thwarted, Mrs. Stone," Mousef told her. "And I do not like being cheated out of goods for which I have paid, and paid handsomely. I fear that if your husband's ship does not arrive soon, you will be the only available target

291

to bear the brunt of my anger."

She shook her head slowly. "I don't think you fear anything," she murmured. "And I don't think you need an excuse. I think you are a petty tyrant who rather enjoys hurting women."

It was only when the words were already spoken that she realized she'd been a fool to say such things to him. His cheeks blotched dark with anger above his beard and she saw a wildness fill his eyes. She backed away from him, nearly falling over a low table as she fled from him.

Luckily for Sam, before he could reach her, the servant returned, this time accompanied by a second man.

"The captain of the *Ghaffir, ya shaikh,*" he announced.

Mousef turned and looked at the newcomer, Sam apparently momentarily forgotten.

"Where is the American ship?" he shouted.

"It must have wandered in the storm, *ya shaikh,*" the pirate captain replied quickly, obviously hoping to ward off his ruler's displeasure. "It was there, my lookouts swear they could see the lights all through the night. But when dawn came, and the weather cleared, it had disappeared."

"Disappeared?" Mousef roared. "How does a clipper ship disappear? It was supposed to have been under your watchful eye. *Ghaffir?* Your ship is badly named. What kind of a watchman loses a ship on the open sea?"

"It will be found, *ya shaikh,*" the captain insisted. "It was manned by ten of my best men. They are probably only a few miles off shore now, bringing her into port."

Despite the captain's protestations, Mousef was far from satisfied. He drew his knife from its sheath and held it out, moving forward slowly until it was close to the other man's face.

Sam saw the terror that filled the pirate captain's eyes as he watched the blade approach. After what the woman Ayesha had shown her, she understood the man's fear.

Mousef pressed the knife to the side of the man's cheek. A long line of red suddenly blossomed beneath it. Sam could see the captain shaking, forcing himself not to pull back, away from the blade.

He didn't, and his bravery seemed to mollify Mousef, at least temporarily. The bashaw pulled the knife away. A line of dark red marked the place where it had been, a line that grew steadily redder, dripping slowly down the pirate captain's cheek and onto the front of his shirt.

"I suggest you set out within the hour, and make sure you are not mistaken," Mousef hissed. "You have one day to find the American ship and bring it back here. If your men have lost control of it to the Americans, or if the fools let the ship founder in the storm, I will make you wish your mother never gave you breath."

'Iywa, ya shaikh," the captain murmured. "We will find her, *ya shaikh.*"

Only when Mousef had turned away, dismissing him, did the captain raise his hand to his cheek, and with the back of it wipe away a thick drop of blood. Then he turned on his heel and marched quickly to the door, obviously glad to have survived with so little harm done him.

Even before he was gone, Mousef returned his attention to Sam.

"You seem amused, Mrs. Stone," he muttered sharply.

"Delighted, not amused," Sam corrected. "Jason *has* escaped."

This time the possibility did not seem so much to anger Mousef as to puzzle him.

"Impossible," he told her after due consideration. "The ship wandered off in the storm."

Sam only shrugged.

"As you like," she murmured.

Mousef approached her.

"In any event, I still have you, Mrs. Stone," he said. "And that makes you very valuable indeed. I doubt there is another woman in Tripoli of so much as a tenth your worth."

Sam arched a brow. "Valuable?" she asked, clearly bewildered. "What do you mean?"

"I mean," Mousef explained slowly, "that one way or another, I will have my rifles."

Sam shook her head. "I don't see how," she said.

"Surely your husband would not be so great a fool as to

293

turn his back on you," Mousef told her. He put his hand on her neck and slid it slowly downward to her breast.

Sam pulled back.

Mousef stood, staring at her in silence for a moment.

"Part of me almost hopes he will," he said. "Twenty-four hours, Mrs. Stone. Either I have my rifles by then, or you will reimburse me for their cost. One way or another, I will not be cheated of what is mine."

"Ye'll never find the way, Captain," Argus muttered as he stared into the darkness that shrouded the long line of beach.

"It'll be dawn soon," Jason assured him. "And by my reckoning, we can't be more than ten miles or so east of Tripoli. Have no fear, Mr. Argus. I'll find my way all right."

Argus turned back to the longboat in which he and Jason had come ashore. He walked to it, but hesitated with his hands on the gunnels before pushing it back into the waves. He turned back to Jason.

"Are ye sure ye won't let me come along, Captain?" he asked. "I'm a good man in a fight."

"The best, Michael," Jason agreed, for once dropping his customary formality with the mate and calling him by his given name. "But I hope I won't find myself depending on my fists. Besides, I need you on the *Lady*. You have to keep her out of sight, and then get her back here in twenty-four hours to pick us up."

"The crew can handle that well enough, Captain."

"Perhaps," Jason ceded. "But there's not a man among them with the talent you have for keeping a ship away from unpleasant company."

Argus permitted himself a grin, knowing that Jason was referring to that period of his youth when he'd piloted a small craft between France and Ireland, following a time-honored tradition of avoiding the excisemen and doing a bit of harmless smuggling. But the grin quickly faded.

"I didn't do such a good job of it last night," he admitted.

"Neither did I, Michael," Jason agreed.

"It's what comes of living totally within the law," Argus confided. "A man stops looking over his shoulder for the excise-man, and sooner or later he starts to actually believe he's in-violate."

"Last night we weren't either of us at our best," Jason said. "And that's all the more reason not to let them do it again. When the fireworks start, keep low. Mousef's pirate fleet won't just sit in the water and allow themselves to be sunk. They'll fight back, and they won't be too fussy about finding military targets for their cannon. I don't want the *Lady* to be in the path of one."

Argus nodded. "I'll keep the *Lady* safe for ye, Captain," he promised. "And we'll be here tomorrow at dawn, waiting for ye."

"Then get back to her," Jason ordered. "And find her some empty waters to hide in."

"Aye, Captain," Argus answered. He pushed the longboat into knee-deep water, and swung himself inside. He glanced up at Jason as he took up the oars.

"Have ye thought of what ye'll be telling them, Captain?" he asked.

Jason shrugged. "I don't know yet, Mr. Argus," he admitted. "I'll have time to consider on my little hike. Hopefully, I'll have come up with something before I find myself knocking at Mousef's door."

"God be with ye, Captain," the mate called as he began rowing back out to the *Lady Alyssa*.

"Amen to that, Mr. Argus," Jason murmured as he turned away and started his walk toward Tripoli.

Chapter Eight

Sam walked quietly at the side of Mousef's servant. She'd decided that he took his cue from his master, inflicting pain with an indifferent pleasure when it appeared to him that Mousef would not call him to task for the action. She decided that prudence was the wisest path to take with him, and was determined to do nothing that could possibly give him an excuse to hurt her.

"The American, *ya shaikh*," the servant murmured as they entered the same room to which he had brought her the day before.

He bowed to Mousef and then pushed Sam forward toward the heap of pillows on which the bashaw sat crosslegged and, to all appearances, deep in thought.

Mousef roused himself at the sound of the servant's voice. He looked up and eyed Sam as she stumbled a few steps forward, propelled by the unexpected shove.

"Come here," Mousef ordered.

Sam took a few more steps forward, then stopped. Her glance had wandered to the window overlooking the bay. A small, frightened voice told her not to look, but it was quickly silenced. She knew she had to see if the *Lady Alyssa* was there in the bay.

She stared through the fretwork, searching out the wharves at the far side of the bay, afraid she might find the *Lady Alyssa*.

She was rewarded for her bravery far beyond her expectation.

The view seemed virtually identical to what she remembered having seen the previous day. The two pirate ships were tied up at the sides of the long wharves. They were alone. There was no sign whatsoever of the clipper.

An incredible weight seemed suddenly to be lifted from her. When she turned back to face Mousef, she found she was no longer afraid of him. Nothing had changed in her situation, she knew, but it no longer seemed to matter to her. Jason was safe, and nothing else was important.

"It's been twenty-four hours," Mousef told her.

Sam stared directly into the bashaw's eyes. She half expected the terror to return when she saw the anger that blazed from them, but it didn't. The knowledge that Jason had indeed escaped somehow left her without any fear for herself. Whatever happened to her now, at least she was free of the guilt that had haunted her since the pirates had first attacked the *Lady Alyssa*, the guilt of knowing she had been the sole cause of what happened.

"And the *Lady Alyssa* is not here to celebrate the hour," she returned with a small, pleased smile.

"Your apparent pleasure at that fact bewilders me, Mrs. Stone," Mousef told her.

"It wouldn't if you'd ever felt anything for anyone but yourself," she replied. "Jason's escaped you, and that's enough."

"Such altruism," he said with a sarcastic sneer. "Perhaps you will be rewarded in your Christian heaven."

"I've already been rewarded by the knowledge that you don't have what you want," she told him.

"I think you may be less smug when you've had a little demonstration of just how unpleasant my anger can be," he told her. He motioned to the servant. "Bring in the captain of the *Ghaffir*."

"Iywa, ya shaikh," the servant answered.

He bowed and turned away, leaving by the door at the far end of the room.

"Come, sit here beside me, Mrs. Stone," Mousef told her. "I think you will be interested in this small demonstration."

Sam had no sooner settled herself where he indicated than

the door opened again, and the servant entered. Immediately behind him were two of Mousef's guards dragging the captain of the pirate ship between them. Sam was shocked to see his face, swollen and covered with dark bruises, bearing almost no resemblance to the man she'd seen the day before save for the long, thin red line Mousef's knife had left on his cheek.

She shuddered.

"What have you done to him?" she asked.

Mousef smiled, apparently delighted to see the effect the sight of the beaten man had on her.

"I've reminded him of the cost of failure, Mrs. Stone," he told her. "And now, with your permission, I'm about to remind you of its ultimate price."

He pushed himself to his feet, strode the few steps that separated him from the pirate captain, and stood staring down at his victim.

Mousef grasped the man's hair and pulled it up, raising his head. The pirate slowly lifted his swollen eyelids and stared dully up at him.

"You have wronged your bashaw," Mousef intoned.

"Iywa, ya shaikh," the pirate whispered through cut and swollen lips. "I have failed you."

"That failure brings you nothing but shame," Mousef went on.

"Iywa, ya shaikh," the other whispered hoarsely.

Mousef glanced back at Sam. He smiled. It was clear to her that he was enjoying himself, and, even worse, that he did not care if she knew. He turned back to face the pirate captain.

"And would you have me be merciful and rid you of that shame?" he asked.

The captain swallowed. His eyes grew wide as he looked up into Mousef's eyes, and then quickly down as though what he had seen there frightened him.

"Iywa, ya shaikh," he finally responded.

Mousef smiled again as he released his hold of the man's head. He turned to Sam.

"A demonstration of my mercy, Mrs. Stone," he hissed at her.

And then he drew his knife and expertly slit the man's throat.

Sam heard a scream, and didn't realize it had come from her throat. When it died away, the room was silent save for a slow, gurgling hiss as the last of the pirate's breath slipped away.

Mousef was wiping his blade on the dead man's shirt when the servant returned to the room.

"Ya shaikh," he said as he bowed. He darted a glance at the dead pirate, but there was no sign in his expression that he felt anything whatsoever at the grisly sight.

"What is it?" Mousef demanded.

"An American has arrived, *ya shaikh,"* the servant replied. "He claims he is Jason Stone, the captain of the American clipper carrying your rifles."

Sam gasped.

"Jason," she whispered half aloud.

She glanced at the body that was being borne out of the room. The beaten face swam before her eyes, and what she saw suddenly became Jason's body, not the pirate captain's. She couldn't bear that, she told herself, couldn't bear seeing another man killed in front of her, couldn't bear to think of what would happen to Jason before Mousef was done with him.

How could he be such a fool as to come here?

Mousef was looking at her, and there was pleasure in his expression as he recognized the fear he saw in hers. He replaced his knife to its sheath as he returned to her, then calmly resettled himself on the heap of pillows at her side. He put his hand on her arm, holding her firmly, letting her know that she was not to move.

"Bring Captain Stone here," he told the servant.

He stared at Sam, smiling smugly, obviously anticipating the meeting with pleasure.

* * *

Mousef glanced at Jason, then back at Sam. He was still holding her arm, still keeping her close to him lest she try to bolt and run to her husband. She was staring at Jason, and he was pleased to see her expression showed the terror that she seemed almost to have lost when she'd entered the room.

"You see, Mrs. Stone," he said, "I told you you were of great value. Here is your husband, ready to barter away a small fortune in arms, all in an attempt to ransom you." He turned to look up at Jason. "Is that not so, Captain Stone?"

Jason tried to ignore him, telling himself to swallow the anger he felt at the way Mousef was handling Sam, at the way the bashaw was deliberately trying to goad him. He knew he couldn't afford to lose his control. With an armed guard on either side of him, he really wasn't in much of a position to help Sam at the moment. He simply had to wait until the right moment. He would have no other chance and he knew it.

"Jason, why did you come?" Sam murmured. "How could you be such a fool as to walk into this madman's hands?"

"Remind me to discuss your lack of manners sometime, Sam," he told her flippantly. "The bashaw is our host, and we owe him certain basic courtesies."

Mousef grinned. "Bravo, Captain. I did not realize you were a man of such style."

Jason ignored him. Staring at Sam, he found he couldn't play Mousef's game. There was very real fear in her eyes, and it pained him to see it there, pained him more than he would have thought possible. More than that, he was afraid to allow himself to think how beautiful she looked in the filmy wrap of soft silk, afraid he would become distracted and do something foolhardy.

He turned his gaze back to Mousef.

"Shall we get down to it?" he growled, any sign of flippancy now vanished from his tone. "We each have something the other wants. I came here to propose an even exchange. So let's set the details of the bargain and be quit of one another."

Mousef held up his hand. "I don't see your position quite so simply as you seem to, Stone," he said. He, too, was now

300

completely serious. "I am told you come here on foot and alone. How do I know you actually have my rifles?"

Jason offered him a sly smile.

"Because I tell you I do," he replied. "Just as I'm willing to take your word that you have my wife."

Mousef laughed. "You are very witty, Captain," he said in a dry, decidedly unamused tone. "But you can see your wife. And I want to see my rifles before I agree to a trade. For all I know, you somehow managed to escape, but my crew still has control of the clipper."

"Your men are dead, Mousef," Jason told him. "And you know it. If they weren't, they'd have brought the *Lady Alyssa* to you by now."

Mousef shrugged. "Very well. I'll grant that you may have regained your ship. I will graciously allow you to leave unhindered so that you may bring it here. Then we will discuss a trade."

"And my wife?" Jason asked.

Mousef smiled. "She will, of course, enjoy my hospitality until you return," he replied. He touched his hand to Sam's cheek. "I could not ask for a more attractive hostage."

Jason bristled, but he forced himself to remain calm.

"I have no intention of sailing the *Lady* into port to display the rifles," he told Mousef. "Whatever you may think, I assure you I am not that much of a fool."

"Come, Stone, be reasonable," Mousef told him. "I could always have you tortured, you know. Eventually you'd tell me where the ship is anchored and I could simply collect my lost cargo."

"You haven't the time," Jason replied. "If my first mate doesn't receive a message within twenty-four hours that both my wife and I are free and out of Tripoli, he has orders to turn the rifles over to the American naval attaché in Alexandria." He smiled, this time a bit smugly. "You could try to collect them from the attaché if you like. Or you can be sensible and deal with me."

"You are a very organized man, Captain."

Jason shook his head. "No," he replied, finally allowing

301

himself to give vent to some of what he was feeling. "What I am is a very angry man. So don't threaten me. And we can dispense with the games. I'm tired, and I'm afraid I don't like you."

"You can't really expect me to allow you to walk out of here with your wife while you give me nothing more than your word?" Mousef asked.

"That is precisely what you'll do if you want to get your hands on those rifles," Jason countered. "Decide, and decide quickly. Release us, or you will never see your rifles."

"I find your tone offensive, Stone," Mousef snarled.

"It's meant to be offensive," Jason replied evenly.

"I don't like being threatened," Mousef said.

"And I tend to lose my manners when I find myself in the company of a filthy, thieving pirate," Jason responded.

"Silence," Mousef shouted.

Sam realized Jason had pushed him too far. "Don't, Jason," she shouted as she tried to squirm away from Mousef's hold.

But Mousef held her fast and her warning came too late. The bashaw motioned to his guards.

They immediately moved back a step, lifting the butts of their rifles as they moved and then bringing them down sharply on the back of Jason's head. He fell forward, sprawling on the floor.

"Jason," Sam screamed.

She flailed and scratched at Mousef's hand, now desperate to free herself of his hold. For a moment he seemed to ignore her, then he abruptly pushed her forward, sending her to her knees on the floor in front of him.

"Go to your husband, Mrs. Stone," he hissed. "Treat him tenderly. Make him realize all he risks losing if he angers me."

She scrambled to her feet, running the distance that separated her from Jason, then falling to her knees at his side. She put her hands on his shoulders and helped him lift himself to his knees.

He groaned, put his hand to the back of his neck, then turned to look at her.

"Does this wifely concern mean that you've decided we're friends again, Sam?" he asked her softly. Illogically, he was grinning foolishly at her.

Sam thought she would dissolve in tears.

"How could you have been so stupid as to come here, Jason?" she whispered. "Now he'll kill us both."

Jason glanced at the window, at the long, slanted shaft of sunlight that made its way through the fretwork. Not yet sunset, he thought. But not that much longer to wait, either. He turned back to her.

"Something strange happened," he told her, and he gave a second of those slightly lopsided, inane grins. "I found I actually missed you."

"You're a fool Jason Stone," she whispered through the tightness that filled her throat.

He put his arm around her, pulling her close to him. How good she felt in his arms, he thought. He swore to himself that he would never again let her out of them.

"No one's going to die," he told her. He looked up at Mousef. "The bashaw knows he can't afford to kill either of us. He just likes to see men on their knees before him."

Sam clung to him, praying he was right. But when she turned her gaze to Mousef's face, she knew that prayers were not going to help.

"Oh, I won't kill you," Mousef told them. "But I will make you wish you were dead."

He motioned to the two guards.

"You have two hours," he told them. "Take them both. Make him talk. I don't care how you do it."

Jason darted a glance at the window. The last of the afternoon was slowly fading into a still-peaceful night. It pained him to realize he had made a mistake by not stalling Mousef just a bit longer.

It was a mistake that might cost both him and Sam their lives.

The guards were hardly gentle as they pushed Sam and Jason to hurry them down the long flight of stone steps. Jason

303

put his arm around Sam, holding her close to keep her from falling.

She felt a wash of pleasure at his touch, a pleasure that only shamed her, for she knew she had been the cause of his coming to Tripoli. She knew equally as well that neither of them would ever leave.

"You shouldn't have come, Jason," she whispered to him.

"You didn't really think I'd leave you here, did you, Sam?" he asked her.

She looked up at his eyes, wondering what he was thinking.

"The *Lady* would have been all yours," she ventured.

"True," he mused softly. He grinned. "But it wouldn't have been the same."

"How can you be so pleased with yourself?" she demanded.

"Because something's about to happen," he said.

She realized that each time they passed one, he had turned to look out the narrow slits that served as windows in the stone walls at the side of the winding staircase. This part of the palace was actually cut into the rock face of the cliff that overlooked the bay, she realized. She strained to peer out as he did, but as far as she could see, there was nothing to look at, only the steadily growing darkness.

"What?" she demanded.

As she looked up at him, waiting for an answer, a series of low, booming sounds shattered what had been the quiet of the early evening. When he heard it, Jason pushed her against the inside wall.

"That," he answered as he pressed himself against her.

The guards raised their rifles, and started threateningly toward him, but they never had the chance to strike. The low booms were followed by a loud shattering explosion, and then another and another. The outside wall shook and the stairs beneath them trembled. Unprepared for the concussions, the guards lost their balance, tumbling one against the other.

But Jason had known precisely what was coming, and he was prepared. He turned and drove his fist into the belly of the closest guard, then grabbed his rifle and wrenched it from his hands. Before the second could aim and fire at him, Jason turned the rifle on him, shooting quickly, sending him reeling backward down the stone steps. The first man lunged to his feet and tried to charge, forcing Jason to fire again. The guard slumped lifeless against the shaking wall.

Jason turned away from them, and moved to Sam's side.

"Are you all right, Sam?" he asked. He reached out for her and caught her in his arms.

She fell against him, shaking at the seemingly endless explosions that shook the stones around them.

"What's happening?" she asked.

"Admiral Preble's bombarding the city," he told her. "And if we don't want to end up dead beneath the rubble, we'd better get out of here."

He wasn't exaggerating, Sam realized. The explosions continued one after another. Already there were large cracks beginning to appear in the wall. It was more than obvious that soon the walls would crumble under the onslaught of the bombardment of cannon shot.

Jason took her hand and pulled her away from the wall. But as soon as she no longer had the support of the wall, as soon as she stood alone and felt the movement beneath her feet, she cringed back.

"Come on, Sam," Jason told her. "There's no time to waste."

She stared up at him. "I can't Jason. I can't."

"Just think about being on the *Lady* in a storm," he told her. He took her hand again. "We have to go now, Sam. If we don't, we'll die here."

She nodded and slowly edged herself away from the wall. Then, holding fast to his hand, she started running at Jason's side back up the long flight of trembling stone steps.

Jason stopped at the top of the stairs, fearing they would be seen and recaptured as soon as they reentered the corridor of the palace proper. He needn't have bothered. Here all was panic, and those guards who had not yet fled were too busy dodging falling debris in their own effort to flee to bother with questioning strangers.

"Which way?" Jason asked Sam.

She looked around, trying to remember. But she found she didn't recognize anything. What little of the palace she had seen was nothing more than a blur to her now, and she had no idea where they were or which way might lead them to the outside.

"I don't know," she admitted.

Jason said nothing, just grasped her hand more firmly and looked around. There didn't appear to be any single direction those guards he saw were tending to follow. Their movement was panicked and seemingly random.

He turned right, nodded to her, and they started to run along the corridor. But they hadn't gone far when they were forced to stop to dodge pieces of falling debris, large slabs of marble that the concussion of the explosions loosened from the walls and sent crashing down to shatter on impact. Jason pressed Sam against the wall, covering her with his body to protect her from the bits of flying stone.

"We'll never get out of here," Sam cried when the echo of the crash had begun to fade.

Jason took her hand and pulled her on again.

"This is no time for you to become timid," he told her. "Where's that argumentative, self-contained Samantha who was such a pain in my neck?"

"I am not argumentative," she retorted.

"We'll argue about it later," he told her. "Come on."

Sam glanced up at the walls with trepidation, but when he took her hand again, she forced herself to swallow her fear. She ran on, determined not to give in to the terror.

But it wasn't easy. The place was bedlam, and there were the sounds of cries now, cries of fear and of pain, added to the near constant sound of the explosions. The knowledge that they were running blindly, without any idea where they were going, only added to the madness.

And then suddenly Sam realized she recognized something. Only hours before she had stood in front of the doors at the far side of the corridor they were now in. There were no guards standing by them now, but she was certain that the barred doors were the entry to Mousef's women's quarters.

If she had any doubts at all, they were quickly banished by the sound of cries from the far side of the door, the sound of female cries. It sickened her to think that the guards had fled without first releasing the women who were trapped inside.

"We've come the wrong way," she told Jason and pointed to the doors. "This is the center of the palace, and that is the women's hall."

"Mousef's harem?" he asked.

She nodded. "And they're trapped in there."

They ran to the doors, and Jason drew away the heavy bar that secured them. Even before he had pulled it free, the doors burst open and women began to push their way out, heedless of the two who had freed them in their frenzy to be away from the place. One glance inside was enough to make Sam realize that she didn't blame them. Half a dozen stone pillars had fallen. There was rubble everywhere and stone dust cast a thick haze in the air. Half a dozen small fires had started where lanterns had fallen. It wouldn't be long, she realized, before they became full-fledged blazes.

"No wonder they were in such a panic to get out," Jason murmured. He put his hand on Sam's arm. "Come on."

But Sam didn't move.

"No," she said. "Look."

She pointed to the center of the room where a woman was kneeling beside one of the broken pillars, then started inside.

Jason ran after her. "There's no time, Sam," he told her.

"It's Ayesha," she replied. "She was kind to me. We can't just leave her there."

Even as she spoke, another explosion rocked the floor beneath her. Weakened by the constant battery, the supports of the palace proper were beginning to crack. It wouldn't be long before the whole of the structure began to crumble.

Sam fell to her knees at Ayesha's side, but before she could speak, she found herself stunned to realize that in front of her

307

was a woman lying with the fallen pillar across her chest. She was Raisa, a woman Ayesha had introduced to Sam the evening before. The two seemed to be close friends. It sickened Sam to think that the still, sightless thing in front of her had been vibrantly alive only a few hours before.

She knew that Raisa was dead, her chest crushed beneath the weight of the pillar, but still Sam put her hand to her neck.

"She's dead, Ayesha," she said gently.

Ayesha turned to her and nodded. Sam knew the words themselves meant nothing to her, but it was obvious that she understood. She reached forward and gently closed the dead woman's eyes, then turned back to face Sam.

"Sam, we have to get out of here."

The two women turned to find Jason standing behind them. A look of shock crossed Ayesha's face, and Sam realized that the sight of a man in this place must be strange and frightening to her. But she managed to recover quickly, and when she saw Sam scramble to her feet, she hurriedly did the same.

The three ran back to the doors. They stopped, and Sam and Jason turned to Ayesha.

"How do we get out of here?" Sam asked her.

"Does she understand English?" Jason asked.

Sam shook her head. "No," she told him. "And unless you speak Arabic, we're lost again."

But Ayesha understood the need to flee, even if she didn't understand what Sam and Jason were saying. She took Sam's hand and motioned.

"Well?" Sam asked Jason. "What shall we do?"

He shrugged. "We don't have much choice," he told her. "We follow her."

Ayesha led them along the corridor, then stopped in front of a small door. She pulled it open, and motioned to Sam and Jason to follow her inside.

Sam looked into the dark passage that lay beyond the open door. It was narrow and low-ceilinged, and there was rubble fallen from the ceiling and walls littering the floor.

Ayesha grasped her arm and began to pull Sam forward.

Sam balked, refusing to move. "We can't go in there," she said. "We'll be trapped."

Jason looked first at Sam, then into Ayesha's eyes.

"She's leading us out of here, Sam," he said finally. "I don't see that we have any choice but to follow her."

"Ayesha, isn't there some other way?" Sam cried. She pointed back in the direction from which they'd come.

But Ayesha shook her head and tugged at Sam's arm.

And then the matter was decided for them. An explosion shook the corridor behind them, sending huge slabs of marble crashing to the floor.

Jason pushed Sam and Ayesha into the narrow passageway, then dove in after them as the walls of the corridor tumbled into rubble behind him.

Chapter Nine

"Jason? Ayesha? Jason where are you?"

Sam was on her knees, and around her was nothing but darkness, a terrifyingly absolute darkness.

"I'm here, Sam."

Jason's voice came out of nowhere in the dark and a hand touched her leg. She offered up a silent prayer of thanks. As she did, she realized that she'd feared him dead, feared he had left her alone in that abyss of inky blackness.

"Samantha?"

It was Ayesha's voice now, and Sam felt movement just in front of her.

"Well," Jason said, "it sounds as though we're all accounted for."

He fumbled in the dark, and finally found Sam's hand with his before he pushed himself to his feet. Clumsy without sight, still he managed to help Sam and Ayesha up.

"What now?" Sam moaned softly.

"Samantha!"

Ayesha's voice was firm and completely calm. Sam felt her hand touch her arm, then grasp her hand.

"We can't go on in here," Sam murmured.

"We can't go back," Jason told her. "The walls are crumbling out there. We'd be crushed."

And then Ayesha raised Sam's hand and placed it on her shoulder.

"*Taala*," she said, holding Sam's hand firmly and starting forward.

Sam realized she was telling them to follow.

"I think she wants us to go with her," she told Jason. "Although where we could go in this darkness is a mystery to me."

"I don't see that we have any choice," Jason said.

Sam shivered. Although the sound of the explosions was muffled, she could still feel the concussion in the trembling of the floor. She didn't like being where she was one little bit. All she could think of was being trapped there in the darkness were the ceiling to fall on them.

But she knew that Jason was right, that they didn't have any choice. Mousef's palace was crumbling into ruins around them, and if they didn't get out of it soon, they would be buried alive. Following Ayesha was their only chance of surviving.

They started forward, Sam holding on to Ayesha's arm and Jason at the rear. Sam could sense Ayesha's fear as she slowly felt her way along the passageway. Strangely, awareness of that fear calmed Sam, for it made her realize that Ayesha was as frightened as she. Even stranger was the tingling warmth that seemed to radiate through her from Jason's touch. He had never held her this gently or this much before. It seemed a bizarre sort of first dance.

Later, she would realize it was those thoughts that kept her from thinking of the real danger they were in. All she could think as they stumbled along in the darkness was how much she wanted to feel both Jason's arms around her and to wonder at the mystery of why he had come after her at all.

She had no idea how long they trudged through the darkness. It seemed endless hours, but it might have been only minutes. In any event, when Ayesha halted and then pushed a thick door open, the stars were shining brilliantly in a black velvet sky and the pale-silver light of a newly crescent moon seemed like daylight to her after the total darkness of the passage.

"Where are we?" she murmured.

Jason turned her so that she could see the walls of the palace, the city beyond, and the bay. The fleet of a half dozen

311

American ships was there, sending off a last few desultory cannon shots now that the palace was in near ruins. Everywhere she looked, Sam could see fires beginning to send bright licks of flames into the air.

"So much destruction," she murmured, aghast at what she saw.

Jason nodded. "Mousef brought it down on himself, but it's sickening that the whole of the city had to suffer for it."

Sam turned to glance at Ayesha, wondering what sort of anguish she must feel to see the destruction. But Ayesha wasn't looking at the city. She had turned to stare up at the walls of the palace, at the growing fingers of flame that were starting to make their way through the cracks the cannon shot had left in the stone.

"Fody," she murmured, and a look a satisfaction filled her wide, dark eyes.

"What did she say?" Jason murmured to Sam.

Sam shook her head. "I don't know," she admitted. "But I think she's saying that she's free." She, too, stared at the flames. She could feel their warmth now, like a dragon's breath pushed into the night air. "Do you think Mousef escaped?" she murmured.

Jason shrugged. "I don't know," he said. He put his hand on her arm and she turned to face him. "I only know I'm glad we did."

With that, he pulled her close to him and kissed her, kissed her with a yearning passion that completely surprised him. When he'd realized Mousef had taken her, he'd come to the reluctant acceptance of the fact that he loved her, but it was only at that moment that he was starting to realize just how much.

A dull, cracking sound in the stone made him end the embrace prematurely. They looked up, and realized the heat of the flames was breaking the wall. The three of them hurried off, retreating to the east and the darkness away from the city.

It was Ayesha who stopped first, and Sam guiltily realized that her limp seemed more pronounced now than it had been.

"We have to slow down," she told Jason. "Ayesha's leg must be paining her."

But Ayesha hadn't stopped because she was in pain or was tired. She pointed to a crossroads that the moonlight picked out of the darkness.

"No, no," Jason told her. He motioned to the beach bordering the coast. "My ship is this way."

Ayesha shook her head and motioned to the road inland. Then she smiled at Sam, opened her arms to her, and embraced her.

"Ma al salama," she murmured as she pulled herself free.

"But won't you come with us?" Sam asked and motioned once more to the beach as Jason had done.

Ayesha shook her head again and smiled. *"Fody,"* she said, just as she had when she'd looked up at Mousef's destroyed palace. Then she turned away and walked off into the night.

Sam and Jason watched her until she'd disappeared.

"I never thought," Sam murmured. "But of course she had a life before Mousef stole her from it."

Jason put his arm around her and they started to walk along the beach.

"And now she's free to return to it," he said.

"Just as we're free to go back to our lives," Sam added.

Jason stopped, put his hands on her shoulders, and turned her to face him.

"Is that what you want to do, Sam?" he asked her. "Go back to the way things were?"

She looked up into his eyes, dark blue in the moonlight, blue like the sea. She smiled as she raised her hands to the back of his neck.

"Not entirely," she whispered. "I can think of a few things we might change if it pleases you, Captain Stone."

Jason smiled.

"It pleases me, Mrs. Stone," he said before he kissed her.

They made love for the first time there on the sand, with the water lapping nearby and the moonlight a gentle silver

313

blanket over them. By its pale light Jason undressed her, and pressed his lips to her neck and her breasts and her belly.

Sam gazed up into his eyes, watching them as he whispered the words, "I love you," and knew that it was true, and even more that she loved him, too.

When he pressed himself to her, when she felt the wonder of that first sweet, fiery thrust and felt herself melting inside, she could only wonder that they had found this joy despite all they'd been through. She realized that much of her life had been a lie, that she'd been wrong to think herself immune to the need of another. But all that was over now. In the act of surrendering to him she came to know that she'd really found herself and to realize that she'd never be whole without him.

She floated on a sea of passion he awakened in her, lost in the throe of tides she had never known existed. She gave herself up to it, willing to trust Jason to keep her safe.

When it came to her, the release was more frightening and more shattering than anything she could ever have imagined feeling, for she knew herself at that moment to be part of him, and he part of her. She clung to him, trembling with the wonder of all she had found.

"You have the wheel, Mr. Argus," Jason said. "We had a long walk last night, and I think we are both in need of a little rest."

Sam realized that Jason was smiling at her in a way she'd never seen before, but which definitely made her think he had something other than sleep in mind. She blushed as she realized the prospect was entirely agreeable to her as well.

"What heading, Captain?" the mate asked.

"East, Mr. Argus," Jason ordered. "Back to Alexandria. We have a draft to collect from the *Constitution's* purser and a bowsprit to repair."

"Aye, Captain."

Sam realized the mate was smiling oddly at her, but she didn't mind. It was perfectly fine with her if he smiled, just as long as Jason was standing beside her with his arm around her. Let Argus be amused if he liked. She supposed she would smile, too, were she in his place.

"And Captain," Argus added, stopping them as they began to turn away. He grinned. "It's good to have you back. Both of you."

Jason smiled. "It's good to be back, Mr. Argus," he said. "Better than words can express."

With that, Jason hurried Sam off the deck and down to their cabin. Once inside, he went directly to the cupboard where his hammock was stowed. Sam watched him open the cupboard, and as he did, she felt her heart grow suddenly achingly heavy inside her. A pang of hurt welled up inside her as she wondered if she had misinterpreted everything that had happened between them. She crossed to the desk, found her spectacles just where she had left them. As Jason took the hammock out of the cupboard, she put them on, feeling suddenly the need for the protection she had always felt they afforded her.

But once Jason had the hammock under his arm, he turned and smiled at her.

"I don't think we'll be needing this anymore," he said as he crossed the cabin to the door. He was grinning when he opened the door and dropped the hammock outside.

Sam smiled. The hurt seeped away and the warmth of a blush crept over her cheeks. When Jason turned back to face her, the blush grew deeper.

"One thing I must admit about Mousef . . ." he murmured as he crossed the cabin to her.

"That is?" she asked.

"He certainly knew how a beautiful woman ought to be dressed," he told her.

"Do you really think I'm beautiful, Jason?" she murmured. She stared up at him, almost afraid he might take back the words.

He touched his hand to her hair, letting his fingers slide through the mass of silky curls.

"Yes," he answered softly. "I think you're more than beautiful."

It was true, he realized, and he knew it had been there all along even if he'd let her hide it from him.

He put his hand on her cheek, caressed it softly, then carefully removed the spectacles.

"You really don't need these just now, do you?" he asked.

Sam smiled and shook her head. "I suppose I only need them when I read," she admitted.

"And you don't want to read at this moment," he told her before he pressed a hungry kiss to her lips.

"No," she agreed a bit breathlessly when he lifted his lips from hers. "I don't want to read just now."

He dropped the spectacles back on the desk, his hand skimming the open page of the ledger she'd left there. He glanced at the row of numbers and smiled, then released her and stepped back.

"There's one more thing I have to do," he told her.

Sam watched him as he pulled out the old trunk that contained her clothes, lifted it, and carried it to the door.

"I've decided to take you shopping while the *Lady*'s bowsprit is being repaired," he told her. He looked at her, and Sam realized his expression was fixed and determined. "You have no objection, have you?"

For an instant she wondered what he would do if she had, but decided it wasn't a matter worthy of an argument. Now that she considered the matter, she realized there had rarely been any real reason for most of their arguments, that she had begun them simply out of a desire to assert herself. Perhaps, she thought slyly, there were other, less antagonistic ways. She smiled at him.

"No, I have no objection," she told him softly.

The trunk soon joined the hammock, and Jason closed the door on the heap, turning the key in the lock before he turned back to her. He seemed, Sam thought, very pleased with himself.

"Now," he said when he'd returned to her and put his arms around her, "where were we?"

"I think we were about here," she replied as she lifted her arms to his shoulders and raised her lips to be kissed.

It was a long, hungry kiss, one that promised them both a good deal.

"I think we should marry," he said softly as he lifted her into his arms. "After all, it's only proper."

Sam laughed.

"We *are* married," she told him.

"Are we?"

He sounded genuinely amazed at that revelation despite the smile that belied the words.

She nodded. "I remember writing about it in my diary," she told him. "June 6th, 1804," she recited. "Today I became the bride of Jason Stone . . ."

"June sixth?" he asked.

"Yes," she assured him. "June sixth."

He grinned as he put her down on his bed and then followed her, pressing his lips to hers, holding her body close to his.

"In that case," he murmured as he put his lips first to her ear and then her neck, "I think it time we began a long overdue honeymoon."

Sam laughed and then reached up to him. She drew him close and answered him with a kiss.

FEEL THE FIRE IN CAROL FINCH'S ROMANCES!

BELOVED BETRAYAL (2346, $3.95)

Sabrina Spencer donned a gray wig and veiled hat before blackmailing rugged Ridge Tanner into guiding her to Fort Canby. But the costume soon became her prison—the beauty had fallen head over heels in love!

LOVE'S HIDDEN TREASURE (2980, $4.50)

Shandra d'Evereux felt her heart throb beneath the stolen map she'd hidden in her bodice when Nolan Elliot swept her out onto the veranda. It was hard to concentrate on her mission with that wily rogue around!

MONTANA MOONFIRE (3263, $4.95)

Just as debutante Victoria Flemming-Cassidy was about to marry an oh-so-suitable mate, the towering preacher, Dru Sullivan flung her over his shoulder and headed West! Suddenly, Tori realized she had been given the best present for a bride: a night of passion with a real man!

THUNDER'S TENDER TOUCH (2809, $4.50)

Refined Piper Malone needed bounty-hunter, Vince Logan to recover her swindled inheritance. She thought she could coolly dismiss him after he did the job, but she never counted on the hot flood of desire she felt whenever he was near!

Available wherever paperbacks are sold, or order direct from the Publisher. Send cover price plus 50¢ per copy for mailing and handling to Zebra Books, Dept. 3780, 475 Park Avenue South, New York, N.Y. 10016. Residents of New York and Tennessee must include sales tax. DO NOT SEND CASH. For a free Zebra/ Pinnacle catalog please write to the above address.

SURRENDER TO THE PASSION

LOVE'S SWEET BOUNTY   (3313, $4.50)
by Colleen Faulkner

Jessica Landon swore revenge of the masked bandits who robbed the train and stole all the money she had in the world. She set out after the thieves without consulting the handsome railroad detective, Adam Stern. When he finally caught up with her, she admitted she needed his assistance. She never imagined that she would also begin to need his scorching kisses and tender caresses.

WILD WESTERN BRIDE   (3140, $4.50)
by Rosalyn Alsobrook

Anna Thomas loved riding the Orphan Train and finding loving homes for her young charges. But when a judge tried to separate two brothers, the dedicated beauty went beyond the call of duty. She proposed to the handsome, blue-eyed Mark Gates, planning to adopt the boys herself! Of course the marriage would be in name only, but yet as time went on, Anna found herself dreaming of being a loving wife in every sense of the word . . .

QUICKSILVER PASSION   (3117, $4.50)
by Georgina Gentry

Beautiful Silver Jones had been called every name in the book, and now that she owned her own tavern in Buckskin Joe, Colorado, the independent didn't care what the townsfolk thought of her. She never let a man touch her and she earned her money fair and square. Then one night handsome Cherokee Evans swaggered up to her bar and destroyed the peace she'd made with herself. For the irresistible miner made her yearn for the melting kisses and satin caresses she had sworn she could live without!

MISSISSIPPI MISTRESS   (3118, $4.50)
by Gina Robins

Cori Pierce was outraged at her father's murder and the loss of her inheritance. She swore revenge and vowed to get her independence back, even if it meant singing as an entertainer on a Mississippi steamboat. But she hadn't reckoned on the swarthy giant in tight buckskins who turned out to be her boss. Jacob Wolf was, after all, the giant of the man Cori vowed to destroy. Though she swore not to forget her mission for even a moment, she was powerfully tempted to submit to Jake's fiery caresses and have one night of passion in his irresistible embrace.